I0588335

CHILDREN OF ASH

CHILDREN OF ASH
BOOK ONE

ALLISON ANDERSON

OLIVERHEBERBOOKS

All rights reserved.

No part of this publication may be sold, copied, distributed, reproduced or transmitted in any form or by any means, mechanical or digital, including photocopying and recording or by any information storage and retrieval system without the prior written permission of both the publisher, Oliver Heber Books and the author, Allison Anderson, except in the case of brief quotations embodied in critical articles and reviews.

NO AI TRAINING: Without in any way limiting the author's [and publisher's] exclusive rights under copyright, any use of this publication to "train" generative artificial intelligence (AI) technologies and/or large language models to generate text, or any other medium, is expressly prohibited. The author reserves all rights to license uses of this work for the training and development of any generative AI and/or large language models.

PUBLISHER'S NOTE: This is a work of fiction. Names, characters, places, and incidents either are the product of the author's imagination or are used fictitiously. Any resemblance to actual persons, living or dead, business establishments, events, or locales is entirely coincidental.

Children of Ash Copyright 2025 © Allison Anderson

Published by Oliver-Heber Books

0 9 8 7 6 5 4 3 2 1

Praise for Children of Ash

"Steeped in Norse mythology, this gem of a fantasy is one pulse-pounding ride from beginning to end. Rich in adventure and romance, Axel and Pet's journey sets an epic stage for an unputdownable and magical series. Highly recommend!"

— Kathryn Purdie, #1 *New York Times* bestselling author of The Forest Grimm series and the Bone Grace duology

"With a charming twist on classic mythology, *Children of Ash* offers an epic filled with heroes, magic, and enough yearning to make your heart ache in the most wonderful way."

— Elizabeth Lowham, award-winning author of *Casters and Crowns*

"*Children of Ash* is a high-stakes epic fantasy mashing up Greek legend and Viking mythos. With grit and tension between the characters and their culture, I tore through this book and anxiously await another. Allison delighted me with The Cartographer's War series. This time, she's going for the jugular."

— Jeff Wheeler, *Wall Street Journal* bestselling author

"Immersive, heart-pounding, and brutal. More, please."

— Jessica Scarlett, author of *Town of Shadows*

"A thrilling fantasy bursting with adventure, secrets, and myths made real."

— KayLynn Flanders, author of *Shielded*

For Tyleah.
You freaking know why.

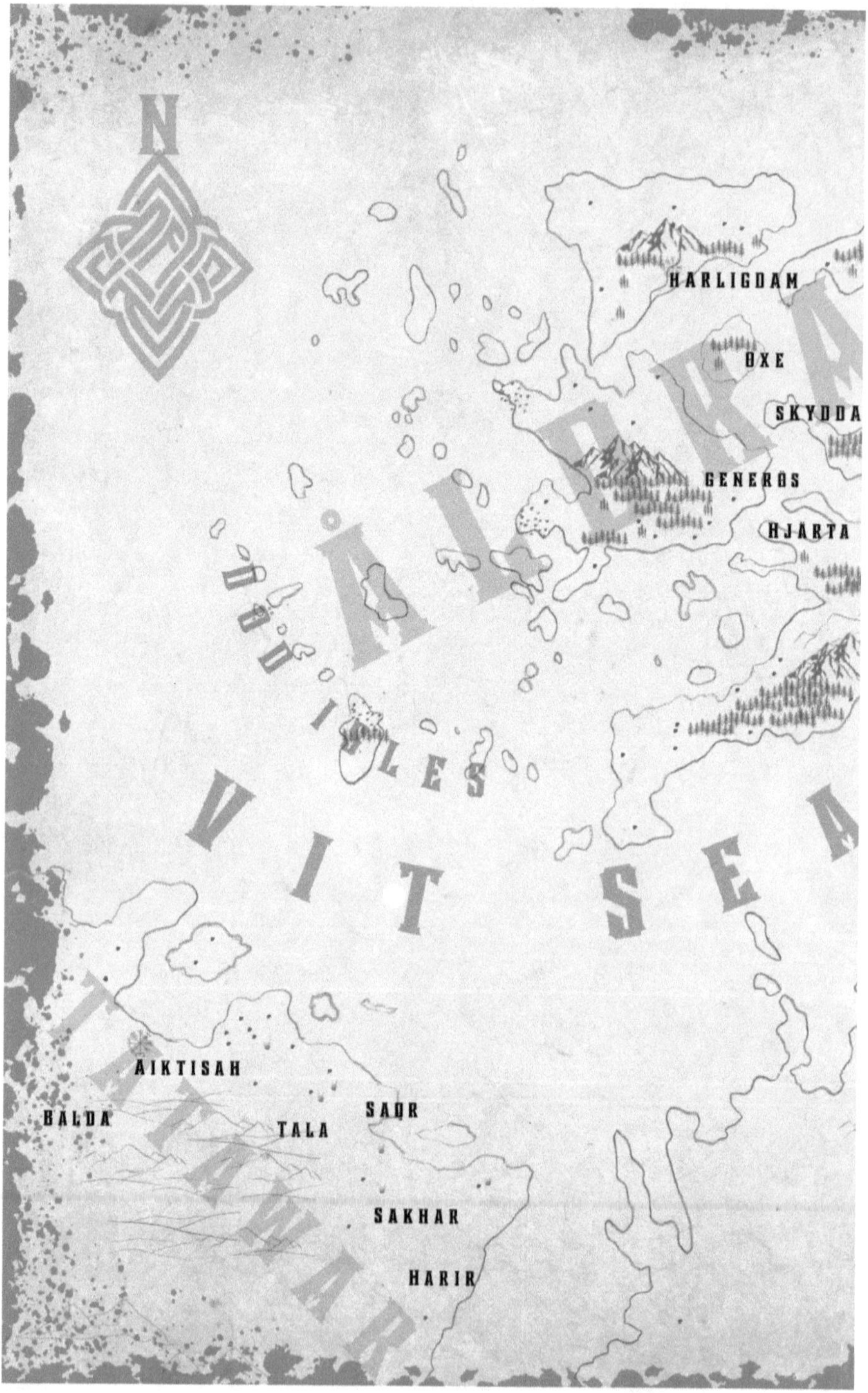
N
HARLIGDAM
OXE
SKYDDA
GENEROS
HJARTA
VIT SEA
AIKTISAH
BALDA
TALA
SAQR
SAKHAR
HARIR

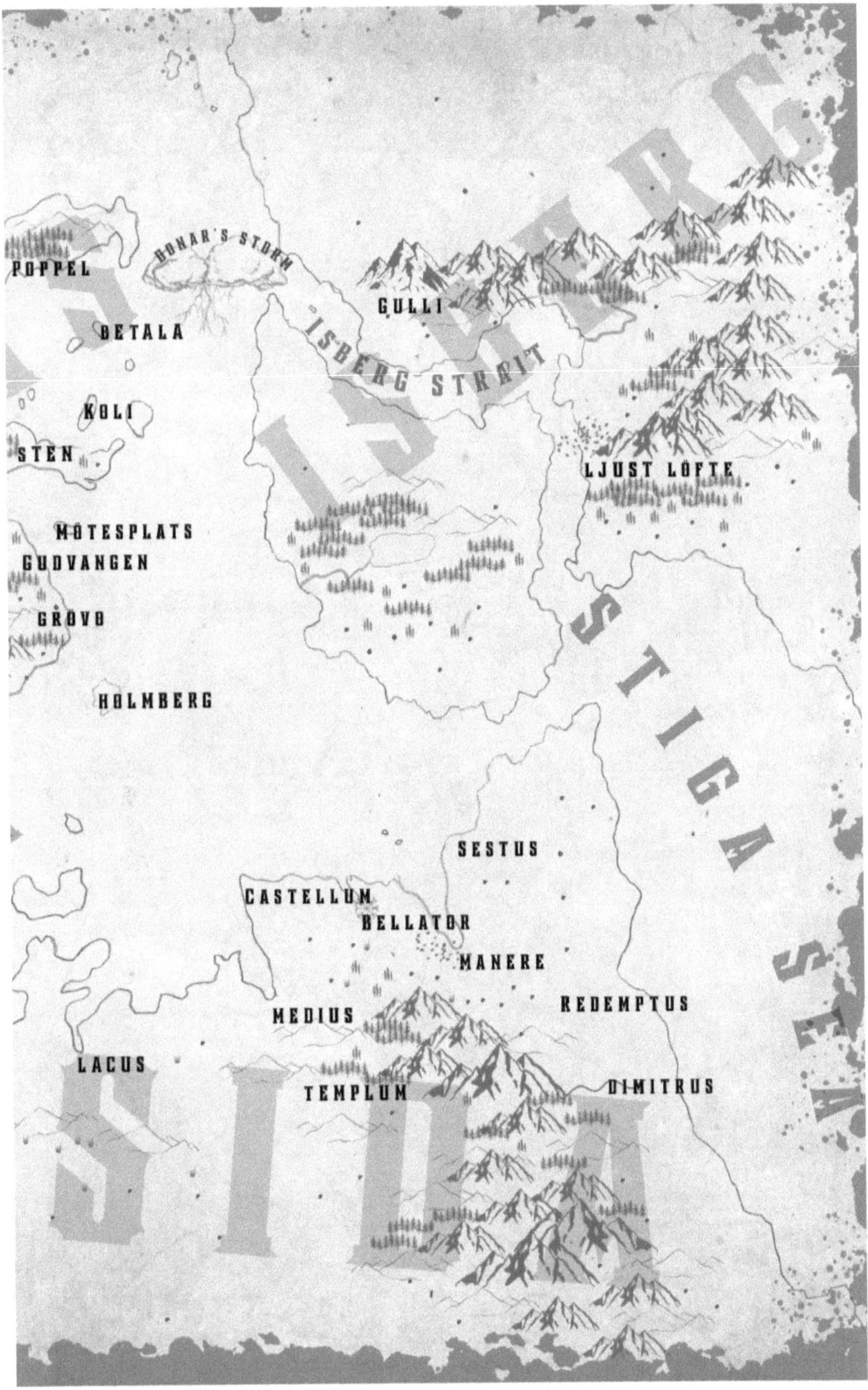
DONAR'S STORM
POPPEL
BETALA
KOLI
STEN
MÖTESPLATS
GUDVANGEN
GRÖVO
HOLMBERG
GULLI
ISBERG STRAIT
LJUST LÖFTE
STIGA
SESTUS
CASTELLUM
BELLATOR
MANERE
REDEMPTUS
MEDIUS
LACUS
TEMPLUM
DIMITRUS
SIDA

Glossary

Häxa Terms:
Häxa—women gifted with power over elements of nature
Animal Shifters—shift into other animals, communicate with animals
Air Whisperers—manipulate the weather, use the air to communicate long distances
Fire Charmers—manipulate fire, self-healing
Plant Healers—grow plants without aid, heal other people's infirmities
Spirit Walkers—walk without their body, commune with the dead
Stone Carvers—manipulate rock, imbue stone with magic
Water Wielders—wield water, see into the future
Ekte—Häxa killers, men who have carved their skin with runes to negate magic
Förändra—the catalyst for a Häxa's gift

Magical Beings:
Dragon—a winged beast of legend
Draugr—undead beings whose bite will kill even the strongest of warriors
Dwarf—creatures with perfect craftsmanship who can enchant the things they create
Elf—a creature of great magic who can wield shadow or light

Fossegrim—a fiddle-playing creature that lures women and children to their deaths

Giant—a humongous creature known to dwell in the most frozen parts of the world

Hafgufa—a ship-eating creature; known for looking like an island and luring desperate sailors to their gaping maws

Hamingja—benevolent spirits that will bestow luck upon those they deem worthy

Huldra—a forest-dwelling creature that takes the form of a woman, distinguished by an animal-like appendage and a large, hollow cavity between her shoulder blades

Jörmungandrson—spawn of Jörmungandr, the Great Serpent, known for dragging ships down into the water depths

Jötunn—another name for the gods who dwell over all of Yggdrasil

Marbendill—a creature with the torso and head of a woman and the tail of a seal

Nixie—water-bound creatures who drag sailors to their doom

Phoenix—a bird that rises from the ashes with new life

Valkyrie—servants of the gods, usher the souls of warriors to Valhalla

Vätte—small creatures often found in the midst of cattle, wear furred hats, and known for killing an entire herd of cattle if displeased

Gods:
Baldr—god of beauty, light, and peace
Donar—god of thunder
Freyja—goddess of beauty, love, death, war, and magic
Freyr—god of the harvest
Frigg—goddess of motherhood, marriage, and prophecy
Fulla—goddess of service
Hel—goddess over the dead
Hermod—messenger god
Hrimthursar—frost giant
Logi—god of fire
Loki—god of mischief and disguise
Máni—goddess of the moon
Njord—god of the wind and sea
Sol—god of the sun

Three Norns—goddesses of fate
Wōden/Allfather—god of all Yggdrasil, father of the gods

Ships:
Langship—Sidan longships, known for their speed and maneuverability over the water
Karve—longship used for both war and cargo, known for its broad hull
Knörr—merchant ship, used for long voyages for trade
Skeid—large longships used to transport soldiers over far distances
Snekkja—small ships, used in battle

CHAPTER 1

A CHILD

The more years that pass, the more I regret rescuing those two little scraps on the glass-covered beach of Holmberg. Those boys have been a thorn in my side since I pulled them onto my ship. I should have dumped them in the ocean the moment Axel started beating every one of the crewmen in that arm-wrestling contest. When Petyr disappeared for hours, even on a bloody karve in the middle of the ocean. Now, I've become nothing but a doddering nursemaid, sent after them every time they do something High King Firmin doesn't approve of. Wōden's golden eye, I'm going to strangle the both of them.

— *FROM THE WRITINGS OF DORAN FINNSSON, THE LAST KING OF GROVÖ*

A cting like a woman was as foreign to Pet as an elk sitting at the head of a feasting table. She adjusted the front of her bodice, still not used to the amount of her chest wrap the garment revealed. Not that there was much chest to show in the first place, but she felt her insides squirming without her usual clothing. Without the weight of her axes at her waist and the tug of the wind on her hair.

Pet dropped an empty basket beside Axel's washbasin. Pretending to be in the process of collecting the sodden clothing to hang, she muttered under her breath, "The contact reached out. We move the cargo tomorrow night." She didn't glance over her shoulder toward the window. It wouldn't do to draw too much attention.

Axel hummed, grabbing a handful of soiled laundry and dumping it into the sudsy water. The image might have been soothing or even domestic...if it weren't for the ill-fitting dress stretched across his broad shoulders. A song bobbed at his throat, one they'd heard in the mead hall they'd become regulars at over the past few weeks. He looked nonchalant, but Pet could see his thoughts rolling in and crashing like the tide. Their time in this town was up.

It had been like this in every town they'd visited over the last three months. Their missions were quick and quiet. They couldn't let anyone know what they were about, or it would be more than just their heads that rolled.

Or burned.

A gaggle of laundresses approached them, the boldest of them shoving forward as they encircled Axel. For the last two weeks, almost every girl in the laundry house had sauntered past Axel to brush an arm or a skirt against him. While he wore a dress, it did nothing to hide the very obvious breadth of his shoulders. The dress was a flimsy disguise anyway, used more to distract from what they were actually doing in the laundry house rather than conceal their identities. There was no hiding Axel no matter where in Åldras they went. Women flocked to him, and the laundresses were no different. They vied for his stolen looks and soft touches like undead draugr fought over living flesh.

"My lord," said the bold one, "we heard you humming and wondered if you would grace us with a song."

A smile curled at the corners of Axel's mouth. "You want me to sing for you?"

The girls nodded so emphatically their heads nearly dunked into the suds at Axel's feet.

"It's so dull in here," another said, "and your voice would be a relief to our boredom."

Pet bit the inside of her cheek. *Girls can be so senseless sometimes.* It seemed all anyone thought they were good for was batting lashes and shaking skirts. And it seemed they all believed it as well. Insipid morons the lot of them. Thank the Allfather Pet knew better.

Axel chuckled. His hum morphed into words, and the shiny-eyed girls grinned.

> *"Gather 'round, oh hearty kinsmen.*
> *Raise a tankard of honey ale*
> *To mighty Axel, son of Asher.*
> *Take a seat and hear his tale."*

The low rumble of his voice danced through the steam of the workroom and straight through Pet's bones. He scrubbed the dirty fabric in his hands across the rutted board the same way the notes rubbed along her spine.

As the laundry girls swayed to the tune, Pet pulled back from the gathering crowd. She didn't need to be suffocated by those flirty smiles or Axel's preening, and she finally let herself look close to the window. Viveca, the girl they had been tasked with rescuing, sat against one of the walls, mending a pair of trousers. A tiny, gray mouse skittered under her chair, but if the child saw it, she didn't so much as flinch. She couldn't be older than eight, but she wielded a bone needle as well as many of the older women. Axel had been doing his best to befriend her, working alongside her and asking about her favorite things. Viveca had grown comfortable around both him and Pet, which would make tomorrow night much easier.

Pet joined her. "Do you like music?" she whispered.

Viveca nodded shyly, peeking out between strands of golden hair, her gaze fixed on Axel as he finished the opening chorus and began the first verse.

> *"Born on his feet, twelve pounds of meat*
> *He'd take no milk from the witch's breast.*
> *Downed half a cask of bitter mead,*
> *Then belched and farted and drank the rest."*

The women gasped in mock outrage, and Axel's emerald eyes glittered as he smirked. Pet tried not to roll her own eyes but failed. He loved singing that verse to get a reaction from the fairer sex. *Well, most of the fairer sex.* Looking at her sun-darkened hands, nobody would categorize her as *fair*. Most days, she pretended she wasn't *female* either. It was that or end up just like these women, locked in a laundry house day in and day out. Or as someone's wife. She shuddered at the very thought.

No, it was better she kept pretending. They were careful. Pet never washed in front of anyone and made sure she always had cover. Never undressed anywhere someone could see her. Axel was the only one to dress her wounds. She told people she couldn't go without clothing because of the scars from the fire—scars she didn't have. As she'd gotten older, the fact she was a woman got harder to hide. When one lived in such close quarters with a group of men, there was bound to be some slip ups. If it wasn't for Axel, Pet's ruse would have been up the moment she stepped off Holmberg's blackened shores.

Fabricating lie after lie kept her alive. Kept her with Axel.

The chorus echoed through the room once again, bringing Pet back to the song weaving the tapestry of the story—a story Pet had not only heard, but seen with her own eyes.

The Sidans to the south of Åldras had come like thieves in the night. There had never been what anyone would describe as peace between the two kingdoms, but no one really understood why the Sidans had gone to Pet and Axel's home eight years ago. Why only two children had survived the onslaught. Why the Sidans had left behind nothing but ruins of a town that had stood as a beacon of strength to many. The Sidans had never offered up an explanation or apology, but they had birthed a legend in those ruins.

Mighty Axel, the only Häxa son to ever be born and the greatest warrior in all of history, had been Åldras's only hope against the Sidans for the last eight years of war. With the ability to perform feats of impossible strength and his imperviousness to injury, he had become a man of legend, giving him the moniker *Mighty Axel*. Many believed he was all that stood between Åldras and Sida. All that kept their kingdom from falling to the murderous invaders.

Axel Ashersson, a hero to everyone.

Everyone but Pet.

The man was a nuisance to say the least.

A group of people jostled about on the street outside. Viveca looked up toward the window, her golden eyes widening with worry, the bone needle clenched tightly in her fingers. Pet stood and took a short step toward the window. A company of men approached the door. One of them pushed forward, charging in the direction of the laundry house with a stormy expression matching the weather outside.

Doran.

"Oh, rocks," Pet cursed, but not loud enough to interrupt Axel's song.

> *"When Sida's rogues lined up to test him,*
> *One by one the raiders fell.*
> *Then once returned to hero's welcome,*
> *Åldras's maids lined up as well."*

The door of the cramped space swung open with a *bang*, sending the laundresses squealing and leaping back to their work areas. The intruder stomped into the room, flicking the hood of his drenched cloak back to reveal his ashy-blond hair and thick beard. His furious gaze turned darker when it landed on a still-singing Axel.

Pet drew back behind the hanging sheets in front of her, obscuring her from view. She tried to give Viveca a reassuring smile, but it likely fell flat. Doran always knew how to find them. Which was likely why Firmin kept sending him. Especially when they ignored the brute's summons.

Like they were now.

The tune strengthened as Axel bellowed out the last verse, completely ignoring the murderous-looking man while smiling at all the girls to distract them. Pet half-heartedly glared at him, and he winked back. *This is too fun,* that wink said. Reading his expressions was as easy as hearing his words.

Bloody idiot she said with her glare. She slunk around another line of laundry, keeping herself concealed from Doran's icy glare.

> *"Tales be told of legends many.*
> *Men of valor, wit and gall.*
> *In epic quests, adventures any,*
> *Mighty Axel bests them all!"*

At the last round of the chorus, Axel's exuberance grew contagious. His charming smile and outrageous volume lightened the laundresses' expressions once again. If Mighty Axel wasn't afraid of the fuming warrior in their midst, why should they be? A few of the more ridiculous girls took up the tune and even Pet's lips danced with the lyrics.

> *"Gather 'round, oh hearty kinsmen.*
> *Raise a tankard of honey ale*
> *To mighty Axel, son of Asher.*
> *Take a seat and hear his tale."*

The women cheered, the grumpy intruder forgotten, and demanded an encore. Axel stood gallantly and folded into a bow, nearly losing the wad of linen Pet had crammed into the bosom of his oversized blouse. A cluster of girls swooned when he flashed them a flirtatious grin. When his gaze caught Pet's again, he smirked. She returned his expression with a crude gesture.

His grin only deepened as he finally turned, his smile falling away with poorly feigned surprise at Doran's presence.

"My lord!" The falsetto of Axel's voice only added to the ridiculousness of his disguise. "An honorable man such as yourself shouldn't be dallying with us common women. Allow me to point you in the direction of the best pleasure house this side of the isle. They should be able to warm you up after being out in such wretched weather."

Pet peeked back around the curtain. Doran's expression darkened further, his cheeks pinking at Axel's implication. He'd always been a bit of a prude.

"Cut the horse dung, Axel." With a swipe of his hand, Doran pulled the cloth off Axel's head, revealing bright blond curls. "I won't be doing any 'dallying' because I'll be dragging you by the ear out to the docks!"

"Such a mood killer," Axel grumbled, his voice resuming its regular deep tone.

Doran shoved him. If not for his quick reflexes, Axel would have landed rump first in the wash bin. Pet almost smiled at the image but wiped the edges of it from her face. She grabbed a shawl hanging from one of the lines and took a silent step out from her hiding place.

Doran continued his tirade. "What in Midgard are you doing here, Axel? Disguised as a *laundress* no less." He gestured at Axel's lumpy ensemble then looked about the room. "And where is Petyr?"

"Here."

Doran jumped at Pet's quiet voice beside him. There was enough noise in the room to cover the sound of her movement. Not that she needed anything to mask her steps.

"Thunder's beard, Petyr! Why do you always have to do that?" He shook his head and gave Pet a little shove. "Such a sneaky little lad."

Pet couldn't help the flat look she gave the back of Doran's head when he turned away. The man was completely oblivious to Pet's true identity and had been for the entire seven years they'd known each other. Freyja's golden tears, she was wearing *a dress*. It should have been obvious, but most people only saw what they wanted, or what others told them to see.

When her eyes met Axel's glittering ones, it was as if he had plucked the very thoughts from her mind. *He really is daft, isn't he?* His lips pursed to conceal his amusement as Doran continued to cluck about like a mother hen. Pet tugged the borrowed shawl tighter around her shoulders.

Even when Doran had saved them from the ruins of their home, he had no inclinations that she was anything other than what they claimed: Axel's *boy* cousin. Which she certainly wasn't. The only familial connection they could claim was their mothers had been friends. Their fathers comrades in arms. Their homes only a stone's throw from each other. They'd been raised with the sea in their lungs and the sun against their skin. They were the last of Holmberg—the isle that had once stood tall in the middle of the Vit Sea, a beacon of hope to those of Åldras and the first line of defense against the kingdom to the south. Now, it was nothing more than an island of crusted ashes and dead dreams.

When they'd been found in the remains of their village at fourteen, it hadn't been too difficult for her and Axel to keep the secret of her gender. It became harder as the other young men their age grew, and even worse as they'd been thrust into the front lines of the bloody war.

The moment Axel had been deemed able enough to fight, Firmin had sent them onto battlefields no mortal man could survive. Ordered them to face foes no army could vanquish. Pet should have died ten times over—had the scars to prove it—but she was nothing if not persevering. She would never be separated from Axel as long as there was breath in her body. She'd walked onto every single battlefield. Killed hundreds of Sidans in the name of her kingdom.

Mighty Axel's shadow.

Åldras's demon.

The girl who fooled kings.

Axel gestured toward a curtained off room at the back. "Could we continue this conversation in private?"

Pet followed Doran and Axel as they wove through the women resuming their tasks. Axel's height made him duck beneath the doorframe. While Pet was the same height as Doran, her above average tallness didn't impede her at doorways. They all shuffled into the storage room. She tried to conceal the three of them with the curtain, but the cramped room already overflowed with barrels and clothing, making it difficult for them to cram into the space. Her back pressed against the curtain barely concealing them.

Axel sat on one of the barrels to make more room. "How did you find us?"

Doran clenched his fist, obviously fighting the urge to smack Axel. "It's not hard to track down a dwarf-made karve with the head of a phoenix when your crew leaves it sitting in plain view at the harbor. Everyone in Åldras knows that boat." He ran a hand down his face. "I thought I taught you both better than to leave tracks like that. I won't even mention the horrendous outfits." He gestured between the two of them. Pet caught herself frowning down at her own dress. It wasn't that bad. She'd found some thick linen that hid the entire bandolier of knives tucked under her bodice. Axel had done a fantastic job sewing the pieces together to hide it all. He was a master with a needle.

She shrugged. "Who said we didn't want to be found?"

Doran pointed back the way they'd come. "Then what was the ridiculous charade for?"

"We're here to poke fun at Firmin," Axel answered, "since he's been trying to get us to go to Harligdam for the last six weeks."

"*Six weeks?*" Doran shouted. The room beyond them quieted, and Doran lowered his voice. "He only told me he was attempting to summon you, not that you'd been ignoring him for six bloody weeks. And it's *High King* Firmin, you ingrate. If the two of you don't get your arses to Harligdam, he's going to put each of you on the end of a pike."

Axel folded his thick arms over his chest. "I don't quite feel the need to attend to his hissy fits at the moment. When he finds out I'm here, dressed up in this very flattering costume, the man is likely to grind his teeth so hard they crack. The idiot deserves to squirm a bit after the stunt he pulled in Koli."

Pet huffed out a breath. Axel had been in a rage when he'd had to go to Koli to fight against a band of huldra after Firmin had killed one of their young in a "hunting accident." However, if Axel thought that would be a satisfying excuse, he was wrong. Doran looked angrier than a bear with an arrow sticking out of his arse.

Axel scratched at the skin under his jaw. "While I'd like to say poking the Firmin beehive was the only reason we're here, it's not."

His green eyes flicked to Pet, and he nodded. *We should tell him.*

She tilted her head. *Are you certain?*

Another nod. *Yes.*

Fine. Pet rubbed at her brow and pushed the curtain open a bit, nudging Doran's shoulder. If Axel wanted to trust Doran with this information, she wasn't going to fight him on it. With her chin, she pointed out Viveca still sitting by the window, stitching up a pair of trousers. Wisps of blonde hair still fell into her face as her honey-brown eyes swept the room every few seconds.

Doran sucked in a sharp breath. "Is that who I think it is?"

"Obviously," drawled Axel as Pet allowed the curtain to fall back into place. "The Great Mother sent us to retrieve her granddaughter. We found her last week but had to make sure we could get her out safely before sending her off to wherever the Great Mother took the rest of the Häxa. The Ekte have been flocking like crows over the last few days."

Young Viveca had been on the Ekte's hunt list for two months now, after her family had been revealed as blood relatives of the Great Mother, leader of the Häxa. As Häxa, all the women in Viveca's imme-

9

diate family had been burned at the stake by Firmin's cadre of Ekte. The king's vile ideals were sweeping across the waters around Åldras. More and more women and children found themselves strapped to a pyre. This girl had only escaped because of her father, who had died trying to save the rest of his family from the bloody witch hunters.

It had taken Axel and Pet an entire month to track her down, only receiving word from the Great Mother that the child had found refuge with one of the laundresses in Stern. But Stern boasted six different laundry houses within its borders, and Viveca's protectors had done almost too good of a job hiding her.

"Are the two of you mad? You could be more than stuck on a pike. There would be a pyre for both of you and that little girl." Doran wagged a finger in Axel's face. "If High King Firmin finds out about this—"

"Relax, *grandfather*." Axel waved his hand dismissively, knocking aside Doran's threatening finger. "No one knows what we've actually been doing. Most folk think I'm here just to annoy *High King* Firmin, not to smuggle Häxa girls out of the city and reunite them with their matriarch."

Doran squeezed the bridge of his nose. "By all the gods in Asgard, you'll be the death of me."

"Look Pet!" Axel pointed at Doran's head. "I think I saw another silver hair sprout up."

Doran glared, but Pet couldn't stop the smile that grew on her lips. It had always been like this since she and Axel had been thrust by the gods into Doran's unprepared arms. Though the man was only fifteen years their senior, they'd certainly aged him in the five years they'd spent under his tutelage, and it only got slightly better in the two years since they had set out on their own.

"Hel's halls, King Firmin is going to have your heads for brushing him off. I know you both like to act as if he's some idiotic buffoon, but he's High King with the backing of every king and warlord in Åldras." Doran gave a sigh. "How long until you drop off the girl?"

"We're supposed to head out tomorrow night," Axel answered, "but we'll hand her off on another island. The smuggler we hired didn't want anyone catching wind of it." Axel shuffled past Pet and swept through the thin curtain. The girls closest to the storage room jumped, but grins broke across their faces when they saw Axel coming out.

Doran let out another long sigh as he glanced at the young girl in the corner. "The girl's rather recognizable and you'd probably be noticed if you tried anything in town. Especially with His Majesty having sent the Ekte after her." He straightened his tunic.

Bloody Ekte. Pet tapped her fingers against the blade she had hidden against her thigh. Of course, they'd gone into this mission knowing the hunters were coming for the Häxa girl. It was why the Great Mother had been so insistent *The Phoenix* sail to the rescue. The girl had already escaped certain death once, and Firmin would hate to be thwarted a second time. The thought made the corners of Pet's lips twitch.

Axel smiled, the stupid smile that had all the other women in the room gawking. He swung one large arm around Doran and the other around Pet's shoulders. "See, my lord? We did learn something from you."

Doran half-heartedly glared and shrugged off Axel's bulky arm as they walked across the room. "Too bad you didn't learn any manners. I thought I taught you to respect your elders."

Axel feigned a thoughtful expression. "I didn't know thirty-seven was considered elderly." He nudged Pet. "We really need to start working on our retirement plan if we're to quit the hero business before we become senile."

Doran elbowed Axel in the gut as they made it to the front door. He looked back toward the little girl with a hint of something deep...or possibly sad. "'The hero business has certainly saved more than a few families from being separated. For the sake of those of us who have lost too many in this war, I recommend sticking around a while."

The words made Pet's chest tighten. Holmberg hadn't been the only city to fall to the Sidans. Grovö had been hit shortly after, leaving Doran without a land to rule or a family to care for. And he wasn't the last to lose what he loved to the bloody Sidans. Eight years was too long for a war, and they were fighting it on two fronts. Axel would never let the Häxa down, but he also wouldn't allow Áldras to fall to Sida. If Axel simply rid Áldras of the Ekte, Firmin's ilk would revolt and the Häxa that would have been saved would burn in droves—not to mention all the women mistakenly charged with possessing magic. He could leave, but then the Häxa left behind would have no one to fight for them against Firmin and the Ekte. If Axel took Firmin and his idiotic brother out of power, Åldras would devolve into civil war, paving the way for the Sidans to come sweeping in and burning the rest of the kingdom to the ground. Pet could see her thoughts mirrored in Axel's eyes.

"We aren't going anywhere," he stated.

Doran shook himself and returned from wherever his thoughts had taken him. "Well, you certainly shouldn't go anywhere dressed like that." He waved a hand at their dingy costumes. "Make sure to wear some proper clothes when we—yes, *we*—meet at the dock tomorrow night. I don't think even the worst mead in this town will be able to wash the image of you two from my mind until we get to Harligdam— which we will after we take the girl to the Great Mother." His eyes flicked between the two of them before he shook his head. "You two make for some horrifying women."

Pet refrained from snorting. *You have no idea.*

Doran walked out the door and joined the men he'd arrived with. A few from Doran's old crew followed him back up the road. They'd likely come with him to fetch Axel in case there was a skirmish. Not that they would be much help. Doran still had the small scar on his cheek from where Pet had sliced him in their last fight and there wasn't much anyone could do to get Axel to do something he didn't want to.

Axel leaned down and picked up a shiny, silver button from the ground. "Well, I guess we get to add one more to the crew for tomorrow night."

Pet nodded, already rearranging the numbers in her head. Depending on how quickly they needed to get out, they would need him either working the sail or at the oars. "I'll let Erik know to put him on the oar rotation."

But Axel probably hadn't been listening. When she turned to look at him, he'd already crossed the few steps to where Viveca sat, offering her the shiny button with a genuine smile on his face.

CHAPTER 2

DRUNKARDS

"That bloody stick ought to watch where it's going." *Hiccup.* "Should know better than to mess with the likes of us."

Though Axel knew Pet was playing the role of a drunkard, he nearly lost his composure. She really did look like a lad who'd been too deep in his cups, but he knew she'd never tasted more than a drop or two of mead in her life. While Axel's magic made it impossible for any mead to ever inebriate him, Pet wanted to avoid the fog that came with it, so neither of them drank.

But it had been important to behave as if nothing were amiss. After Doran had stormed in the day before, it had been better for Axel and Pet to avoid the laundry house. Besides, Viveca wasn't at the laundry house that day. Axel had tasked her guardian with keeping her hidden until he and Pet could retrieve her. So, to the mead hall they'd gone and wasted good silver on watered-down mead.

"All right, little man," Axel said, loud enough for everyone on the street to hear, "let's get back to the house and leave the poor, innocent stick alone."

"Innocent!" Pet screeched, her scratchy voice taking on a pitch only a very put-out young man—or girl—could. "You wouldn't know innocent if it looked you in the eyes, you giant oaf. Innocence runs when you come calling. It has nightmares about you and your non-innocence-ness. Women weep and children scurry when they smell the faintest whiff of your foul stench."

Axel leaned down as if giving her a talking to. "Over-selling it much?"

Pet's keen, steel gaze looked up at him through half-lidded eyes. The blue-green hazel of her irises brightened with mirth. "Why? Do they look suspicious?"

Axel looked around, pretending he didn't know where they were walking, and spotted the two men who had followed them from the mead hall they'd used to begin their ruse. Neither man had a weapon in hand, and both looked bored rather than wary. *Good.*

Why they were being tailed, Axel could only guess. It could be that Firmin wanted to keep better tabs on them. Or the Sidans had sent them to watch them. Or maybe the bloody Ekte had sniffed out the little girl and they were waiting for Axel to make a move for her. But Axel had spotted the two men watching them a little too closely at the mead hall. While being the only man ever born by a Häxa, the only man who couldn't be killed by any blade or poison, certainly gave him notoriety, these stalkers had way too many blades hidden in their cloaks to be Mighty Axel devotees.

After Doran was able to find them the day before, it shouldn't have been surprising that the bloody vultures swarmed. The whole kingdom knew Doran only ever showed up when he was sent to mediate between Axel and Firmin. Doran, the peacekeeper king. Freyja's golden tears, if Axel could find a way to put him in Firmin's place, he would. If the title of High King didn't pass through a family line, he would have displaced both Firmin and his insipid brother years ago, but Firmin had a whole litter of brats that didn't deserve Axel's ire. It wasn't their fault their father was a maggot.

Axel would simply figure out how to get rid of the Häxa killer after they stopped the Sidans from burning the rest of Åldras to the ground. Priorities and all that.

He wrapped his arm back around Pet's neck. "Let's just get to bed," he boomed. "My head's already starting to ache."

"Can't hold your drink, eh?" Pet prodded his side, almost making him jump. He gave her a sharp look. He hated being tickled and she knew it.

They walked—well, exaggeratedly staggered—through the small streets of the town. Being this close to the edge of their kingdom, signs of the war with the invading country were more prevalent in Stern. The Sidans had raided many of the towns on the edges of Åldras, stealing away women and children, and bringing military force into the towns. Axel's pulse spiked whenever he saw the empty husks of burned houses or the thin limbs of the children crawling out of the shadows. While he might have been grateful for the temporary armistice between Åldras and Sida, something in his chest still burned at the fact that these people only had a couple of seasons to prepare for another onslaught.

One year wasn't enough. Nothing would be enough until this war was finally over.

"Keep it together," Pet hissed. The short hairs of Pet's dark locks brushed against his arm as she looked up at him, centering him a bit.

Axel loosened his stiff muscles once again. It would all be done tonight. He wouldn't have to worry about getting Viveca out of this place even one more night. The child had stolen a little piece of his heart over the last few weeks. She was a quiet little mouse, such a contrast to her grandmother who had more than enough words.

They turned down the street leading to the tall visiting house where they were staying. Stern was one of the smallest towns to have such a place, and Axel viewed it as a miracle that it hadn't been torn down in any of the skirmishes. Three men stood outside, attempting to hide their interest at Axel and Pet's arrival. Pet tapped him on the arm twice, making the total number of stalkers seven. Pet pinched him and let out a loud belch. Even after all these years, it was still impressive she could do that on command.

Axel's attention snagged on the beggar man who let out two sneezes from the shadows of the house. The cue.

"I hope you don't snore like a pack of wild animals tonight," Axel said, loudly.

Pet spluttered. "*Me?* You're the mouth-breather!"

"*I'm* the mouth-breather? You're the one that bugles like a deranged elk!"

Pet gave him a halfhearted shove, but Axel made it look like she'd nearly toppled him. He shoved her back, knowing she expected it, but still winced when she landed in the trash pile next to the inn. He took a step toward her. Sometimes he forgot his own strength.

With a very authentic roar, she jumped up from the refuse and pounced on him. Of course, if they were doing this for real, she wouldn't have even moved him. However, since he was supposed to be drunk, he fell with her. He did his best to take the brunt of the fall, knowing he wouldn't even get a scratch. They landed with a thud on the ground and rolled through the garbage.

Pet landed on top. "How do you like it, you *stupid troll*?"

"I'm a very intelligent troll, you dwarfish half-breed. Now, get off me!" He bucked her off and she landed with her legs sprawled next to the grubby man in the shadows. Axel stood and barely saw the flash of white pass from the man's soiled hands into Pet's boot.

Pet jumped up and came at him again, her hazel eyes flashing bright. Pet took him by the front of his shirt. "How dare you call me that?" She breathed heavily and sloppily punched at him as he purposefully batted away half of her attempts. Soon, both of them slowed as if growing tired and slumped down on the ground in front of the steps.

"I'm not a half-breed," Pet griped in her most masculine, whiny voice. She'd really perfected it over the years. As everyone else believed she was barely eighteen, she had trod the fine line between adolescent and man for years. She'd even mastered the little squeak boys got when their voice changed.

"I know." Axel slurred his words. "I didn't mean it."

"It hurts when you say stuff like that." Pet gave an exaggerated sniff.

Axel almost snorted. "I know. I'm sorry."

"I didn't mean it when I said you were a troll." Pet wiped her sleeve over her eyes. "You're my best friend. You're the best cousin a man like me could ask for. I love you so much."

That was when Axel heard it. The sniggers of disgust...and dismissal.

He looked about as if perusing the world in front of his supposedly hazy eyes. The three men still stood at the front of the inn, but all of them had turned toward one another and began whispering. The two tailing them turned back the way they'd come. One on the rooftop across from them crawled down the side of the thatched roof.

Axel heaved himself up to standing, sticking his hand out to Pet. "Let's get inside. I don't want to sleep on the ground."

Pet grabbed his proffered hand and stood, swaying like reeds in water. They thumped up the steps to the house side by side, nearly smashing face first into the wooden door as it swung open, and a raucous group came pouring out. Pet let her head drop back in feigned exhaustion as Axel held the door, the candlelight from within illuminating the skin of her throat. He swallowed hard and turned away. Sometimes, the late night picked at his resolve. Every now and again, he couldn't help looking at her like he shouldn't. Couldn't help the swoop in his stomach or the stutter of his heart.

Once the door cleared, the two of them stumbled into the building. The public room on the bottom floor of the house still teemed with people despite the late hour. The owner of the large house was known for having mead nights every so often for his guests. Town guards just getting off shift huddled in a corner as dogs lapped up drips of grease from the floor at their feet. Each bench was filled by the rump of a man holding tightly to a tankard of mead.

It was the trio of Ekte against the back wall that had Axel's fingers curling into fists. *Bloody Häxa killers.* The tall flame atop the candle at their table flickered, casting light onto the scars dotting their faces. Each rune nullified a type of magic. Each scar made it easier for them to kill a Häxa.

"*Och*, my lord, I didn't know if you'd be coming home tonight," said the owner from where he stood near the fire. Where most houses in Åldras placed their fires in the middle and used a hole in the roof to rid the building of the worst of the smoke, this house had a towering stone box tucked into the corner of the building. There was a hole at the top for the smoke to go out, allowing the house to be two stories tall and offer more rooms for visitors of the small town. It was also one of the cleanest houses Axel had ever visited. When he'd asked about the unique design, the owner had said it was common across the Vit Sea in Tatawar and even making its way into Sida.

Axel pushed his most unconcerned grin onto his face, pretending to stumble a bit and nearly knocking Pet into one of the tables. "Pet here had one too many drinks, and we decided it best to get to our beds before we had to work in the morning."

The innkeeper shook his head. "Odd lads," he mumbled, but Axel could hear him over the din of the great room even if no one else could. The innkeeper shook off his misgivings and gave Axel a smile anyway, his desire for coin likely overriding any complaints he had about their roughed-up appearance. Wōden's one good eye, Pet had nearly torn Axel's sleeve from his shoulder.

Pet pretended to trip over her boots as she wove through the crowd beside him. Axel wouldn't be surprised if she arrived at their room with a handful of coin purses and a few new knives. Since Holmberg, she'd picked up the nasty habit of picking pockets. Axel couldn't really blame her. Those first few months after they'd left home had been brutal. Especially for her.

While no one had known she was a girl, the boys they'd trained with had found her wanting, weak. Those boys had gained quite a few broken bones, and Axel hadn't even had to get involved...*much*. He looked over at Pet, the bump on her nose from the few times it had been broken catching the candlelight in the hallway. With Axel's gifts, not even his nose had ever been broken. Pet wore scars enough for the both of them it seemed.

"Stop gawking at me," she hissed. "We need to get into the Ektes' room."

Right. The plan.

The steps leading up to the second story squeaked in protest as they stomped up them. They'd chosen this particular guesthouse because of its proximity to the docks, as well as its reputation for housing traveling Ekte. *Bloody witch hunters.* While the Ekte order had been around for decades, it wasn't until Firmin was crowned High King that they had any real foothold in Åldras. Now, the bloody heathens were everywhere.

Pet stopped at a door and quietly tried the knob. It didn't budge.

"Rocks," Pet bit out and dug about in the pocket of her trousers. She fished out a sleeve of lock picks. "Watch the stairs, will you?"

Axel didn't need to turn around to do as she asked. His heightened senses allowed him to hear more than a normal person. Pet was well aware of this, but he obliged her anyway. She never liked working with an audience.

Even turned around, he was acutely aware of her movements. Her fingers deftly moved the pins in the locks with small clicks, and she adjusted her weight on the floorboards under her boots. She'd always been a clever thing. As the only girl in a family of five older brothers, she'd had to keep up with them. Mallory—Pet's Da—had known the best way was through her wit rather than her brawn. He'd trained his daughter to be a fox in the den of wolves he'd raised.

"Got it," she said, and the door swung open.

"Finally!" he said, feigning exasperation. "I could have done that in half the time."

Pet rolled her eyes. "Sure you could."

Axel stepped into the room, taking the lead in case someone waited for them on the other side, though he hadn't heard anyone. When they found the room empty, Pet pocketed her pins and began rifling through trunks, tossing the contents all over the floor. Axel set to work on the bedding, tearing the sheets in half with his hands.

"Show off," Pet muttered.

When the room was effectively tossed, Axel turned back toward the door. Hopefully, the Ektes search for whoever had wrecked their room would keep them busy long enough for them to get the girl out of the city.

"Hey Axel, look at this."

He turned back and found Pet looming over the wash bowl on one of the tables. Quick as an adder, she snatched a half-burned piece of parchment out of the bowl. Her brows lowered as she read it. With a growl, she passed it to him. "The Ekte are going for the girl tonight."

Axel took the paper and read it over. The Ekte were indeed going after their charge. Axel and Pet weren't the only ones that knew the child was in the city, but they'd be the first ones to get to her. He crumpled the partial note and tossed it onto the shredded bed linens. "Bloody Ekte."

Pet grabbed his sleeve. "Come on. Our timetable just moved up."

Axel followed her out, stomping on every piece of shredded bed sheet or broken pottery he could see. The Ekte would pay a pretty penny to the house owner when he saw this. Axel paused at the sound of the creaking steps of the stairs. He pushed Pet toward their room. "Incoming."

The door to their room swung most of the way closed just as the

Ekte arrived in the hallway. Axel stood above Pet and watched through the tiniest crack of the door as the trio took in the destruction. They marched back down the stairs in an uproar.

When they were out of sight, Pet shut the door the rest of the way. "Time to go."

ᚠᚾᚲᛟᚠᚤᚱ

MOST PEOPLE BELIEVED Axel's favorite part of his work was the fighting. With his unmatched skill with a blade and his unbreakable skin, he was a born warrior, an unconquerable foe. People thought he relished the victory over regular men, wrote songs about how he delighted in the clash of swords and reveled in the spray of blood.

He didn't.

Pet stopped at a crooked looking door, ducking her head to peer down at the crumpled note in her hand. The one she'd received from the beggar in the alley. She tossed the note into the pile of garbage next to the front step and knocked quietly. Two raps of her knuckles, then three, then two again.

The door opened and an older woman peered out into the midnight darkness. Without a word, she gestured for someone behind her, and a little bundle of dark cloth waddled into the doorway. A pair of honey eyes peeked out from under the thick hood.

Pet exchanged a few quiet words with the older woman and nudged the small girl toward Axel. He crouched down and offered her a smile. The crinkle of her eyes returned the expression. He held out his arms and she went to him, trust and hope in the skip of her step.

No, the fighting was not his favorite part.

The saving was.

The crooked door snicked shut, and Pet pointed her chin in the direction they needed to go. She always had a plan. While Axel might be the brawn of the operations, Pet had always been the brains. With the little girl scooped up in one arm and his hand on the hilt of his sword, he charged after Pet through the muddy streets. The girl wrapped her arms around his neck, eyes fixed on Pet's cloaked form in front of them as much as Axel's were.

Pet wove through the streets ahead of him, following a path only she could see in her mind. Since the Ekte were also there for the child, it wouldn't do to walk straight to the boat. The docks would be watched, the ships searched before leaving port. Which was why Axel had sent word ahead for the crew to leave the harbor and meet them a short way down the river.

"Over here," Pet hissed as she pulled them into a deeply shadowed doorway.

A pair of Ekte in their long cloaks sauntered down the length of the road on the other side. The hairs on Axel's skin rose at the glimpse of the runes carved into their cheeks. One held a sword and the other a halberd, though the marks on their skin were more of a weapon than either blade. Those marks made them impervious to Häxa gifts, the very magic repelled by simple lines. It was the one thing that made them the largest threat to a Häxa. Those bloody marks. If a single mark was made on a Häxa, it blocked their magic. He'd seen arms carved with fresh marks before they were strapped onto a pyre. Thank the Allfather his skin couldn't be marred. It was likely the only reason Firmin hadn't killed him off yet.

Pet's eyes flicked over the two men as she picked at the cracked skin of her bottom lip.

Axel swatted her hand away. "Stop that."

She glared at him but didn't keep picking. "There wasn't supposed to be a patrol on this road right now. They should be on the other side of the square."

"So, someone figured out what we're up to." Axel frowned as she stared at the Ekte, her eyes gleaming a bit wickedly. "Don't be getting any ideas. We can't attack them outright. I'm down a hand and this mud would be terrible to run through, no matter that it would slow them down too."

Pet shook her head. "I know, but if we keep running into Ekte on the road, we won't make it to *The Phoenix* in time. I told Erik to meet us before dawn, and we still have a three-hour walk ahead of us."

Axel adjusted his grip on the child. She'd laid her head on his shoulder as her form had gone limp a few minutes ago. *Poor thing.* They would get her to her grandmother, and she would finally be able to rest easy.

"They're gone," Pet said, pointing toward the end of the road. The

Häxa hunters had walked out of sight. Axel crept out into the moon-light. Of course, the storms that had plagued Stern for the last three days had abated by that evening, taking the cover the clouds would have provided. Axel's boots squelched in the mud under his feet as he raced over the unprotected road.

A shout went up from behind him.

Pet spun. "Hel's bloody halls."

Axel looked over his shoulder and found the Ekte they'd just watched disappear come back into sight, weapons in hand.

Quickly, Pet grabbed Axel's arm and swung it around her shoulder. A jolt shot from his fingers all the way to his toes. She tucked herself into his side and laid a small hand on the little girl's sleeping form.

Play along the widening of her eyes said.

The Ekte, one looking to be middle aged and the other likely just out of training, trudged through the mud toward them, their faces shifting from angry to confused as they took in Axel and Pet.

"Good evening," Axel said as the men drew closer.

The one on the right, the younger, adjusted his helmet to see them better. "A bit late to call it evening."

Axel pushed out his most charming laugh and adjusted his hold on the girl. She had stiffened, woken by the sound of the new voices. "My son agrees with you. We were just on our way home from my father's house." He gave a little frown. "We don't often see patrolmen on this road. Anything we should be concerned about?"

The Ektes both shared a look, their suspicions dissipating. "Nothing you folks should be worried about. Just some slight distur-bances out by the docks. We wanted to do our part to help the people of Stern feel safe."

"How thoughtful." Axel settled a hand on Pet's back. "We'll be on our way then. Need to get the little one into bed before it gets any later."

The guards nodded and walked past them. The younger one stepped right beside Axel and nodded. "Nice sword."

Axel froze as the older guard stiffened. Hel's bloody halls, of course the rockhead would recognize the sword. The lysande blade was only one of few, the swirls in the steel distinct. Only a dwarf made sword looked like this and only a handful of men could claim to wield one.

"Rocks," Pet cursed.

Before Axel could draw his blade, Pet had her axes in hand and her hood back.

"Get the child!" barked the elder and lifted his halberd.

One of Pet's short throwing knives spun in the air toward him as she pounced on the younger one like a wolverine. The older Ekte dodged the flying blade. Axel drew his sword, his arm still wrapped around the little girl hanging from his neck.

"Give us the girl," the Ekte said. "We don't want anyone to get hurt."

Axel scoffed. "I don't think I believe you." He struck before the older man could say another word. His sword sang as it swung through the air, the tune one of justice and imminent death. Wōden's one good eye, he hated these hunters.

His sword met the shaft of the halberd, digging a deep notch into the hardwood. The guard twisted his long ax, dislodging the sword, and swung at Axel's head. Axel ducked to avoid the blow. He came up quickly, sword swinging. The sharp edge glanced off the guard's leather armor. If Axel had been bearing the sword with two hands, it would have gone straight through to the skin.

The little girl clung to him tightly as he readjusted his footing in the slippery mud and retreated from the guard's attack.

An ax flew past his shoulder and stuck into the Ekte's helmet.

The Ekte fell, the blow sending him back and killing him on impact.

Axel spun and found Pet, her fingers still outstretched from the throw.

She straightened, wiping the blade of her other ax on the tunic of the dead Ekte at her feet. "You're growing lax in your old age."

Axel rolled his eyes and sheathed his sword. "I turn twenty-two at the end of Heyannir and suddenly I'm ancient? What does that make you?"

Pet walked over to retrieve her other ax. "Aged like the fine wine those Sidans are so fond of." She grinned at him. Pet was in fact seven weeks older than him, much to his chagrin. She'd always lorded it over him, making sure to remind him often that he knew she was the one in charge.

Axel turned to the child in his arms and peeked under the cowl covering her wheat-blonde hair. Her eyes were scrunched shut. Axel took several steps down the street, turning away from where Pet riffled through the dead men's pockets for any information.

"Are you still with me, little mouse?"

The girl peeked through one eyelid. After a quick glance around to check for any other danger, she opened her eyes fully.

"Are you all right?" he asked.

She nodded, but her tiny frame shook against him.

Pet came up beside them, tucking a few coins into her pocket. She was going to be rich after this trip. "Nothing of any consequence," she reported.

Axel tucked the child's head under his chin. "Then let's get to the boat and deliver this girl to her grandmother."

CHAPTER 3

A STORY

The splash of the oars sliding through the water settled Pet's beating heart. Her eyes still scanned the shore for more Ekte to come pouncing out of the fading shadows, but the farther they sailed from Stern, the less her pulse jumped. A calm breeze wound through the morning air around the ship, cooling the sweat-soaked back of her shirt and sweeping the tips of her hair up to tickle her jaw. Her arms moved rhythmically with the other men on the oars.

"Ah, Pet," Axel sighed. "Isn't this great? The open sky, the salty air. It's like a song taken life."

She glanced up. "The view would certainly be better if you would sit your arse down and help us row."

Axel plunked down on his trunk across from her, jostling Viveca seated there. Her bright eyes took in the scene around them, likely looking for whatever song Axel saw in the night-darkened world around them. He grabbed the wooden oar lying at his feet and gave the girl a genuine smile, which she tried to match. Dropping the large oar back down without touching the water, he reached into the pack he had crammed between his trunk and the gunwale.

Pet gritted her teeth and pushed her oar through the water. The bloody thing was over ten ells long—a single ell measuring about fingertip to elbow. The current going out into the sea carried them forward, but the cliffs on either side of the ship funneled the wind in the wrong direction for the sail and they needed to leave the island behind them before anyone got the idea to try to track them.

"Here," Axel whispered, pulling out a small cloth bundle and holding it out to Viveca. "I was saving these for later, but you look like you might enjoy them more than I will. Might even help you stay awake until we get out to open waters. Having something to munch on always helps me."

Viveca hesitated before slowly reaching her hand out to grab the sack. She pulled it open and found the dried peaches and walnut bits within. An excited gasp escaped her as her thin fingers plucked out one of the peaches. Pet's lips twitched at the child's obvious delight. At least they could be counted on for sweets. Axel never went anywhere without at least three of those snack bags on his person and a dozen more scattered throughout his trunk and satchel. Pet had a few mixed in with her supplies as well.

"All right, men!" Erik, the ship's skipper, hollered from his perch at the tiller. "Ready the sail!"

While Axel was *The Phoenix's* steersman with command over where *The Phoenix* went and what missions the crew undertook, Erik directed the ship through the water, charting the course and leading the men through rough seas. The old man ran a tight ship, one of the reasons Pet had convinced Axel to take him on almost three years ago. Lucky for them, no one had wanted a legless man to steer their ships, even if he could move at the same speed as the rest of the crew with the sliding platform the dwarf craftsmen had made him when they built *The Phoenix*. But he kept them out of more scrapes than any other skipper sailing the Vit Sea. Pet had sung praises to Allfather ever since.

The crew not on the oars scurried about. Little Hal, the youngest member on their ship at age twelve, scrambled to the edge of the deck and looked over the side. Erik barked at him to grab one of the stays and the lad jumped into action.

Big Hal, who shared the same name as Little Hal—*Halvor*—stood next to the gunwale, his arms straining as he pulled at the shroud and fastened the sail into place. Big Hal made it look easy when Pet knew it wasn't. The man's shoulders were slightly broader than Axel's, though he stood a few inches shorter, and his arms were thicker than tree trunks. He was in regular competition with Axel in strength, though he never won. However, he was wicked with a war hammer and could take out five Sidans with a single swing.

Doran rowed at one of the oar slots across from Olav, Little Hal's grandfather who talked at Doran without taking a breath. While most ships had a bard to tell tales of their crew's noble deeds, *The Phoenix* had, well, *Olav.*

"The people who are called 'shepherds' herd sheep," Olav mused. "Does that mean the people who herd cows are 'cowards?'"

Doran gritted his teeth, eyes flashing up at Olav, but the older man didn't even take a breath.

"I had a herd of cows once. Best cows in Åldras. Little Hal's ma named every one of them. My daughter had a thing for flowers. There was Campion, Poppy, Willow, Saxifrage, Tulip, Bluebell, Lilac. Oh, what were the others? We had a dozen or so. Our big bull was named Buttercup."

"Steady men!" Erik called just as the sail snapped into place.

Pet closed her eyes and took in a deep breath as their ship broke from the walls of the cliff and pushed out to sea. The salt in the air always reminded her of Holmberg in a way nothing else ever could. The fresh scent of the ocean brought back the memories of home, of warm days and happy nights with her brothers gathered around the table. A song on Mama's lips. Da's booming laugh.

So unlike the visions of ash and smoke, saved for when she slept.

Erik quietly called for the oarsmen to fasten the oars down inside the hull as the sail took them into the water and toward their destination. Pet pulled her oar through the oar port and tied it down. Doran finished tying his off and came to sit by Axel. Sweat gleamed on his forehead as he guzzled from a waterskin.

"Where are we to meet the smuggler?" he asked, breathing heavy. He'd obviously grown lax in his new position as councilor to Firmin if such a short row had him this worn out. It had been just before the armistice was called that Firmin finally realized Doran's silver tongue was sharper than his sword. Wōden's eye, the armistice only happened because of Doran. Grovö's king might have been young, but he had wisdom in droves. It was one of the only reasons he'd been able to put up with Axel and Pet as they grew.

Perhaps she'd tell Erik to put him on double oar rotations to bulk him back up. He'd done it to her and Axel enough times growing up.

"We'll make the drop a little way off the coast of Mötesplats," Axel responded nonchalantly.

"You're joking, right?"

Pet shrugged. "Of course."

Axel nudged Doran. "Don't listen to Pet. They just repaired the port on Mötesplats last week. There are boats in and out of there at all times right now. We'll be a leaf floating downriver in the middle of autumn."

"Yes, except your leaf looks like a bloody phoenix and your cargo is one of High King Firmin's most sought-after fugitives. The Ekte are likely swarming these waters for the lot of you even now."

"And that's why we're the ones taking Viveca home," Axel cut in. "The Great Mother would never have allowed anyone but kin to deliver her. It certainly helps that her only son is also the greatest hero in all of Åldras." He winked at Viveca, and she gave him a timid smile, the small bag in her hand empty.

Pet reached into her own satchel and grabbed another pouch. Axel got cranky when he was hungry, so she made sure to always be prepared. Viveca's mouth stretched into an eager smile when Pet placed it in her palm.

Doran snorted. "It seems not all your Häxa kin are so loyal. This one is easily bribed out of your good graces."

Axel leaned back against the side of the ship. "Well, who couldn't fall to Pet's irresistible charms?"

Pet kicked Axel in the shin as Doran let out a chortle. "Only you would dare call a wolverine charming."

"Pet *is* charming. At least, when he's not trying to gouge your eyes out or chop your head off." A manic grin cracked Axel's face as Pet bared her teeth.

Moron. Sometimes, she couldn't tell who the real liar was, her or Axel. Especially when he said things like her being *charming*.

"I can honestly say I don't miss watching over you two. You squabble nearly as much as High King Firmin and King Anders."

Axel squawked indignantly. "How dare you compare us to those idiots! They only squabble because neither of them has any brains to sit down and have a civilized conversation without trying to stab each other."

"'Civilized' is not a word I would use to describe Petyr or you. 'Reckless' or 'hot-headed' fit the bill much better."

"Pet, did you hear?" Axel leaned over toward her conspiratorially. "Doran thinks you're reckless and hot-headed."

Pet sent Axel a flat look as Doran gave in to his impulses and finally smacked Axel upside the head.

"Why do you call him 'Pet?'" asked a small voice.

All three of their heads turned toward Viveca's small form as she continued munching on the snack in her hands. It was a question many had asked. Pet had answered with a number of things, none of them true. No one would ever learn the truth.

Axel cleared his throat. "I've always called him that, since we were even younger than you. It's a 'pet-name' I guess you could say."

Olav crowed in laughter from across the deck.

Viveca's shoulders shook in silent giggles in the overly large cloak draped over her shoulders to keep the chill of Njord's breath from freezing her.

It was the small laugh that kept Pet from kicking Axel again. She leaned over toward the child instead. "He thinks if he keeps calling me that, I might start listening to what he says like any other good pet would."

Viveca's smile fell, and she looked down at her toes. "I used to fight with my sisters too."

Pet met Axel's softened gaze across the small foot space.

He tucked his arm around the girl's small frame. "You won't believe me yet, but I promise that where you're going, there will be family for you again. Your grandmother is a crazy old bat, who says some rather odd things, but she loves with her whole heart."

Sniffles accompanied Viveca's quaking. Silver limned eyes met Pet's. The quiver of the girl's lip nearly undid her steely resolve. "I don't want to love anyone else. Mama and Papa and Sorscha and Lottie are all I want."

Pet reached out and grabbed Viveca's hand. It was so tiny and soft in Pet's calloused one. They sat in that position for several minutes as quiet sobs broke from the child's thin chest. It wasn't fair. This war wasn't fair. This girl's fear wasn't fair. The scars on Pet's soul ached with her own loss, calloused over the years. Her eyes turned on Axel and she saw the wounds of their past plain on his face.

He understood Viveca's pain too.

Even though the odd Häxa magic he'd been blessed with made him impervious to death, he felt every Häxa death keenly. It was why he strived to help them get to the Great Mother. Why he risked the lives of the crew to help them escape. The virtuous idiot would give up his own magic if it would mean finding peace for everyone in Åldras—human and Häxa alike.

Axel leaned toward Viveca, his own eyes glistening with bits of ash and smoke. "Have you ever heard the story about your grandmother and the bear?"

The little girl's head turned to look up at him, and she shook it softly.

Axel's face broke into a grin. "Olav! We are in need of a tale."

Olav looked up from where he had a string dangling off the side of the ship. "A tale, you say? Would you like to hear the one of you defeating the ice bear? Or the one about you saving the daughter of King Agnar from the clutches of the dreaded Sidans? Perhaps the one about the man cursed to be a ferret?"

A twitch grabbed the corner of Pet's lips. Olav's job on the ship was to maintain morale, which he did with much aplomb. He regularly retold stories of the crew's adventures, though the ferret curse story he told because it was Little Hal's favorite.

Axel flapped a hand at him. "We want the one about the Great Mother's origin. For our guest here."

"Ah, a magical tale." Olav dusted off his tunic and settled himself onto his trunk, spreading his cloak like wings behind him. A light sparked in his eye as he met Viveca's gaze, his knobby fingers weaving through the air as if he could hold the story itself.

"Once, a long time ago, the Great Mother was not the brave and illustrious leader of the Häxa. Once, she was a little girl, just like you, with a big well of curiosity. The Great Mother was then known simply as Gyllene. Back then, the Häxa lived in the villages of Åldras like everyone else, and we all gave tribute to the jötunn, the great gods of Asgard, under their watchful care. One day, after she had done her chores around the house, Gyllene decided to go adventuring in the woods around her home. Gyllene wanted to prove to her mother that she was a powerful Häxa, even though she had not found her förändra."

Viveca gasped and leaned toward Olav. Every good Häxa knew not to tempt fate when on the hunt for their förändra. At least, that was what Pet had heard. She didn't actually know, as she hadn't been raised to understand the ways of the Häxa as a child.

"That's right, Little One. Gyllene hadn't experienced the change from witchling to those with magic from the elements of the world around them—though not for a lack of trying. All her young friends had found the catalyst to their gifts. The forest around their village held creeks, plants, and rocks aplenty to help the girls find their source of magic and begin using them. Gyllene however, had found nothing worked. So, on this particular day, she decided to jump across the creek near her house and embark on a quest."

Everyone on the boat grew quiet. While Olav drove most of the crew mad with his ramblings, he could weave a story like no other. It made one feel like maybe there was a little magic in everyone. That maybe elements weren't the only gifts given to humankind.

"For an entire day, Gyllene walked deeper into the wood. As the light of the day faded, creatures of the night called to one another. The girl stumbled blindly through the trees, doing her best to let Máni's light guide her steps. It's said that as she walked, her journey was witnessed by the Two Crows who delivered the tale to Wōden's ears themselves."

Viveca's eyes widened farther, and the crew leaned in. Olav held the entire ship in the palm of his hand. Even Pet lost herself to his voice though she'd heard this story a hundred times growing up.

"Gyllene stumbled out into a grove to be met with the sound of snuffling and grunting. Not ten ells in front of her lumbered a great, brown bear. The animal turned its muzzle in the direction of Gyllene, his dark eyes staring at her quivering spirit. Gyllene knew Häxa could speak with nature more than regular folk, but without proper training and without her *förändra*, she knew nothing could help her in the face of this giant beast."

Viveca's hand tightened around Pet's.

Olav lifted his arms overhead, knobby fingers curled like claws. "The brown mass of fur stood up on his two hind legs, taller than a mighty tree. Gyllene took a step back only to trip and fall. As she placed her hand on the ground to stand, her fingers met with something hard and white in the moonlight. It's said that when her skin touched the bones of the deer, the whole forest erupted into a cacophony of sound. The birds chorused together with the howl of the wolves and bugle of the elk. When the noise settled and the animals of the forest nestled back in their beds, Gyllene found herself in the skin of a great white wolf and heard the voice of the bear as she would her own mother's."

Viveca sprang up. "That's why Mormor wears bones. They help her shift and speak with the animals just like me." She reached into the neck of her shirt and pulled out a small piece of chicken bone attached to a cord of leather. Her eyes sparkled as she showed off her prized possession.

Pet looked to Axel and found the mirror of her own surprise on his face. Animal shifting was one of the rarest gifts the Häxa had, and many believed it had gone extinct along with the gifts of fire charming and spirit walking. The Great Mother was the first in generations to be blessed with the gift to shift. It was no wonder why the Ekte were after the child in the first place.

Olav's sun-wrinkled face softened. "It'll be good to have something in common with your mormor. She'll love to teach you more about your gift once you meet her."

Viveca spun around to look up at Pet. "Do you like her?"

"Not particularly," Pet stated bluntly. The lie rolled off her tongue before she thought too hard about it.

Axel poked her shoulder. "Yes, you do." He turned back to the girl. "Why, your *mormor* always tells me to look after Pet here in every letter she sends me. I think she thinks I'm going to get him into trouble."

Viveca's brows drew together. "Are you going to get him in trouble?"

"Maybe," Pet replied, "but it'll only be because I have to get him out of it."

ᛈᚾᚲᚩᚠᚤᛚ

"LAND!" Big Hal called overhead.

Pet stood, the handles of her short axes tapping her thighs, and urged Viveca to stand with her as the coast of Mötesplats came into view. The island glowed with moonlight, the black sands sparkling. Tall trees crowded together at the edge, but Pet could see the glow of life from the small harbor town sticking out along the shore.

The journey had taken them a full day, and the stars danced in the sky once again. It had been the smoothest sailing they'd had in months, the winter storms finally behind them as Åldras welcomed the warmth of spring.

"Hold steady," called Erik to the crew. "We're to meet with our contact on the west side of the island."

Pet stepped away to take her place with Erik at the tiller when little hands grasped onto hers. Viveca looked up to Pet with pleading eyes. "Do you think she'll love me?"

Pet glanced up at Axel. She'd never been as good with children as him, but he wasn't paying her any attention as he watched the coastline from the stem of the ship. She sank into a crouch. Instead of trying to come up with an answer, she asked, "What do you think?"

Small hands wiped tears from a dust-stained face. While Viveca seemed fearful of what was to come, Pet could also see courage and hope light the girl's golden eyes.

Viveca clenched her fingers around the small bone hanging from her neck. "She will."

"All right," Axel called. "Let's go see some real Häxa."

Pet brought Viveca to Axel's side. When the child walked within arm's reach, Axel hoisted her up on his shoulders so she could see over the sides of the gunwale. At first, her big eyes widened in fear but wonder soon took its place, and a smile brought out a dimple in her left cheek.

As the boat swung around the island, they spotted a karve waiting in the bay, right where their note said it would be. Axel directed the men to sidle up next to the boat so they could make the exchange on the beach. Erik made the adjustments, and it wasn't long until the two boats were tucked into the small cove. Axel let the girl down from his shoulders before calling for ropes and directing the men to prepare for them to disembark.

Pet's eyes remained glued to the other boat as a group left the confines of the karve and landed on the beach. A flash of white hair appeared in the crowd of silhouettes.

"Axel!" she called. She pointed in the direction of the beach and heard him swear when he caught sight of the Great Mother.

"I'm not wearing my best clothes!" Axel ran for a pack near his trunk. Pet had to quickly usher Viveca in the opposite direction as Axel's shirt went flying over his head. He had absolutely no shame when it came to his modesty.

Pet guided Viveca toward the edge of the ship and held her steady as the hull met sand. After traveling as much as Pet did, she'd accustomed herself to the rough beaching, but Viveca wobbled as the ship skidded to a stop. After a moment, Axel joined them in his black tunic and pants with the most hideous, green, homespun cowl Pet knew to exist. When she saw him, Viveca laughed.

"Oh, that cowl really suits you," Pet said.

Axel looked down at his ensemble. "You're the only one who doesn't like the look of this cowl."

"No, he's not," Doran called from the opposite side of the boat.

Axel gave an aggrieved sigh and shrugged the fabric from his shoulders before jumping over the edge—spinning in an elaborate front flip —and landing on his feet in the shallow waters below.

Pet rolled her eyes.

Never can pass up the chance to show off.

CHAPTER 4

PROPHECIES

There are many mysteries surrounding the Häxa and their children. In the old lore, it was said they were women gifted by the gods with magic so intrinsically linked to the world around us that they were set as overseers over all of Midgard. They have been part of the world since Ymir's body was used to create the earth, born from our first parents, the same as any other. We believed we knew everything there was to know about the women and the types of magic their daughters wield. The world has seen gifts manifest and disappear like seasons and tides. The gifts of fire and spirit have faded to nothing but memory, and the shifters and healers have taken their place. Man has seen many wonders of magic in the centuries we have walked the earth. But there has never been anything like Axel Ashersson, the first Häxa son, nor the horrendous prophecy that bears his name.

— FROM THE WRITINGS OF DORAN FINNSSON, THE LAST KING OF GROVÖ

"Great Mother, you honor us with your presence," Axel called over the crash of the surf as they stepped out of the shallows and onto the dry beach. He ignored the impulse to shake the water from his boots as they approached. Pet caught up to him only a few moments later, Viveca clinging to her hand.

"Speak of the troll and he appears on the porch." The Great

Mother left her retinue and came to stand a few paces out from the water, her hands on her hips. Axel folded into his most gallant bow and the Great Mother's eyebrows rose. "Well, my son, it seems someone has been teaching you manners." A small quirk of her lips belied the severe tone with which she spoke.

"Pet has been doing a wonderful job, wouldn't you agree? Always going on about how uncouth I am. I suppose some things have begun to stick."

Pet came up alongside him, and Viveca tucked herself behind Pet's legs.

The Great Mother's eyes widened at the sight of the bundled-up girl and knelt down in the sand. "It's all right, Viveca. I have come to take you home with me. Would you like that?"

Viveca peeked out. Pet settled her hand on the girl's back and nudged her toward the elderly woman. Viveca looked up at Pet, a plea in her eyes, to which Pet gave a confident nod. Axel couldn't help the beat of pride in his chest. The confidence on her face would have driven the most cowardly man into the face of danger. Viveca glanced back at the Great Mother and took a shy step toward her.

A little peep came from Viveca. "I can't curtsy."

Axel chuckled as the Great Mother's lips split into a smile. "And I wouldn't expect you to. You're not just my child, like all the Häxa, but also my blood. My granddaughter."

The Great Mother reached into the pocket of her robe and drew out a bone. One moment, an old woman stood before them. Next, there was a white wolf standing in the sand. If Axel hadn't been staring at the woman, he wouldn't have believed it.

Viveca's eyes widened and she grabbed the tiny bone around her neck. She, too, turned into a wolf, though she stood much smaller with a tawny coat.

The white wolf gave a playful yip, spinning in the sand. Her long tail whipped back and forth.

The tawny wolf yipped in return, and she bounded toward the Great Mother. The two wolves playfully zipped around the beach, their howls twining with each other as they frolicked.

Axel laughed when Viveca dodged the Great Mother and playfully snapped her teeth around the Great Mother's fluffy, white tail. How was something like this deemed evil? How could a child playing with her grandmother be anything but love? Firmin's propaganda claimed the Häxa were nothing more than wicked women seeking to overthrow mankind. But they were as human as the next person. They loved and needed love. He should know. He was one of them.

The two wolves transformed back when they returned to where Pet and Axel stood. The Great Mother scooped Viveca into a fierce hug. Axel's own eyes prickled as he watched a tear leak from the corner of the older woman's lashes. Longing hooked Axel's gut as the two smiled at one another. It had been so long since he'd felt what they had.

"Oh, I'm happy as an egg yolk." The old matriarch really did say the oddest things. The Great Mother gave one more tight squeeze before she stood and tucked Viveca against her side. "Thank you, my son, for bringing your sister home. I knew I could count on Constance's child to deliver my most beloved to me."

Axel looked at the sand beneath his feet. "I'm sure my mother would be proud to hear those words." Not that he would actually know. He didn't even know what the woman looked like, let alone what she cared about.

The Great Mother looked on him with sadness. "I know you never had the chance to know her. She was a powerful woman. A little ambitious, but I'm sure she wished to have remained by your side after she received the vision."

Viveca looked back and forth between Axel and the Great Mother. "What vision, *Mormor*?"

The Great Mother smiled down at her granddaughter. "Perhaps he'll make a trade." She looked up to Axel. "A riddle for a map?"

"A map to what?" Pet asked.

The Great Mother smiled at her. "It's nothing to hang on the yule tree, but since you've done so much for us, the elders have agreed to gift you the directions to Ljust Löfte."

Axel took an involuntary step forward. "Are you certain?" Having the trust of the elders had been hard earned over the years. It had taken the crew ages to prove they weren't in league with King Firmin, that they truly wished to help the gifted women escape persecution. The fact that the elders were willing to reveal the way to their safe haven was certainly something to hang on the yule tree.

The Great Mother waved him off. "Your crew has proven themselves worthy of such a secret." She pulled a roll of parchment from her sleeve. "Give this to your skipper. I'm sure he's smart enough to know what to do with it."

Pet took it from her hand and unfurled it. Axel looked over her shoulder to see a hand-drawn map, coded with directions and notes. The lines of ink stretched over the page, shadowing the coastlines of Isberg and highlighting the peaks of mountains Axel had never laid eyes on. Erik would eat this up when he got his hands on it.

"Now, will you trade with us?" the Great Mother asked.

Axel smiled before bending down to Viveca's level. "My mother was known as Constance of the River before she married my father. You can imagine the shock that came when I was born a boy instead of a girl, as most Häxa. My mother used her power with the water to gaze into the future of her impossible son and returned to my cradle with a song.

> *"Behold, the yield of the witch's womb.*
> *The she-bear's shield, the eagle's doom.*
> *Sent to save the land that bore him.*
> *No mortal foe dares stand before him.*
> *True, born below, yet godly made,*
> *Unchallenged in bow, unmatched in blade.*
> *Too strong to bend in battle's din,*
> *With flame his friend and death his kin.*
> *In war's dark fray, steadfast, unharmed*
> *Until one day by love disarmed.*
> *When, with a maid his heart is traded,*
> *By gods betrayed—in war unaided*
> *The hero's strength in battle fails him.*
> *At last, at length, his foe impales him.*
> *The reaper calls from deathly hollows,*
> *The hero falls, the she-bear follows."*

Axel let the waves of the prophecy wash over him as he did any time he told it. Pet stood quiet beside him, doing the same. The prophecy was the one thing from their childhood they regularly talked about. It had almost become a game, guessing what would happen when. The words were practically scarred onto Axel's heart, seared into his mind. When he'd been a lad, Father had made sure he knew what the gods had decided for him. Knew that Axel's fate would decide the future of their kingdom.

Would Father be right and Axel would be the one who truly determined the fate of Åldras? Or was there more to it? He preferred to focus on the beginning, pitting himself against the greatest warriors Åldras had to offer to see if there was anyone that could match him. So far, the prophecy had proven true. The last part, however, he had a few guesses about, but nothing he really discussed with Pet. She'd probably stab him if he did.

Viveca's eyebrows drew together in concentration. "What does it mean?"

Axel laughed. "Maybe you can tell me. I've been trying to figure it out since I was a babe."

The Great Mother shifted, drawing every eye in her direction. "That's the way of Häxa prophecy. None but those who received the song have clear answers."

"If the witch who bore me ever does show up," said Axel, careful to keep his tone light, "please send her my way. I have a long list of questions I'd like to ask." Like why she would leave Father and him behind. Or why she'd never returned. Was she dead? Or was the thought of Axel's prophecy so awful she couldn't bear to watch it come to pass?

The Great Mother held Viveca close. "Now don't go jumping on your own nose. Your mother likely left believing it would be safer for you. Her gift with the water foretold many things. Even news of the exodus to our new home fell from Constance's lips before that murderer you call a king was fitted for his crown. You'll need to let go of your anger eventually, my son. The riddle is a warning to protect you."

"Riddles," griped Axel. "Is that all Häxa magic is good for?"

The Great Mother quirked an eyebrow and a large crab scuttled up from the sand beneath Axel's feet. *Thunder's beard.* He barely ducked out of the way as a pair of osprey talons came streaking over his head. He made a hasty circle around the sand as a group of crabs chased after him.

"I concede!" he called as something began moving quickly through the water in their direction and the crew all ran to the side of the ship. Was that a bloody killer whale? The large creature disappeared before he could get a glimpse at it.

"That'll show you where a chicken pees from." The Great Mother chuckled and directed Viveca toward the boat that would take them home. Axel went to Pet, and she shifted in his direction when the Great Mother gently touched her shoulder. "Take care of him."

Pet nodded, dutiful as always.

The Great Mother turned her attention to Axel, moving her hand from Pet's shoulder to his forearm. "Take care of Pet."

Axel met the wizened, golden eyes of the leader with a heart big enough to love an entire race of people as her own children. In those rings of honey and amber, Axel saw the heartache caused by the magic gifted to her by the gods—or rather, the persecution of that gift. The delicate hand touching his arm belied the weight this woman carried with it.

He gave the only response he could to such a request. "Of course."

The Great Mother dropped her hand and began leading Viveca toward their boat, leaving them to stand in the sand. Axel looked up to the stars glittering across the sky. His lungs filled with the salty air, and he couldn't help but close his eyes to take it in. At least he'd done something good today. He'd saved someone.

"Are you gonna stand there all night or can we get a move on?" called Pet. "This boat isn't going to get off the beach on its own, you self-important goose."

Axel let out a sigh before slapping on his most playful smile and chasing after her. "And I was under the impression that you liked me."

Pet rolled her eyes, but he saw the small curl at her lips. She could try to hide her laughter all she wanted, but Axel could see through every façade, every lie. He knew her better than he knew himself. His very heart silently beat her name.

He joined her and the other crewmates under the stem of the ship. The open-mouthed phoenix head called silently down to them, ready to be off toward Harligdam and Firmin. Axel placed his hands on the feathered breast of the bird and pushed. While the rest of the crew's faces were strained with the force, Axel slid the boat back into the sea as easily as pushing Pet into it.

The crew waded into the water until *The Phoenix* bobbed on the waves. Pet and Big Hal easily clambered over the gunwale. Little Hal was the only one on Axel's crew allowed to use the rope ladder hanging over the side—he still wasn't tall enough to reach the top of the gunwale. Axel always said if you couldn't haul yourself onto the ship at a moment's notice, you'd be left behind.

Little Hal passed out breakfast rations even though the sun hadn't risen yet. The lad was young, but he knew how to season up a halibut a thousand different ways and made the porridge rations bearable. Today, they all swallowed down brown bread and pickled eggs, fare they didn't have to cook, in order to get away from Mötesplats and the Great Mother as quickly as they could. Erik directed the ship smoothly through the water, his arm draped over the tiller as he brushed crumbs from his chest-length beard.

Gray began to stain the horizon, putting the stars to sleep. Axel rubbed his eyes. He hadn't had a good night's sleep in days, and it was beginning to weigh on him. He blinked his weariness away and found Pet watching him.

"What?" he asked.

"We'll hit Gudvangen at lunchtime, and we can probably rest up while Little Hal cooks some real food." She nudged her bowl of pickled eggs with the toe of her boot.

Axel picked them up and bit into one. "We need to figure out what we're going to do when we arrive in Harligdam."

"Yes, I'd like to know that as well." Doran grabbed his flat-topped trunk and slid it beside Pet's. "I don't imagine King Firmin will be all too pleased with how you've been ignoring him."

"Firmin can jump in a draugr bog for all I bloody care," Axel grumbled, then bit into another egg. Honestly, the fact that idiot thought he could snap his fingers and expect Axel to come running was ludicrous. The vision of a livid Firmin pulled a smile onto Axel's lips. The brute would be ripe for a blow up once *The Phoenix* arrived.

"I don't think it'll be too hard to get back into his good graces." Pet tugged the hood of her cloak tighter around her face. "He obviously wants Axel to do something for him. He knows if he bugs Axel too much, we'll just leave."

Axel pulled up one of his eyebrows and looked at Doran. "Do you know what he wants?"

Doran sighed. "No. I did ask around, but whatever he's up to is all very secretive. I did hear rumors of a curse, but I don't know what exactly that means."

Axel set the empty bowl back down by his feet. "If he thinks I'm going to appeal to the gods again because he killed a sacred animal or whatnot, he's got another thing coming." While Åldras didn't have a patron god everyone worshipped the way the Sidans did, Axel knew which ones to supplicate when he needed things done. Pet's mama had held a healthy respect for the deities that watched over them and taught Axel more than a few ways to gain a god's favor.

"You know I would give you more information if I had any," Doran said.

Axel nodded and leaned back to rest his head against the side of the ship. Doran wouldn't ever keep vital information from them, what with his whole identity revolving around sharing knowledge with others. But the small knot in Axel's gut still said this summons wasn't something he was going to enjoy. Not that he ever particularly enjoyed being at Firmin's beck and call.

They just had to get through this war. Then, Axel could live out his wildest fantasies of sailing around Åldras as a trader with a fat belly and thick beard. He could help more Häxa get out of Åldras and work toward getting rid of the bloody Ekte. Once the Sidans were taken care of, Axel would finally be able to help the people of Åldras.

"Luckily, we won't be walking in on any celebrations," Pet mused. "Sigrblót was over six weeks ago, and we still have a good two months until Mid-Summer."

Axel feigned a pout. "Just because you don't like to revel during the holidays doesn't mean the rest of us wouldn't enjoy it."

Pet brought a boot up onto her trunk and laid her chin on her knee. "Better to get into the city without the hoopla. With the number of adoring fans you have, it'll be hard enough to get in and out of the city."

Axel tried to look put out, but inwardly he was pleased. "I can't help being adored, Pet."

Her expression didn't change but he could see her internally roll her eyes.

"So, what's your plan for Harligdam?" Doran asked.

Axel grabbed a lump of light aspen wood from the small pile near his trunk. The horse he was carving still didn't look quite right. "We go in, allow Firmin to pontificate to his heart's content, then leave." He turned to Little Hal who was in the process of collecting everyone's bowls. "Send the raven to Harligdam and let them know we'll be there in three days."

Little Hal bounded for the back of the ship where the messenger raven was kept. Axel would have to check Little Hal's writing, but it would be a good opportunity for the lad to practice his letters.

"And what about High King Firmin's mission for you?" asked Doran. "Will you accept it?"

"That," Axel answered, "will depend entirely on how long Firmin is able to keep from saying something that makes me punch him in the nose."

CHAPTER 5

A KING

Firmin Witchkiller, High King of Åldras, son of the late High King Vilgot the Steadfast, is one few men would wish to cross. The man's girth could rival that of an ice bear's, but his mind is that of a wolf. While not particularly quick-witted, he does not forget wrongs against him, and he is swift in restoring that balance. His early succession to the throne after the murder of his father has taken its toll, but he is a warrior of the highest caliber, rivaled by few. We would not have made it this far into the war without his machinations, but I often wonder if this war would have even started if he weren't king.

— *FROM THE WRITINGS OF DORAN FINNSSON, THE LAST KING OF GROVÖ*

P et glared at the back of Axel's neck, skirting past a trio of ladies throwing spring blossoms up at him from their baskets. The Three Norns must have been cackling at her from their spinning wheel on Yggdrasil.

Harligdam was always a crush of people, but this was getting out of hand.

Axel sat on what had to be the biggest warhorse in the three kingdoms, it's long, black tail swishing right in front of Pet's nose. None of the crew owned horses, the long voyages and the upkeep of the animals not worth the investment. This mass of horseflesh had been waiting for

45

them at the harbor with a note signed by the High King himself. Axel waved at the adoring crowd as the red-and-brown banner of Åldras fluttered in every doorway. Men hollered his name, their voices taking up the song he'd sung in the laundry house in Stern, while the women threw flowers and blew kisses at him with abandon.

Pet was going to throw up.

It was always like this when they returned to Harligdam. The capital city sat nestled in the northernmost corner of the kingdom, far from the edges of war. Far away from the Sidan threat that loomed closer with every sunset. All these people cared about was getting a glimpse at the man they thought would be their savior, the very same man their bloody king would sooner stab than actually praise.

But he couldn't take one drop of Axel's blood, so he settled for threatening the rest of them instead. While Axel denied it, Firmin had him on a tighter leash than the rest of the bloody kingdom because Axel couldn't live with the idea of anyone suffering because of him. He would juggle horse dung while walking through the city street stark naked if he believed it would save someone.

Of course, everyone would just love him all the more for it too.

Doran led their procession on a shorter—but no less grand—horse at the front while the rest of the crew of *The Phoenix* trudged closely behind Pet. Big Hal and Olav walked on either side of Erik to insure none of the incensed crowd kicked his canes and peg legs out from beneath him.

When they finally reached the circle of Firmin's fortress, Pet had to hold back a snort. The walls surrounding the fortress were a new installment in Harligdam, one the people had likely been coerced into creating over the last few months. The wooden walls stood twenty ells in the air, each forming the outer crust of the king's perfect pie. A large gate loomed ahead of them, allowing the people in and out of Firmin's outrageous compound.

"Does the king really believe this will protect him from the Sidans?" Big Hal asked.

Erik grunted. "It's like he forgot fire exists."

Pet's gut twisted as a vision of flames flashed across her eyes. The smell of smoke burned her nostrils. It hit her at random moments, that night in Holmberg all those years ago. It felt like it was only yesterday she'd been standing beside Mama. When the Sidans had burst into their house. She breathed deeply, squashing the sensation stirring in her gut. It was fine. She was fine.

The sound of hammering replaced the cheers of the crowd as they pushed through the unfinished gate. Buildings in every stage of construction squatted all around the compound. Harligdam had been the capital of Åldras for generations, but it likely hadn't seen this level of construction since its establishment. Harligdam itself was a hodge-podge of old and new—some of the homes with new rooms built onto decades-old walls as families grew or buildings took on new residents. Most of the fortress was recently constructed, excepting the great hall that had stood on this ground for generations. Other residences boasted the flags of several kings, giving the traveling rulers a home within the capital when they visited. Pet didn't see Holmberg's helm stitched onto any of the flags. A blacksmith's forge puffed smoke under an open-walled smithy. Some kind of storage building took up a large section close to the center. There were frames put up of larger build-ings all around, but they could be for any number of things. It was a city within a city.

If the Sidans did make it all the way to Harligdam, where would the citizens outside the walls go? Had Firmin even considered that?

The finished hall stood at the epicenter of the fortress. The carved head of a she-bear roared from the apex of the shingled roof. A dozen stone stairs led up to the humongous doors, wide open to let the evening air cool the inside.

Axel dismounted, frowning up at the intricate pillars and gaudy paint. "I really do hate this place."

Pet could only agree. They only had another few months to prepare to go to war again and Firmin thought now was the time to build himself a fancy compound? The whole fortress was a waste of time and resources.

She pushed Axel toward the door. "Then let's get this over with so we can leave."

He pretended to drag his feet—she wouldn't have been able to push him unless he let her. "Do you think he's called us to tell us the war is over?"

"As if we'd be so lucky," Doran grumbled from behind them.

Axel sighed and pulled forward, so Pet wasn't actually pushing him any longer. "Perhaps we can convince him to turn this ridiculous monstrosity into an orphanage."

"Aye," Pet scoffed, "and then get him to take an oath of silence." Firmin would likely gag on all the words he wouldn't be able to say.

Pet and Axel had taken one for a year under Doran's tutelage. He'd told them it helped warriors understand how to communicate when talking was impossible, though Pet still suspected it was more because he'd wished for peace and quiet. Not that he'd gotten it. The practice taught them to listen as well as how to come up with new solutions to problems. Like how to forge Doran's handwriting to get them access to raid the storehouses in the war camps they'd frequented.

The crew crossed over the threshold, and the chill of early spring died as the blazing fire in the middle of the large hall kept the room at a sweltering temperature. Harligdam's Great Hall boasted wide chairs to fit the largest of warriors, tables so thick they could take the brunt of an ax, and enough tapestries and furs to clothe the entire city through winter. One large chair sat at the back of the room, intricately designed and taller than any other seat in the room. A throne, but no one wanted to call it such. That would create a power imbalance and Firmin was a firm believer in equality—or so he spouted. While the title of king was tossed about to any man who claimed leadership over a town within the borders of Åldras, Firmin was at the top of the food chain. The Council of Kings had been created by the first High King as a way to sow peace through the somewhat spread-out kingdom. Technically, Axel should have inherited the title of king when his father, Asher Redbeard, had died. But Firmin would rather eat his own crown than give Axel the title.

The not-a-throne sat empty at the moment, but Pet new it wouldn't remain so for long. The rest of the crew spread out, Big Hal taking a post by the door while Erik and Olav settled at one of the tables across from each other, pulling out a deck of cards. Little Hal slipped back out the door, on the hunt for information. The lad was a fiend at collecting gossip and starting up rumors, which Pet had supplied him with before they'd stepped off the ship. It would be better for the city to believe Axel had come to pay his respects to Firmin rather than think he'd had to be dragged here. They needed to keep eyes and ears off them as much as possible, though people would be waiting to hear what havoc Mighty Axel would wreak in Firmin's presence. Doran found a small table to have to himself and took out his leather-bound writing kit. Axel circled around the fire and approached the not-a-throne.

"What are you doing?" Pet asked.

Axel gave a dramatic flourish of his cloak and sat right in Firmin's not-a-throne. He wiggled his body, pretending to nestle into the padded seat, and swung one leg over the thick arm of the chair shaped like a bear's front paw. With a purse of his lips, he looked over the room as if taking stock of the place.

"I can see why he would pick this chair," he said. "It gives such a good view of the room, and the seat would very easily fit his rather humongous—"

The door behind the throne flew open and Firmin swaggered into the room. The man was nearly twice as big as he had been the last time Pet had seen him, and that had only been three months ago. His shoulders were wide, but the paunch of his belly now spilled over the buckle of his belt.

Seemed someone had been gorging himself during the armistice.

"My friends!" Firmin opened his arms. "Welcome!"

He was followed by his usual retinue. The High King never went anywhere without his little herd of sheep. His four advisors, a pair of Ekte, the trio of wolfhounds, the messenger lad, and, of course, his younger brother. Firmin and Anders could have been twins if Anders's eyes weren't narrowed like a weasel's and Firmin wasn't dressed to his teeth in expensive fabric. With guts the size of boulders and shoulders the width of the bears' that decorated their family's sigil, the two stood shoulder to shoulder like Trouble and her twin, Chaos.

Firmin turned to the entourage and ordered them to leave. Pet watched them go, their bleats of surprise fading as they disappeared back through the doorway. Everyone but his brother scurried out of the room. She turned to look at Axel, her gut twisting uncomfortably.

He met her gaze, his brow quirking just slightly. *Well, that's different.*

Firmin's eyes narrowed on Axel lounging in the not-a-throne. "Axel, my boy, I'm glad to see you've made yourself at home."

Axel gave his most guileless smile. "With Åldras as my home, it's easy to feel such ease in her bosom. But don't stand about on my account." He waved at the chairs gathered around the room. "Pull up another chair, and let's discuss why we've all gathered here."

The king's cheeks mottled with red, but he held his tongue as he gestured for the rest of their party to sit. Pet moved to grab a chair, but Axel's voice cut her off. "Ah, thank you, Your Majesty, for supplying Pet with a chair. I'm sure he's most humbled by your offer."

Pet turned to see Firmin halfway into a seat beside Axel. The High King's eyes flared wide with incredulity, but he gritted his teeth and stood back up. Hel's halls, Firmin really did need them. He wouldn't have given up his chair otherwise. Axel waved Pet over and she took her seat, ready to leap into action when whatever little game Axel was playing at ran its course. When Anders arrived with his chair, Firmin snatched it from him and sat on Axel's other side.

"So, Axel," the High King began, "I've been trying to summon you for weeks. I have very urgent matters I need you to attend to."

Axel turned to where Doran sat. "Doran, why did you not tell me there were *urgent matters*?"

Doran didn't look up from his writing, but he shook his head in exasperation. Pet suppressed her smirk, but it was difficult. Even Doran wasn't going to poke holes in Axel's obvious act.

"Axel," Firmin said in a controlled voice, though the side of his jaw twitched. "I have something that needs to be taken care of and you're the only man that can see it done."

"Oh? There are many things I can do that no other man can. You'll have to elaborate."

Firmin scooted his chair closer. "It's about the Häxa."

Pet's fingers twitched, ready to reach for the ax at her hip. This would not end well. Axel did a decent job keeping his temper under control, but there were some things he wouldn't tolerate. Firmin's stance on the Häxa was one of them. She looked about the room, waiting for guards to come barging in.

Axel went very still. "And pray tell, what kind of *trouble* are you in? I was under the impression you had the Häxa under control, carving your evil marks into the flesh of women and children. Making fathers and husbands watch their loved ones get eaten by flames."

Pet could hear the steel in his voice. This wasn't something that would go over well if Firmin didn't tread lightly. Axel had no problem vocalizing his complaints and as an unkillable warrior, Firmin had to let him. They'd been playing this game for years, each toeing the line of civility and cruelty. There was no love lost between either of them.

"There has been a, uh, *new* development." Firmin scratched at the beard under his jaw. He turned toward the side doors. "Bring her in!"

The side doors opened, and Pet jumped to her feet. Her hand fell from her ax as a trio of women walked in. Pet recognized the first: Firmin's wife, Queen Eva. The second was a girl, likely not much older than Little Hal, with Queen Eva's bright red hair but Firmin's wide nose. Firmin had many children, though Pet couldn't say she knew any of their names.

The last arrival was Lady Idalia, Anders's newest wife—his *third* wife. Pet only remembered her name because the last time they'd been to Harligdam, Big Hal had come back to the ship waxing poetic about her beauty and grace. It had driven the crew mad for days. Erik had nearly kicked him off the ship at the next harbor. But now, Pet could understand the man's obsession. The woman was only just past being a girl, perhaps a year or so younger than Pet. The skin of her shoulders and her unwrinkled face still held onto her youth. The combination of copper skin and dark hair from one of the southern kingdoms was practically exotic this far north. The lady's dark eyes flashed at the group, defiance spitting sparks even as she held her chin low in deference. Pet immediately felt a kinship with the lesser king's wife.

"Surely," Axel said, voice low with warning, "not even you are low enough to get rid of your wife by stating she is a witch."

King Firmin drew back. "Of course not. I've had the Ekte test her. Multiple times, in fact. She is free from any magic." He turned to the women. "Ella, come here my girl."

His daughter stepped timidly toward them, blue eyes flicking from face to face.

"Show them, child."

Her chin wobbled, but she fidgeted with a pocket in her skirt until she drew out a handful of seeds and a piece of wood. She held out the seeds and they started growing. Tears streamed down her cheeks as clover spread through her fingers and cascaded down onto the floor.

Axel stood up beside Pet and both of Princess Ella's companions stepped forward to flank her. Pet felt a single brow on her forehead rise but quickly schooled her features back to neutrality. The women's obvious defense of the princess was to be commended, but it was more than surprising considering their husbands were the strongest advocates of the Ekte.

"You can see my problem," King Firmin said. He stood as if to stretch and slid into the not-a-throne Axel had vacated. Pet nearly shoved him off but withheld the urge. Not only was the man triple her size, but he was High King for a reason. He'd snap her neck without batting an eye.

"A problem you created," Lady Idalia muttered.

If the High King hadn't ordered every girl with magic murdered, this moment would have been celebrated. It wasn't unheard of for a girl to discover she had magic when her mother didn't. There was no rhyme or reason to who the gods bestowed their gifts on. Axel was simply another testament to it. If the princess had been born to a family without magic only a few decades before, the family would have found their daughter's gift a blessing.

But they didn't live when the Häxa had been revered. They lived when the princess's magic was nothing more than a curse.

Pet watched for a reaction from Firmin, but the High King ignored Lady Idalia. "It has turned from bad to worse. The Sidan delegation arrived three weeks ago to propose an extension to the armistice—which you would have known about if you'd arrived when I asked for you. I have agreed to nothing, but with them here, I worry about them discovering Ella's curse. They could take her and use her against me in more ways than just with her forbidden magic."

The Sidans had no qualms about the Häxa. Pet had fought a few witches on the battlefield, taking up arms alongside the Sidans as the kingdom to the south recruited men and women alike into their forces. Åldran women weren't allowed to go into battle with the men, and as the Häxa were more than simple women, they *definitely* weren't allowed to march under the she-bear's colors even before they'd started being hunted for their magic.

Pet stepped away from the circle, edging toward the back of the room and leaving her chair empty. She needed to keep an eye on the door the women had come through. If anyone snuck into this meeting, it could become very dangerous very quickly.

"This certainly is a conundrum." Axel picked up a piece of clover and twirled it between his thumb and forefinger. "If you hadn't had the gall to demand the Häxa's heads, you would find yourself most proud to have a daughter gifted with such power." He smiled down at Ella and tucked the clover behind her ear. The girl's watery eyes glanced up at him, wide with obvious awe. "The Sidan delegation does pose a problem. If you rescinded the law, perhaps you wouldn't be in such a precarious situation."

"The law is the law," Firmin snapped. "I cannot take back what has already come to pass."

Axel whirled. "No, you can't, but now you must deal with the consequences. Now, your daughter's life is in danger because the Allfather saw fit to grant her this boon, and you would have her and everyone else in this bloody kingdom believe it to be a curse."

"But it is a curse," Anders piped in, "and the only reason the girl isn't being bound to a pyre this instant is because of the insistence of our wives."

Pet glanced between the two women. Had they truly kept their husbands from sentencing the princess to death? Their stance at Princess Ella's back looked as formidable as the wolves guarding the gates to Valhalla.

Lady Idalia glowered. "This is a warning from the gods," she spat. "This land will pay penance for the souls that have suffered at the hands of your witch hunters."

"We didn't ask for your opinion, *wife*," Anders shot back. "If you cannot leash that tongue, I'll do it for you."

Lady Idalia bowed her head, but Pet didn't believe the meek act for one moment. That woman looked ready to tear out her husband's throat if she could. *More's the pity.* She'd get charged with witchcraft, like any other wife who disobeyed their disagreeable husbands. It happened enough. Brutes that didn't want to deal with the semantics of petitioning the elders of their towns for divorce would whisper in the Ektes' ear and the wife he didn't want to deal with anymore would find herself either ruined by reputation or dead.

Queen Eva stepped up beside her daughter. "I will not have Ella harmed when there are other ways to keep her magic out of Åldras."

Of course the queen was the voice of reason in this situation. She made up the heart of the kingdom, though Pet couldn't even begin to guess what she was feeling now. Was she angry with King Firmin for putting their daughter in this situation? Most Häxa found their *förändra* at a young age. Had they been hiding it from him? Pet almost snorted. It would serve the High King right to have his own daughter practicing magic under his roof.

"And what do you suggest?" Axel asked.

"We know you're associated with the Häxa," Firmin said, but he raised a hand to forestall any of Axel's denials. "I'm not blind. I know you just smuggled a child out of Stern. One that has been the most dangerous target of the Ekte for months. But because I am a fair king, I won't make you face trial for the death of two of my best Ekte."

"Two Ekte given the charge to kill a child—"

"Axel, if you interrupt me right now," Firmin ground out, "you're going to find that not all pain is done to one's physical body." He glanced at Pet and the rest of the crew.

While bodily harm might have not been much of a threat to Axel, the rest of the crew couldn't claim the same. It was one of the only reasons Axel still put up with the arrogant High King. If he didn't, there would be consequences.

Firmin knew exactly how to push him.

If it were up to Pet, the bloody tyrant would be dead already.

Axel scowled but kept his mouth shut.

Firmin pinched the bridge of his nose. "If you take the girl to Ljust Löfte, we'll allow her to live."

Pet stepped forward as Axel closed in on the king, ready to pull him back should he attempt anything foolish. And he would if Firmin continued down this path. The only thing that kept Axel from tearing the man's head from his shoulders was the consequences that would rain down on the crew's head for the High King's death.

"How do you know about that place?" Axel asked. His hands clenched into fists at his side, his knuckles white with strain.

Firmin held up his hands placatingly. "I think you forget I am *High King*, boys. I have many voices whispering in my ears, doing their best to get into my good graces. Of course I know of the colony, and so long as it remains outside my kingdom, the Häxa can stay there."

Pet scrutinized him. High King Anselm Häxasbane, Firmin's grandfather, had outlawed the use of magic long before even Da and Axel's father had been born. The old king had punished any practicing Häxa, cutting off hands or even allowing the Ekte to carve runes into their skin. Those who were found guilty of practicing multiple times were beheaded. It was Firmin who actually began hunting the gifted women after his father, High King Vilgot, was supposedly murdered by a Häxa. It was Firmin who stuck the women and children on pyres for even a whisper of magic. Pet remembered her parents' anger over the establishment of the Ekte throughout the kingdom, and Axel's father fought against allowing them into Holmberg. Too much blood had been shed for Firmin to be so flippant about the colony.

Axel tilted his head to the side. "And you wish for us to take your daughter there?"

"Of course. In fact, I insist. I cannot allow her to stay, lest someone discover her magic, but I also can't bring myself to kill my own flesh and blood. What a father would I be to do such a thing?"

Pet could have laughed. She doubted he was a better father than he was a king. While he might have been an acceptable general, he had a true lack of compassion for his people. No, this likely had nothing to do with the High King's heart and everything to do with the two steely eyed women flanking his daughter.

Axel folded his arms over his chest, his gaze drawn to a spot on the floor. His body remained still, but Pet could see the tumult spinning through his head. This mission wouldn't be a simple one. It was a bloody miracle they'd only just received the map—a miracle that was beginning to look like a set up on the Great Mother's part. She had water wielders scouring time for new Häxa all the time. There was no way she hadn't known about the princess.

Axel looked up at her. "What do you think, Pet?"

Everyone turned to her, even Doran. Pet yanked on her most unaffected mask, but she still curled her toes in her boots at the attention. She met Axel's gaze.

I want to do it, his eyes said.

Pet tilted her head. *Seriously?* This could be a setup for Firmin to get them out of Åldras to do something dastardly. This could be a death trap for the rest of the crew. Hel's bloody halls, this could be a ploy by Firmin to get the Häxa's location and exterminate them all. With the Sidans hanging around, there could be major problems. Not to mention Erik had yet to decode the map's directions. And it was *Firmin*. Nothing about this situated added up.

Axel quirked a brow. *Why not?*

Pet could think of a dozen more reasons why not, but with Axel's steady gaze and the sniffles of the young lady on the other side of the room, none of her concerns mattered. Not when there was someone who needed saving.

"We'll do it," she said, "if our *queen* commands it."

She refused to do it for Firmin, refused to do it for the bloody Ekte. This wasn't about a king and his false heart, but a mother protecting her child. Pet wouldn't say no to that, no matter how much she believed this mission to be a bad idea.

Anders hissed at the obvious slight to his brother, but Queen Eva lifted her chin.

"I do."

CHAPTER 6

COMPLICATIONS

Axel looked the timid princess up and down. She couldn't have been more than fourteen, maybe fifteen, years old. Her shoulders sagged as she stood in front of them, worry and helplessness seeming to weigh her down. But he swore there was a little steel in her gaze when it met his.

He tried to give her a reassuring smile. "If it's all right with you, Princess, we can leave within the hour."

"You have to wait to leave until the morning," Lady Idalia quickly answered.

Axel turned back to him. "Why on Midgard would we need to wait until tomorrow?" It wasn't as if the ship weren't ready, and it would be hours before Sol's light gave way to the night. The quicker they left, the better. If the Sidans got even one whiff of what was going on, there would be trouble simply because it was the Sidans, and they could sniff out weakness like a wolf could scent blood.

"Tonight is the feast we've been putting together all week," Queen Eva said. "If Ella were to simply disappear before then, it would raise too many questions."

"Say she died," Axel suggested.

Firmin scoffed. "And have a funeral with no body?"

"We can procure a body," Pet answered in her usual monotone.

Anders' face blanched, but Axel pressed forward before anyone else could give that suggestion more thought. "She could feign an illness or something."

"Do you think the Sidans would be so easily fooled?" Firmin asked. "All I'm saying is that you wait until morning. The Sidan delegation will be packing up to visit Oxe with Anders, and no one will notice a ragtag group of sailors running around the docks."

Axel found Pet's narrowed gaze. *Ragtag?* that look said.

He crossed his arms over his chest. "You think we're just going to be able to jump on our ship and leave after the parade you just threw for our arrival?"

Firmin frowned. "I don't care how you manage it, but my daughter won't be leaving until after the feasting."

Axel leaned forward. "Who is she staying to impress?"

Firmin narrowed his eyes. "I don't know what you mean."

"A pretty girl like that would be quite a distraction if used the right way with the right sort of lad." Axel sat down in the chair Pet had vacated. "Who's here that has caught such a fancy toward her?"

Lady Idalia stepped forward. "Prince Roman," she said in her warm tone, "has come with the Sidan delegation."

The crew around the room hissed.

Axel felt his teeth grind against one another. "You mean to tell me that you're allowing your daughter to entertain the bloody Prince of Sida? Under your very roof?"

"She's not being used in such a way," Queen Eva said, obviously offended.

"Then what are you insinuating?"

"We're saying," Firmin drawled, "that the prince has forged a *friendship* with our Ella and if she disappears before the feast, we worry things could get...complicated."

"They're not complicated now?" Doran asked, fully invested in the conversation now that Firmin had shown what an absolute lout he was. Naturally. Sometimes, Axel wondered how the High King hadn't found himself with a knife in his gullet already.

"They're uncomfortable now," Firmin said, "but it will get worse if His Highness has reason to make it so. We're doing our utmost to make sure this armistice stays intact long enough for the crops to take root in the southern isles. Once we have enough food for our men, then we can discuss kicking the beehive."

Axel had to breathe in and out through his nose for several seconds until he could open his mouth without calling Firmin a bloody idiot to his face. "So, how will us waiting help?"

Anders leaned forward. "If she stays, continues on as if nothing has changed, the complication will disappear when Prince Roman is off to Oxe."

"Fine." Axel was ready to hit something. "We let Roman prance about the fortress and see what he needs to see, then we take off with the princess after he's gone to take his luxury tour."

"Don't take this so lightly, Axel," Doran said. "Prince Roman may be the younger son, but he's just as cunning as his older brother. Some say he's even worse than Prince Enzo in some ways. It would be best if we didn't aggravate an already tremulous situation."

"But essentially, yes, that's precisely what we'll do," Firmin added.

Axel slapped his hands on his thighs. "I expect my crew to be lodged together, and this feast better outshine Little Hal's cooking or I'm leaving."

Firmin grinned through his large, blond beard. "Excellent. The feast starts at sundown."

ᚠᚼᚲᛟᚠᛦᛏ

AXEL STOOD in the dressing room he and Pet had been given and pulled his ugly green cowl down over his head.

"If the prince sees you in that, he'll definitely be scared."

He turned to see Pet pulling together the fabric at the neck of her blue tunic. A slip of her wrappings peeked above the low collar, which she hated. Any exposure of her lie made her touchy. Even though they'd explained away the need for her wrappings—saying she'd suffered severe scarring from the fires of Holmberg—she still hated anyone looking too closely. If they did, they might notice the extra padding around her middle to make her look stouter or the lack of scars peeking up over the edges of the wrap. It wasn't the best lie, having been fabricated when they were only fourteen, but anyone that wanted to test any theories had to contend with Axel's reputation and

Pet's cunning. The very few that had even thought to torment Pet about it had been dealt with. Severely.

"Stop before you make it worse." He walked over to his trunk and pulled out a lace-up vest he'd been gifted by a father of a Häxa child they had saved last year. "Here," he said, holding it out to her.

Pet snatched it from him and yanked it on over her head, eyes flashing more blue than green, reflecting the color of the tunic. Her eyes always changed with what she wore or whatever emotion she was feeling. Right now, Axel could see her frustration in the depths of that blue as fathomless as the sea. When she tied off the string at the top, she huffed out a breath. "All these morons trying to show off the three chest hairs under their collar are going to be the death of me."

"Oh, it can't be that bad," Axel said. "At least you don't have to worry about showing off your chest hairs. One look at that scowl and no one will even want to get close enough to check." Pet shoved him, but he only laughed. "Honestly, Pet, I don't think anyone would have noticed if you left the vest off."

"I'm not going to risk it just because I don't want to sweat to death at the feast."

Axel pursed his lips to hide his smile. "But maybe if you swoon, it will get us out of having to stare at the Sidan prince's ugly mug all night."

Pet glared at him, but before she could attempt to stab him, someone pounded on the door.

"Hurry up, you two!" Big Hal called from the other side. "The rest of us are *starving*."

Which meant Olav had just finished getting dressed after Big Hal had shoved a fresh tunic on him and threw him into the hall. Little Hal still raced about the city on whatever errands Pet sent him off on, and Erik had firmly stated he would meet them at the feast. He likely had gone in early to get a comfortable seat close to the feasting tables so he wouldn't have to move for the rest of the night.

Axel laughed and slung his arm around Pet's shoulders. "You good?"

Pet shoved his arm off and slammed her elbow into his side. "I suppose."

They opened the door to a frenzy-eyed Big Hal. "Let's go. Let's go. *Let's go.*"

Axel shut the door behind them and followed their motley crew members toward the clatter of feasting. As they drew closer, the sounds began to distinguish themselves from one another. Smacking lips. The thump of tankards on wooden tables. The slosh of mead onto the floor. Laughter. Yells. Whispers. When they reached the hall, the stench of a hundred men and burnt fat poured out from the spacious room.

Big Hal groaned. "I could eat an entire elk, I'm so hungry."

"Technically," Olav piped in, "you could live the rest of your life without eating."

Big Hal frowned. "What? No, you can't."

"Ah, but can't you? If you starve to death, it would legitimately be the rest of your life."

Big Hal looked at Olav like the man was a complete moron, and Olav met his gaze with a wicked gleam in his eye. The old man took every opportunity to poke fun at Big Hal. Honestly, it was Big Hal's fault. He fell for it too often. All four of them filed into the feasting hall, spreading out like a pod of killer whales on the hunt. Axel circled to the right, Pet not far behind him.

Firmin sat at the head of the largest table, his not-a-throne positioned as the center of attention. Queen Eva and Princess Ella sat to the left of him, and Anders sat to the right. Lady Idalia's seat was vacant next to her husband.

"There's the prince," Pet said, pointing to a corner of the room.

Axel felt his brows rising but pulled them down to school his features. Prince Roman was not so young, perhaps a year older than Axel himself. He shared the familiar attributes with many of the Sidans Axel had stood across from on a battlefield over the years. Bronze skin, hawkish nose, dark eyes. His black hair soaked up the light from the fires in the hall like ink, but his smile was inviting. Too inviting for a man in enemy territory, certainly.

The prince sat at a somewhat smaller table than Firmin's, but his company was just as prestigious. Two of Åldras's lesser kings as well as Lady Idalia circled the prince's table. As Axel watched, the prince spoke, hands waving in the air. He must have said something funny, because the entire table erupted into laughter and showered the prince with good natured cajoling. Prince Roman had never fought on any of the battlefields, at least, not that Axel had heard. But he wielded his charisma like a weapon, which could be just as deadly.

Pet nudged him in the side. "Stop staring and go say hello."

Axel looked down at her. "And why in Hel's halls would I do that?"

"Because if you don't, everyone here will view it as a snub and all their delicate sensibilities will be offended."

"Wōden forbid," Axel muttered and made his way toward the prince. He could see the heads turning and feel the eyes following as he walked through the throng. If these sniveling dogs thought they were about to get a show, they'd be sorely disappointed. Axel could keep his head for one evening. Probably.

As Axel drew closer, the prince looked up. The man's charming smile slipped for just a moment, a crack appearing in the veneer of his charm. Axel felt his own lips pull up, the prince's faltering smile fueling his own. He stopped at the head of the table but did not bow.

"Prince Roman."

"The Mighty Axel Ashersson, I presume." Prince Roman stood and held out a hand. "I find it quite a pleasure to meet you tonight."

Axel let the prince's hand remain aloft until the air between them grew almost uncomfortable before he took it. "I hope the company has not been so dull. I know King Agnar here can be a bit of a bore." He slapped the older king on the shoulder.

King Agnar chuckled good-naturedly. "Aye lad, but when you get to be my age, you've earned the right to be as boring as you like."

"Yes, but our Axel wouldn't know boring if it tried to sneak up his nose!" chortled King Gudrun from beside him. "The lad practically summons trouble by breathing."

"You're likely right," Axel said, pulling a chair up next to King Agnar. Pet slunk around the table, silent as a cat, and tucked herself into the shadows against the wall farthest away from the fire.

"And who can we thank for the pleasure of your company, King Axel?" Prince Roman asked.

"*Pshaw!*" one of the other men at the table said. "King? Axel hasn't been *king* of anything since King Doran picked him up. Holmberg's been a graveyard since you Sidans showed up."

Prince Roman nodded as if they discussed the weather. "I recall hearing you're from Holmberg." He didn't try to apologize or make light of the situation, which Axel could almost respect. The prince was a diplomat for sure.

"And what brings you here, Your Highness?" Axel asked.

Prince Roman gestured to the room. "Why the fine company, of course." The table laughed, but he raised his hands placatingly. "Truly. There aren't so many as half as interesting men in Sida as there are here."

"And women?" Lady Idalia asked.

Prince Roman nodded in her direction. "Yes, and women."

"Why are you here now?" Axel asked.

Prince Roman leaned back in his chair. "My father thought it best I come to visit on his behalf. With winter comes battle, and my people wish for this war to end sooner rather than later."

Axel folded his arms over his chest. "So, you're here to surrender?" Firmin had mentioned the Sidan prince was there to explore lengthening the armistice. Could this war come to an end before the winter storms even came?

"I'd say *negotiate* would be a better term. Eight years is a long time to be at war. This armistice is a boon for many in our kingdom. There's quite a number of our citizens who wish to end this conflict and go back to how things were before."

Axel felt his teeth grinding together, but he kept the words he'd like to say shut behind them. Aye, eight bloody years was a long time. If only the Sidans had kept their hawkish noses out of Åldras, none of this would be happening. They'd been eyeing Åldras for years before the war from what Doran had said. Always reaching out with different trade agreements or petitioning to acquire lands on the south end of the kingdom.

"Has the High King been amicable to your terms?" Lady Idalia asked.

Prince Roman smiled disarmingly, though his eyes still glittered with intelligence. "That I cannot confirm or deny."

Axel met Pet's eyes over the prince's shoulder. Pet watched the Sidan princeling, head tilted to the side as if by doing so she could hear his heartbeat.

Her eyes met his. *What do you think?*

Axel couldn't settle on an answer to the question. The Sidans had gotten them all into this mess, and they'd better be paying a king's ransom to get them all out. And it would hurt. After all, they'd been just as eager to accept the armistice as Åldras had been to introduce it. War was expensive to even swaggering, overly charming princes.

"I have to admit," Prince Roman said, bringing Axel's attention back to him, "I've heard many a tale of Axel Ashersson's mighty deeds. I had hoped to meet you in the flesh, and I find myself surprised by you."

"Oh?" Axel asked. "And what about me is not meeting your expectations?"

Prince Roman chuckled. "It's not like that, I can assure you. Only my brother and his men return home with tales of facing you on the battlefield. I'm having a hard time attaching the bloodthirsty monster they say you are to the congenial man sitting across from me."

Axel flashed his own charming smile like he would one blade against another. "Pray tell, what stories do they come home with? I know the feats get a bit exaggerated." Not by much, but he wasn't going to admit that. Best to be underestimated where he could.

Prince Roman leaned forward in his chair. "Is it true what they say about your heritage? That you're Häxa born?"

"My mother was Häxa, aye."

"And you're the only male to ever be born to a Häxa?"

Axel shrugged. "I've never heard of any others." There were women born to a Häxa who inherited none of the gifts of their mothers who would birth sons. But Axel was the only son in their known history born to a woman with powers and the only male ever to have powers of his own. And those powers were completely different from his sisters'. His magic came from inside him, his förändra, his heart, rather than the elements of the earth around him. At least, that was what he guessed based on his prophecy and what he'd experienced. No one had any real answers for why he was what he was, except that the will of the gods was a mystery and other bloody nonsense.

True interest flashed in the prince's eyes. "And your abilities?"

"What of them?"

"Do they truly make you impervious to harm?"

Axel grabbed the small blade tucked into the sheath under his shirt.

A Sidan guard stepped toward the prince, but Axel flipped the knife and held out the handle. "Why don't you see for yourself?"

Prince Roman reached forward and grabbed the blade tentatively. His fingers wrapped around the hilt in a way that said he knew how to use such a weapon but didn't know what to do in this situation. When he looked up at Axel, his expression turned contemplative. Perhaps he didn't actually believe the legends. They were far-fetched for certain, but not any more extraordinary than a girl changing into a wolf. Or perhaps he was just weighing out the costs if he actually drew blood.

"You really want me to stab you?" Prince Roman asked.

Axel stretched out his arm. "Go ahead. Try it."

The prince touched the knife to Axel's skin.

Axel smirked. "Come now, even King Agnar's grandmother could do better than that." The table broke out in laughter. "Try a little harder."

Prince Roman met his eyes. It was then that Axel finally saw the bloodthirsty Sidan under the veneer. Saw the man who would draw blood because he believed it would give him something in return. Believed the shedding of blood entitled him to some kind of gift. Glory. Power.

The prince slashed the blade over Axel's skin. On any other man, it would have opened up half his arm. But Axel's skin remained unblemished, only the slight indent of the knife's presence receded from his skin.

Prince Roman returned the blade to Axel, the princely mask falling back into place. "That's incredible. You're indestructible."

"Except by age and wounded pride." And supposedly being madly in love, but unless she reciprocated, there wasn't much threat of that.

Axel's quip elicited another round of laughs. Even the prince was grinning ear to ear.

"So, it's true," Prince Roman said. "About Holmberg, I mean. You survived the fire when everyone else perished."

Axel's smile vanished. "Aye. Pet and I are the last ones." Axel looked to where Pet stood in the shadows.

Prince Roman turned around, obviously surprised to see her there. "You're Petyr Mallorysson, yes?"

Axel could see Pet's eyes narrow at the attention, but she didn't let more than that glimpse of her irritation show. She gave a curt nod.

"And are you Häxa born as well?"

The table erupted in laughter.

"Petyr?" one of the older soldiers said. "No, Petyr's a wee demon, that's what he is. Lives in the shadows and pops up in your nightmares like a being sent from the goddess Hel herself."

The table roared with approval, each man adding his own anecdote about Pet. She was a shadow, a wraith, a creature of darkness. Everyone knew it. Everyone had seen it. She'd put as many Sidans in a shallow grave as Axel had. Had taken out every threat to Åldras that crossed her path. While Axel had the privilege of deciding who was a threat, Pet didn't. She'd had to become something much darker than him. He'd helped her become it.

She could take the mockery, but it still rankled on him that she had to. That he was the glorious hero while she was the infamous shadow. But it kept their secret safe. It kept her safe.

Axel cleared his throat as the noise died down. "Well, if he's a demon, perhaps Hel's domain isn't so bad after all."

Prince Roman continued to watch her in the shadows. "Perhaps all of us are demons in our own way." He gave her a slight nod and turned back in his seat to start up another conversation. Something about the summer storms.

Everyone else took on the new topic, but Axel watched Pet. Her eyes remained on the prince, but her curiosity had vanished.

Prince Roman had passed some kind of test.

Or perhaps he'd proven to be exactly what Pet had expected him to be.

Axel certainly wouldn't be taking his eyes off the prince if he could help it.

CHAPTER 7

A PARTY

Wōden's one good eye, parties were the worst thing the gods had ever invented. The only thing worth going to a party for was picking pockets, but the pockets surrounding Pet were unpickable. She'd lose her bloody hand if she tried to steal from any of the kings or commanders in the room.

She stayed close to the wall as Axel stood from the prince's table and began making his rounds. It had always been interesting to watch, the way he strutted through a crowd like a god come down from Asgard. The way the crowd reacted to him as if he was something to be worshipped. Someone handed him a plate of food, and he followed them toward another empty seat. Everyone tracked him. It was like watching the tulips that had once graced Mama's garden chase after the sun.

He looked back to where she stood, tilting his head at the empty chair next to his. *Join me?*

Pet shook her head. The last thing she wanted was to be smushed between him and Vilhelm, one of Firmin's best steersmen. The man bugled like a bloody elk when he got deep enough into his cups.

She broke away from her spot on the wall to find her own plate of food. While Little Hal's cooking was unmatched by any other crew's cook, she needed something other than barley and fish in her stomach for one night.

On quick steps, she slid along a banquet table, snatching goods as she went. Legs of venison and grouse glistened on platters next to bowls of sweet sauces. Baskets of flatbread, brown bread, and bean cakes covered with linen to keep the bread soft. There were bowls of nuts, fruits, and pots of boiled vegetables. Firmin's belt would likely snap by the end of the night, and Pet wouldn't be mad if hers followed after it. When her plate was heavy enough to make her arm ache, she snuck away to find a spot somewhere out of sight once again. Prince Roman's attention had been uncomfortable to say the least. When she'd spotted him at first, he'd seemed like the preening prince the rumors said he was, but she'd seen something. A sharpness in the way he moved. When he'd attempted to slice Axel's arm right where the large artery flowed from his fingers to his shoulder, it only proved what she'd suspected. Sidans were never to be trusted. And he'd taken too much of an interest in her after their conversation, his eyes never straying from the conversation around the table even as he kept her in his peripherals. She didn't need another Sidan to remember her face. It was better when everyone forgot she existed.

She spotted Doran sitting at a table far from the fire with a single candle flickering above the pages of his journal. If the man hadn't become King of Grovö when he was younger, he'd likely have been a scholar, endeavoring to record the oral records of Åldran history. He was always spouting on about how the kingdom's traditions would be lost if no one wrote them down. The cost of paper meant nothing to him so long as he could record what he believed to be important for the people who came after them.

Pet set her plate down beside his empty one, careful to keep it far from the flickering candle.

"Good evening, Petyr," he said, not looking up from the leather-bound tome in front of him. "Have you lost your other half so soon into the feast?"

Pet pointed her leg of grouse at where Axel regaled his table with some kind of war story. There was enough jabbing with the pig rib in his hand to have slaughtered an entire infantry.

Doran looked up and followed where she pointed. "I'm glad he can find such enjoyment in a situation like this." He set his quill to the side and pulled out a small pouch of sand.

Pet had seen him do it enough times that she pulled her plate away as he dusted the wet ink with the fine grains. She set the plate back down as he funneled his sand back into its pouch and flipped to the next page. The two of them sat quietly with one another as the room grew loud around them. While Doran had always been a man of words, he used them carefully. As if he understood the gravity of each one he used. Well, unless he was angry. Then no one could get him to shut up.

But at that moment, they sat together in companionable silence, which Pet took to mean he wasn't mad at her or Axel. A miracle to be sure.

"That poor girl," he said after Pet had nearly finished her plate of food, watching the princess sit beside her mother. "Her entire life has been snatched out from under her, and for what? Because her father and men like him can't lay pride and hatred aside." Pet tore apart the last bean cake on her plate as he turned in her direction. "What do you think about all of this?"

Pet bit into the cake, one of the beans popping between her teeth. "I don't think about it."

Doran snorted. "Please. I know you better than that, Petyr. Out of the entirety of your crew, you're probably the only one who has more than a dozen thoughts in their head."

Pet looked up at him then. "Why does it matter?"

Doran's face softened. "Because most of the time, your thoughts portray something in a light I didn't see them in before."

"Don't get mushy." Pet ducked over her plate. "I'll throw up everything I just ate."

"Oh, what a child you still are." He shook his head. "Eighteen really is such an interesting age. Not quite a man but not a child either."

Pet's mouth twitched. When Doran had found them, she and Axel had agreed to tell everyone she was simply younger than him which explained her fairer looks. The truth was that she would turn twenty-two during Sólmánuður, the hottest days of the year. A whole seven weeks before Axel, though he enjoyed pretending he was older than her.

"Do you and the crew have any other plans to keep you distracted until tomorrow?" Doran asked.

Pet shrugged. Axel had wanted to shop around for some new boots, and Erik had been inquiring about new sails since they left Mötesplats, but neither of those were real plans, and Pet didn't feel the urge to divulge them. Especially because it was likely they wouldn't have the time to do any of it if they were going to be smuggling a princess out under the Sidan's noses.

"Perhaps you can get Axel to acquire a new cowl," Doran said.

At that, Pet smiled. "Not likely." He'd been given the ugly thing by a little girl in one of the villages they'd visited right after the armistice had been called. The village had been one of the most recently attacked and the crew had taken the first month of the armistice hauling timber around the kingdom to help with rebuilding. The child's village had been left nearly empty, but the girl had woven Axel the cowl in the three days they'd been there trying to frame some buildings. She'd gifted it to him right before they left, tying off the very last knot before putting it in Axel's hands.

Doran chuckled and turned back to his notes. A few months after he'd brought them onto his crew, Pet had stolen his writings to see what on Frigg's lands he could possibly be writing about. She'd been shocked when she'd found his innermost thoughts mingled in with the tactics and written histories from other cities in Åldras. Many of them were stories about his life in Grovö. His time as king. As a husband. A father. Grovö had been the closest city to Holmberg. Doran had been away on a hunt when his city was attacked by the Sidans. When he and his men had returned, the streets had been empty, excepting the blood that had stained the walls of the pillaged houses. From what she could tell, Doran had run and hadn't returned to his home since.

Pet soaked up the last bits of gravy from her plate with a piece of flatbread and moved it to the side to lean over the table towards Doran. "So, the princess?"

Doran sighed and looked around them before putting down his quill. "It'll probably be best to try to get her out before sunup, once everyone has been deep in their cups and the city quiets. We don't know if any more Sidans will decide to join their prince here, and we need to avoid their attention as much as possible."

Pet picked at the skin of her lip. "It'll be difficult getting past any patrols they have running the channel near Bellator too." She could picture it all in her head. Isberg's lands stretched south, nearly touching the Sidan lands across the channel between the Stiga Sea and the Vit Sea.

"As long as we aren't caught by surprise, I don't think *The Phoenix* will have any problems outrunning anything."

But if anyone caught wind of it, there would be trouble for sure. If the Sidans learned about the princess, who knew what would happen. They might simply offer her asylum in Sida, but that wasn't likely. Not if they could use her against Firmin in some way. If the Ekte found out, the girl would die, no matter what Firmin said. It was best for everyone if the princess got to Ljust Löfte, and that was the end of it.

"We'll need more men," Pet mumbled.

Doran nodded. "I've already reached out to a few of the old crew here in the city. I know Ludvig, Hemming, and Ulf are able to come, though I don't know how many more you want to add besides the four of us."

Pet's brows rose. "You're coming as well?"

"I can't just leave you two to your fate after I was the one that dragged you back here. I'll see it through."

That would give the ship ten men. Erik would probably like a couple more just for security purposes, but he would make do with what they had. If Pet had longer in the city, she probably could have found a few more, but there wasn't time to properly vet them for such a sensitive mission.

"What is he doing now?" Doran grumbled.

Pet's head jerked up. Axel stood toe to toe with Anders, who had a very firm grip on his wife's arm. Lady Idalia's cheeks were flushed pink, her dark eyes flicking about the room. Pet was out of her seat and at Axel's side in the time it took for her to draw a knife.

Anders's face was mottled purple as he spat. "You can't tell me what to do with my wife, boy."

"I won't to tolerate a pig like you talking to a lady like that." Anger radiated off Axel in waves. The king must have really crossed a line.

Anders spluttered. "How dare—"

His words cut off as Axel's hand shot out and grabbed his wrist. A knife flashed in Anders's hand. The blade hit Axel's arm hard enough to make the lesser king wince when it bounced off Axel's impenetrable skin.

Axel completely ignored the attack and pried Anders' fingers from Lady Idalia's arm. Pet felt her own fury join Axel's when she spotted the marks the king's grip left on the lady's skin.

Firmin decided then to make his appearance. "What in Hel's halls is going on here?"

Pet took a step forward, knife in hand, but Axel's arm shot out to stop her.

"Pet, please escort Lady Idalia out of the hall. She should not have to cavort with such...*men*." The last word came out as a curse more than anything else.

When she looked up at Axel, he didn't meet her eye, but she saw the pleading in his face. *Please get her out of here so I don't have to kill them.* Pet bowed to the lady and offered her an elbow. Lady Idalia let out a shaky breath and took it. The lady's fingers trembled through the fabric of Pet's tunic as she led her to the door.

"Axel," Firmin snapped, "you have no right to tell any man here what they can or cannot do with their prop—"

Pet slammed the door behind them before Firmin's sentence could finish. Axel would have his hands full with that. Leaving him behind felt a bit wrong, but Big Hal would have his back if the situation escalated further. Doran would step in before too long and use that silver tongue of his to convince everyone they were in the right and cool off. Olav would probably have them all singing a ballad together in a few minutes anyway, the moment forgotten.

She led Lady Idalia farther away, taking the roundabout path leading around the great hall toward the royal houses. If she could get the lady settled, she could return to her meal.

Lady Idalia pulled Pet's arm. "Please, not there. Not yet."

Pet stopped and looked at the woman holding her arm in a vice. As if she would sink into the very earth under their feet if she let go. Two tears fell, each on either side of her face, but her dark eyes bored into Pet's.

"All right," Pet mumbled, turning away from the great hall. Axel would tan her hide if she left a lady crying alone in the dark.

They walked for a bit, the night air turning their breaths to fog in front of their faces. While the snow on the mountains melted during the day, the air was still cold at night. Eventually, Pet led the lady to one of the fires flickering in the iron baskets staked down around the fortress. Pet didn't get close to the fire but stayed just on the edges of the ring of light so the lady could still see her.

"Thank you, Lord Petyr," Lady Idalia said. She finally brushed the tears away from her cheeks. "I'm sure I'll be much more myself in a moment."

Pet watched as the princess tried to pull herself back together, piece by piece. The tremble in her hands slowed, her breathing taking a more even pattern. The mask slowly slid back into place, the poised lady once again smothering the scared woman underneath.

"I don't know how you do it," Pet said.

Lady Idalia met her eye. "Do what?"

"Live like that." She pointed back toward the great hall. "Married to a tyrant that treats you worse than a bag of dirt."

A breath of a laugh slipped between Lady Idalia's lips. "I suppose it's because I don't have much choice, do I?"

"Of course you do." Pet flipped a dagger through the air, the fire glinting off its sharp edges, and caught it by the tip of the blade. "Just stick one of these between his ribs. Problem solved."

A smile touched the corner of the lady's mouth. "And get framed as a witch and burned at the stake?" She shook her head. "No, I still have at least that much self-preservation."

"I'm sure there's someone who would do it for you." Freyja's golden tears, Pet would have done it herself if she could have gotten away with Axel not knowing. Pet flipped the knife again. He would be upset if she killed the lesser king without enough cause—though with the way he'd been fuming, that might not be too far off now.

Lady Idalia stared back at the great hall. "I'm sure there would be, but I'm one of the few in this bloody kingdom that believes violence is not the answer to everything."

Pet caught the knife again and paused.

Lady Idalia smiled, watching her. "Are you surprised? Do you believe violence is the answer to illness, to a war that no one can determine the reason behind?"

Pet shrugged, doing her best to remain nonchalant even as her heart pounded at the lady's words. "Hard to be a pacifist when you've been in the fight, watching men get slaughtered in their homes."

"But why does it have to be sword against sword? Why can't we be civil and sit down for a plain conversation?"

"How does a wolf become alpha, or an ice bear claim its territory?"

The lady's lips thinned into a line. "Is that what we are then? Animals meant to tear each other apart over scraps?"

"We can't always talk ourselves out of any situation. Not when the enemy is holding a sword to our throat."

Lady Idalia folded her arms over her chest. "Sida isn't holding a sword to our throat now."

Pet bit the inside of her cheek. *No, just a noose.* But she could see the lady felt differently. Perhaps if there were more people like her, people in a position where they could actually use their wits instead of their swords, the world could be different.

But wherever that world was, it wasn't here.

"Lady Idalia!" a call sounded out from the dark.

Pet's fingers wrapped tightly around the hilt of her dagger as a shadow loped from the great hall and joined them. Pet stepped farther back into the shadows as Prince Roman jogged into the light. That sharpness she'd seen earlier faded behind the furrow in his brow and the obvious anxiety over Lady Idalia. What on Midgard was he doing chasing after her?

"Are you all right, my lady?" He reached for Lady Idalia's hand, tucking it gently between his own.

"Yes, Your Highness." Lady Idalia looked up at him, eyes wide as she took a step toward him. "I apologize for my candidness back in the hall. Sometimes, my words run away with me when I talk of my homeland. I hope I didn't offend—"

The Sidan prince waved her off. "There was no offense. I only wish my question hadn't elicited such a reaction from your husband. I shouldn't have acted so familiarly with you in front of him."

Pet's gaze flicked between the two of them. They were far more familiar with each other than any two royals should be. The prince acted like he cared a little too deeply for an already married woman.

One very obviously shackled to a man he should think twice about offending if he wanted this armistice to last.

Lady Idalia ducked her head, her dark hair hiding her face from Pet's view in the shadows. "If only my husband wasn't so offended by my culture, it wouldn't have been a problem. Asking such a simple thing about my life before my marriage shouldn't have prompted such a public scene."

A sour taste grew in Pet's mouth. Anders was the stupidest man in Åldras, to be so prejudiced of his own wife's people. She'd seen it in both the lesser king and his elder brother, the disdain they held for anyone different. It didn't matter that they were all created by the same gods, only that the two brothers wished to degrade anything that didn't make them look better.

"I hope there's something I can do to make it up to you." Prince Roman set his hands to his heart. "It wounds me to know I caused a lady as lovely as you such distress."

Lady Idalia smiled.

What in Hel's bloody halls is going on between these two? It would serve Anders right that his wife would seek comfort in another man's company. Of course, Lady Idalia was playing a dangerous game if she was ever caught smiling like that at anyone, let alone a Sidan prince.

"Pet!" Axel called from the door of the great hall.

Both the prince and Lady Idalia jumped at the sound. Prince Roman's face turned a bit pale when Pet stepped out of the shadows. Even Lady Idalia blinked in surprise as she straightened and gave a slight curtsey. "If you gentlemen will excuse me, I think it's time for me to retire." Pet took a step toward her, but the lady raised a hand. "I'll be fine on my own. Thank you, Lord Petyr, for your assistance and your company this evening." She nodded and glided in the direction of the royal houses, only looking back at them once.

"Pet," Axel repeated, close enough now that she could easily hear him at a normal tone, "we've officially been uninvited to tonight's events."

Pet withheld a sigh and circled the fire and the prince. With a short bow, she swept past him. The sensation of the prince's attention followed her until she disappeared around a corner.

CHAPTER 8

SURPRISES

I have been one of the lucky few to have studied Mighty Axel Ashersson and his unique gifts up close. The first time I saw him use his abilities, I must admit, I was frightened. A boy with such power would be the ruin of any kingdom. I was surprised, however, when he proved to be not only intelligent but charitable as well. It is not often one finds a man that is both powerful and humble. He is a hero in every sense of the word, and I couldn't be gladder for it. I only pray he remain so for as long as it takes the Allfather to accomplish what He needs the lad to do.

— *FROM THE WRITINGS OF DORAN FINNSSON, THE LAST KING OF GROVÖ*

Axel led the crew through the fortress and away from the party, leaving Doran to attend to Firmin's oncoming tantrum. Big Hal stood at the rear, acting as shield. Olav was happily chattering, his words halfway between speech and song. Erik swung his canes in a steady rhythm, the sound settling Axel's still-racing heart. A pair of serving girls passed by, tittering and batting their lashes at him and the rest of the crew. Axel nearly growled at them. He needed to get away from all these people and sharpen his sword. Or carve something. Anything to keep his hands busy enough to forget how much they wanted to throttle Firmin and Anders. *Those bloody idiots.* When he'd seen Anders shake Lady Idalia like a limp doll, he'd nearly taken the king's head off.

The rapid thump of his heart in his ears lessened the farther they got away from the feast. Spring had already started pushing herself onto Åldras, even as the mountains farther inland held onto their snow. Axel could just make out the glittering peaks in the moonlight as he took a deep breath of crisp air.

Seven months of peace left, and what did they have to show for it?

If he didn't think every single one of his crew would be slaughtered for it and the kingdom wouldn't fall to the bloody Sidans, he'd have killed Firmin and Anders years ago. But even if he was unkillable, his crew wasn't. He'd seen what happened to those who betrayed the kings. No one was safe. Not even him.

Once they were far enough away from listening ears, Axel turned to Pet. "How are we going to get the princess out of here tomorrow?"

"The Sidans might pose a serious problem for us if they are as deeply involved with the princess's family as Prince Roman looked," Pet said as they marched across the firelit grass.

He shrugged. "We'll simply have to be a problem for them as well."

But Pet was right. If they were seen shuffling the princess—Freyja's golden tears, what was the lass's name again?—off toward *The Phoenix*, the Sidans would certainly start asking questions. If they started asking questions, Firmin would get antsy, and the gods only knew what he'd do.

"I'd wager there's something else going on here," said Erik.

Axel paused and turned back to their skipper. "And why would you be suspicious?"

"The wind feels off to me."

Erik's instincts were nothing to scoff at. His feel for danger had saved their sorry hides more than once in the two years since they'd started sailing together. He'd proven his mettle when they'd faced their first storm together and he'd gotten them through the Död Isles on the western side of Åldras. Besides, there was no other skipper on the Vit Sea that could get a karve to outpace a skeid on the water.

"There's little else we can do," Big Hal said, flicking his mane of strawberry-blond hair over his shoulder. "If the king wants his daughter—his *Häxa* daughter—taken to the Great Mother, we're the only ones who can do it."

Olav sighed. "Do you know what songs I could write about a Häxa princess? If it wouldn't get her hunted by the Ekte, I'd be rich."

Axel gestured for them to pick up speed, only going as fast as Erik could on his canes. Though, for a man on two peg legs, he could be quick when the moment warranted it.

They slipped into the hut they'd been shown to after they arrived. It stood close enough to the great hall to be convenient, though not so close that Axel would take the attention too far from Firmin. *Bloody narcissist.* But, while Firmin might have been a thorn in his side, the man did know how to host guests—or at least his underlings did. Thick furs and stuffed mattresses lined the walls on each side. A fire crackled in the pit at the center, the smoke twirling up toward the hole in the domed ceiling. A washbasin squatted in one corner. They'd passed outhouses on the way in, so Axel wasn't surprised by the lack of chamber pot. The outhouses were also somewhat private, which would be good for Pet. He knew she'd appreciate not having to find a place in the woods somewhere.

The men scrambled to lay claim to their space. Erik took the bed closest to the door as usual, unbuckling the wooden pegs extending from his mid-thighs and massaging the scarred flesh. Big Hal and Olav squabbled over the beds closest to the fire. Little Hal would probably curl up next to Olav once he got back from whatever errand Axel had sent him on. Pet threw down her pack on top of the pile in the farthest corner, even grabbing the mattress and tucking it as close to the wall as she could. The spot next to her was left vacant. Axel was the only one ever allowed to sleep anywhere near her. Not only would she have punched anyone else for trying to get close to her, but she also might have tried slitting someone's throat in her sleep. Axel had woken to Pet's dagger bouncing off his chest more than once, though it had lessened as the years went. Perhaps, one day, she wouldn't be plagued by nightmares.

Olav and Big Hal finally settled, and Olav looked out from under a mountain of furs. "So have we come up with a plan?"

Big Hal scoffed. "Please. We all know Pet has been plotting since we learned of this quest. It's stupid to think otherwise."

Olav took up his *pondering face*. "If a stupid person knows they're stupid, does it make them less stupid than a person who doesn't know they're stupid?"

Big Hal stood up, hands clenched at his sides. "Are you calling me stupid?"

"Both of you, shut up." Axel rubbed his eyes with his thumb and forefinger as he tried to recall the Great Mother's map in his mind. "We're going to need a bigger crew. The six of us won't make it to Ljust Löfte without a few more hands on the ship."

"Doran already agreed to dust off some of his old crew," Pet said.

Axel straightened. "Doran's coming?" It had been years since they'd all gone on a voyage together. Hopefully, some of the old crew could join and it would feel like old times.

She nodded. "He's got another three and there are probably half a dozen drinking off their sorrows somewhere in this pit of flesh-eating maggots if you want them."

"Ah, Pet, you make Harligdam sound like paradise," Axel said. She'd always had such a way with words. When they were younger, she'd picked up many a phrase from her older brothers, then come running to teach him. Axel got his ears boxed more than once by Father for repeating something she'd taught him.

She shot a glare in his direction but grabbed a clay tablet to begin jotting down a list at the same time Erik pulled out the precious slip of parchment he kept close to his chest. He unfurled it to reveal the detailed map of the continents around them, Tatawar and Sida to the south and Isberg to the northeast. He then pulled out the smaller piece of parchment, the one the Great Mother had given them.

"From what little I've been able to gather from the map, there are two paths to Ljust Löfte." Erik pointed at the top of the map, where dark waves tattooed the paper. "Taking the northern pass through Donar's Storm would be suicide. Even if we made it out of the storm, the Isberg Strait is nearly impossible to navigate through."

Axel scrubbed a hand over the stubble taking root on his jaw. Erik was right. Donar's Storm had been there since the gods only knew when. It was said the storm had been brewed by the jötunn Donar himself after being offended by a crew who had cursed him when rain had started up during their voyage. Donar had crafted an eternal storm that never abated, and only the most foolish of men ever attempted to cross.

"So we take the easier way." Big Hal pointed at the southern route. "Likely the path the Great Mother just took to get home."

Erik shook his head. "There are notes throughout the page, but most of them have been written in a way I can't tell what they mean."

"Either way, it's a risk," Pet said, using the tip of her dagger to draw attention to Bellator, the Sidan capital along the coast. "If we get close to Bellator, we'll have Sidans on our rears faster than Anders on a slice of honey cake."

The other men snickered, but Axel shook his head. "We'll have to take a chance on the southern route. With the princess as cargo, I wouldn't want to risk the storm, no matter how fun it looks."

Erik gave him an evil eye at the suggestion that they would take his precious ship into such a dangerous place, but the other men only nodded and shuffled around their sleeping areas.

Big Hal shucked off his boots and snuggled down into his furs. "Don't wake me up until we have to leave tomorrow," he said, tugging on one of his thick fur hats and covering his eyes. "I haven't slept on dry ground in ages."

"You slept in a house less than a week ago," Pet mumbled.

Big Hal grabbed one of the boots and chucked it across the room at her. Pet caught the boot before it hit her in the face and lobbed it back at him. The heel smashed into his giant hat and knocked it off his head. Big Hal grabbed for his other boot when the door burst open.

Little Hal crashed into the room. "The Sidans! They've got a fleet coming into harbor not two hours out."

Big Hal's boot fell from his hand and landed with a *thump*.

Little Hal closed the door behind him. "Watchmen say *Sida's Shield* leads them."

"Of course it does," Erik said, shuffling back toward his peg legs.

Sida's Shield. The one Sidan ship nearly as infamous as *The Phoenix* herself and for very good reason. It was Crown Prince Enzo's—or rather, Enzo the Scourge's—ship after all.

"I guess it's time to go!" Axel said in his cheeriest voice. If Enzo caught even a whiff of their plans, the chances of getting *The Phoenix* out of Harligdam would go up in flames. Especially with such precious cargo. Luckily, the crew was used to packing up to go at a moment's notice.

Pet tossed him his sword and crouched down to help Erik strap his peg legs back on. "You think his brother told him we arrived?"

Axel buckled the sword to his waist. "You don't?"

ᚠᚾ<◇ᚠᚤᛚ

BIG HAL LAUNCHED Erik into the ship as Doran came running up the dock. "So, first a Häxa princess, now the Sidans. Is there any chance you could stop for just a second and let the rest of us relax?"

Axel scowled. "You're the one who said I had to be a hero all the time."

Doran let out a chuckle. "Well, I'll make sure Little Hal serves those words up with my next bowl of porridge." He turned to the three men accompanying him. "You remember Ludvig, Ulf, and Hemming. Hopefully, the four of us will be enough."

Axel had served with all three of them under Doran's command, and he'd beaten each in multiple arm-wrestling contests over the years. Ulf was the oldest, having served under Doran as his lead armorer. The man could make a shield out of anything. His wide girth could rival even Firmin's, but the man could haul an entire pack of weapons on his back without breaking a sweat. Ludvig had served as one of twenty oarsmen, but his wild hair had always made him stand out. He'd taken to keeping it long on the top, twisting the golden locks into intricate braids, but the sides were shaved. A long scar stretched from his right temple toward the back of his head, a wound from one of many fights on the open sea. Hemming stood taller than even Axel, though he was built like a bean pole. Everything about him was thin except the wild mane of hair on his head. Red curls shot out in every direction and blended almost seamlessly into his beard.

Axel shook hands with each man. "We're glad to have you."

The four men grabbed their trunks and pulled themselves over the side of the ship.

Axel tossed his trunk up after them just as the sound of sobbing echoed down the dock.

"Please, Father! I haven't even said goodbye!"

Firmin pulled a crying Princess Ella across the rough planks of the dock by her arm. "Stop your blubbering, you stupid girl. By the gods, this is no time to get weepy."

The princess cried harder. She tripped over one of the warped planks and fell to her knees, making Firmin stumble. A few of the guards behind them jumped to help her up, but the High King pushed them off.

"Ella!" Firmin snapped, hauling her up by the wrist. "You will cease your whining and get your arse on that ship, or I will throw you in the harbor for the whales to eat."

Axel felt the air beside him shift, and Pet materialized beside the girl. She threw a glare sharp as the daggers on her vest at the king before offering her hand to the crying girl.

Princess Ella took her hand, small sobs still shaking her shoulders as she walked toward *The Phoenix*. Her wrist had gone red where Firmin had clamped his large fingers over her skin. It would likely purple by the time the sun came up.

Axel stormed towards Firmin, his chest burning at the haughty expression on the High King's face. "And here I figured you only used that tone on your men. I didn't take you for one to be so hard on your children."

Firmin jutted out his chin. "Take your indignant smirk and be off, Axel. You can charm the rest of Åldras with your self-righteous candor, but I don't have need of it here."

Axel stopped only a step away, leaning down so he could be eye level with the king. "Then perhaps you should reevaluate."

"Perhaps you're the one who needs to *reevaluate*. You forget, *I* am High King here. My word is law and a simple whisper from me could have you and your crew shipped off to Tatawar's slavers before sunset tomorrow."

A dark chuckle rubbed up Axel's throat. His hand snapped out, and he grabbed the king by the wrist. "Someday, you're going to run out of threats, Your Majesty."

He felt Firmin's blade do its best to dig into the flesh of his gut, but it couldn't break past his skin.

The king's jaw tightened. "There isn't a day that goes by that I

ALLISON ANDERSON

don't wish I could just gut you and feed your innards to the bloody sharks."

A few of the guards reached for their blades, but one look from Axel froze them. He bared his teeth at Firmin.

"You may be High King, but *I* am the one with the real power here. With Sida knocking on your door, I imagine you would be remiss to get rid of your peoples' greatest hero. My patience with your pathetic existence grows thin."

Firmin's eyes narrowed, but he said nothing. *Smart man.* Too bad he didn't have the same sense of preservation for his kingdom that he did for himself.

"Put your legs on your neck, Axel!" Erik hollered. "Time to get paddling."

Axel dropped Firmin's arm and took a step back toward the ship.

Firmin's hand snapped out and grabbed the front of Axel's shirt. "Don't forget, the only reason I haven't slaughtered every single one of those men on your ship is thanks to my patience. It would be wise not to keep testing me, Axel. You might find yourself wishing I could slit your throat."

Axel yanked his shirt from Firmin's grip. "One of these days, you're going to find yourself on the wrong end of a sword, and I'm going to clap with bloody glee when it happens."

"We'll see, won't we?" The king's face darkened as he clenched the blade tightly in his fist.

Oh, how lovely it would feel to slide a blade between his ribs. It was the only death he would relish in. The only blood spilled that would actually make the world a better place. But not yet. Not in front of his child. Not before this war was over and they could move onto better things.

"Axel!" Erik's voice snapped.

"I'm coming!" Axel snapped back. He hoisted himself over the edge of the ship and bounded to his place in the rowing line, leaving the fuming king behind him.

CHAPTER 9

A PRINCESS

Petyr Mallorysson is the perfect contrast to Axel Ashersson and some-times I wonder if they are actually related at all. Petyr has always been a quiet lad, content to allow Axel the spotlight, though the boy deserves far more credit than he receives. I've never seen a quicker wit, nor a quicker blade. I am glad he has Axel to temper him, to negate the dark-ness I sometimes see in him. I wonder what abysmal hole he would have haunted without his cousin to pull him into the light. I also wonder how much damage Axel would have done without Petyr to knock some sense into him.

— FROM THE WRITINGS OF DORAN FINNSSON, THE
LAST KING OF GROVÖ

"Freyja's golden tears," Pet muttered as she led the still-sobbing princess toward the cargo pit in the middle of *The Phoenix*. Hauling a soggy girl down into the belly of the ship was the last thing Pet wanted to do that evening, but the crew didn't need this small, dainty girl getting trampled underfoot before their journey even started.

Princess Ella looked over Pet's shoulder then around at the men. Big Hal nearly barreled into the princess, the trunk in his arms big enough to fit her inside. Pet yanked her out of the way and into the cargo pit in the middle of the ship. It wasn't a true hold like those on a knörr, but it was big enough to carry the cargo the crew needed.

The princess shrank back. "What is that?"

Pet followed her gaze to a net full of grayish-blue blubber. "Hafgufa skin."

Princess Ella cringed. "What is a 'hafgufa?'"

"They're also known as *ship eaters*." The nasty creature had nearly swallowed *The Phoenix* whole before Axel had climbed up its back and cut the creature down the middle. The skin was good for making temporary patches on the ship. Besides the skin, there were many trophies from the crew's adventures as well as a few mementos. Along with pelts of fur from an ice bear, the tail of a huldra, and a vätte's hat, they also had a large tapestry from Erik's homeland, Little Hal's cradle that Olav had hand carved, and the shield of King Asher Redbeard— Axel's father. Firmin had been asking for it for ages to put up in his great hall, but Axel kept it in the hold. Rather honor his father by taking it with him than allowing Firmin to mar the dead king's memory.

Before the princess could ask anything else, Pet pulled her past the center of the hold, where the mast was secured to the keelson, and led the princess toward a netted pile of sacks filled with grain and other supplies for their journey. The princess's eyes widened as she tried to take it all in. She flinched every time Erik barked an order, and Pet could easily see the small tremble in her shoulders she attempted to hide.

"Here," Pet said, grabbing an armful of furs from one of the trunks. She knew exactly where they were because she usually slept down there when Olav snored like a bear or Erik thrashed at the ghosts of pain from his missing legs.

Princess Ella took the furs when Pet offered them and slumped down on the bags. "Why are you being so nice to me?"

Pet paused. Was she being nice? She shrugged. "Just doing my job, princess."

The princess ducked her head. "Thank you. And please, just call me Ella."

Pet went to walk away but stopped and pulled a small dagger from her vest. She held it out, pommel first. "For emergencies."

Princess Ella tucked the knife against her chest. Hopefully, her father hadn't neglected her so much she didn't have any training with a blade. However, the steel Pet had seen in Queen Eva's spine might have made up for the king's folly. If he hadn't at least given his daughter a blade, the queen had likely taught her what to do if handed one.

"Petyr," Erik hollered, "stop your flirting and get up here!"

Pet rolled her eyes and bounded up onto the deck, leaving the princess to her own devices. She would check on her again after they got out into open water. The crew had the oars through the oar holes and Pet joined the lineup.

"Row!" Erik called the beat over the deck. "Row!"

Pet moved her arms with the rhythm of his voice. Doran sat in front of her, his arms in sync with hers. Axel and Big Hal each took the oars at the front. Olav sat behind Ludvig and his ugly haircut. The remaining men sprinted across the deck, strapping down cargo and prepping the sails to unfurl when they hit the winds.

They left Harligdam behind them, with the Sidan prince still snug in his bed and his incoming older brother none the wiser. *Easier than sneaking a bowl of pudding from under Ander's bulbous nose.*

ᚠᚾᚲᛟᛒᛏ

"PRINCESS." Pet poked the girl's arm a third time. "You should wake up now." The sun had reached its peak nearly an hour ago. *The Phoenix* would be stopping near the northern coast of Skydda so Little Hal could serve the crew a proper meal. The men would need it after the day they'd had. While they'd gotten out of Harligdam without issue, none of them had rested enough the night before and all they'd eaten was what they'd been served at the feast. It also didn't help that they were working against the wind, Erik having to resort to tacking for most of the journey. It would be a long voyage to Ljust Löfte.

The princess groaned and turned away from Pet. Right by her face lay a sack of grain. The moment she touched it, the entire thing burst open, leaves and roots shooting out in every direction. The princess yelped as the sprouts covered her. Pet jumped back, doing her best not to get caught in the wave of plants, and climbed out of the hold.

"What on Midgard?" Axel said from somewhere behind her.

The plants grew up and over the edge of the hold, their green roots twining around the cargo. Shouts went up behind Pet as she kept stepping away from the exploding plants. The stalks faded from green to gold. When the plants stopped growing, Pet slid back down into the hold and waded through the stalks of what looked like oats.

"Princess?" she called.

The plants ahead of Pet shuddered until a small, freckled hand shot out of the mound, followed by a head of gnarled red hair. "What happened?" Princess Ella cried.

"Looks like you got too close to some of the grain," Olav called out. "Should have thought about that one after the girl we'd saved last spring nearly sank the boat with the spruce cone Little Hal had tucked away down there."

"At least oats are lighter than a bloody spruce tree," Axel said, jumping down from the deck. He joined Pet in stomping down the stalks to reach the princess. "We'll just have the chore of cleaning this all up."

"I'll absolutely help," Princess Ella said. She looked down at her hands, face pale. "I still can't believe I can do that."

The girl likely thought she was some kind of abomination. With a father like Firmin yapping on about how evil the Häxa were and hearing about all the women the Ekte murdered in the name of good, she wouldn't know otherwise. Not without someone to teach her. To help her know what to expect.

But Princess Ella was one of the lucky ones. She'd had a mother and an aunt on her side. There were plenty of others who were on their own, just trying to survive in the wicked world they lived in.

The crew got to work throwing the stalks out of the boat. Pet toiled beside Princess Ella, heaping armfuls of the grain and tossing them overboard. Olav had found the princess a pair of gloves, which kept her soft hands from getting sliced up by the sharp edges of the oat leaves, and prevented her from accidentally growing any more. The work continued until Erik pulled *The Phoenix* into a small cove to stop for lunch.

Pet strapped her axes back to her waist as everyone else hopped out of the ship. The gods only knew what lurked in the brush. Big Hal grumbled about not making it to one of the coastal towns closer to

Skydda, but there was little to be done. They'd cleaned up at least a third of the hold, giving Little Hal access to a barrel of fish and a sack of beets. The lad was in the process of whipping up a simple meal as the rest of them stretched aching muscles.

Hemming, one of Doran's old crew, disappeared inland for five minutes before returning with a handful of green leaves and a rabbit slung over his shoulder. The man could find food anywhere.

The princess placed a hand on her lower back and groaned. "How do people do that during the harvest months?"

Olav chuckled from his seat on a large rock where he was scaling some of the fish. "Why do you think they call farming 'back-breaking' work, lass?"

The crew slowly encircled the fire as the aroma of Little Hal's cooking wafted toward them. Pet did her best to remain as far from the flames as her rumbling stomach would allow though. She could get food once there weren't so many people gathered around the cookfire.

"And the plants grew so fast." Princess Ella looked to Pet, drawing her back into the conversation with Olav. "Can other Häxa do things like that? Grow crops? Water plants?"

"No," Pet answered. "You're just special."

Axel flapped his hand at Pet. "Don't listen to him. There are other Häxa with all those gifts. And more. I've seen women transform into animals. Drive away storms. Even heal a bleeding wound with a touch."

"Idalia said I might be able to do that."

How did Lady Idalia know so much about the Häxa? Pet hadn't been around the lady since she arrived from Tatawar to marry Anders only a year before the armistice. Tatawar was known for their ingenuity, but Åldras had always been the most populated with magic users.

At least, until Firmin and the Ekte started killing them off.

Doran sauntered over and sat on Pet's other side. "How long have you known about your gift, Your Highness?"

"Please, you must all call me Ella," she said. "I discovered it about six months ago."

"And your father only just found out?" Axel asked.

She nodded. "My mother and Idalia did their best to hide it. It was harder in the beginning. I had little control, and I feared even going outside would give me away. We had to fake a 'woman's illness' for six weeks before I could finally leave my room without losing control. Even after that, it was difficult to hide, especially once the snow thawed and the plants started popping up everywhere."

Axel leaned forward. "Did you plan on hiding it forever?"

"We knew we couldn't, and it was that kind of thinking that eventually got us caught. We knew there were people smuggling Häxa out of Åldras, though we didn't specifically know you and your crew were the ones doing it. My father never said anything to us about it until he discovered my mother attempting to find you."

Pet held back a snort. "I imagine that went marvelously." Wōden's eye, the girl was lucky to be alive. There were more than a few stories about the atrocities done to Häxa under Firmin's roof. His witch hunters were merciless.

Ella looked down at her still-gloved hands. "He did not take it well."

Little Hal called for lunch, ending their conversation, but something in Pet's gut still churned. This was why she could never be anything but a man. Women in Åldras were nothing but a piece of a man's household, only good for cleaning and bedding. The moment they were an inconvenience they were thrown to the wolves.

The only people Pet had seen that hadn't been like that were Mama and Da—and maybe King Asher—but their somewhat forward thinking hadn't kept them alive when the Sidans came to Holmberg.

No, it had been quite the opposite.

Pet grabbed her bowl of fried fish and beets from Little Hal and found a place on the outskirts of the group. She watched Princess Ella sit next to Olav and stare down at the bowl in her hands.

If Pet hadn't listened to Axel when Doran came to Holmberg, if she hadn't learned to fight or pretended to be Axel's boy cousin, there was a very real possibility she would have turned out just like the princess.

Small.

Weak.

Adrift.

It had been a close thing when Axel had pulled her from the rubble of her house. Pet could almost see her thirteen-year-old self in the princess's vacant gaze. That loneliness that ate away at a soul. Knowing she'd never see her family again. Knowing she'd never be the child she once was and had to become something new. Something hated. Something feared.

Because that was where the real power came from. It wasn't in being able to grow plants at a whim or call a storm with a thought. No, power was in what one could do with those things. In what they did when the light had vanished and no one could see them. In how they snapped back once pushed into a corner. Power was being something that someone blamed when the forest burned. Power was being something that someone praised when the rain came to squelch the flames. There was power in being hated. There was power in being feared.

And Pet would never be powerless again. Not like her thirteen-year-old self, and not like the shunned princess.

CHAPTER 10

RIDDLES

"What if we just aren't reading it the right way?" Axel flipped the map upside down. The jumbled letters looked worse that way. With only the light of the fire to see by, it was even harder to read the rune-like figures the Great Mother had jotted all over the map.

Erik snatched it back. "You don't think I've tried that?" The gruff man smoothed the small wrinkles in the parchment. "I think there's a code, but I haven't been able to figure it out yet."

They'd been going over the map since Little Hal had collected their dishes. The lad had already cleaned up supper and was fast asleep in the sleeping mat next to Olav, who was deep in his whale-like snores. They'd stopped just on the tip of the isle outside of Generös, away from the docks where the Sidans could potentially pop up since they were scheduled to head there today anyway.

Pet stepped closer, leaning over Erik's head from where he sat on a low rock. "What are these bits around the edge?"

Erik shrugged. "I haven't been able to figure those out either. The only thing I can read is this bottom bit right here."

Axel circled both of them so he could view the page. At the very bottom was a small phrase, situated in a box that reflected another box of bolded runes at the top of the page.

Jackdaws quietly vex the bold nixie grazing frozen thyme atop lush, breezy mountain cliffs.

"What?" Axel muttered. "Nixie can't even get up a mountain." The nasty creatures were water bound, barely able to breathe air without having to submerge themselves in water every five minutes.

Pet picked at her lip. "I don't think it needs to make sense."

"So, it's a riddle?" Axel asked. *Bloody Häxa and their riddles.* Was it not enough that he had to decipher his own prophecy?

"I thought that at first," Erik answered, "but there's nothing else it could possibly attach to."

Pet drew close enough to Axel that the hairs on his arms stood up. "Are any of the symbols a jackdaw?"

Erik shook his head. "None."

"Perhaps we're supposed to be using constellations," Axel said, looking up. "I know there's a vixen, but I don't remember there being a jackdaw."

"No stars on the map," Pet said.

"The Great Mother speaks to animals," Erik said. "Could it have something to do with her magic?"

"Perhaps." Axel tapped a beat against his thigh with the tips of his fingers. "Or it could be a million other things."

Erik ran a hand through his graying hair. "What exactly did she tell you when she gave you the map?"

Axel repeated the experience, with Pet filling in what he forgot. He hadn't thought anything much about the Great Mother's words. His mind had been filled with the bloody prophecy he wished he could forget. What sane man would want to live with the knowledge that he was the savior of a land that hated his kind? He was almost positive part of the reason Firmin hadn't found an excuse to get rid of him was because of the prophecy. It wasn't like no one talked about it. When Doran had first brought them to Harligdam, it seemed it was all anyone talked about. The boy who would bring down the Sidans. The boy that would sacrifice everything to keep his kingdom from destruction. The man everyone wanted to be but no one could touch. He was blessed and cursed for Åldras's sake, and if he was any other man, he would have left the bloody place to ruin the moment he stepped foot on *The Phoenix.*

But here he was, saving an Åldran princess and once again stopping ruin from coming to the kingdom.

He really ought to get paid more for it.

"May I?" Pet stuck out her hand, the sleeve of her tunic brushing against Axel's arm as she reached for the map. It made Axel's skin prickle with gooseflesh.

"Have at it," Erik sighed.

Pet took the paper and twisted so she could clearly see the symbols in the firelight. The orange glow danced over her form, bringing out the small bits of gold in her otherwise brown hair. The light softened her edges just a bit, making Axel's mouth go a bit dry.

He shook his head and turned back to Erik. "What do you suggest we do if we can't read the map?"

Erik shrugged. "The way she wrote the instructions make it plain Ljust Löfte is located somewhere in Isberg's mountains, but there are too many things she's written to narrow down exactly where or what the other symbols mean. Some of them could be notes, but most maps like this warn of hazards we may come across on the journey—like Donar's Storm. There's a small line of symbols right where the storm should be, so I know she's taken account of that."

"It didn't seem like there were very many notes near the southern route."

"Aye, but that could mean any number of things. We just won't know until we figure out what it all says."

Axel turned to the fire. If it was just him, he wouldn't even bat an eye about traveling through whatever the Great Mother had thought to warn or not warn them about on the map. However, he wouldn't subject the crew to anything until he knew what they might face. Not to mention Pet. She would follow him into Hel's bloody halls herself if he charged in there, axes swinging. *Stubborn woman.*

"Axel," Pet said, breaking through his musings, "will you grab my clay tablet out of my satchel."

Axel found the small plate of clay and brought it to her. She settled into the sand with the map in her lap and the writing tablet in her hands. With the small bit of bone she had tied to the plate, she began jotting down letters. "It's not a riddle, it's a code."

Erik slid from his rock and shuffled over to where Pet sat. "Show me."

Pet explained how the phrase contained every letter of the alphabet and how each letter matched with a corresponding symbol in the text below it. Seeing the repetition of those symbols matched the repetition of the letters in the riddle, she quickly created a key. However, when she applied it to the text on the rest of the map it still didn't make sense. Axel's smile grew as she showed Erik what she did. She really was a marvel.

"But when you said you noticed the note over Donar's Storm," Pet said, "I decoded it and realized they aren't just coded, but also backwards." She wrote out the translation, which read *MORTS SRANOD.*

"That Great Mother really is something else," Erik mumbled.

Axel laughed. "I suppose you can't keep a race from genocide on animal magic and eclectic idioms alone."

"Axel," Pet cut in, "it seems like the symbols on the outside of the map are for us." She pointed to a spot on the top of the page, where a gap separated one chunk of text from the next.

Axel looked to the sleeping crew, then back to Erik.

The skipper took the hint. "I'll let you two decipher that and go catch some shut eye myself. I'll have time on the ship tomorrow to go through the notes. It'll be another three or four days before we pass Grovö, so I won't need it until then anyway."

"Goodnight," Axel said.

Erik shuffled over to his bedroll, brushing sand from his trousers where what was left of his legs had dragged along the beach.

Pet yanked on the edge of Axel's tunic. "Sit."

He obliged her, sitting as close to her as he could. "So, what ominous message has our illustrious matriarch left for us?"

"Not ominous so much as somewhat generous."

Axel watched the tablet as she decoded the message.

Axel and Pet,

I figured I could kill two flies with one swat by giving this map to you and the men of your crew. I want you to know that, above all else, I trust you. You have done much for our people and this was one of the greatest ways I could express that appreciation. Secondly, I want to extend to you an invitation. I hope that with this map, you might find yourselves more willing to visit Ljust Löfte and eventually call it home. There is more to life than war and bloodshed. Perhaps someday, you'll allow me to show you.

Axel couldn't smother the smile he felt growing on his face. The Great Mother's words were a balm on old wounds. It had been a long time since Axel had a home, a people that welcomed him as one of their own. A leader who trusted him because he did what was right and not because they knew they couldn't kill him. While he had *The Phoenix* and her crew, there was something about the Great Mother's invitation that filled a little of the hole inside him.

"It's a nice offer," Pet said. "Too bad we won't ever be able to take her up on it."

Axel's mood dampened. "And why not?"

"Because we won't ever leave Åldras while the Sidans are still a threat." She stood and erased the grooves she'd made in the clay tablet.

Axel stood next to her. "But what about after?"

"You think there will be an after for us?"

She walked away before Axel could reply. Really, he couldn't find an answer anyway. He'd always imagined there would be something after this war. That Åldras would eventually fight off the invading Sidans and be safe. Maybe he and Pet would return to Holmberg. Rebuild. Maybe they could take *The Phoenix* and start a trading company, as the boat was built to handle the cargo—not to mention it would make saving Häxa easier.

The possibilities were endless, and the sky was the limit. All he had to do was convince Pet to come with him.

CHAPTER 11

AN ENEMY

They were making good time, praise the Allfather. Pet held a hand to her brow as she watched the coastline of Mötesplats come into view. Once they passed to the south of the island, it would be smooth sailing to Isberg.

Little Hal waved his thin arms at the back of the ship. "Axel! Sidan ships."

Pet's stomach dropped into her toes as Axel stood from his trunk beside her.

"Where?" he demanded, striding toward the lad. Pet followed on Axel's heels as he met Little Hal at the stern.

Three Sidan vessels glided through the water toward them from the northwest, skirting along the coast of Gudvangen with sails full of wind. Axel growled beside her, his expression darkening. He pointed out the ship leading the small fleet. Pet had to watch it for a moment before the morning sun hit the golden beak of the screeching eagle at its stem. *Sida's Shield.*

"Oh, rocks," Pet hissed. How had the elder prince followed them? He must have turned right around the moment he'd stepped foot on the dock at Harligdam. Had Firmin even tried to stall him?

"What is it?" Erik asked from the tiller, tightening the straps over his chest that attached him to his sliding platform.

Axel turned back to the crew. "Grab the oars! If we don't outrun them, we'll have Enzo the Scourge on our stern before you can kiss your sorry lives goodbye!"

Pet's stomach twinged, and she raced for the oar locked next to her trunk. She'd fought against Crown Prince Enzo of Sida once, after she and Axel had left Doran's tutelage. The Sidans had pushed for more land that summer, nearly wiping out three villages in the southern region of Åldras and working their way north past Grovö. *The Phoenix* and her crew had been sent to take care of it. Between their team and the three others that joined them, they shoved the Sidans back. But Enzo had gotten in quite a cut to her abdomen. Axel had stitched her up as he usually did, but he'd said any deeper and her guts would have been on the ground at her feet. The long, purple scar across her stomach attested to it.

Pet followed Axel to his seat. "If we turn around, we might be able to go the long way, skim past Skydda and lose him in the smaller isles."

Axel shook his head, grabbing his oar and sliding it through the port and into the water. "We'd risk getting boxed in by Prince Roman's crew on their way to Oxe."

Rocks, he was right. If Prince Enzo was here, it likely meant he'd gotten word from his brother. It would make sense the two of them would attempt to trap them in the bottleneck created by the two larger land masses.

Erik called out a faster beat and the ship picked up speed.

"We could try to swing around Mötesplats and sneak past him." Pet sat behind Doran and grabbed the oar out of its spot on the deck. "We could skirt around Skydda and Betala then turn south. We'd probably have him on our tail the whole time, but we could outrun him."

Axel shot her an incredulous look. "And go right past Bellator on the way?" He shook his head. "Not on your life. Most of the reason we snuck the princess out was so we could get past Sida without them knowing. Chances of that are nil now. We both know if we get anywhere near Sida now, they'll set a trap. We'll be sitting ducks in the middle of the Vit Sea."

"What do you want to do then?"

Axel kept his count going on the oar but looked back at the tiller. Pet followed his gaze to find Erik staring back, his gray brows pulled low over his stormy blue eyes. He nodded and yelled, "Unfurl the sail! Pull the sheet!"

Pet whipped her head back in Axel's direction. He couldn't be thinking what he was thinking. It was impossible. *Suicidal.*

Axel's teeth flashed. "Onto Donar's Storm, boys!"

Hel's bloody halls, he was going to get them killed. Donar's Storm wasn't another beast to be vanquished or adrenaline high to chase. It was insane to even think they would make it out of there alive.

Pet threw down the oar and stomped up to him. She so desperately wanted to cuff him on the back of the head that she had to cross her arms not to give in to the temptation. "I knew you were an idiot, but I never imagined you would be this stupid."

Axel kept rowing but looked up at her. *You know I'm right.*

She narrowed her eyes. *You're going to get us killed.*

One of his golden brows rose. *Are you scared?*

She nearly threw up her hands. *Yes!*

He laughed.

She growled and Olav snickered next to them.

She glared at the old man and jabbed a finger in Axel's face. "Just don't come crying to me when this entire thing goes completely to the fish."

"Petyr!" Erik called. "Get back to your post!"

Pet sent Erik a sharp nod and left Axel to his rowing. Over the side of the ship, she watched the Sidans skip across the water toward them.

ᚠᚾᚲᛟᚠᛁᛚ

FOR AS MUCH AS she hated them, Pet had to admit the Sidans were competent sailors. As *The Phoenix* raced through the eastern isles of Åldras, the trio of Sidan langships were right behind them. *The Phoenix* was a truly masterful ship, but it wasn't built for short sprints. Sidan langships, however, were built for speed. The only thing *The Phoenix's* crew had over their pursuers was Erik.

"Pull the bowline! Keep that sail steady!" It was like he knew exactly which way the wind would turn at which moment. Little Hal stood right beside him, his eyes glued to the ships tailing them and reporting to Erik every move they made.

Enzo's ship led the trio. With the oars pushing them through the water and the wind whipping at their heads, Pet watched the ships draw closer and closer. But her worries didn't remain on the ships behind them for long. *The Phoenix* had made it all the way through the night and into the next day, but now the evening sun was cloaked by roiling black clouds, casting the boat into darkness only broken by veins of white lightning.

The wind grabbed them next.

"Strap in everyone!" Axel's booming voice called over the gale. He tossed Pet a nest of leather, which she detangled into a harness much like the one Erik wore to keep him tethered to his perch. The leather was slick with oil to keep it from cracking, but it also made it difficult to handle when her fingers trembled. She fitted the straps around her legs and across her torso.

Then came the rain.

Pet slammed into the side of the ship, holding tight to the line attached to the mast. Water trailed down her cheeks. The rain soaked through her clothing as she knotted the rope through the rings going around her waist.

"Pull, boys! We need that sail shut as tight as the gates to Valhalla!" Erik called from the back of the ship. A wave crashed over him, but he lifted the handle of the tiller and slid it into the next slot on his rail to lock it in place. The water under the boat rocked, sending men tumbling around the deck. Most of them were already harnessed in, and Pet set to buckling the rest of them.

"Pet!" She turned and found Axel pointing toward the cargo pit. "Make sure that princess isn't going anywhere."

Pet skidded over the soaked deck and nearly fell into the open hold. The storm made it dark enough that she had to feel her way around. Nets, crates, and sacks led her through. She stopped when she found the lump of furs huddled on the floor.

"Ella?"

"This is *madness*!" Ella's voice was barely audible over the crash of the waves, her cheeks pale and eyes wide as her fingers clutched her harness.

Pet grabbed one of the ropes tied down to the keel and began tying knots around the princess's waist and legs. "If something happens to the ship, pull this buckle loose and yank the ring off the harness. It will detach you from the rope, but don't unravel it unless absolutely necessary. Stay down here unless there's water pooling, you understand? There shouldn't be rocks this far out, but we won't have you getting in the way of the crew."

Ella grabbed onto her arm. "Please don't leave me down here."

Pet pulled away. "I need you to promise to stay here unless something happens to the ship."

The princess stared up at her, fear stark in the lines of her face. Slowly, she dropped her hand, that steel Pet had seen in the queen entering the princess's expression.

"I trust you, Petyr," Ella said.

Pet stiffened. The princess trusted her? Why on Midgard would she do something so foolish?

She shook her head. "I'll come let you out after."

If there was going to be an after.

Pet pushed her way back up onto the deck. The wind yanked at her clothes, her hair. She squinted against the gale to get a look at the crew. Thank the Allfather everyone on this ship, including Doran's crewmates, were all seasoned sailors. They found their storm legs and lunged about the deck, making sure lines were tight and the oars were locked into their slots. Little Hal zipped about, getting the lanterns around the gunwale lit with small amounts of Åldran fire, the only substance that wouldn't go out in the rain. He moved past her, intent on the lantern hanging from the stem a few ells away.

"Petyr!" Big Hal cried. Before Pet could even blink, he threw a coil of rope in her direction. The wind caught it, pulling it sideways. She lunged for it, but it bumped straight into Little Hal. The boy staggered, tripping over the ropes and sending the small iron bucket of Åldran fire flying through the air. It dumped onto the deck only a step away from Pet.

The oil splashed toward her, and the flames followed.

Pet's entire mind went blank as the orange and yellow fingers reached for her, longing to touch her.

Flashes of charred bodies and ashen earth zipped through her mind.

Her mother's blue eyes ringed with fear.

The crash of Sidan soldiers banging on their door.

The heat scorching her throat as she screamed.

She scrambled blindly over the slick wood of the deck, but the liquid fire spread through the water, giving the flames more paths to take. Though the flames grew smaller, they were no less deadly. No less hungry.

Rough hands hoisted her to her feet and turned her away so she couldn't see the begging flames. Fingers tightened around her arms as they held her up. Axel's green eyes replaced the flicker of the fire.

She couldn't breathe. The ashes choked her, coating her throat and blackening her lungs until all that was left was fire.

Fire.

Fire.

Fire.

"*Pet!*" He shook her a bit and the jolt helped center her. His eyes blinked against the squall as he studied her. He set his hands on either side of her head, blocking all the sound around them, but she could read his lips.

"It's not going to touch you. Little Hal's already put it out. It's gone. I won't let it touch you."

Pet gulped down what felt like her first lungful of air. She nodded, her hair whipping into her eyes. It wouldn't touch her. It wouldn't get her.

Axel pulled his hands away from her ears. "You good?"

"Aye." Pet shuddered, wiping her hands down her face and feeling anything but. "Aye, I'm good."

"Look out!" Erik yelled.

Pet swung in his direction as a wave crashed into the deck of the ship.

Chapter 12

Storms

Axel gasped in a lungful of air, holding onto the straps of Pet's harness as the boat returned to an upright position. Pet regained her footing, allowing Axel to let go and grab one of the ropes flapping in the wind. He couldn't even tell where the other end was attached, the sky was so dark.

A holler broke through the water of Axel's clogged ears. He whirled and found Ulf hauling Little Hal away from the side of the ship. Little Hal strained to get to the edge, his face contorted in anguish.

Olav's rope hung over the side.

Axel ran, eyes scanning what little of the black waters he could see through the rain as he grabbed the line. His heart shot to his throat as the rope came to him with ease. In moments, the end came up out of the waves, tied around a single, iron ring.

Little Hal screamed and it rattled Axel's ribs.

The waves around them rocked the ship, and Axel held onto the gunwale as he searched the water for the shine of Olav's gray hair. The sunbaked skin of his hand. The flash of iron from the rings.

Olav was nowhere to be seen.

Axel grabbed the buckle at his waist. Olav couldn't have gotten far.

A vice gripped his wrist, and he found Pet standing before him, her gaze dark. *Don't.*

He looked out at the water. She was right to stop him. There was no way he'd find him. Not in this. Not with the ship in the throes of the waves. Not with the inky blackness of the water. Not when the crew needed him to get them to safety.

"Axel!" Erik barked. "I need a second line on the oars!"

War brought loss to everyone. Kings lost crowns. Lords lost lands. Families, homes. Mothers, sons. Soldiers, brothers. One would think after losing so much, the scars would harden the soul, make the future losses more manageable. If that was the case, Axel's soul must have remained as unscarred as his body. He sliced the rope in his hand and tucked the empty ring into his pocket. He'd already lost so many brothers. So many men that had fought beside him. Good, Åldran warriors.

And now, another had joined their ranks.

So often, it happened like this. Quick as lightning and without a moment to truly mourn. There was no way Olav would last through this storm.

Axel released his hold on his buckle and watched the waves with a reverence so opposite to the chaos billowing around them. "We'll see you in Valhalla, brother."

"Axel!" Erik hollered.

With his heart still stuck in his throat, Axel slipped the iron ring into the pocket of his vest and ran down the ship. If the tiller broke, they could use the oars to navigate, but if the storm took both, it would take all of Erik's skill and Wōden's own hand to get them out of this mess.

Axel tied down the last oar as another wave crashed over the side of the ship. The briny water stole every bit of oxygen from his lungs. The wave receded, and the crew came up coughing. Pet staggered toward the hold, lightning lighting up her silhouette in the pitch black of the storm in flashes. He took a step toward her.

"Axel!" Erik yelled.

Turning away from Pet, Axel squinted through the deluge of water until he saw Erik, pointing off the port quarter.

He squinted as lightning flashed again.

A Sidan ship crested a wave.

Hel's halls. They'd followed them into the bloody storm! Axel kept them in view as they bobbed over the waves, their lighter ship swaying in the maelstrom. It wasn't Enzo's ship, thank the Allfather, but it was a Sidan ship, nonetheless. Another problem.

"Can we lose them?" Axel yelled over the boom of thunder.

Erik's eyes darted about, taking in the scene and doing whatever brilliant thinking went on in that head of his. Once, he had explained how he measured the speed and direction of the ship to determine where they were, but Axel still couldn't guess how the man kept it all straight in his head. Erik used one of his tiller locks to hold their course and detached his harness from his perch. He grabbed one of the extra tie downs and tied it around the ring of his harness. With just his arms, he scrambled into the hold and pulled himself up the thick mast, using the pegs they'd had installed to allow Erik to climb up the mast to see.

"What's he doing up there?" Pet hollered.

Axel threw up his hands. "No clue!"

Erik shimmied back down, hair plastered against the sides of his face. "We've got to head further south! If we get out of the bloody storm, we can lose them in the strait!"

Axel nodded and headed for the tiller. Erik shuffled ahead of him, aiming for his seat.

A shout ripped through the air.

Axel whipped around, searching for the source of the sound. Little Hal was on the ground, his hands over his head as a rope swung over him. Axel raced toward him, the sound of snapping ropes matching the furious beat of his boots against the planks.

The main sail unfurled over his head, catching the blustering wind and yanking the ship forward.

Axel lost his footing and went down on one knee, only a few steps from Little Hal. The boy's fingers now dug into the hardwood of the deck, keeping him from rolling as the sail jerked the ship about.

"Get that sail secured, *now!*" Erik bellowed.

Axel grabbed the back of Little Hal's shirt and tossed him toward the hold. "Get down there! Keep an eye on the princess!"

Little Hal nodded, obviously ready to accept any task to get him into safer quarters. Once the lad was off, Axel joined Big Hal and Doran as they scrambled for the lines to tie up the sail.

Another shout rang out over the water.

The Sidans were drawing nearer.

"Erik!" Axel pointed behind them.

"It's going completely to the fish, I know!" Erik strained at the tiller, Pet bracing herself on the other side to keep it straight.

Her eyes flashed dark as they met his. *I bloody told you this was a mistake.*

If they could just get out of the storm, they could deal with the Sidans.

Axel dropped the length of rope he'd been holding and began scaling the mast as Erik had. He tried to grab at the sail as it flicked past him, but the wind pulled it out of reach. At the top, he let his eyes scan the horizon. All he needed was a—*there*. The whites of cliffs peeked out in the dark, invisible to any other man's eyes but his. He pointed in the direction of the cliffs and looked down at where Erik steered the ship.

"There! Just—"

Blinding white suffused everything around him.

Axel swore he heard Pet scream. Not the sound of rage or pain as he was accustomed to from her, but of fear.

The next thing he felt was cold.

But he had to get to Pet.

He didn't realize he was in the sea until he tried to breathe and promptly choked. The sensation was uncomfortable, but the lack of air wouldn't kill him. He looked about in the water, trying to find anything that would indicate which direction the surface was.

Light flashed above him.

He kicked toward it, propelling himself as quickly as he could.

When he surfaced, water spewed from his lips and he gave a hard cough, expelling the liquid from his lungs.

"Thank you for nothing, Njord." He spat out the last of the water and looked around.

The Phoenix bobbed in the waves a dozen ells away, her silhouette skewed in the darkness. He swam for her, but it wasn't until he got closer that he figured out why she looked so wrong. The mast hung over one side, the sail sliding into the sea. He could see the crew trying to pull it back onto the deck, but they were losing the battle

Axel cut through the water as quickly as he could, diving below the surface as large waves crested between him and his ship. He approached the hull from the opposite side of where the mast hung and pulled himself up onto the deck. As soon as his feet were under him, he ran to where the crew was doing their best to keep the water from pulling the sail under.

"About bloody time you showed up!" Pet hollered from her place at the front of the group. She had a tight grip on one of the ropes, her face screwed up in a snarl.

Axel grabbed the broken end of the mast beam. "I get struck by lightning and the greeting I get when I return whole and hale is *'about bloody time'*?"

"Shut up and pull!" she snapped.

He dug his feet into the deck and yanked the beam back. The water tugged at the wide fabric of the sail, making it weigh as much as a bloody frost giant. Axel roared, the sound ripping from his chest to contend with the howl of the storm around him and he hauled the mast from Njord's watery hands. The crew helped guide the mast onto the deck, tying it down as they would the oars. Another wave crashed over them, but their gazes were focused on the task before them as the water receded once again.

Ludvig called from the stem of the ship. "Look there!"

A wall of white rock split in two towered above the water.

"Get on those oars, boys!" Erik's voice called over the screaming wind. "We head for the strait!"

Axel hopped to the task with the rest of the crew, finding his place at his trunk and tying his harness to one of the rings used to strap down the oars. He glanced back at Pet to see her brows furrowed in concentration, her hair plastered to her face.

When he looked over her head for any sign of the Sidan ship, he found none.

CHAPTER 13

A SHIPWRECK

There are many creatures that have made their homes above or below the surface of Midgard. In man's earliest years, giants, dwarves, dragons, and elves toiled under Sol's heat and danced under Máni's soft light. As man took to their boats with metal swords and the hope of glory shining in their eyes, the creatures of magic slowly faded into bedtime songs. In my travels, I have seen much evidence of the frost giants, and the dwarves have not made themselves impossible to find, but their numbers dwindle as man turns to pride and innovation instead of tradition and enchantment. I don't know how many more generations we have left to live in a world of magic.

— FROM THE WRITINGS OF DORAN FINNSSON, THE LAST KING OF GROVÖ

Pet, with Hemming's help, swung the heavy barrel of kraken blubber from the ship onto the small patch of pebbled beach. With a thump, the large barrel joined the others in the pile of supplies on the shore. Pet dug a splinter out of her palm with the tip of her knife and turned back to the mess that was their camp.

Little Hal sat next to Ella by the fire, the two of them soaking up whatever warmth their small bodies could get from the flames. Big Hal, Doran, and big-bellied Ulf hauled supplies from *The Phoenix* where she was beached in the small inlet Erik had limped her into. Thankfully, nothing in the hold had been seriously damaged when the mast broke, but the wood of the hull underneath was severely burned from the lightning. Praise the Allfather they'd even made it into the strait.

"Pet!" Axel called from where he sat next to Erik on a sun-bleached log.

She jogged over to where they huddled, looking over the map Erik had kept in oilskin to keep safe alongside his other important documents for the ship.

Erik pointed down at the map the Great Mother had given them. "The strait goes on for miles. It'll likely take us a full four or five days to make it with all the maneuvering we'll have to do. Some of the passes look awful narrow."

Axel slapped him on the back. "If anyone can get us through it, you can."

"Those aren't even the biggest concerns. Look here." His thick finger followed the edge of the strait until it turned south. "I haven't cracked all the codes the Great Mother wove into this map, but if the drawing is anything to go by, that looks like a bog to me."

"We can walk it," Pet said.

Erik shook his head. "This land is strange, full of creatures some of us have only heard about in song and story. We need to be wary wherever we go. Can't trust anything you see."

Pet's lips twitched. *Eyes lie just as much as hearts do.*

"Ship repairs first, then we can worry over nefarious landmasses," Axel quipped. He stood from his crouch and stretched. A sliver of his stomach showed as he lifted his arms above his head. A small gasp sounded from behind Pet, and she turned to see Ella staring in Axel's direction, her face slowly reddening.

Pet almost couldn't contain her eye roll, but she managed. "If you could stop strutting around like a bull elk with the fanciest antlers in the herd and help get camp set for the night, that would be great."

Axel swung an arm up over her shoulder. "You think I would have fancy antlers?"

With an elbow to the gut and a level kick to his knee, she left him behind, laughing.

ᚠᚢᚳᛟᚠᚤᛈ

"PETYR."

A hand to her shoulder had Pet sitting straight up, dagger swinging. Had the Sidans caught up? Where was Axel?

Doran dodged the swipe, having woken her from slumber in the past. He'd only nearly lost an eye once.

Pet sheathed the dagger, squinting up at Doran and the backdrop of glittering stars behind him. It wasn't even daylight yet. "What?"

"The princess has asked for your assistance."

Pet looked over his shoulder to find a fidgeting Ella only a few paces behind him.

What on Midgard...

"I believe the princess is in need of a washroom, Pet," Axel mumbled from his bedroll near hers.

"And why am I the one being woken up hours before my watch to take care of it? Isn't Hemming supposed to be up with you?" They were to take patrols in rotations of two every three hours in the hopes that everyone would get enough sleep to start the journey the next morning. All except Little Hal who would be up early in the morning to prepare breakfast. Though, perhaps Big Hal would take that role for the morning and everyone would eat his chewy porridge without complaint. Little Hal deserved to have a moment. The gods knew not everyone had time to grieve when their loved ones were ripped from them.

But that meant everyone else was relegated to princess duty.

Doran rubbed a hand over the back of his neck. "Because she trusts you and *I* trust you."

Pet groaned and unburied herself from her bedroll, grumbling. Why had the bloody princess put her trust in Pet out of everyone else? Wouldn't the girl want someone big and strong to scare off all the spooky shadows? Ulf would have been bloody perfect for the job with his wide girth and mighty arms. Or even Big Hal and his stupid hammer. What was the point in having all these crew members if she still had to do everything? She grabbed her cloak, the inlet having significantly chilled since she fell asleep.

Pet met Ella's eye and nodded toward a copse of trees next to the cliff face. She'd found it earlier when looking for a place to relieve herself before she'd laid down for the night.

Relief eased Ella's features as they trudged through the pebbles. "I'm sorry King Doran had to wake you. I didn't feel comfortable asking anyone else to accompany me."

"I trust most of these men with my life." Pet tried to scrub the weariness from her eyes. Even Ulf, Ludvig, and Hemming were some of the most honorable men she knew. She'd fought alongside each of them when she was under Doran's charge. While Ulf had a penchant for good mead, Ludvig could cheat a man out of his life's savings in a gambling ring, and Hemming...well, there wasn't anything wrong with Hemming. He was too much like Doran. Honorable to a fault. The two of them would have been mistaken for being the same man if Hemming didn't have a red beard to rival Firmin's and eyes as dark as black peat.

There had been plenty of warriors Pet had crossed paths with over the years that she wouldn't trust with a pile of horse dung. War had the potential to bring out the best and the worst in people. There were many stories about Åldran commanders who would just as quickly take advantage of someone like Princess Ella as they would deliver her to safety. Stories about Sidan warriors pillaging more than houses when they took a village. It had been a bloody miracle Pet and Axel had been picked up by Doran. His crews had always been honorable, and any cruelty was dealt with swiftly, usually by Doran's own sword. He had no tolerance for perfidy, even in morals.

"Besides," Pet continued, "I don't imagine much could happen on this chunk of land without Axel hearing it."

Ella glanced back over her shoulder. "Can he really hear as well as an owl? I've heard tales, but he looks so...*normal*."

Pet quirked a brow. "You look normal and can sprout trees with a thought." Though, if she were being honest, he probably listened in on their conversation right then, but Pet wasn't going to tell the princess.

"I suppose you're right."

They made it to the group of trees, and Pet leaned back against one of the trunks. "Don't wander too far."

With a grateful smile, Ella disappeared into the brush.

Pet rested her head against the smooth tree but kept her eyes open. The stars danced overhead, twinkling softly as if whispering gossip to one another as they watched the world below them. It would be interesting to know what they spoke about. Did they talk about her? Did they titter and laugh as she walked about in boys' clothing, trying to fool everyone but only fooling herself? It was laughable to be sure.

She glanced over at Axel, his golden hair shining in the moonlight. If she didn't know better, she would have said he bargained with Máni, goddess of the moon, to shed her light on him that way. To make him look like some kind of god sent down from Asgard. But she knew it was just him. The gods couldn't even take credit for him being so loved by the world they lived in.

The tumble of a rock behind her caused Pet to turn, but Ella remained hidden in the foliage.

How long was this going to take?

"You done yet?" Pet asked

Nothing.

Pet straightened, peering through the leaves. "Ella?" She shoved her way through the thick branches, but the princess wasn't anywhere.

"Axel!" Pet hollered.

She found traces of where the princess had been, but the thick layer of pebbles on the ground made it difficult to track where she could have gone. It was almost like she'd simply flown—

A small pebble bounced off the top of Pet's shoulder.

Her head snapped up.

Hanging twenty ells above, Ella kicked at a small mass directly below her. In the short amount of time the princess had been out of sight, the dwarves had grabbed her, gagged her, and pulled her up the cliff.

Axel burst through the foliage and Pet pointed.

"Bloody dwarves!" Axel swore. He jumped, grabbing the slivers of handholds he could find on the cliff face. "Get Doran."

Pet ran back out of the brush and found Doran and the rest of the crew already rushing in their direction.

She looked back at the cliff and pointed. "There. Dwarves."

"Rocks," Doran hissed. He grabbed the large, unstrung bow at his back and bent it to get the string attached. Big Hal ran past her, followed by Ulf and Ludvig, with one of the largest of their furs.

Doran pulled up the bow.

"Can you hit them without hitting her?" Pet asked.

Doran notched an arrow. "The problem isn't if I can't hit her. It's what happens when I hit all of them and she falls."

Pet's gaze shot back up to the scurry of shadows along the white cliff. There were four dwarves from what she could tell, all using a system of climbing and then passing Ella up like a bag of grain instead of a squirming young woman. They moved up the sheer face as if it were stairs, never once slowing. They had to be over fifty ells up now, nearly halfway.

A few trees dotted the edge and the whole thing sloped down on the side leading to the mouth of the strait. The small inlet they were in ended about three *Phoenix* lengths from a crevice in the cliff, reaching only twenty or so ells up before it hit where the top of the cliff sloped down.

Pet ripped off her cloak and ran toward the water. If she could climb it in time and get up to the top, she might be able to stop the dwarves at the edge and keep Ella from falling to her death. With a burst of speed, she leaped into the black waters. Teeth-chattering cold sluiced through her clothing, but Pet pushed through. She'd swam in colder before, and she was sure to swim in colder again. Her arms cut through the water, propelling her forward at a slower rate than she would like. If she'd shed her blades and boots, it would have been easier, but she would need both if she was to save the princess.

The crevice she'd spotted opened at the bottom just enough for her to squeeze through. Her boots scraped against the rock on either side as she pushed forward through the water. Praise Máni that she could still see anything inside the crevice. The moon stood just overhead, blessing Pet with enough light to see that the back of the crevice sloped up. Climbing could actually be easier than she thought.

Pet grabbed hold of the sharp rocks jutting out from either side and hauled her way up the crevice.

CHAPTER 14

CLIFFS

Axel reached one arm up over his head, his fingernails digging into the needle-thin ridges in the cliff. It was a good thing his magic made him so strong, or he would have fallen thirty ells ago. Not that a thirty-ell fall would have done anything worse than set him back to the beginning of this climb.

Dust rained down on his head and he had to duck in order to keep it from getting in his eyes.

Bloody dwarves.

Bloody princesses.

If he'd been anyone else, he would have never had to do this job. He would be sitting at the bottom of the cliff, watching someone else make this climb. Or he'd be sleeping on a warm, comfortable bed hundreds of miles from this bloody place. But of course, he wasn't anyone else. He was Mighty Axel Ashersson, the greatest man to ever live.

And he was being outrun by bloody dwarves.

He pulled himself up to another handhold, pressing his body against the rough face of the rock. The hilt of his sword jabbed into his side, but he ignored the discomfort. Máni's moon hung high in the sky, allowing him to get a good picture of the group ahead of him.

Each dwarf wore a tunic in a mixture of leather and chain mail. The armor would prove difficult for Doran to shoot through. Each also wore a black or perhaps dark-blue sash around their waists. Axel had spent a little time around dwarves. There was a clan near Harligdam, in the mountains north of the capital, where Axel had commissioned *The Phoenix*. While they were quiet folk, their clothing told stories. The fact that all these dwarves matched said they were from a group of trained fighters. The sashes around their waists were even more telling. They worked for a sovereign. Every dwarven clan had a leader boasting a collection of colors to declare their family lines, but only a select few had a king with a solid standard color.

One of the dwarves cocked back a hand and threw a rock. Right at Axel's head.

Axel ducked, the rock grazing his ear. "Great. Now I've become target practice." He pushed himself up onto a small shelf, his arms and chest taking up the entirety of it. His muscles didn't grow fatigued, but his magic didn't keep him from sweating or breathing hard. Besides, he was definitely more of a "strike quickly and get it over with" kind of man.

Another rock sailed over his shoulder, and he heaved himself higher up the cliff.

"Hey!" Axel hollered. "If you lot simply hand my charge back to me, I'll quit chasing you and we can all get back to our warm beds."

A fist-sized rock crashed into his shoulder.

"I suppose that's a 'no' then," he muttered.

Only another dozen ells separated them now, but the dwarves had less than that to climb before they reached the top of the cliff.

Another rock hit him on the crown of his head, breaking into smaller pieces.

"Hey now! That's bad form."

He got close enough to hear them chitter to one another. Their voices were quiet, used to the echo of the mountain tunnels they usually lived in.

"Hurry up," one of them hissed. "The brute is gaining on us."

A light illuminated the rocks at Axel's hands. At the top, a trio of dwarves peered over the edge, and let down a rope.

"Oh, rocks." Axel picked up the pace of his climb. There was sure to be an entrance into a network of tunnels somewhere up there and if he didn't get to the princess before they reached the opening, he would lose her.

Only a few paces away, the dwarves hauled Princess Ella over the edge and out of sight.

Axel grabbed a large stone protruding out of the cliff face, only for it to give way and leave him hanging by the tips of his fingers. He swung his arm up and grabbed the now empty spot of earth. A yelp sounded above him, and he only had a moment to squish himself against the side of the cliff to avoid a falling dwarf.

A few voices shouted, the ring of blades swinging and bodies crashing to the ground.

Pulling his torso over the edge, Axel paused.

Pet, hair as wild as the snarl on her face, cut down one of the dwarven guards with a dagger as she swung a long branch into the face of another. Half a dozen dwarves, some only as tall as her waist, swarmed her. Another group had Princess Ella trussed up like a prized pig and lifted her into the air above their heads.

Axel swung his legs up and landed a two-booted kick to the dwarf closest to him. With a roar, he got to his feet and drew his sword. But instead of the fight he expected, all the dwarves stopped, even those holding a wide-eyed Princess Ella.

Every one of them turned tail and ran, still carrying the princess.

"Ella!" Pet threw one of her knives, the blade sinking into the back of one of the running dwarves holding the princess aloft. The dwarf went down, but another quickly took their place.

Axel gave chase, only a step ahead of Pet.

"How did you get up here?" he couldn't help asking.

"Climbed," she said, as if that were a sufficient answer.

Axel shook his head and ran faster. She would tell him after they saved the princess. He met the slowest dwarf at the back, kicking out his foot to topple the creature. They went down with a shriek, but Axel left it behind. It was hard to tell if they were male or female, all of them having a propensity for facial hair.

Pet hurled her branch at another, knocking them and the dwarf in front of them over. Only a dozen or so continued forward.

Axel pushed ahead, leaving Pet behind to catch up to where

Princess Ella still tried to escape the dwarves' grasp at the front. He trampled one, two, three dwarves under his boots as he bulled his way through their ranks.

A dwarf at the front stopped, waving an arm over his head at the mouth of a cavern.

Rocks.

Axel shoved forward, hammers and axes hitting his flesh but never tearing it. Sharp curses sounded from behind him, but if Pet was cursing, it was because she was angry, not hurt. Princess Ella crossed over the threshold of the cave, only two dwarf heads ahead of Axel.

The dark was almost instant. If he didn't have keener vision, he would have been absolutely lost the moment he stepped into the cave. The ground beneath him declined, sending everyone down into the earth. The tunnel narrowed as he trailed the larger group of dwarves, batting away the ones that turned to face him. It took precious time and Princess Ella got farther away.

Up ahead, three different arches opened up, leading to only Wōden knew where. The dwarves scattered, each taking a different route.

They took the princess down the left tunnel.

Axel turned to follow but slowed as a rumble started up the middle tunnel. He skidded to a stop as a large crack slithered over the ceiling above him and continued down toward the opening.

Oh, bloody rocks.

He spun around and bolted toward the entrance. The cacophony of falling rocks met his ears as he strained to hear the whistle of swinging knives. A few of the straggling dwarves jumped to the side, already racing to hidden alcoves and other tunnels. But Axel found what he was looking for.

"Come back here you bloody little—"

Axel grabbed Pet by the middle and hoisted her over his shoulder. He could feel the dust and splinters of rock shooting at his heels as the roof of the cave broke apart right behind them. The incline of the tunnel steepened, and a sliver of moonlight glittered at the mouth of the cave.

"Almost there," Axel huffed.

Two paces from the inviting light, the growing crack above their heads circled a massive boulder making up a large portion of the ceiling. Dirt trickled from its edges as it shifted and began to fall.

Axel pulled Pet from his shoulder down to his chest and ducked under the falling rock. With one last push, he leaped toward the mouth of the cave. He did his best to soften the landing as he caged Pet between his body and the ground. They landed just outside the mouth of the entrance. The falling rock closed the tunnel, sending a spray of dust over them.

Under him, Pet remained completely still, but he could feel her breathing, his own lungs gasping for air he could barely find. When the ground fully settled and the rumble behind them ceased, Axel moved to get a look at Pet. He had to know if she'd been injured at all. His arms trembled a bit, as he released her and looked at her face.

Her dusty, blood-smeared, furious face.

Axel's chest tightened. "What's wrong? Are you hurt?"

"No, I'm not bloody hurt!" She finally got her arms up enough between them to shove him off. He let her. "They took her, and now we have no idea where." Cursing worse than Erik when the tiller jammed, she got to her feet and stomped toward the entrance.

Axel shook out his tunic, debris having sneaked through every opening in his clothing. At least she was still cursing. His eyes flicked about, scanning for any dwarves waiting for them in the shadows, but he didn't see any. *Sneaky rockheads.*

Pet whirled, her hands on her hips the way her mother had put them whenever she was especially cross. "You idiot. If you'd just kept going, we wouldn't have lost her. She's probably halfway across the bloody continent already. What were you thinking?"

Shaking out his hair, he pointed back toward the cliffs. "Show me how you got up here. Then, we're going to meet up with the rest of the crew and figure out how we're going to find the dwarf king scuttling about in these cliffs."

ᚠᚾᚲᛟᚠᚤᛈ

THE DESCENT DOWN to camp had been much easier than the climb up. It could have been a lot nicer without Pet's crazed mumbling all the way down, but Axel wouldn't complain. She probably had seventeen different plans crafted in that head of hers by the time they made it back to the crew. Ulf had a large shield strapped to his back and a sword hanging from his belt. Ludvig had two lengths of rope hanging from his shoulders and Doran stood at the side of the ship while Hemming tossed down a quiver and a bow.

"At least the lot of you weren't just going to leave us up there," Axel joked. It actually did his heart a little good to see the chaos of the camp and the coils of rope all taking up the ground around the fire. He found a spot on the log closest to the fire and plopped himself down.

Doran scowled as he threw the quiver next to Axel. "Where is the princess?"

"Likely snug in a dwarf king's tower by now." He pursed his lips. "Would it be a tower if it's underground?"

"Tower or dungeon, do we know where said dwarf king is?" Doran asked.

"And do we know why they targeted Ella?" Erik added.

Axel shrugged. "They took her through a cave at the top of the cliff. There were plenty of offshoots to the tunnel we were in, but with its collapse, we won't be able to use it to gain entrance to their city."

As to why they took her, there could be a hundred reasons. Perhaps they wished to hold her for ransom. Or they believed she'd decided to relieve herself on sacred ground. Or the king sought to draw the rest of the crew out. Dwarves weren't inherently malicious. At least, none Axel had ever met. They were creatures that thrived on creativity and community. He didn't know these dwarves or if they were anything like those in Åldras, but he didn't remember ever reading anything about kidnapping maidens.

Big Hal lumbered through the patch of trees against the cliff, a large fur sack wiggling against his back. Little Hal thumped it with a stick.

"What do you have there?" Axel asked.

Big Hal dumped the fur on the ground and out rolled a trussed-up dwarf, beady eyes narrowed over a round nose and flat teeth bared over his gag.

Axel jumped to his feet. "How did you manage such a catch?"

"Landed right in my lap," Big Hal said with a grin. "We had the fur out to catch you or the princess if either of you fell, but we ended up with this fellow."

The dwarf growled, words unintelligible with the large wad of cloth in his mouth.

Axel knelt by the dwarf's head and removed the gag.

Teeth met his hand.

Pet appeared on the other side of the dwarf, knife drawn, but just as Axel had suspected, the large, flat teeth did nothing. The dwarf's jaw quaked until he realized that his teeth broke no skin. They let go with a sharp breath and wide eyes.

"Jötunn," the dwarf said.

Axel opened his mouth, a denial on his tongue, but Pet shook her head. Her eyes flicked down to the dwarf then back to Axel.

Don't correct him.

Axel chafed a little at the idea of impersonating one of the gods. Bloody rocks, he could get cursed for even suggesting he could be related to one of the Allfather's children. The jötunn were known for being easily offended. But he didn't have to accept or deny the claim, did he? Perhaps simply allowing the creature to assume would keep him from the gods' displeasure at least a little.

"Tell me," Axel said, "what does your king want with the girl he has stolen from me?"

The dwarf trembled slightly. "Apologies, Great One. I am sure my liege was unaware—"

Axel cut him off, a bit of bite in his voice. "What does the king want?"

"A bride, Merciful One!" Sweat beaded along the dwarf's wiry hairline. "He wishes to take a bride and when we saw such a beautiful maiden in your company, we could not let the chance to appease our king pass us by."

At least the princess wasn't to be offered up as some kind of sacrifice or something awful. Axel's brows drew together. Well, perhaps being married to a dwarf king that lived in the middle of nowhere was like being a sacrifice. But if the king wanted to marry her, that meant she would be alive by the time they got to her.

Axel looked to Pet, who glanced around at the others. They needed a plan, and he could see her mind working through what to do. She met his gaze, her face lined with weariness.

Drawing himself up to look a bit menacing, Axel demanded, "At sunrise, you'll take me and my companions to your king."

The dwarf bowed his head, as much as he could lying on his back. "Of course, Great One."

Axel felt his lips pull wide. He clapped and stood, garnering the attention of the camp. "Rest up! Come morning, our new friend will be escorting us to the dwarven city."

CHAPTER 15

A HUNT

A s soon as the sun brushed the sky, Pet was awake. It wasn't true sunrise, but it was close enough. She stirred from her bedroll, jostling enough to wake Axel in the process. He'd always been a light sleeper, though touching him to rouse him was unwise. He didn't have any control over his strength until he'd been alert for a good two minutes.

Once they were both up and moving, Pet found her voice. "Do you really think this dwarf is going to lead us right into his home?" Axel's idea wasn't strategically sound. They could be walking right into a trap. What if the guards simply turned them away at the gate? Or their fortress was an impossible maze guarded by a monster? There were too many variables to consider.

"You forget, my good Pet, that I am a master of disguise. It should be easy enough to weave a story about how darling Princess Ella has found herself in good favor with the gods and they sent servants down to attend her."

Pet tied back the front of her hair with a strip of leather. "I don't think your *that* good."

Axel scoffed, but Pet left him to speak with Doran. At least the old king would come up with a better plan than bloody acting. He and Erik were closest to the fire, Erik having taken last watch and Doran, as predictable as a bindweed flower, wakening at the first hint of sunshine like Pet. Both shared space on the wide log Big Hal had dragged over to use as seating the night before. The rest of the crew lay scattered about, and the dwarf remained tied to the base of the tree about twenty paces from them.

"Good morning, Petyr," Doran greeted.

Pet gave a small nod and turned to Erik. "How long will it take for ship repairs?" Any plans they came up with would revolve around how long it would take *The Phoenix* to be operational again. Especially if they needed to make a quick getaway with the princess after freeing her from the dwarves.

Erik tugged at the end of his beard. "We've got a full barrel of tar and the wood from the cliff to repair the hull. The sail needs a few stitches, but it won't take too long. The big problem will be crafting the mast and repairing the hull underneath."

"How long?" Pet asked.

"Five days." Erik sighed. "Maybe six."

Pet folded her arms over her chest. "We don't have six days." In fact, not even the ship would save them if they did escape the dwarf king's fortress. Those tunnels she and Axel had glimpsed last night likely spanned miles of the cliffs around them. This was the dwarves' home. Any strategic advantage would be theirs.

Erik frowned but didn't contradict her.

"Anything from the dwarf?" she asked.

Both men shook their heads. "He's been quite content," Erik said. "Even dozed for a bit on my watch."

The dwarf watched the crew stir, his gaze flicking over every man again and again. If Pet was in his position, she would be watching too. What kind of men did a supposed jötunn allow to attend them? How long would he believe the lie?

She turned back to Erik. "How many hands can we spare to chase after the princess?"

"None, but then where would that leave Ella?" Erik asked.

Pet picked at her bottom lip. "Hemming comes with Axel and me. The three of us might be able to handle bamboozling a kingdom of dwarves." Hemming would also be helpful finding the dwarves if their little friend proved himself to be a problem. The man could travel through uncharted lands as if he'd lived there his entire life.

It was too bad they'd lost Olav in the storm. The man would have been a great help in distracting the dwarves. Axel could weave a tale fine, but Olav would have pulled it off seamlessly. The old man was likely watching them from Valhalla, laughing around a mouthful of roasted walnuts.

"I'm flattered you think so highly of my capabilities," Doran said. "However, I think it will take more than three men to break the princess out."

A heavy arm fell over Pet's shoulders. "Well, it's a good thing we won't need to break her out," Axel responded. "In fact, we probably won't even need our blades."

Pet looked over the rest of the crew. It was always wise to take Doran to meet foreign dignitaries, but he would be more use here if he needed to rally the crew to come after them. Ulf could or Big Hal would be helpful in a fight, but they weren't exactly subtle. Ludvig could be of assistance if they needed to get out of a bind, but he'd be more help to Erik and the ship than he would be on an extraction mission.

It would just have to be her, Axel, and Hemming.

Doran cocked a dark eyebrow. "And how do you think you're going to manage to free her?"

Pet shoved Axel off her. "This brute has it in his head that we'll simply ask."

Doran looked up at Axel. "No swords swinging? No heroic endeavors? Just walk in and ask?"

"Shouldn't be that hard." Axel shrugged. "Besides, we don't know what kind of people this dwarf king rules over. I wouldn't want to barge into their city without getting a lay of the land first."

"Then interrogate the dwarf," Erik said.

Axel glanced over at their captive. "If we treat him like a threat, he'll know we're up to something."

"Then don't treat him like a threat," Pet said. "Treat him like a guide. If we can convince him we aren't a threat to his kingdom, then he'll want to act as emissary to a bloody god. Let him think he's doing something honorable while he's leading us right where we want to go. Basking in others' admiration is at least within your abilities, Axel. Once we get to wherever the dwarves have burrowed down, Hemming and I can find the princess while you go flatter a king."

A smile bloomed on Axel's lips. "I'm glad you at least realize I'm a good flatterer."

Pet rolled her eyes. "You certainly flatter yourself enough. Soon, your head will get so big you'll topple over."

ᛋᚺᚲᛟᚠᛁᛏ

THE DWARF—WHO had introduced himself to Axel as Adalfuns— practically skipped at Axel's side, an eager pup ready to impress his new master.

And Axel was eating it up.

"I hope Your Greatness will not be too offended by my forward- ness," Adalfuns said, "but I am most eager to be the one to guide you to my home."

"You do your king and your people justice." Axel's chest puffed up. "I'm looking forward to seeing it all with my own eyes."

By all the gods in Asgard, this journey was going to drive Pet to kill something. After using the route Pet had taken when climbing the cliff, they marched through the rocky terrain. Thin trees and shrubs took up any open ground not overrun by boulders. Snow still coated the shadowed parts of the earth, melting down into small creeks. Pet walked a few paces behind them, Hemming at her side. He had been as quiet as she had, but his eyes scanned their surroundings, and he jotted notes down as they went.

"Tell me," Axel said, "what kind of fortress does your master live in? Does it compare to the halls of Asgard?"

Adalfuns shook his head vehemently. "Of course not, Great One. Nothing on this planet could compare to the beauty of the gods' home. My liege does boast a large fortress for a sovereign, but he is as humble as they come."

Pet refrained from snorting. If there was one thing she'd never seen, it was a humble royal. Well, that wasn't necessarily true. Doran was technically royal, but Pet would never stick him in the same lot as King Firmin or King Anders. He also wasn't technically a ruler over anything. At least, not anymore.

"Does the fortress have many doors?" Hemming asked. Pet frowned at him, but he ignored her.

"There are three main entrances to the castle proper, though I know there are more ways in and out since the castle itself butts up against a straight cliff face. There is no telling how many tunnels the kings of the past have created for their own use."

Pet set her hands on the heads of her axes. The halls of the dwarf king near Harligdam had been deep within the mountain outside the capital. One couldn't even tell they'd passed into the castle except the halls were guarded, and the walls were better polished. She'd nearly lost herself in the maze of it when she and Axel had gone to petition for *The Phoenix*. One had to approach the dwarf king if they wanted to buy such a large craft from his clan.

"What about gates?" Axel asked next. "Do the gates around the castle glitter like the gates of Valhalla?"

"Oh no. What need have we for gates?"

Axel pulled back a thick branch blocking their path. "How do you protect what's important to you?"

"We have the dragon for that."

Hemming and Pet both stumbled to a halt.

"A dragon?" Hemming asked.

Rocks. They couldn't face down a bloody dragon. There were many creatures Pet and Axel had seen in their time since leaving Holmberg. There had been the gargantuan wolf outside of Oxe. Pet and Axel had hunted the beast for three months until they'd found its den. There had also been the giant's footprint they'd glimpsed off the western coast of Isberg. They'd even faced off with a group of marbendill with their human upper-halves and seal tails.

But never a dragon.

The ferocious beasts were things of legend. Like the frost giants, dragons weren't native to Åldras or the kingdoms around it. There were tales of distant kingdoms where dragons had once dwelled with men. There were even stories about the miraculous things they could do, having been bestowed with the powers of the gods. Dragons supposedly had magic over the elements, much like the Häxa did, but they were also able to do any number of things. There was a tale she'd heard as a child about a dragon that could create magic with its breath. Most of the stories felt distant from Åldras's shores.

But it seemed they weren't just stories.

Adalfuns nodded. "Biggest dragon on this side of Isberg. Our king is very mighty and has tamed the beast to listen only to his command."

Hemming shook himself from his stupor. "What happens when the king dies?"

"Well, his heir would take over. Of course, the king does not have an heir at the moment. The last one he fed to the dragon."

So not only would they be facing off with a king in control of a dragon, but a *mad* king in control of a dragon.

Pet grabbed Hemming's shoulder and slowed, allowing Axel and Adalfuns to get ahead of them. "Axel's plan isn't going to work. A mad king isn't going to care about appeasing a god, let alone a false one."

Hemming pursed his lips. "Or it will work too well. Such a king may revel in the fact that he's kidnapped the charge of such a god. It will be the ultimate prize."

Hel's bloody halls. If Axel got himself captured, there would be little they could do to get Princess Ella out. Pet gritted her teeth. Sometimes, it was more a burden to have Axel around than it was a boon. He practically spawned tricky situations. Pet couldn't even count how many brawls they'd been drawn into because someone thought fighting Axel might be fun. Fighting their way out of a dwarf stronghold would add to the tally.

How were they going to convince a dragon-keeping king to let go of a supposed god? It wasn't possible. Perhaps they could sneak into the fortress. With Axel's abilities, they might get out. But where would that leave the crew? The dwarves knew where the ship was beached. It could be worth it to simply get to this dwarf king and wait out the repairs. If they tried it right, they could grab the princess in a few days and make a run for it once they could be sure *The Phoenix* was repaired. So long as the king hadn't made Princess Ella marry him already and they didn't get fed to a bloody dragon.

Rocks.

"What are you thinking?" Hemming asked.

Pet let out a breath. "That we're probably all going to die."

They followed Adalfuns for half the day, the rocky plains climbing into steep mountains. They could see the peaks over the tops of the hills and trees. One of the mountains had a flat top, the peak dusted with snow. Adalfuns pointed at it.

"There is Gulli, the great mountain."

The dwarf city would be somewhere inside the mountain. The real challenge would be figuring out where they were holding the princess. If the dwarf king was mad, he might have her hanging from a cage right above his bloody dragon.

"Thank you, Adalfuns," Axel said. "You've been very helpful." In a flash, he lifted his fist and smacked it on the top of Adalfun's head. The dwarf dropped like a bag of stones.

Hemming crouched down and checked the dwarf's breathing. "Why did you do that?"

"I heard you two whispering like a pair of ravens back there. We definitely can't go in there with the lie that I'm some kind of god." He pulled his bright, golden hair into a knot on the top of his head. "The king will likely throw me in with the dragon just to check, and I really don't want to find out what it feels like to be a lizard snack."

Hemming grabbed the dwarf under the armpits. "We'll need to tie him up if we want a good head start."

Pet folded her arms over her chest. They could just kill him, keep him from running home and ruining whatever new plan they would come up with. It was the only way to ensure a particle of success. But that suggestion would be shot down in present company.

Instead, she found rope in her pack, and Axel set to work strapping Adalfuns to a thick tree. When he awoke, the dwarf wouldn't have too much trouble escaping his binds, especially if he was as strong as he looked. It wouldn't give them much of a head start, but they would use it to the best of their advantage.

Hemming shaded his eyes with his hand and looked in the direction they were headed. "We've probably got another three-hour journey until we hit the base of the mountain."

"Good," Pet said. "That will give us three hours to come up with a new plan."

Chapter 16

Intruders

I've had the opportunity to stroll through the dwarven cities under Áldras. There is a small town in the mountains near Grovö that my father took me to as a boy. The largest is north of Harligdam, home of the dwarf king, Alfríkr. The dwarves are industrious, but they are suspicious by nature. There is a reason they have lived so long on Midgard while the other races have slowly faded from the face of it.

— FROM THE WRITINGS OF DORAN FINNSSON, THE LAST KING OF GROVÖ

A xel peered over the top of a boulder.

On the other side, at the base of the mountain, stood two burly dwarves with halberd heads on poles twice as tall as they were. The entrance to the cave was extravagant for, well, a *cave*. An archway of runes curved over the guards, nearly as tall as Firmin's ridiculous wooden wall. Torchlight flickered from behind them, making their chain armor glow in the darkening light. This far north, the days were still short in the spring, providing the perfect cover.

A hand grabbed the back of Axel's tunic, pulling him down.

"Quit gawking!" Pet snapped. "We don't need them seeing you until Hemming is in place."

Axel glanced up the mountain. He could just see Hemming's

outline dart from rock to rock, making his way slowly to the top of the arch of runes. It had been his idea to spook the guards. Luckily, there were only two. Any more and it would have made the plan more complicated. Axel didn't want to hurt anyone he didn't have to.

Hemming made it to the top of the arch, a large bundle in his hands. He carefully opened the sack he held and dumped the contents out over the guards' heads.

A feathered lump smacked into their helmets.

Axel had spotted the cormorant flying back toward the cliffs earlier that day and Hemming had brought it down with a slingshot. While he wasn't superstitious about the wilds of the dark elves or the portents of death, he knew dwarves were. They were notorious for their suspicious nature, but Axel couldn't fault them for it. There had to be a reason their kind had outlived so many others.

One of the guards lifted a black wing. Blood coated his fingers, and he jumped back, wiping his hands on his pant leg. His companion, however, looked up. Grabbing a torch, he pulled his comrade forward and lifted the light to try to see the top of the archway. They missed Hemming, already skittering down the side, out of reach of the light. Axel could make out his form in the shadows.

But the dwarf was undeterred. He ordered his companion to grab another torch and stepped fully over the bird.

Rocks. Of course they got the least superstitious dwarf in the mountain.

"Act two," Pet whispered.

Axel undid his sword belt. His entire soul balked at the nakedness he felt without it secure around his waist, but he ignored the crawling sensation over his skin and tucked the blade under a bush next to the pile of fur he'd stuffed there earlier. The disguise wouldn't be convincing if he had a giant sword strapped to his side. Pet's axes joined it.

She met his eye, her lips a crooked smirk as she took him in. He likely looked quite the mess, just as Pet did. Dirt smeared across her face along with some of the blood they'd gotten from the bird. She'd gnarled sticks into her hair and covered her shirt in lichen to make it look more ragged than it was. Her steps bounced as she hurried away to find a better position. Axel readjusted the crown of tree roots on his head. He'd deemed himself King of the Draugr.

Did the undead creatures have any sort of hierarchy? Axel shook his head. Probably not. They were too savage for that.

Right on time, a deep moan started up to the west of them. Hemming's low tones carried over the rocks as he got closer. Pet added to the noise, her voice coming in from the east, farther than what she should have been able to get to in such a short amount of time. Axel rustled the bush hiding his blade and took up his own moan.

The guards at the cave shifted, the links of their armor clinking as they shook. Axel couldn't see them, but he could hear their gasps.

"Quick," one of them said, "we need to—"

The voice cut off.

Pet had struck.

Axel leaped from his hiding place, allowing his limbs to sway and his feet to stumble. Draugr were quick but clumsy creatures, their entire focus on sinking their teeth into living flesh. There probably wasn't much reason to be careful about fumbling about and bashing your head in when you were already dead. Pet had ahold of one of the dwarves, dragging him by the foot as his companion swung his halberd at her head. She ducked it, of course, but she had to let go of the dwarf to dodge a well-aimed kick to her knee.

Axel stepped in, grabbing the guard's halberd from behind.

He nearly laughed when the dwarf came with it.

The guard dangled from the end of the halberd and shifted his gaze toward Axel and his crown. Refraining from smiling, Axel gnashed his teeth in the dwarf's face, making it seem like he was ready to bite their nose off. The dwarf dropped to the ground, scuttling out of reach.

Hemming joined them, his moans loud over the fight.

With the added foe, both dwarven guards got to their feet and bolted for the cave entrance.

Axel smiled as he watched their retreating forms turn down a tunnel. "Well, that went better than expected." He pulled the crown from his head and dropped it in the dirt.

It was time for act three.

ᚠᚢᚲᛟᚠᚤᛚ

ALLISON ANDERSON

THE DWARVES TOOK LONGER to regroup than Axel thought they would, giving him, Hemming, and Pet plenty of time to set the scene. While Axel had found the cormorant, Hemming had been the one to spot the polecat. The creature had given them just enough gore to make it look like a fight had taken place. After a clean-up of his skin and the return of the sword to his hip, Axel hoped he looked the part of a seasoned monster hunter. If only he hadn't left his cowl back at the ship. Pet might have hated it, but the thing was certainly eye catching.

A company of dwarf guards clogged the mouth of the cave. Axel popped the last walnut he'd had in his little snack pouch into his mouth as he faced down who he assumed to be their captain, based on the extravagant helmet he wore.

Axel raised a hand. "Greetings, friends."

The helmeted dwarf tilted his head. "Odd, I did not know one could be friends without an introduction."

Axel gave his most dazzling smile. "I think the common goal of safety for the living makes us friends, don't you?"

The dwarf looked about, eying the blood on the ground. "I came to face demons and am met instead by humans. Pray, what kind of men hunt monsters outside the boundaries of man's kingdom?"

Axel bowed. "I'm only a servant, good sir. I came with a party of men escorting a young maiden. We've come looking for her only to find these creatures at your door."

They had decided playing the role of humble servants would attract less ire. If anything, it was only flattering to the princess that she would have such faithful servants and hopefully the king would like her all the more, knowing she encouraged such loyalty from her followers. It also helped that Axel couldn't die, so murdering them to keep Princess Ella from knowing they came to rescue her wasn't an option.

The lead dwarf studied Axel. "We were told the princess had more than three men to serve her."

Axel bowed again. "There is a crew tasked with the princess's escort, but we three are her most humble servants. We've been charged with delivering her to the Häxa, as she is to study under the Great Mother and live out her days in piety."

He could feel Pet's glare at the back of his head. *That was not part*

136

of the plan, that look likely said. But if the king knew Princess Ella was indeed a person of some standing and she was expected elsewhere—by the Great Mother herself no less—perhaps the king would be more lenient about letting them go.

The dwarf frowned. "The Great Mother, you say? Why I believe King Thrum is most interested in hearing more of this news." He waved a hand forward and his retinue surrounded Axel, Pet, and Hemming. "Come. We will take you to the throne room."

That couldn't have been any easier. Axel trailed after the dwarf leader through the archway. They would speak with the king directly, convince him of their quest, and would all be on their way come morning. Axel turned back to Pet, a large grin on his face.

Her wary expression darkened as she met his gaze.

He withheld the urge to stick out his tongue at her. Just because he'd been right not to barge into the dwarf fortress, blades swinging, didn't mean she needed to be such a mood killer.

They followed the dwarves, leaving the open air and torchlight behind them. While the flames would keep most creatures away from the entrance, the dwarves didn't actually need the firelight. When they turned a corner, they walked into complete darkness. Axel could barely make out the rough forms of the dwarves ahead of him. The smoothed rock of the tunnel made the walk easier, but he heard Pet's careful shuffle change to keep her from running into anything.

Without a word, he reached back and grabbed her hand.

Like they always did when they touched, shivers raced up his arm. It had since he was twelve years old, and the sensation had only grown more intense as the years passed. He didn't know if it was the same for Pet, but he would never dare to ask. Not if he wanted to keep her safe. Her fingers squeezed his in silent thanks, and he felt her reach back to take hold of Hemming's hand. Their small chain would keep them together and assist them in making their way through the darkness.

A low hum took root in Axel's boots, growing and ebbing as they followed the maze of twists and turns. The dwarves led them through the tunnels in zigzags, attempting to confuse them. Axel passed a small pillar for the third time.

"How much farther?" he asked.

"We will be there soon," the lead dwarf announced.

Axel refrained from sighing. If they kept up this game, they could be stuck in the tunnels all night. It would have been nice to sit down for a moment.

After another half an hour of walking in endless circles, the hum in Axel's boots steadily grew louder. It was a constant rumble, vibrating through the soles of his feet and up into his chest. Pet's hand tightened around his, signaling she heard it now too.

The tunnel around them lightened, the silhouettes of the dwarves taking on more distinct shapes. Axel blinked the darkness away and, when they reached the end of the tunnel, what air he had in his lungs left him.

This was nothing like the dwarf kingdom in Åldras.

Glowing moss coated every inch of the rocky walls, soaring up until they reached the stars above them. A waterfall, the rumble that had sunk into Axel's bones, fell from a hundred ells up the side of the rock face, crashing down into the black rocks at the base of the hole. The water must have been from the snow melt, as it made no sense there should be water falling into the middle of a volcano.

A volcano. Somehow, they were standing inside a volcano.

It looked like it had been dormant for long before even the Åldrans had sailed the seas, but it still made Axel's palm grow sweaty in Pet's hand. How would she react to being in a mountain made of dead fire? He glanced back at her, but her attention was trained on the dwarves around them.

"Come," called the leader, pointing across the volcano's vent. "We should get to the castle."

A black castle towered over a village, torchlight and luminous moss brightening windows and lining streets. While the castle was made from dark stone, it had an air of artistry. Cylindrical towers with turrets framed the face of the castle, which had rounded windows that invited instead of warded. The village below was even more welcoming. Colorful banners hung over cobbled streets, clean of any refuse. Dwarves sauntered along the streets, passing carts pulled by what looked like giant voles. Axel could just make out a tune, music playing somewhere within the crush of buildings.

Now that they were out of the complete darkness, Pet released

Axel's hand. He flexed his fingers, resisting the urge to reach for her again.

The dwarves led them down the side of the vent, stairs and ramps carved into the black rock down to the smooth crust of the volcano floor. If there hadn't been an entire village nestled on top, he would have been tempted to trod very lightly. It wasn't that he was actually afraid that the crust would break and he would plummet down into the magma that might boil below. It couldn't actually harm him, after all. At least, he didn't think it could, but he'd never swan-dived into lava before to test the theory and he didn't plan on doing it now.

"Welcome to Gulli," the dwarf leader said.

Axel stepped forward. "We wish to see our lady."

The dwarf waved a nonchalant hand. "All in good time. We will go to the throne room first."

They circumvented the center of the village, instead taking a route around the outskirts and toward the castle's northern entrance. Máni's moon hovered high over the mouth of the volcano when they finally arrived at the entrance. The guards there barely glanced their way when the company of dwarves led them through the entrance.

The hall they entered wasn't like anything Axel had ever seen.

The walls weren't made of slabs or bricks, but of seamless stone, not a crack or crevice in sight. Images of fighting dragons, elves, and giants were carved on the walls, drops of ruby dripped along the stone, ivory teeth bared in fearsome visages. War and death sprang from the walls, more gruesome than any ballad Axel had ever heard. This was not a kingdom built on peace but on war. And from the way the walls told it, the dwarves were the victors.

The head dwarf led them to a set of large wooden doors; the only ornamentation carved in anything but stone. The dwarf thrust the doors open, not even announcing himself as he strode into the room.

Pet grabbed the back of Axel's shirt, slowing him. When he met her gaze, she furrowed her brows. *Something's wrong.*

Axel felt it too. The small twist in his gut. The rise of hairs on the back of his neck.

The lead dwarf strode to the end of the room where a tall throne towered on top of a dais. The throne was not black like the rest of the castle but white. Bone white.

The lead dwarf took the half dozen steps up the dais.

A side door opened, and two guards escorted a dusty, furious Adalfuns into the room.

The twist in Axel's stomach became a full knot.

The lead dwarf sat in the bone throne, a smirk nestled within the tangles of his beard.

CHAPTER 17

A TRAP

Oh, bloody rocks.

Pet's eyes flicked about the room, taking in the exits, and returning to the lead dwarf who was apparently King Thrum. It had been obvious something was off the moment they'd entered the castle. If only she'd said something earlier.

Dwarves began trickling in, first a couple, then a multitude. It wasn't long until Pet was nearly suffocating in the giant hall. Dwarves surrounded them on every side, waiting to hear what the king would say. Guards blocked each door. There might be an exit behind the throne, but Pet hadn't spotted it yet.

Adalfuns pointed a thick finger at Axel. "The jötunn, My King."

King Thrum stroked his fingers over the length of his black beard. "Yes, I could spot the god, Adalfuns. Though I am a bit...*unconvinced*." He rubbed his palms over the arm of his throne, the end capped with a human skull. "Tell me, *jötunn*, why have you come?"

Axel took a step forward and gave a small bow. "As I said before, we've come for the princess, Your Majesty. I have been tasked with her safety and am honor bound to deliver her to the Great Mother."

Whispers bounced about the room.

Pet stayed right at back. Just because he couldn't die didn't mean he couldn't get captured. Didn't mean they couldn't take him from her. She gripped the top of her axes with white knuckles.

"The Great Mother's power does not reach this far north, jötunn," the king said. "Why should I concern myself with her and her little coven?"

Axel stiffened next to Pet, and she had to refrain from poking him in the side. He got his pants in a twist over the smallest slights directed toward the Great Mother. However, a fight right here in the throne room would not end well for any of them.

Hemming stepped forward, his gait slow but confident. "Your Majesty, are you aware of who stands before you?"

The king lifted a thick brow. "I was under the assumption he was a godling."

Hemming smiled a very kingly, political smile. Probably something he'd learned from Doran. "This is the Mighty Axel Ashersson, son of King Asher Redbeard, and the pride of Åldras."

Rocks. Pet glared at the back of Hemming's head. He was going off script, which meant he saw something in this king that made him change tactics. Hemming wasn't a complete idiot which was why she'd brought him, but if he got them killed, she would skin him alive in the afterlife.

The king's other eyebrow rose to meet its pair. "I've heard tales of an Åldran called Axel—a man that cannot be slain by blade or poison, though many have tried."

Hemming gestured toward Axel. "Before you stands that very man. A man who cannot be slain or harmed in any way a mortal can."

"I see." The king's eyes darkened. "And what brings such a being to my realm?"

"It's as I told you, Your Majesty." Axel turned to address the rest of the room as well. "We're to take the girl to the Great Mother to continue her training in the arts of the Häxa." He took up the tale of their journey, embellishing where needed. While Olav would have had the entire crowd eating dirt out of his hand, Axel wasn't a terrible storyteller.

Pet's stomach twisted. Instinct buzzed about in her limbs, telling her to fight. Telling her to flee. The way the king's eyes continued to flick between Axel and Hemming had Pet reaching for her axes. Something was very wrong.

Guards at the door held their spears high, their eyes trained on

Axel. The stream of attendees had lessened, only a trickle now, but gave enough movement in the room to draw eyes. Would everyone in the castle have come to view the spectacle? Was anyone guarding Ella?

She took a single step back.

Axel met her eye and gave a subtle nod of his head. Perhaps he was, in fact, worried about this king. Pet slipped into the crowd. They'd played this game a number of times. He stepped toward the engaged crowd, taking up the part of the story where Enzo the Scourge showed up. The dwarves stared up at him with starry eyes. Freyja's golden tears, it was like they'd never seen a man before. Though, being sequestered in this volcano, perhaps they hadn't.

Taking another step back, Pet watched the dwarves around her. As everyone did when Axel turned on the charm, their eyes glazed over. There had to be some kind of magic in his smile. It could make even the most straitlaced of people weak at the knees.

Pet took another step, and a pair of dwarves took the space she'd just vacated. She crouched down, diminishing her height and doing her best to blend in with the people nearly two heads shorter than her. There were so many in the crowd, elbowing her way back wasn't an issue and neither was slipping things off shoulders. She stepped on a harried mother's toe, snatching the loose apron hanging from her plump waist. Then came the blanket off the elderly dwarf's lap when she knocked into his companion, causing him to hang off the back of the elder's wheeled chair. A basket of limp carrots. A couple of bracelets. A handful of coins. She received a few grunts and elbows of her own, but with Axel in the room, it was oh so easy to be overlooked. Tucking herself against the wall, she shrugged into the stolen clothing, blending in easily with the crowd around her.

A guard stood not ten paces from her, the curve of his helmet blinding his peripheral and hiding her from view. It had to be one of the worst helmets for a guard ever made. The guard on the other side of the doorway stood enraptured by Axel's retelling, which had reached the lightning strike in Donar's Storm. Pet didn't remember seeing Donar's face in the clouds—or even catching a glimpse of a face at all— but Axel knew how to tell a story much better than she did.

Pet took a step into the guards' line of sight, doing her best to look natural. That was what distrustful people never suspected. If she'd tiptoed or tried climbing the wall, it would draw eyes. Walking along the wall as if she'd been there the whole time? Anyone could get away with murder if they acted as if they had permission.

Neither helmeted head turned to follow as she walked past them and out of the throne room.

ᚠᚾᚲᚩᚠᚤᛚ

ELLA WAS NOT in the towers.

Of course not. It wasn't as if the dastardly dwarf king with the dragon pet could have kept to the cliches. No, he had to make Pet's job difficult.

Pet slinked down a darkened staircase, ears peeled for the sound of pursuit. She'd been working her way up the southern tower when she'd heard mention of Ella from the chatter of a pair of what looked like servants. Now, she was going as far beneath the castle as she could.

The dungeon. What man put the girl he wanted to marry in a dungeon?

The faint flicker of torchlight on the steps below slowed her pace. She heard the hushed tones of a light voice, the sound reverberating against the black stone under her hand even though whoever spoke was obviously attempting to be quiet. A soft voice followed. Pet recognized it instantly. She let go of the wall, drawing the ax from under the apron wrapped around her waist.

Stepping lightly, she reached the bottom of the staircase and found a row of barred doors. At the end, a dwarf with dark skin and hair blacker than King Thurm's peered into the opening of the door to the left. The same helmet the guards in the throne room had rested on their head. Pet tried to look past them but couldn't see another glint of steel or flicker of torchlight. It looked like it was only Ella and the guard.

And now Pet.

She hung the ax back at her side and grabbed one of the daggers at her waist. She flipped it in her palm, eyeing the dwarf's neck. The base of the skull was always the best in these situations. Creeping up behind him, she skimmed the torchlight as much as possible and got into position.

The dwarf swung around before she could land the blow.

He sprang at her, his solid arms coming around Pet's torso and knocking her into the sturdy door behind her. Pet's head smacked into the barred window, but she kept her wits and swung the dagger down toward the dwarf's spine. His arms released Pet, and he rolled away, the dagger slashing through open air. Popping up a moment later, he lunged for her again, this time going for her ankles instead.

Pet fell in a heap on top of him but twisted out of his hold and grabbed her ax. She rolled back into a crouch just as the dwarf got to his feet.

"Petyr!" Ella's voice rang out. "Roald, wait! He's my friend!"

Roald paused, his eyes flicking from Ella to the ax in Pet's hand. "I did not realize a princess would have friends that would strike when their opponent's back is turned." He dropped his hands. "Who are you?"

Pet slid the ax back in place but didn't take her hand off it. "I'm one of the men leading Princess Ella to the Great Mother."

Roald folded his arms. "You are her guard?"

Pet nodded.

"You have come to free her from King Thrum."

"Indeed." Pet took a step toward Ella, but Roald blocked her path.

"He will not let you take her."

Pet cocked her head to the side, sliding the ax from its loop. "The only thing I see between me and her is *you*."

"Listen, boy—"

Pet set the blade of her ax under his chin. "Let me make one thing perfectly clear. I'll be leaving this castle with the princess. You get to decide if that happens with you still breathing." Who was this dwarf? Seriously, the situation was almost laughable. Ella had made an ally within the confines of the dungeon in the single day it had taken them to get to her.

Roald raised his hands and stepped away. Pet pushed a smirk onto her face. It was how male posturing went. One guy puffed up his chest. The other pulled an ax. Big chest deflated and ax wielder smirked.

Pet faced Ella through the bars.

The princess's eyes puffed red with tears. "You came," she whispered.

Pet looked down at the lock on the door. A solid piece of iron. Reaching into one of the pockets of her vest, she withdrew her lock picks.

"Listen to me," Roald said over her shoulder. "You may get her out of that cell but getting her out of the castle is an entirely different story."

Pet selected three of the picks. "I got in here, didn't I?"

"Yes, but I also imagine you were invited in. Leaving, on the other hand, will be much more difficult."

Something in his tone made Pet pause. She turned away from her task to study him. "Why are you so sure?"

Roald's eyes flicked to the dungeon's entrance then back to her. "Because once he heard about him, it was imperative to the king to let the jötunn in. He never had plans of letting him out."

Pursing her lips, Pet turned back to the lock, the three prongs pressing up on the springs while she shimmied the middle piece up. "What's your role in all of this, dwarf?"

Roald bristled, but Ella spoke up. "He's leading a coup."

Pet's fingers slipped and she cursed. Had they really walked right into a rebellion plot? She groaned. *Rocks, once Axel hears about this he will never want to leave.* One look at the crazy dwarf king and she should have known a coup was already in the works.

"Princess Ella has told me of your journey," Roald said. "Even if you get out of the castle, you do not have a ship."

With a grumble, Pet wriggled her picks from the lock, leaving it in place. "It seems you have all of this thought out. But it doesn't explain why you were in here trying to break her out first."

Roald shook his head. "I was not trying to break her out. I was letting her in on the plan."

Ella's hopeful smile shone between the bars of her cell. Freyja's golden tears, the girl was so easily won over. It was almost painful to watch.

Pet sighed. "All right, what is this plan?"

"I will reveal all in due time, but first we must get you back to the throne room. If your absence has not been noted yet, it will be very soon."

Pet tucked away her tools and pointed a finger at Ella. "Don't do anything stupid while I'm gone. Like befriend dwarf guards." She'd already gotten chummy with one. They didn't need her blabbing the plan to anyone else.

Ella blushed but nodded. Hopefully, that would be enough.

Pet turned and followed Roald out of the dungeon.

"We must be quick," he said, leading her down one of the many tunnels in the cavernous castle. "Pray to whatever gods you worship they have not—"

The sound of shouts cut him off.

CHAPTER 18

PRISONERS

Axel trailed behind the king, doing his best to look casual as the bands around his ribs grew tighter with every second. It was normal for Pet to slip away to complete a mission. He just didn't love the idea of her running around when there might be a fire-breathing dragon roaming the halls. They needed to find Princess Ella and get out of here.

Axel walked beside King Thrum, speaking with him as he would any foreign ruler. "Your Majesty, I'm sure our comrade simply got lost in the hubbub. He's sure to be around here somewhere, probably walking circles around your impressive abode."

King Thrum's frown deepened another fraction as he turned to meet Axel's eye. "Do all your men get so easily turned around, Mighty Axel? I would assume one as prestigious as you would surround himself with only the wisest of companions."

Axel bobbed his head. "Yes, but Pet is special in his own way."

King Thrum arched a brow. "What self-respecting man allows himself to be called another man's 'pet?'"

Axel tried to suppress a grin but felt it tugging at the corners of his mouth. "Pet is certainly the least self-respecting man I know."

King Thrum gave him a befuddled look and marched on, the dwarves around him shooting down tunnels and returning with no sign of Pet or the princess. Axel's stomach twisted tighter as they began

149

their descent on another set of stairs. Where on Midgard could she possibly be? He'd assumed she would have made her way to the tower, but the king wasn't leading them in that direction. He was leading them deeper into the castle. Would there be a lava pool at the bottom?

Another dwarf approached and gave the king another empty report. King Thrum shoved the dwarf away, his face turning an alarming shade of red. "How did one measly human get past all of you?" He began shouting orders, his voice filling the entirety of the cavern.

Something tingled at Axel's back.

He turned and found Pet walking down the corridor, a dwarf in a guard's uniform following behind her.

Her eyes met his and she gave a subtle nod. *Found her.*

Praise the Allfather.

"Your Majesty," the dwarf accompanying her called, "I have found the missing human."

King Thrum spun, his eyes narrowed as he took in the new arrivals. "Captain Roald, I did not realize you were on duty this evening."

Pet stopped a few paces away. She wasn't cursing which might have been a good sign. Axel's eyes roved over her, but she held herself straight and there wasn't any visible blood. Though, the small velvet pouch hanging from her belt was new.

Captain Roald stepped around her. "When I heard about the arrival of our guests, I thought it wise to make sure the men were all at their stations." He gestured to Pet. "I found this one wandering around near the kitchens."

King Thrum tugged on the end of his beard. "Well, good that you found him. I was concerned he would get lost in the tunnels."

Axel held back a snort. He hadn't known this king very long and he could already tell the dwarf lacked a soul. It was more likely King Thrum was hiding more than just Princess Ella in this castle.

Captain Roald bowed. "That is most gracious of you, Your Majesty. I am sure our guests appreciate your hospitality." He fell in beside Pet and led her forward.

King Thrum's eyes flicked to her as if he had forgotten she existed for a moment. "Let us get you men into some rooms, shall we? The hour is most late, and I am sure you would like a place to lie your heads."

"I can escort them, Sire," Captain Roald offered.

King Thrum waved him off. "No need. The rooms are not so far, and I am happy to play host to our guests."

Axel watched the captain, but the dwarf's expression remained placid. It was the king's stiff shoulders that made Axel frown. Some kind of tension brewed between the king and his captain. Axel looked to Pet for some kind of hint as to what could be between them, but she watched them as closely as he did. Hopefully, they hadn't just walked into the middle of a coup.

Hemming came to Axel's side. "What of the princess, Your Majesty?"

"I am sure she is resting," King Thrum answered. "Preparing for our nuptials."

The loosening twist in Axel's stomach went cold. He shoved his way past the dwarves surrounding the king. One of them jabbed him with the tip of their halberd, but Axel batted it away. "Nuptials? What of our quest to deliver her to her people?"

King Thrum shrugged. "I suppose your quest will simply have to end here. I am sure there are many other witches in need of your assistance."

Axel clenched his hands at his sides and gritted his teeth. Who did this king think he was? Freyja's golden tears, the arrogance of kings was beginning to chafe under Axel's skin. Just because one wore a crown and had been given authority over a people did not entitle them to treat others like objects. Axel opened his mouth to argue, but a hand on his shoulder pulled him back.

"Leave it," Pet whispered.

Axel turned, blood beginning to boil. He met her eyes, more green than blue in the darker light of the castle. She winked at him and the boiling in his blood turned into something else. Something he wouldn't put words to.

He pushed the feeling down under all the other ones. Focus. He needed to focus.

Meeting her eye, he tilted his head. *What do we do?*

Pet's gaze flicked toward the captain, and she smirked. *I have a plan.*

Their party stopped at the mouth of a hallway. The squash-shaped lanterns hanging on the walls barely illuminated the plain rock of the hall. Four nondescript doors stood no taller than Axel's chest, each facing another across the hallway. Hopefully, the ceilings were higher in the rooms, or he would have to crouch.

"Your rooms," the king said, gesturing to the doors. "We will be holding the ceremony at high noon, with the sun shining down through the mouth of the volcano. It is going to be a glorious day."

The guards pushed the three of them toward separate doors, but Axel grabbed Pet's arm. "Your hospitality is most appreciated, Your Majesty. Pet and I will take this room." Axel pulled Pet toward the farthest door on the right. He opened it and shoved her in ahead of him. "Good night!"

"Both of you?" King Thrum asked. "But there's only one—"

Axel shut the door, cutting off the king's words.

Pet yanked her arm from his grasp and spun on him. "What on Midgard are you doing?"

Axel pressed his ear against the door, the rustle of the guards and Hemming's beleaguered sigh coming through from the other side. They'd have to sneak into Hemming's room later if they came up with a plan. "All right, they've got Hemming just across from us. It sounds like there will be two guards at the end of the hall. I don't know that two guards are going to be much of a detriment, but whatever makes them feel—"

A pillow slammed into the back of his head, smashing his nose into the door.

"Ow." The word slipped from him more in surprise than in actual pain. Axel turned, raising a hand to block another swing. He grabbed the pillow and ripped it from Pet's hands. "What was that for?"

"For being a rockhead!" She pointed to the far corner of the room. "There's only one bed!"

Axel looked over his shoulder and took in the room. A small oil lamp flickered on a table by the door, illuminating the space. It was larger than he'd thought it would be, boasting a high ceiling and room enough for a desk, three large chairs, and a couple of chests. There was even a tapestry hanging from one wall and a bear rug on the floor. His gaze landed on the single bed, and a wicked grin spread across his face. "Oh, dear. Whatever are we going to do?"

Pet tried to shove him, but he kept his footing. "You're sleeping on the floor," she said, yanking the pillow from his hand.

He snatched the pillow back. "No, I certainly am not. I had to climb a bloody cliff last night, hike through this wasteland, and entertain a mad king. I'm tired and grumpy, and I will be sleeping on that bed."

"I also did all of those things, you ungrateful maggot."

"You're right. So, both of us should try to get what little rest we're going to find in this creepy hole in the ground before we have to pummel some dwarves or, Wōden forbid, fight a bloody dragon."

"Fine!" Pet scowled and stomped over to the left side of the bed and pulled the blanket back. "But if you kick me, I swear I'll knock you off faster than you can say 'bloody rocks in my socks.'"

She removed her vest, taking the time to check each blade tucked into it and even jabbing some under the stuffed mattress. Her boots and socks went next, thumping onto the floor. Then her arm bracers. Without removing her tunic, she loosened the bindings around her torso and breathed a sigh of relief. That sigh did strange things to Axel's chest. He hated that she had to hide who she was. Hated that he was the one keeping her hidden.

Shaking himself, Axel strode toward her, shucking his boots from his feet as fast as he could and throwing his sword on top of her pile of weapons. His vest went next. It made a small *clink* as something rattled in his pocket. He checked the pocket and found the ring from Olav's harness. The sight of it formed a lump in his throat. He needed to speak with Little Hal when they got back to the ship. Needed to do something.

"Axel?"

He stuffed the ring back in the vest pocket and ripped off his tunic. Pet reached for the blankets, and he jumped on the top of them, bunching them up. "If you can keep your nose whistle under control," he said, "I'll keep my feet to myself."

Pet tried to pull the blanket out from under him. "I don't have a nose whistle."

Axel didn't move. "Yes, you do. Ever since you broke your nose fighting in Hjärta last year." It had been during one of the ever-increasing Sidan raids that had grown in the southern part of Åldras over the years. *The Phoenix* had been posted in Hjärta for three of the winter months, just waiting for the Sidans to make a move. They'd attacked after the first heavy snow of the season, trying to take the harbor in order to get a foothold closer to Harligdam. During the fight, Pet had spotted a bowman on the roof of a watchmen's tower and had gone after him. She'd killed him, but he'd broken her nose for the third time.

Pet gave up and laid on the pillow, the thick blanket barely covering her left side. "We should take watch shifts—which would be much easier if we aren't both in the bed. There's a lot to do tomorrow, and I'd like to get some rest while we can."

Which was Pet code for *I'll explain my super amazing plan that I know you're dying to hear once I feel like it.* Well, fine. Axel wiggled his way around the bed until he was under the blanket, feet dangling off the edge. Dwarfish beds weren't meant for pretend jötunn. Pet had curled onto her side away from him. She looked almost cozy lying there, the blanket bunched next to her ear.

He couldn't help himself. He shoved his feet between hers.

"Ack! Get your icicle toes off me!" She kicked his feet away and curled up tighter on her side. "That's it. You get to take first watch."

He withheld a snicker and burrowed into the blankets. Pet's warmth had already started seeping into the bed, and he scooted as close as he could without touching her. He definitely couldn't cuddle her. No matter how unkillable he might have been, she'd find a way to slaughter him if he tried. But that was for the best anyway. He wouldn't put that kind of pressure on her. Wouldn't give her one more thing she'd have to hide.

Eventually, Pet's breaths evened out, her body finding sleep easily after the taxing day. He had complained about needing good rest, but she needed it more than him. After all, she had to work three times as hard as he did simply to keep up with him. Even after all these years, he still couldn't believe she stayed with him. He couldn't offer her anything besides a life of heroics. A life of war. Of death. There was no place in his world for stability or even a home. Not until the Sidans were stopped. Until this war was over.

One of his fingers brushed the very tips of her shoulder-length hair, some of the strands glittering golden brown in the low light. He couldn't give her the life he wished she could have, but he couldn't give her up either. He hadn't been strong enough to do it when they'd left Holmberg, and he wasn't strong enough now.

They lay there for what felt like an entire night, but Axel knew it was only maybe one or two hours. Being underground always disoriented him. He liked living under the stars where he could count the hours as they passed. The silence of Gulli felt like a tomb. A tomb with skittering rats in the walls. He turned his head, listening closer. No, they were bigger than rats. Perhaps the voles? His gaze found the large tapestry hanging on the wall to the left of the bed, on Pet's side.

No, not voles.

He had one foot out of bed when the scuff of boots came from near the door. Axel grabbed his sword from where it lay on the ground next to the bed, unsheathing it silently and grabbing one of Pet's small knives from her vest. The knob on their door turned, and Axel positioned himself to the side where the door would open into the room and conceal him from the still-flickering lamp on the table.

The door opened enough to let a squat form in. *Definitely not Hemming.* The dwarf slipped into the room and shut the door behind him.

Axel's sword was at his throat the moment the door clicked shut. The dwarf stilled at the touch.

"On your knees," Axel demanded.

The dwarf slowly got to his knees and Pet sat up. Without a word, she shrugged on her vest and grabbed one of her axes.

"Sir Petyr," the dwarf said.

Pet stilled. "Roald?"

Axel looked down at the dwarf, recalling his dark hair and serious face. What was the captain of the guard doing in their room? And why was Pet on a first-name basis with him?

"I came as quickly as I could manage. If we are to save Princess Ella, we must hurry. I fear the king may be growing suspicious."

So, one of the king's men was on their side. He met Pet's eye, and she nodded. They must have met when Pet found Princess Ella. This must have been how Pet had come up with a plan.

Pet grabbed Axel's forearm to draw the sword away from the dwarf's neck. "What's happened?"

Captain Roald nodded his thanks, prodding the side of his neck as if Axel had nicked him—which he most certainly hadn't. "When I left you, His Majesty demanded the castle be searched for any other intruders. He demanded all our men be at their posts until the wedding and if anyone was out of place, he would know."

"Did he say why?" Pet asked.

Axel raised a hand. "Wait, how would he know?"

Captain Roald shook his head. "The king has spies, though I am not privy to their methods."

Axel narrowed his eyes on the captain, tilting his head to count the heartbeats in the room. *One. Two. Three. Four.* "Did you come alone, Captain? You told no one else you were coming here?" His fingers curled around the knife in his hand.

Captain Roald nodded. "I could not risk my men with—"

Axel raised the knife he'd taken from Pet's vest and threw it at the tapestry. The blade sank through the fabric and into the wall until only the hilt stuck out.

"My lord!" Captain Roald rounded on him. "That tapestry is likely older than your great grandfather."

Pet moved across the room and yanked the knife out of the tapestry. The last third of the blade came away bloody. Axel heard the body slump on the other side of the wall. She wiped the blade clean on the tapestry and thrust the fabric aside, finding the spy hole on the other side.

Captain Roald muttered a curse and turned back to Axel. "The king. He already knows."

Axel strode over and grabbed his belt and tunic. "I was afraid you would say that."

CHAPTER 19

A DRAGON

Pet stayed behind to retie her bindings while Axel and Roald hopped across the hall to wake Hemming. It was a good thing she'd left the fabric on under her tunic. She'd gotten away with wearing the vest in an emergency, but it always felt safer with the bindings. Praise Freyja for her small chest.

The men—and the dwarf—met her in the hall, swords at the ready.

"If the princess is in the dungeons," Hemming said, "then we need to work our way carefully through the castle."

"You don't think King Thrum will simply lock us up with her if he catches us, do you?" Axel asked as they turned a corner, not a guard in sight.

Roald scoffed. "You would be a dragon's snack before he would put you in the same space as her. Besides, I have the key to the guards' entrance into the dungeon. If we are lucky, we can use that doorway to get her out, and I can hopefully get my men to help fight the king's."

"So, the dragon is definitely real?" Axel asked.

Roald's lips thinned into a straight line. "You think I would make something like that up?"

They ran down the corridor, flying past door after door. Roald took them through several servant tunnels, guiding them through the maze and avoiding the guards he knew were stationed around the area. Pet took the rear, watching over her shoulder for any signs of attack, but none came. They couldn't avoid the rest of the guards forever, could they? It would make sense the king would have this place swarming with dwarves. Axel led from the front, taking direction from Roald but acting as shield for the rest of them. He could hear when others approached them, and Roald knew all the best places to tuck into until the danger passed. Pet didn't even have to kill anyone. Axel was likely happy about that.

"What about the guards *in* the dungeon?" Pet asked. "How will we get past them?"

Roald pointed down another hallway, this one ending in a large door. "The men there are some of my most trusted guards and members of the rebellion. I tried to spread out those who's loyalties I couldn't be sure of throughout the castle."

Axel stopped at the door, pressing his ear to it. "What room is this?"

"The ballroom," Roald answered. "No one's been in there for ages, and it cuts our route in half."

Axel backed away from it, raising his sword and turning back toward where they'd come. "Well, there's plenty of folks in there now. Not to mention the ones coming up behind us."

Pet whirled as a dozen guards came around the corner. They all wore full sets of metal armor, their halberds held high. How had she not seen them when she'd run past there? Had the guards been waiting for them? With a curse, Pet drew both of her axes.

The doors behind her opened with a rumbling groan. The four of them fell into formation, Hemming and Roald facing the hallway while Axel and Pet turned to face the ballroom. Guards pulled open the doors fully, revealing a robed king with three dozen fully armed men behind him.

King Thrum's beard split wide with his smile. "Well, this is a surprise. My captain of the guard taking our guests on a grand tour?"

Roald shifted behind Pet. "Of course, Your Majesty."

King Thrum threw back his head and laughed. "Oh, Roald, you always were such a jokester. I just never realized what a *fool* you were."

"Not a fool, Sire. Just a dwarf who wishes for more than what his king is willing to give."

King Thrum leered at them, his smile growing wider than what should have been possible for his face. Pet looked to Hemming, whose mouth had gone slack.

"That is very unfortunate," the king rumbled, his voice growing raspy. "Because now, I have to kill all of you."

His teeth lengthened. Then his arms, his legs. His hair disappeared and the skin of his neck grew golden. Ragged wings flared from his back and his robe fell in tatters at his feet. Stretching up toward the ceiling, two large horns crashed into the sparkling candelabras suspended above their heads. Dark crystals shattered on the ground near his claws.

Hel's bloody rock-strewn halls. Pet's mouth went dry.

The king didn't *own* a dragon.

The king *was* the dragon.

King Thrum thrust his humongous maw toward them and let out a thunderous roar. Hot spittle splashed against Pet's cheek; the creature's breath reeked of sulfur. The guards behind him shuffled to the side, doing their best to stay as far from the scaled hide as they could, but a few of them got whacked by the spiked tail swishing behind the beast.

Pet squeezed the handles of her axes until her fingers ached. There were no windows, the ballroom being positioned in the part of the castle inside the walls of the volcano, lit only by the torches hanging off the black pillars. If the walls were thinner, she'd have Axel break through them, but the black stone making up most of the building had to be an ell thick. There were three doors in plain sight: one at their back, one ahead of them, and one to their right which must have led into the main part of the castle.

King Thrum's head rose up once again, black eyes on them. He took a step in their direction, his long talons clicking on the polished floor. The creature could probably skewer a man with those things. His mouth opened again in a grin of blackened teeth. The base of his throat bulged.

"Move!" Pet shouted, shoving Hemming to the side as molten black lava shot from the dragon's mouth.

Of course, the bloody dwarf king was the dragon.

A lot of things started to make sense.

The fear of the king. The volcano. The princess stealing.

It was a curse.

There was no other explanation. Besides the Häxa, there weren't too many tales of shapeshifters. But there were more than a few stories about beings cursed by the gods to transform into any number of things. Wōden's eye, Little Hal's favorite story was about a man cursed to be a ferret. There were men turned into ravens, snakes, bears.

And, apparently, dragons.

If Pet wasn't in the middle of trying to stay alive, she would have smacked herself.

The dwarves in the corridor cried out as they were caught by the splash of lava. The stench of burning flesh combined with the stink of the liquid fire made Pet's stomach churn. She raced behind Roald and Hemming. Axel brandished his sword ahead of them, charging toward the group of dwarves guarding the main entrance. Helmets went flying, but the crush of dwarven guards slowed Axel down.

Pet's ax met the top of a guard's head, ringing the metal headpiece like a bell. She felt the shift of giant dragon hide behind her and spun to face the king.

The king's long neck slithered toward them, eyes flashing as he followed Axel's progress through the room. A line of dead dwarves stretched toward the door, where Axel was fighting the last three left in his path.

The dragon hissed and struck like a snake.

Pet dove out of the way, but he wasn't going for her.

"*Axel!*" she bellowed.

But he was already moving.

King Thrum's jaws snapped shut where he'd been standing a moment ago. Axel hurdled over the dwarf in front of him, taking three inhumanly fast steps and using the main door as a springboard.

King Thrum remained stretched out as Axel nimbly landed between two spikes along the top of his spine. The dragon roared, rearing his head back to try and bite Axel off.

Axel grabbed his sword and raised it high above his head. He brought it down toward the golden scales of the dragon's neck.

Pet heard Roald shout from somewhere behind her, but she couldn't make out what he said.

Axel's sword bounced right off the scales.

"Swords cannot cut through the scales!" Roald yelled again.

Axel's eyes flew wide as King Thrum let out another roar and bucked. Axel held tight to the spike in front of him, his surprise turning into all-out glee. He'd be bragging for ages about being the first man this side of the Vit Sea to ever ride a dragon. He was probably already drafting a ballad in his big head.

Pet grabbed her axes and ran toward him. A dwarf attempted to waylay her, but with a swing of her ax, he fell. The rest of the guards did their best to rally at the doors, but Hemming and Roald kept them occupied. The screeching, writhing dragon didn't pay any heed to his men and brought more than a few down before they could assist their comrades.

Pet got as close as she could to King Thrum, watching and waiting.

The beast curved his head back, exposing the soft flesh of his chest.

The ax flew from Pet's hand and struck.

King Thrum howled, black blood dribbling down his chest as he convulsed. He hacked, ash pluming out of his mouth. Axel slid from his back, nimbly dodging a flailing wing.

The ax fell free from the dragon's neck, landing on the floor between his talons.

Those beady, black eyes narrowed on her.

She raised her other ax and drew one of the knives from her vest.

The dragon leaped, his wings stretching out as his jaws opened wide.

Gritting her teeth, she raised her ax higher, aiming for the soulless pupils.

A flash of steel and gold came between them.

Pet flew away from the dragon, skidding over the slippery floor. She didn't even stop moving before she saw the dragon close its jaws around Axel, swallowing him whole.

Pet screamed, the flames of the torches in the corners of her vision seeming to flare along the walls. That bloody dragon did not just *eat* him! Her blood boiled under her skin as she let out another raging roar and got to her feet.

Hemming raced for the dragon, jabbing his sword at the beast's chest where Pet had already left a wound.

King Thrum backpedaled, his talons leaving gouges in the stone.

Pet's ax met the halberd of one of the guards. The blade of her ax sliced through the wooden shaft with ease and the sharpened end plopped to the ground behind her. With a twist of her wrist, she stabbed a dagger into the dwarf's throat and moved forward. She raced to grab the other ax that lay between her and King Thrum. A loud crash sounded behind her, but she only had eyes for the dragon that had eaten the only thing she cared about on this bloody planet.

Axel might have lived through several monster fights, but a dragon? They were creatures of magic. Something inside of them could nullify whatever magic it was that protected Axel. Who knew what that would do to his body? And what if they couldn't get him out?

With a bellow that came from somewhere deep within her, Pet joined Hemming in the fight, looking for any soft spot of flesh she could find. Her short axes weren't the optimal weapon for battling a dragon, but she made enough damage for King Thrum to pay attention to her and allow Hemming to make deeper cuts with his sword. Pet just needed an opening, which she knew Hemming would do his best to facilitate.

The dragon snapped his jaws at Hemming, who skittered to the side. King Thrum's head twisted that way, lifting his chest up and revealing the unscaled flesh of his stomach. Pet took a few steps back, then raced toward the dragon. As his head turned back, Pet kicked her feet out in front of her and slid under the beast. The bloodied floor of the ballroom slipped under her like lard. With her ax, she sliced the skin all the way down his torso, hot black blood streaming onto her hands and face as she allowed the momentum to carry her forward. She didn't make it all the way down before the dragon rose up on his hind legs, yowling in pain and fury.

Pet rolled to the side as the dragon came crashing down, his claws scrabbling after her. The blade of her ax hadn't gone deep enough to stop him, but the long black slice bled profusely.

Leaping to her feet, Pet dodged another swipe of the dragon's claws. He didn't even flinch when Hemming hacked at his armored leg with a sword, trying to draw his attention away from her.

Pet scurried back, axes swinging at anything within reach. One of the dragon's talons tore through the thick leather of her bracers, leaving a thin trail of red blood along her left arm. Her mind didn't even have time to register that it was her blood before the beast spouted bubbling lava from his gaping maw. Pet jumped out of the line of fire, crashing into Roald who was coming to her aid.

Roald helped Pet back to her feet, grabbing her arm with one hand while his other held a war hammer high.

King Thrum bared his teeth at Roald and roared.

Pet shoved Roald to the side, lifting her ax to throw.

The roar cut off.

The dragon's black eyes bulged, showing the thinnest line of white around his irises. His mouth opened and shut. He coughed, bringing his shoulders up with a shudder. His neck convulsed as he took staggering steps back. Black blood sprayed onto the floor as he hacked, his claws coming up around his throat.

Pet stilled.

A long, lysande blade stuck out halfway down the dragon's neck.

Pet's ribs squeezed together as the blade slowly sawed its way down the length of the dragon's throat and chest.

King Thrum's clawing grew weaker and weaker as blood spurted across the floor. He slumped to the side, the convulsing slowing as the life slowly went out of his onyx eyes.

Pet raced to where the chest was still being sliced open and used her ax to make the cut wider.

A black slicked hand shot out of the slit and grabbed her arm.

She hissed at the heat but wrapped both of her hands around his as Roald and Doran joined her. The three of them pulled.

Axel slid out of the dragon's carcass hale and whole.

And almost completely nude.

"Hel's bloody halls, that was *hot*!" he screeched. He shook out his arms, black blood flying from his skin. He looked down at himself. "Bloody dragon stomach burned through my favorite pair of socks!"

Pet took her first full breath. He was fine. He hadn't died because of her. He was fine.

She turned her back to him, averting her eyes. There had been times when she'd seen him in nothing. Being as close as they were and facing as many dangers as they had, bare flesh had lost much of its novelty very early on. Survival had taken as much of the innocence of youth that it could. That didn't mean she wouldn't give him privacy when it was warranted. None of the others around her probably cared as much, but she was still a woman, and Axel was still a man. There was still a sense of propriety carved into her brain from Mama and Da.

Roald collected a cloak from one of the guards, which had multiplied since Pet had checked last. These new guards, however, were rounding up the wounded and a few of the other guards that had been in the room with King Thrum. Their eyes continued to flick to Roald, who was issuing orders to get the dragon taken care of.

The rebel guards then.

She turned back around, having given Axel ample time to get decent. She looked him over, from the black goo in his hair to the toes sticking out of the scraps of leather boot that had survived the dragon's boiling gut. "You good?" she asked.

"Thunder's beard, Pet," Axel said. "Never, *ever* let me get eaten by a dragon again. I don't think I'll be able to take a hot bath for months after that."

She grimaced and wiped his cheek to show him the black sludge caked there.

"Maybe just one hot bath?"

CHAPTER 20

DISAGREEMENTS

There has been much speculation to Axel's prophecy since it became public knowledge. The lad had been raised by it. His mother, a Häxa water seer, left it to King Asher before she mysteriously disappeared. It is said a Häxa's prophecy can mean many things, and no one but the seer herself can decipher it. I have often thought about Axel's prophecy, trying to twist the words this way and that to figure out what his future may hold. All I see is sorrow and pain.

— *FROM THE WRITINGS OF DORAN FINNSSON, THE LAST KING OF GROVÖ*

Axel pretended to nearly fall over as Princess Ella plowed into him. If he hadn't, she would have felt like she ran into a stone wall. Probably would have broken one of her gapped teeth.

"Praise the Allfather, I thought you were all dead!" She pulled away from him and turned back to Pet who had already received an overly eager hug when the girl had been brought up by Roald to the throne room—*after* Axel had had a proper cleaning. "When I heard the roars, I thought for sure the dragon had eaten one of you."

"Well..." Roald trailed off, meeting Axel's eye.

Axel grinned, masking his shudder. In all seriousness, being swallowed by a dragon and having to cut himself out of the thing's neck was something he hoped to prevent from ever happening to him again.

Freyja's golden tears, he was still expelling the black goo from his nostrils.

"We'll tell you the whole of it later," Pet cut in. "We have an entire trip back to the crew, and a ship still to fix."

Axel's mouth pulled down in a frown. "Erik's likely not even close to finished. We should see if there's anything we can find in the village to help."

They would be able to sail all the way around the Stiga Sea with the repairs Erik was capable of overseeing, but *The Phoenix* would look rough until they could get it back to the dwarven crafters who had originally built her. Axel massaged the back of his neck. It would likely be months before they could make it over to the dwarves near Harligdam and the repairs would take longer since they'd have to tear out the rough patches before they could fix her up. Not to mention the price. Dwarves were not cheap craftsmen.

"Quit frowning." Pet slung an arm up onto his shoulder. "She'll be ugly for a bit, but she'll get the job done."

Axel pursed his lips. "Stop reading my mind and let me wallow about my beautiful ship having to look like two-faced Hel."

Roald took a step forward. "You know, I may be able to help with that."

ᛈᚻᚲᛟᚻᛁᛚ

THE SOUND of shouting stilled Axel's movements as he clung to the side of the crevice. It sounded like the voices were coming from the direction of the beach. Had the Sidans made it through the storm and found the crew? Axel strained his ears for any sound of blades.

Pet stopped above him. When he looked up, her dark brows furrowed. *What's the problem?*

Axel began moving again, his hands and feet grabbing the rocks jutting out of the cliff wall. The crevice flattened out the further down they went, and his climb took up speed. He reached the base when the shouts took up a fury Axel did not like. It wasn't far to the bottom of the cliff, maybe a story or two. He jumped, his boots breaking through the driftwood that had gathered at the base of the crevice. The shouting escalated, but Axel caught the bark of Big Hal's voice and

Erik's growling reply. Axel wiped his hands on his trousers, his heart returning to a normal speed. He should have known.

Tilting his head up, he called, "I'm going to head to the beach."

Pet waved him off, her other hand in Princess Ella's as she guided her down the rocky path. Hemming gave him a sharp nod as well, following the princess's steps, ready to catch her if she slipped. Four guards and a dozen workmen scuttled after him, Roald bringing up the rear of the party.

They had it covered. Axel made his way through the opening in the cliff, water pooling around his ankles. Once he squeezed through the narrow exit, he took in the scene.

On the pebbled beach stood Big Hal, purple faced and screaming down at Erik as Doran stood between them, his brows low as he held Big Hal back.

"It's been three days!" Big Hal threw his arms in the air. "We can't just keep sitting here while Axel has his glory moment. We ought to have been allowed to go up there and save the princess too."

Erik glared back. "That's not what we were told to do, Halvor, and you know it. We were tasked with getting the ship repaired."

"No, *you* were supposed to get the ship repaired."

Doran finally shoved Big Hal back. "No one is going to get the ship repaired if we keep fighting. Let's not lose our heads."

Axel waded through the water. "Of course they're fighting like imbeciles," he muttered. It wasn't that he didn't want the crew to fight. It was good for men to air their grievances with one another. He just hated always acting as the mediator between all of them. They were grown men—Pet and Little Hal excluded of course. They needed to deal with their own problems. Since Axel had signed Big Hal onto the crew two years ago, the man had stirred up his fair share of drama, but he also offered a number of solutions. He was a decent fighter, and his stature had thieves and thugs thinking twice before they tried anything with the rest of the crew. However, days like today had Axel wishing he'd gone with the mute, one-eyed arena fighter that had been on the run from Tatawar who had approached him at the same time as Big Hal. But that also would have come with its own set of problems.

"And it might have been done already," Erik bit out, "if you didn't keep arguing with me every five seconds."

"Both of you stop it!" Little Hal threw down the spoon in his hand. "Axel's coming back and he's going to bash both of your heads in if we don't have this bloody ship done."

Axel finally made it to the beach. "Little Hal's right."

All three of their heads whipped in his direction. Big Hal's face went a bit pale, his mouth twisting in a grimace. Erik's mustache rose up his cheeks with his smile.

"Good to see you, Axel."

Axel set his fists on his waist. "Well? Are we going to get this ship fixed up, or am I going to have to bash in some heads?"

ᚠᚾᚲᛟᚠᛁᛚ

THE PHOENIX CRASHED into the black water, star-studded waves breaking from her wings as if she were flying through the night sky. The crowd of dwarves joined the crew's cheers as she bobbed in the water, the mast looking splendid after the dwarves had aided in the repair. It only took them two days to get her ready for the journey, a much shorter time than the crew could have managed on their own.

Big Hal and Erik had still picked at each other during the rest of the time it took to finish repairs, but now the two of them slapped each other on the back, toothy grins stretching ear to ear.

Axel turned to Roald standing at his side. "Thank you."

Roald shook his head. "This is the least we could do. You slayed the tyrant we'd been living under for decades. Without you, our rebellion would have taken years to finally reclaim Gulli. You did what no other man could have." He offered his hand.

Axel took it firmly in his own. "It was an honor, Captain—though, I imagine you won't be holding that title for too much longer."

Roald took a step back, running a hand through his dark hair. "I want there to be a vote. Gulli has been ruled by a tyrant for too long. It will be good to give the people their own power."

Axel shrugged. "I'll believe it when I see it." Captain Roald was too good a leader to not be put in a position of power. That was simply how it worked. Well, at least until someone else came along and changed everyone's mind. Like Roald had with King Thrum. Like Firmin's grandfather had with the Häxa.

"Axel!"

He followed the call, finding Little Hal waving a torch as he jogged across the small beach. The lad's face was still drawn but having something to do seemed to help him keep his grief from surfacing.

Olav's loss hit Axel right in the chest again. Olav and Little Hal had been some of the first to join the crew—when Little Hal had only been nine. Axel hadn't ever seen the two of them separated for more than a few hours. He could only imagine how the lad was feeling. Losing a loved one wasn't a wound that faded quickly. Even nine years later, Axel still woke up some mornings feeling like his chest had been hollowed out. He'd have to find some time to sit down with the lad.

"Axel," Little Hal repeated a little out of breath, "Erik's asking about getting the rest of the supplies on."

With a nod, Axel bade Roald farewell and followed Little Hal to the pile of goods the dwarves had brought down as a parting gift. Food, clothing, medical supplies. Gulli's citizens had restocked *The Phoenix's* hold twice over. Pet would say slaying an evil dragon overlord paid well. Axel grabbed one of the boxes, filled to the brim with salted meat of somewhat questionable origin. He hefted the box onto his shoulder. Little Hal would know what to do with it.

Axel's toes sank into the pebbled beach as he trudged through the water to the ship. With the boat mostly on dry land for repairs, it was easier to get her into the water with a lighter load and put the rest of the cargo on after. Pet marched ahead of him, dragging her waterlogged boots through the waist-high water. Axel could put up with the rough rocks and would be grateful for dry boots later. Praise Wōden's one good eye for invincible bare feet.

They had the ship loaded and the crew dripping onto the planks within the hour. Apparently, Axel wasn't the only one eager to get off that beach because every man took to an oar and pushed through the strait at a fast clip, Erik's voice calling encouragement from the tiller. They would likely stop to sleep in a few hours and then be back up with Sol's sun.

Pet sat beside Axel, her lean arms moving at the same rhythm as his. Most of the crew had doubled up on the oars. Her gaze was trained on Little Hal in the row across from them. The lad's eyes were red, a few tears lingering on his chin as he sat beside Big Hal and rowed.

"Do you ever think," Pet whispered, "this war isn't worth the lives it costs?"

Axel looked back at her. "I don't think war is ever worth the cost. War has no winners or losers. All that's left in the aftermath are those still living and the bodies of those that should be."

Pet's face turned toward the stars, moonlight softening the sharp edges of her face. "What if this war was just some big misunderstanding? What would you do?"

"I would do everything I could to fix it. If I had the cure for this, I'd give it in a heartbeat."

Silence stretched between them. This topic had come up in the past, not so much in the exact same words, but similar. Both of them trying to make sense of a situation that just didn't. Who could truly grasp what war did to people? How could one reconcile humanity with such brutality? It was true that the war had started seemingly out of nowhere. While Sida had always pestered Åldras, they'd never outright attacked them. There had been heated conversations over trade agreements and especially about the Häxa prejudices. There had been skirmishes over the years, but nothing like Holmberg. There would never be a day when Axel could sit down across from a Sidan without seeing death and destruction.

If this war truly had been some misunderstanding, Axel would do anything in his power to see it put to rights. He'd rip his own beating heart out of his chest if it would ensure an end to this bloody fight. But the war between Sida and Åldras was not a mistake. Not when the Sidans had killed so many just to take over lands that weren't theirs. Not when they'd burned down an entire island simply because they believed they could.

"Sometimes I wish you weren't such a hero."

The break in silence threw him and he had to readjust his movements to hers. "What is that supposed to mean?"

Pet shook her head, hiding her face with a curtain of brown hair. "I don't know. I'm probably just tired."

Axel leaned down. "I can row—"

"*No,*" she bit out. "I'm not tired of rowing. I'm just tired of watching everyone die."

Chapter 21

A Pest

The callouses of Pet's hands protested as she moved the oar up out of the water for what felt like the millionth time. But she didn't complain. She didn't complain about the raw skin of her knuckles and nose as the noonday sun crisped her skin red. The other men had already shed most of their layers, sweat pouring down the bare skin of their backs as they rowed.

Pet kept her shirt on.

It wasn't often they had to row like this. Most of their voyages happened on open water, where the wind filled their sail, and the current swept them towards their next destination. In the channel, the water carried them forward, searching for the Stiga Sea as it tumbled beneath the ship. However, the current changed often, the water shooting in and out of springs hidden beneath the surface. The wind wasn't much help either. It came in gusts every so often, but not enough to fill the sail or cool their necks. Their oars stuck out of the oar ports more than they laid in the ship.

A hand settled on her shoulder and Pet about leaped out of her skin. Before she could even think, she had dropped the oar, and a dagger was in her hand.

"Oh!" Ella raised her hands with a squeak. "I'm sorry, Petyr."

Axel's booming laugh echoed off the cliff walls around them, even startling a few puffins from a nest above their heads. He swaggered up between the rowers from where he'd been talking to Erik. "You know, it's dangerous to pop up on Pet. He'll gouge out your eye before he even recognizes you."

Ella's sunburned face paled. "I really am so sorry. I truly didn't mean to frighten you."

Pet slid the dagger back into the sheath at her waist, refraining from glaring at Axel as she resumed rowing. But Ella didn't leave. Instead, she moved into Pet's line of sight. Pet tilted her head. "Is there a problem?"

The princess looked over her shoulder at Axel and the others then back at Pet. "Um, well, I was wondering if you wouldn't mind if I sat next to you."

The sore skin of Pet's nose scrunched up. What in Hel's bloody halls? There wasn't a logical reason for her to say no, but allowing the princess to think Pet might want company would certainly give the wrong message.

She opened her mouth, but Axel cut her off.

"Of course you should sit with Pet," he said, smarmy smile and all. "Here, sit on my trunk."

Pet glared at him. *Idiot.*

Ella's answering smile stretched wide, showing the small gap between her two front teeth. She swept up her now dingy skirts and sat on Axel's trunk beside Pet's. Why on Midgard did the girl want to sit there? The view was terrible, Pet's side being closest to the cliff. There wasn't much to see besides white rock and the occasional bird colony.

Axel watched Ella, his eyes narrowing in thought then going wide.

Pet's brow quirked. *What?*

Axel smirked. A very arrogant, dangerous smirk. "Your Highness, I didn't realize you and Pet here had formed such strong feelings for one another."

Pet frowned at him. Strong feelings? She'd barely said more than a handful of words to the princess. It wasn't like they were great bosom friends now just because Pet handed her a knife and had been apparently assigned her special protector—not of her own volition even.

Axel tilted his head toward Ella, his smirk morphing to a full out grin.

Ella's face had turned a very splotchy shade of red, and she ducked her head when Pet met her gaze.

She looked...bashful.

Pet's throat went dry. Oh, Donar strike her now. She snapped her gaze forward, staring at Ludvig's back. This could not be happening.

But the princess didn't leave. The hair of Pet's head prickled, her entire body wincing every time Ella glanced at her. How did this happen? Pet was usually good at warding off the girls that seemed to trail in every Åldran warrior's wake. She'd always done her best to be the prickliest crewmember aboard *The Phoenix*. It was made even easier by being on Axel's crew, considering he could even give the celestially handsome Baldr a run for his money. Pet wasn't as blind as she wished to be sometimes. She knew why the women flocked to him and avoided her. It helped that she also looked like a teenager, not that it was much of a deterrent for some of the more lascivious women.

Pet couldn't tell Ella she wasn't what she appeared to be. If she rejected the princess, there would be no telling what the girl would do. Having her trust made Pet's job a lot easier than it would be without it. Being withdrawn obviously wasn't working and there wasn't much space on the ship to hide from a young princess's advances.

Freyja's golden tears, they'd better get to Ljust Löfte soon.

ᚠᚾᚲᛟᚠᛁᛚ

THEY TRAVELED down the channel for two more days before Pet was ready to jump overboard and let whatever sharp-toothed creatures living in the water eat her. Ella was at every turn. One might think being on a ship that only stretched thirty-six ells would make it difficult to avoid someone, but Pet hadn't rubbed shoulders with Little Hal or Erik in that entire time. Instead, Ella attached to her like bloody lichen to a tree.

And Axel wasn't much better.

What had started out as a fun thing to tease Pet about had slowly turned into something else. Ella would arrive at Pet's elbow, asking about her family or her favorite kind of stew, then Axel would pop up, telling Ella ridiculous stories from their childhood and practically feeding the girl compliments to give Pet. It was nearly impossible to hide from them, but she made it work as well as she could.

"You can't avoid them forever, Petyr," Ulf said from beside her.

The man's wide shoulders did a fine job concealing Pet from the eyes of the rest of the crew. He also wasn't ever one for much conversation. Unlike Doran, who had started lecturing her on the proper way to address someone else's feelings.

Pet pulled the hood of her cloak farther down her face. "But I can try."

"It's a very small boat."

"Don't I bloody know it."

Ulf elbowed her. "Mind that tongue."

Pet squashed the urge to stick out said tongue, if only so he wouldn't kick her out of her hiding spot.

Blue ice reflected the glow of the dying sun. They'd began seeing glaciers along the sides of the cliffs, paying homage to their continent's name. Pet remembered Da telling stories of his travels as a young man. He'd told of mountains made of ice to the north of Åldras. Black-and-white killer whales swimming under floating icebergs and giants roaming the expanse of white. She didn't know if Da had ever actually seen a giant, but with the way he described the creatures, she wouldn't have been surprised. If only she could ask him.

"Ouch!"

Pet spun and found Ella standing right behind her for what had to have been the hundredth time that day. A pile of furs lay at her feet, and she held up one hand. Pet squinted in the waning light and saw the massive splinter sticking out of the princess's palm.

Hel's bloody rock-covered halls.

Ella quickly recovered and gathered the fallen furs from the deck, one-handed. "Skipper Erik suggested I bring out some furs before the sun starts going down. I didn't know which one you preferred, so I brought them all to you to pick from." Her freckled cheeks went rosy, and she ducked her head as she held out the pile.

"Are one of those furs for Pet, Your Highness?" Axel swaggered over, a handful of nuts in his hand. "You truly are so kind. Pet absolutely deserves to be spoiled by those that care about him."

Great gods. Pet withheld a groan.

Ella smiled, her cheeks even redder than before. "Of course, I care for all the crew. I only hope to show all of you as much kindness as you've shown me."

Axel's face flashed with something Pet couldn't really guess at. He covered it with his most charming smile which he directed at the princess. With a flourish, he took the first fur on the top of the pile. "Here you are, dearest Pet. The warmest fur on the boat."

Pet glared at him. "I'm fine."

"Oh, don't be modest." Axel practically dumped the fur on top of her head. "We all know you like to act tough, but you don't need to pretend in front of Princess Ella."

Pet clenched her jaw, doing her best not to bare her teeth at him. Honestly, she would stab him if it would make a mark. She met the princess's eye. The girl's face had fallen slightly.

Ulf elbowed her.

Freyja's golden tears...

"Thank you, Your Highness," Pet said.

Ella's crestfallen expression lit back up. "You're very welcome, Pet. Is there anything else I can—"

"You know," Ulf said, "you ought to have Little Hal dig that splinter out of your hand. He's in charge of the bandages should you need one."

Her attention shifted to where Little Hal sat at the front of the ship. "Oh, yes. You're probably right." She carried the rest of the furs away, a new spring in her step.

Axel's eyes trailed after her, and Pet did her best to ignore the growing sparks in his eyes. Seriously, what was his deal?

He turned back to her, that stupid smile still plastered on his face. "Erik wants to discuss our next few days."

Pet shrugged the fur off and handed it to Ulf. "If the princess comes back, tell her I'm indisposed."

Ulf chuckled and settled the fur on his lap. "Good luck."

Pet tucked the edges of her cloak around her, more to ward off Axel's attention than the chill dusk air. She followed him as he wove his way through the cargo and the men. Well, maybe *swaggered* was a more accurate description. The man practically preened as he passed by Ella, who had already distributed furs to half the crew.

Pet stomped to catch up to him. "What is your problem?" she asked under her breath.

Axel attempted to look perplexed, but he was failing at it because his pursed lips turned smug. "Whatever do you mean?"

Pet grabbed his arm and pulled him to a stop. "I *mean* that you've been acting crazy for the last two days and it's going to drive *me* crazy if you don't knock it off."

"I'm not acting crazy."

Pet scoffed. "You dove into the water yesterday and wrestled a bloody blue shark simply to pull out one of its teeth, which you promptly tried to convince the princess to give to me as if it were a gold medallion from Frigg herself."

"I distinctly remember you collecting shark teeth as a child." He popped one of the walnuts in his hand into his mouth.

"Not with the godsforsaken gums still attached!" Pet drew in a deep breath and kept walking. "All I'm saying is you need to let go of whatever ridiculous scheme you have in that thick skull of yours and leave me alone. I'm already trying to figure out how to get Ella off my back without having to worry about you as well."

"Why? Do you not like the attentions of someone who cares about you?"

Pet's mouth dropped open. "Are you kidding me? Axel, she *can't* care about me. Not in the way you're insinuating."

Axel looked taken aback. "I'm not insinuating anything. I'm just trying to show you that people can care about you, Pet. That you're worth being cared for."

"Oh, by the Allfather." He really was crazy. "I don't need a child pining after me, and I certainly don't need you encouraging it. It's cruel."

Axel stilled. "I'm sorry, Pet. I didn't mean for it to make you so cross. I just wanted you to feel valued."

"Then stop treating me like a puppy that gets passed around for cuddles. I might start biting." Pet stomped off to where Erik sat, his hand guiding the rudder through the current carrying them. "How's everything looking?"

Erik pursed his lips but kept his eye on the front of the ship. "We ought to be past the glacier by midnight. If we push through tonight, we should be able to get some wind in our sail."

"Is that why you have the princess passing out furs?" Axel asked, coming up beside Pet. "I don't know that we can ask the crew to keep up all night. They've been running themselves ragged the past two days."

"We can't very well sleep on the glacier either. We could throw anchor, but we don't want to be sitting ducks for what's in these waters."

Pet took a step closer. "What do you mean?"

Erik slid a hand to the inside of his vest and pulled out the map from the Great Mother. He unfolded it part way and pointed at a small island tucked into the bay that acted as the elbow to the channel before the water turned fully south. "See the note here? It warns of fossegrim on that island."

Pet leaned in closer. A fossegrim? Truly? She'd never seen one. Fossegrim were reclusive creatures, not usually found within hundreds of miles of one another. They had been more of a problem in the past, but Pet couldn't remember much else about them besides the fact they were not to be trifled with.

Axel's mouth turned down. "I haven't heard of a fossegrim sighting since before my father was born."

"Aye," Erik agreed, "they left much of Åldras before our grandfathers began voyaging."

"Should we be concerned?" Axel asked.

"Maybe not us, but we should guard the princess and even Little Hal well for the next day or two. We don't know what such a creature may attempt to do."

CHAPTER 22

LURES

Axel stared at the black water over the edge of the ship. It was so still, only *The Phoenix* stirred the top of the glasslike surface. The susurrus ripples spread out from the ship, reaching for the edges of the channel. Not even Máni allowed the moon's white face to reflect off the waters. As they'd traveled the channel over the last couple days, there had been fish and birds, otters and beavers, all kinds of curious animals wandering after their ship in such uncharted waters. But now there was nothing but the quiet murmur of the water. The hollowness sent a cold shiver down Axel's spine.

The scratch of leather against wood proceeded Doran's hand on his shoulder.

"You're supposed to be on last watch."

"I'm going to be on every bloody watch until we get past this turn."

"Language." Doran sat next to him on Pet's trunk. Pet had found a spot to lie down near Erik so she could take a turn at the rudder to give the skipper a break later on. Better for her to do it anyhow. It gave Axel the perfect opportunity to watch the rest of the ship.

"Petyr is very put out with you, you know."

Oh, great gods. Axel looked to the heavens. The last time Doran had involved himself in one of their spats, he'd locked them in a prison cell to make them talk it out. That had lasted all of five seconds because

Pet simply picked the lock and Axel knocked out the guard standing watch. Yes, they regularly argued, but they always worked it out no matter what. Pet could be awfully stubborn when she wanted to, but she always came around.

Doran crossed his arms over his chest. "Is there a specific reason you've been tormenting him?"

"Not especially. It's not my fault he's being sensitive."

"Since the moment Ella started showing him interest, you've been pestering him. Don't try to argue that you aren't. I can see it in your face. Are you jealous of her attentions to him? You're not secretly pining after a fifteen-year-old princess, are you?"

"Gods, no!" Axel could gag at the very thought. She was a *child*. His type was older than him anyway.

"Well, what then?" Doran urged.

Axel shook his head. "What do you want me to say? He's being a grump like always and I'll eventually do something to make him blow up, and it'll be over."

Doran sighed. "That's not a healthy way to go about arguing with your family."

"It's worked out this long and neither of us have killed the other." Not for lack of trying on Pet's part. It probably helped her blow off more steam giving Axel the full measure of her anger rather than holding back, but he couldn't hurt her. It would be like stabbing himself in the chest.

"I still think you should apologize," Doran insisted.

Axel rolled his eyes. "I'll stop urging the princess on, but I didn't even do anything worth saying sorry over."

Doran punched his arm. "Then you ought to say sorry to me for making me put up with him for the last two days. The boy is pricklier than a hedgehog when he gets puffed up. You really should know better than to torment him."

"If you want me to stop, I'll stop. However, I still think Pet needs to lighten up."

Now it was Doran's turn to look heavenward. "You're likely right. That boy has always had a darkness about him."

Axel's back straightened, mouth open and ready to defend Pet, but a long moan interrupted him. It wasn't a moan like an animal in agony.

It was like a moan of calling. Of wanting. It was the sound a soul made when they dreamed of going to Valhalla.

A splash disrupted the noise, jostling Axel and bringing his mind back to the ship. Water rippled out from the side where the splash had come from, and Big Hal was already hanging over the gunwale. Axel raced to the edge to see Little Hal's head bob up above the water before going back down again. With hurried movements, the lad swam away from the ship.

"Little Hal!" Axel called. "What are you doing?"

"He just jumped overboard." Big Hal looked around as if he were making sure he hadn't just imagined it. "Didn't say a word."

The boat jostled as the rudder turned. "Get him!" Erik shouted. "It's the fossegrim!"

What did the creature on the map have to do with it? Axel jumped out of the boat, the sounds of Erik's barking commands chasing him into the water. Whatever the creature was doing to Little Hal, it couldn't be good if the lad was willing to jump out of the boat for no reason. The bubbles blinded Axel as he tried to find any trace of the lad. A flash of white slipped through the rocks beneath him, but it disappeared before he could tell what it was. The sound of splashing limbs drew his attention upward and he made out the outline of Little Hal's silhouette.

When he surfaced, he found Little Hal ahead of him, arms cutting through the water toward an island not far off. The low moan that had pierced Axel's soul took up a livelier tune, a welcoming ditty. Axel nearly breathed in some of the water. It was a fiddle. Little Hal moved with a grace and determination Axel had never seen the gangly boy ever show. Axel cut through the water and caught Little Hal by the scruff of his shirt.

"What on Midgard are you doing?"

But Little Hal's eyes were glazed over, his face turned toward the island and the song sweeping through the air. Axel followed that empty gaze and nearly lost his hold on Little Hal when he saw the creature, a fiddle at his chin and an unnatural smile flashing yellowed teeth. Furry legs ending in hooves splashed at the edge of the water as he danced to the tune he played.

The fossegrim.

Axel's heart dropped. *Rocks.*

Rocks, rocks, rocks.

Little Hal cried out as Axel dragged him back toward the ship. The boy's fingernails tried to dig into the flesh of Axel's arm but to no avail. Axel struggled with him as he twisted around like an eel, using any avenue of escape he could find.

"Don't listen to it!" Axel snapped. "That thing will kill you the moment you set foot on that beach."

Little Hal paid him no heed. The enchantment overcame any kind of mental fortitude he might have had. It was a good thing the lad was only twelve. Axel would have had a harder time dragging him through the water if Little Hal had an extra ten pounds on him.

A scrap of wood about an arm's length long floated in the water a few paces from them. With his free hand, Axel grabbed it. He spun around, catching sight of the fossegrim on the beach, the creature's goat-hooved feet prancing as it played its eerie tune. Axel brought his arm back and threw the driftwood. The end of the stick didn't hit the fossegrim's head as Axel had intended, but it knocked the bow from the fiddler's hands into the reeds behind it. The fossegrim screeched and dove for the instrument.

Little Hal's fight left him, but he was somewhat limp in Axel's grip. At least he wasn't squirming anymore. That should keep the beast occupied at least long enough for Axel to get Little Hal back to the ship.

A scream pierced the air, the sharp screech making Axel's ears ring.

White, nearly translucent hands pushed at the sides of *The Phoenix*, tilting the boat from side to side. Axel could see the heads of black hair thick as kelp sway near the surface. One of the heads shot out of the water, black eyes fixed on Axel as the creature bared its razor-sharp teeth with a hiss.

The fossegrim wasn't working alone then. He had a group of nixies helping him.

Axel held tighter to Little Hal and searched the water. He didn't know how he would get through the nixies without losing the lad to them. He could make it through the group, they'd even let him go once they realized they couldn't do anything to him, but he couldn't let Little Hal get hurt.

A bellow thundered over the nixies' squeals. Big Hal raised a long halberd over his head and began stabbing at the creatures in the water near the stem. The nixies fled from the blade, having nothing to fight with besides their hands and teeth.

Axel took the opening. He tucked Little Hal against his chest and sliced through the water. He could have done it in half the time if he'd had his other arm, but he was still faster one handed than anyone else on the ship.

Big Hal waited for him at the stem, his eyes wide as they scoured the water, the tip of the halberd stabbing at anything that moved. Axel made it to the side and Ludvig appeared, rope in hand.

"Put the loop around his waist," Ludvig said, throwing the rope over the side of the ship. "I'll tie him to the mast with the princess."

Axel handed him up. Not a moment later, the sweet notes of a fiddle resumed.

Wōden's eye, they needed to get out of there.

Axel pulled his chest up over the edge. A nixie grabbed for his ankle, but a swift kick of his boot sent the creature careening back into the water. Axel pulled one leg up in time to watch Little Hal resume his enchanted insanity as the bloody fossegrim resumed its tune. He snarled as Ludvig grappled with him, trying to get him tied to the mast where the princess had also taken up a careening song. Tears streamed down her face as she cried. Doran jumped over to help and with Ludvig was able to get Little Hal tied.

Axel cursed. "What on bloody Midgard is this?"

"The fossegrim's enchantment," answered Erik. "The song may be alluring to men, but only children and women are enthralled by its tune. Why do you think some believe it to be bad luck to have them aboard a ship?"

Axel's heart stopped in his chest.

Children and *women*.

He frantically searched the faces on the ship. "Where's Pet? *Where in Hel's bloody halls is Pet?*"

Everyone looked about, dumb expressions on their faces as they searched for the woman Axel already knew wasn't there. He swung his leg back over the side of the ship and jumped again into the water.

The nixies were on him in an instant.

Teeth flashed and fingers clawed at his clothing. They dragged him deeper into the water, but he grappled with them, breaking fingers and smashing in teeth. One got their jaw around his wrist, but Axel punched the beast right in the temple and dislodged it. He pushed again for the surface. All he could think about was Pet. He needed to get to Pet.

The nixies grew warier as he continued to gain ground even though they outnumbered him. He could hear their savage shrieks growing more outraged, then annoyed. Soon, only a few remained to attempt to subdue him, but that didn't last long. He finally surfaced, his body shaking.

Doran hollered over the nixie, pointing. "There! He's just there!"

Axel spun and found Pet stroking through the water followed by nixies. They pushed her toward the island and the fossegrim's welcoming melody.

Axel took off after her. Nixies sprang up out of the water, doing their best to slow him, but he fought his way through every single one, never faltering.

He wasn't fast enough.

Pet crawled onto the island, her dark hair matted to her cheeks as she gazed longingly up at the fossegrim, who still held that bloody fiddle between his chin and shoulder. Pet reached up toward the beast.

Something in Axel snapped.

Another nixie dove at him and Axel grabbed the creature by the hair. The nixie screeched as he pulled it back and threw it at the bloody shore. The nixie flew through the air and knocked the fossegrim to the ground.

Axel's feet met sand as he pushed himself out of the water and onto the island. The fossegrim and the nixie were tangled together, the nixie shrieking as the fossegrim tried to detangle itself from the thick, black hair. Axel grabbed one of the many pieces of driftwood lying on the shore and broke it over one knee as he came up to the wrestling creatures. With a roar, he raised both pieces in the air and brought them down on the fossegrim and the nix, impaling them both.

CHAPTER 23

A MEMORY

I can still see Holmberg that day so vividly in my mind, even all these years after. I can still see the two starving boys standing like statues within the ruins, the sunken skeletons of their attempts to escape sticking out of the sea. How they had survived for so long before we arrived, I still can't fathom. How my men survived that first interaction, I can only give credit to Wōden. Those two boys would have killed three of my men if I hadn't been able to talk them down. This war has taken much from many, myself included, but Axel Ashersson and Petyr Mallorysson died on that island, reborn into something new.

— *FROM THE WRITINGS OF DORAN FINNSSON, THE LAST KING OF GROVÖ*

Pet felt herself awaken, but she didn't know how she had been sleeping upright, on her knees, on an unfamiliar beach. A whisp of a breeze blew into her sodden clothing, making her shiver.

The crunch of boots came from her right and she looked up to see Axel as he crouched next to her.

"You good?"

Pet blinked at him. "I...I think so."

A scream shot through the air. Pet jumped and turned toward the edge of the water where a head popped out and shrieked at her.

A large rock slammed into its face, making Pet jump again.

"Go scream at someone else, you bloody banshee!" Axel threw another rock which must have been enough of a warning because the creature swam away.

"What happened?" Pet asked. How had she gotten onto the island? Why was she soaking wet when she had no recollection of leaving the ship? Pet found *The Phoenix* bobbing in the water offshore a little way. Farther than it should have been if everyone else was getting off.

Axel sat down. "A fossegrim."

Pet's mouth pulled down. "We reached the spot on the map? Where's the creature?"

Axel pointed behind him. Pet glanced over her shoulder and saw two bodies tangled together, two wooden stakes skewering them.

"Oh."

Axel rubbed a hand down his face. "Aye."

Her toes squelched in her soggy boots as she pushed herself to her feet. *Bloody fossegrim.* Her gaze snagged on the shiny wood of the instrument still clutched in the creature's hand.

"You think that fiddle is worth anything?" she asked.

Axel turned and spotted the instrument. He marched toward the bodies and ripped it from the fossegrim's limp hand. Without any consideration, he smashed it right onto the beach. Strings popped with a *clang* and the wooden body broke into a thousand tiny shards, the bit with the pegs the only thing still left somewhat intact. He brushed a few stray pieces from his pants. "Not worth more than my peace of mind." He slung an arm around her shoulders. "Let's get back to the boat. The nixies can claim them once we're gone."

"What nixies?" Pet looked about. There wasn't a single other creature in the water around them. At least, none that she could see.

Axel frowned. "Seems we've scared them off."

Pet looked over at the skewered creatures a few feet away. "Not surprising. I wouldn't want to end up being stick meat either."

The splash of oars drew Pet's attention back to the ship. Doran stood at the stem, and when Pet could make out his eyes, he cupped a hand around his mouth. "You two all right?"

Axel waved him off. "We're fine, grandfather. Just catching our breaths."

Doran tossed his hands up in annoyance and left the stem. A few of the crew popped their heads over the side of the ship, glancing in their direction. *Nosy little weasels, the lot of them.*

The Phoenix glided as close as she could get without full beaching. Pet still had to swim a bit before she reached the side, where Ludvig held the end of a rope and helped haul her back into the boat. She usually managed the task on her own, but her limbs still trembled from the freezing water and whatever magic the goat-man had used on her.

Axel leaped over the side in the usual Axel fashion, showing off and acting as cavalier as possible.

"You gave us quite a scare there, lad." Doran set a hand on Pet's shoulder. "You all right?"

Pet shrugged off his hand. "Just fine."

Doran frowned but nodded anyway. The man knew better than to push.

Axel crouched next to his trunk, rifling around for dry clothing. Lucky him. Pet would have to sit in her wet things until most of the crew was asleep and she could use her bedroll as a changing cover.

"What was that thing?" Ella asked from where she was still strapped to the mast, Big Hal untying the knots. "I've never been so confused in my life."

"A fossegrim, though I've heard others call them simply 'grims,'" Erik answered. "Their music is dangerous. Downright irresistible to women and children."

Big Hal stilled where he was crouched next to the princess. "Women and children, you say?" He looked to Little Hal untying the ropes from the mast, then to Ella beside him, and back to Pet. "Well, Petyr? I knew your lack of whiskers was telling, but I thought you more of a man than that!"

A few of the crewmembers joined in his laugh.

Axel was on his feet in an instant, but Pet was faster.

A knife embedded itself into the deck right between Big Hal's legs.

His laugh choked off instantly.

"Careful, Big Hal," Pet growled, "or you'll be less of a man than I am."

The entire crew fell into fits of laughter, Axel even throwing a grin her way. Big Hal's face reddened, and he stood with a huff, leaving the knife stuck into the deck.

ᚠᚾᚲᛟᚠᛈᛏ

TRAVEL GREW EASIER as they turned south with the wind and the land around them leveled out. It grew warmer as they went, the nights still cool but nothing like they would have been out on the open sea or around Åldras. The sail remained full of wind, rounding like Da's belly after the Midsummer Festival in Holmberg. He'd always said the extra pounds were food storage for the winter months.

Pet prodded the leather of her boots hanging off the side of her trunk. Still wet. She pushed the extra stockings she'd stuffed in there down tighter. She had two other pairs of boots, but these were her favorite. As long as they didn't shrink too much, she should be able to stretch them back into shape.

Ella sat next to Pet, her fingers working a bone needle through loops and knots of spun wool. Axel sat across from her, doing the same. The two of them had been rather quiet since the battle with the fossegrim the night before, though how long it would last, Pet couldn't tell. Nålbinding was one of Axel's least used but most enjoyed pastimes. It was a social hobby, one he had taken up with Mama when he'd visited Pet's home as a child. Pet had always thought it was to charm all the older women into giving him treats, but she realized over the years that he actually enjoyed it. There was an entire crate in the hold dedicated to yarn. He made the crew new scarves and mittens for every Yuletide. One year, he'd knitted together bright-blue covers for Erik's peg legs and canes. Erik had protested the ridiculousness of them, but Pet caught glimpses of them at the bottom of his trunk from time to time.

Axel's elbow bumped Doran, who was writing yet again in his precious journal. Honestly, the man probably spent every coin that came to him for the amount of paper he used. It was surprising he ever had money for food. The rest of the crew sat in much the same repose. Little Hal sat beside a short pile of sacks, shelling walnuts. Big Hal and Hemming sat across from each other with rags in hand, polishing their swords. Ulf had three lengths of rope and was twisting them together to make a thicker line for one of the sails. Ludvig had a bucket of suds at the stem of the ship, scrubbing at a dark spot on the deck. There was always work to do on the ship—mending, cleaning, oiling, sharpening—and a hum took from somewhere near the stem.

Axel's own rumble joined in, twining with the melody. Ella sat straighter, looking around as the music swelled. The melody was a familiar one. Pet's foot took on the beat as Axel's voice rose above it all.

> *"In southern lands,*
> *A city stands.*
> *A beacon to the*
> *Proud and free.*
> *Men of zeal,*
> *Of stone and steel,*
> *Come home to Holmberg,*
> *By the sea."*

The song kept up around them, the other men's voices joining in with Axel's. Their voices crashed against the inside of the boat unlike the calm waves on the outside of it. Pet closed her eyes, allowing her mind to wander back in time.

> *"'Mid mighty walls*
> *And hallowed halls,*
> *A people, place,*
> *And spirit stands.*
> *A stalwart town*
> *Of grand renown*
> *E'er watches over*
> *My kindreds' lands."*

Pet could almost hear her brothers goading one another. The rumble of Da's laugh. The wind tugged at her hair like Mama's soft fingers. Her chest ached as the song pushed the sensations further into her mind.

> *"Hail Holmberg!*
> *Blessed Holmberg!*
> *Beautiful city*

By the sea.
Though Njord and Tyr
Bring blood and fire,
My cherished home
She'll always be."

"Aren't you from Holmberg?"

Pet jumped at the sound of Ella's voice right next to her. "Aye," she said, a bit breathless.

"I've heard stories about what happened." Ella set her project onto her lap. "It must have been horrible."

"'Horrible' is the most basic term I would use for what happened to Holmberg." Doran shoved his papers into the oiled tube he kept them in to protect them from water. "The destruction looked like Logi the Jötunn had left his lonesome cave and smashed Holmberg to dust. No boats bobbed at the shore. No homes stood on the hill. The farther you ventured in, the more desolate it became. In the very heart of the city, only the shadows of the victims remained, forever painted onto the rocks there."

The song had quieted as their conversation took hold of the ship. Pet shifted, her chest tightening. She tried to shove the sensation away like she always did. Tried to breathe normally.

Ella turned to Pet. "How old were you when it happened?"

"Ten." The lie slipped easily off her tongue. She'd been thirteen when Holmberg burned.

"How long where you trapped on the isle after?"

Axel set the wool and needle aside. "Nearly a year."

"A *year*?" Ella gasped. "Why were you there so long?"

"The Sidans didn't attack again until they took Grovö three months later," answered Doran. "When they did, we had to wonder why they hadn't attacked Holmberg first. Once we regrouped, I went looking and discovered that no one had heard news from Holmberg for some time. Once I was able, I departed for their island. When we beached at the island, Axel and Petyr nearly tore my men to shreds."

Pet tried not to think of that time. Tried not to remember how awful it had been. She'd shivered through those first months, not even allowing Axel to light a single spark anywhere near her. He'd had to go to the beach those first weeks to cook fish while Pet had hidden in the small shelter they'd made for themselves. It wasn't until she'd caught a fever in the winter months that she let Axel drag her next to a fire, and it was only because she'd been delirious. Axel had forced her to stay near the fire, though she made him sleep between them as a barrier.

"But how could the Sidans do such a thing?" Ella asked. "How could they kill so callously?"

Doran sighed. "From what they claim, they didn't do it."

"Liars, the lot of them," Axel bit out.

Pet kept her head down, shielding her face from whatever emotions might be surfacing. She could never look at Axel when this topic came up. Bands around her chest made it so she couldn't breathe. She couldn't relive what had happened. Couldn't see the grief in Axel's eyes when he remembered what had been left of their home. Their families.

"I'm sorry, I just can't imagine it," Ella said. "I know what the stories say. The war reaches even the nursery where my younger siblings sleep. I just can't put the two images together. I've never met a Sidan that wasn't kind to me."

"They were playing you for a fool, princess," Axel said. "Of course they'd be nice to you. You're the High King's daughter. They're trying to sweep Åldras out from under our feet by whatever methods they can, even if that means kissing your father's shiny boots simply to steal his belt from under his belly."

"It's just all so horrible." Ella set her own needle down, her brows drawn together. "Why do people have to fight? Can't we all be happy with what the Allfather has given us?"

Pet interjected, trying to cut the conversation short. "Not everyone views their blessings as such, and as long as there's power to be had, there will always be those doing their best to abuse it."

Doran set a hand on Ella's knee. "We cannot always understand why others make the choices they do. We'll never be able to see into their minds or hearts. All we can do is decide who we want to be and do right by others."

"Which is why we fight the Sidans," Axel said. "Because we want to do what's right, even if that means making hard choices. We don't want people to suffer anymore, but we can't guarantee anyone's safety while those with powers like what we witnessed at Holmberg remain unchecked."

"But if they have such powers, why wouldn't they simply raze all of Åldras to the ground with it?"

Axel huffed a laugh. "Well, it didn't go so well for them the first time. They set off whatever magic they had, but it killed all their men too."

Pet's heart picked up speed. Flashes of fire and smoke raced across her thoughts. Her home alight with flames. The Sidans' screams. Mama's tear-filled expression. She closed her eyes, trying to block out the images, but they just came faster. The smell of burning flesh. The heat of the flames against her skin.

Ella's hand came up to cover her mouth. "So much death."

Pet stood, finally having enough.

"Petyr?" Ella asked.

Pet shook her head, nearly tripping over the sack of yarn near her feet.

"Wait, Petyr. I'm sorry." Ella reached out and set her hand on Pet's arm. "I didn't realize how difficult this must be for you. I shouldn't have asked."

Pet ripped her arm away. Stepping over their legs, she escaped the conversation and practically ran toward the back of the ship.

CHAPTER 24

FATHERS

The scrape of the hull jarred Axel from his very comfortable snooze against Pet's leg. He wiped a bit of drool from the corner of his mouth. Wōden's eye, he really must have passed out. He hadn't had a good drool since before they got the Häxa girl out of Stern. With a groan, he stretched out his legs, wiggling his bare toes against the rough wood of Ludvig's trunk.

"About time you woke up," said Pet. Before Axel could ask the question on the tip of his tongue, Pet had already answered it. "Erik's taking us to shore."

Axel rubbed at his cheek, the stubble on his jaw scratching at his palm. He'd have to shave that night. He glanced at Doran, whose golden beard shone in the sunlight.

Doran's beard was glorious.

Axel didn't have beard envy. He didn't. He could grow a beard. He'd done it once when he'd been eighteen. It had been a glorious thing, redder than the gold of his hair, but not as red as Father's had been. He'd grown it a finger's length down his neck before he'd shaved it off. Pet couldn't grow one, after all. It would be too much of a contrast to see him standing next to her. Not if they wanted to keep up this ruse. He'd shaved it the day someone had asked Pet if she'd gotten her first whisker yet. When the other fighters in Doran's battalion had asked why she didn't at least try to grow one, Pet had spun the story that she did it as a show of honor to their village. That she would shave her beard until the bloody Sidans that had killed their families were brought to justice. The lie was effective, but the shaving was tedious.

Shaking off the small bit of tightness in his chest, he got to his knees to unlock his trunk. He'd shave off his stubble, just as he had for the last six years that his beard had tried to grow in. He found the box of runed shaving supplies in his trunk sitting under the ring of iron from Olav's harness. Gods, he really needed to sit down with Little Hal.

With the box in hand, Axel jumped from the side of the ship, following Pet through the ankle-deep water onto the shore. Little Hal already had a fire going and was prepping to catch some fish if the spear on his back and the strung pole in his hand had anything to say about it. He passed Princess Ella their net, showing her the needle and where the holes were. Olav had gotten trapped in the thing on the way to Harligdam and Little Hal had had to cut him out.

Axel's gaze lifted to the waters they'd already journeyed through and back to Little Hal. The lad's shoulders drooped, the load of grief still heavy as he walked back toward the water. Axel set his shaving supplies near the fire next to Pet.

"Don't let Big Hal touch these." The idiot still thought using Axel's enchanted shaving kit would somehow make his beard grow in thicker, but the only magic the knife and shears contained was the ability to trim Axel's uncuttable hair and nails. He couldn't remember who had given him the set, but he'd had it all his life and Father had made sure Axel knew to take care of it. It had been one of the only things to survive the fire.

Pet tilted her head. *Where are you going?*

Axel grabbed the extra pole Little Hal had brought to shore and dug through the soft ground at their feet for a grub. The beach wasn't as rocky this far south. He found a fat little beasty in the loam and lifted it for Pet to see. She didn't obviously recoil, but a wrinkle formed right between her brows. She'd never liked insects much.

He stuck the squirmy grub on the hook and chased after Little Hal, who had already made his way waist deep into the river and cast his line out. A small piece of birchwood bobbed in the water, showing where the line sat under the surface. Olav had been a master fisherman before he'd joined Axel's crew. When Little Hal was too small to use the nets, Olav had engineered this method of fishing so the boy could join him. It only caught one fish at a time, unlike the nets that would catch multiple, but a few of Axel's crew had learned how to do it and regularly enjoyed the peace it brought over the spearing or netting of the fish.

Axel joined Little Hal, the water barely reaching his thighs. "I saw some herring off the side of the boat a bit earlier. The water's warm enough we might even get a few cod close to the shore."

Little Hal nodded but didn't say anything. He slowly pulled his line back in, a thread made of a mixture of horsehair and Axel's own hair clippings. The horsehair worked for a time, but it would slowly break down. With Axel's hair in the mix, the line remained strong and didn't break apart as easily. Little Hal had a small bag of golden hair tucked in his own trunk to use to make new line.

A good size herring—maybe about half an ell or so long—hung from Little Hal's hook. The fish flapped about in the air before Little Hal grabbed hold of the silver body and popped the hook from its mouth. With the swing of a rock, he gave the fish a swift death.

Axel cast his hook. The fat grub hit the water with a *plop* and sank. Axel let the birchwood bob in the water, slowly moving south with the current. It had only been a week since they'd lost Olav, and while Little Hal had still done his job, Axel could see the weight of the grief pulling him down further every day. He wouldn't push the lad into talking. Sometimes, the talking made the loss worse. But Axel didn't want to leave him alone. Not after the trials he'd been through.

Little Hal finished gutting the fish and rinsed his hands in the river. His eyes were glassy as he watched the cloudy water clear under his fingers. He found another worm in the soft soil at their feet and baited his hook. He brought the rod back, the hook dangling longer than Axel would have let it. The line swished to the right, then swung over and grabbed the back of Axel's shirt.

Axel felt the scrape against his skin and gave a yelp as Little Hal flicked the fishing rod forward to cast but instead pulled Axel's shirt up over his head. Axel's fishing rod dropped from his hands. The tunic got caught under his armpits, but the fabric bunched up around his face and exposed most of his bare back. The pulling stopped, and Axel heard the clatter of wood on rocks.

"I'm so sorry!" Little Hal grabbed the tunic and pulled it back down. "I didn't realize..."

Axel twisted to try to locate the hook still attached to him. "That you'd caught the wrong kind of fish?" A laugh burst from his chest. "At least you didn't beat me over the head with a rock like you did that poor fellow." He pointed to Little Hal's catch.

The lad's face turned bright red. "Here, let me just..." With a tug, he freed the hook from Axel's tunic, brandishing the still wriggling worm wrapped around the hook.

Axel tugged his tunic back into place and grabbed his fishing rod off the ground where he'd dropped it. He checked the bobber. Still floating.

He did his best not to flinch as Little Hal recast his hook. Tears pooled in the lad's eyes.

"Want to talk about it?" Axel asked once both of their bobbers floated in the water.

Little Hal wiped his nose with his sleeve. "I don't know how to talk about it."

"I understand."

Little Hal looked up at him, a small hint of silver lining his eyelid. "You do?"

Axel took a deep breath and prayed to whatever gods watching them that he'd have the right words. "Aye, probably better than most. Witnessing your father—even if they aren't your true father—being taken from this world right before your eyes is not something I wish upon anyone. And I watched two of my fathers die in one slew."

Little Hal's brows drew together. "Two?"

Axel nodded. "My father and Pet's da both played major roles in my childhood. My father was King of Holmberg, king of some of the greatest warriors in Åldras after the wars with the giants. He was a strong man, but he needed help raising me. Pet's family did that for him. I was as much his brother as his other brothers were."

"And you saw both your fathers die?"

Axel's heart sank at the memory. "War always brings heartache in its shadow. You know the story of how Holmberg burned down. The walls of fire that decimated everything in their wake. I was on the beach with both of them, fighting off the Sidan invaders when it hit. I watched my father and Pet's da succumb to the flames."

The line on Axel's rod pulled tight. He quickly tugged it back, hoping the hook grabbed the fish's cheek. He slowly pulled the line back in, wrapping it around the spoke at the base. An ell-long cod flopped onto the beach. Axel did his best to deliver a swift death to the creature, thanking the gods for its delivery as he did.

Little Hal offered his thin fillet knife. "How do you live with it?"

Axel crouched over the fish, taking Little Hal's knife. "Some days are worse than others. I'll still wake up in the middle of the night, my chest tight and my heart screaming, knowing something is missing from this world that can't be replaced. But the pain does lessen. I don't think it will ever go away. Frigg's all-seeing gaze, I hope it won't. I don't want to wake up without feeling that loss at least a little bit, but I do my best to not let it destroy me. I do my best to make them proud, knowing that one day I'll face the Allfather and He will decide if I join them in Valhalla."

Little Hal gazed out at his bobber, the last rays of sunlight sparkling off the water's surface. "I want to make him proud."

Axel slapped a hand on his shoulder. "You will, lad. I know you will."

ᚠᚾᚲᛟᚠᛃᛚ

AXEL STARED up at the sky above him. The stars winked down on their stretch of beach, watching over the crew as they slept. Did the gods watch from up there as well? If Axel squinted hard enough, he swore he could see the upper branches of Yggdrasil.

Pet shifted next to him, turning onto her side in her bedroll. "Quit sighing like a lovesick girl over there."

Axel moved his hands from behind his head to lay over his stomach. "Do you think they're watching over us?"

"Who?"

"The gods, our fathers, your mother and brothers. Do you think they see what goes on down here? Do you think they care?"

Pet groaned and plopped onto her back. "Does it matter?"

"Of course it matters. If they don't care, then what's the point in trying to preserve a legacy they don't even think of anymore?"

"I don't know, Axel." Pet rubbed a hand down her face. "Mama always said the Allfather watched over His creations. She said the gods played into our lives far more than we ever realized. That most of them want to see us succeed in this life and join them in Valhalla."

"And what do you think? Do you think we'll make it there?"

Silence stretched out between them. It felt like the stars brightened above them, as if those watchful eyes widened in preparation for Pet's answer. Axel's own heartbeat increased with every second that remained silent between them.

Pet finally let out a breath. "I can only pray that I do. If nothing else, I hope that I can at least help others get there."

Axel frowned. "That's not very hopeful."

"It doesn't matter." Pet shook her head and turned, putting her back to him. "What does matter is that we get enough sleep to push the boat back out into the water in the morning. Not all of us got to take a drooly nap today."

Axel snickered and tucked himself down into the thick furs in his bedroll. Pet's snores cut through the quiet only a few minutes later, and Axel couldn't help but smile. She might not be hopeful, but Axel would have enough hope for the both of them. He would do everything in his power to make sure Pet made it to Valhalla, even if he had to drag her out of Hel's halls and climb the entire world tree and break down the gates. He would make sure she got the world, even if that meant he had to lay it at her feet himself.

Chapter 25

A Pursuit

P et hiked up the crest of the hill, pushing through the brambles that caught at her clothing. She joined Axel as he surveyed the scene before them. Pet couldn't see as far as he could, but she saw enough. Thick bog covered the land south of them. Mist curled up over the willows and birch trees before evaporating in the sunlight above the canopy. On the other side, tall mountains towered into the sky, their peaks still holding on to their white powder from the winter. Ljust Löfte was somewhere in those mountains.

"What do you think?" she asked.

Axel turned back, his gaze narrowed at the path behind them. "I think we should go around."

"How? We can't just leave the ship." They'd already faced enough creatures on this one journey. Who knew what other monsters would come upon *The Phoenix* and rip her to shreds simply for the fun of it? "Besides, it would take us weeks to walk around the perimeter and get to Ljust Löfte."

"I didn't say we *would* go around, just that we *should*."

Pet set a hand on the tip of her ax and shaded her eyes against the sun with the other. "Do you think she'll make it through that?"

"With Erik at the tiller, I think she can make it through anything. The biggest challenge we'll face is making sure Erik *stays* on the tiller.

We'll need to fashion some poles for the shallow bits, but with all the runoff from the mountains, there should be plenty of water."

"And the draugr?"

Axel folded his arms over his chest, his back still to the bog. "They're not the beasts I'm worried about at the moment."

Pet followed his gaze. From where they stood, they could see a long stretch of the strait they'd traversed. Pet couldn't see all the way to where they'd slain the fossegrim, but she could see where a large longship crept through the water. The screeching eagle at the stem of the Sidan ship glimmered as it swept across a section of sunlight not even two sea-miles out.

Pet recognized it instantly. "How did Enzo get through the bloody storm?"

Axel's lips drew into a thin line. "The man isn't known for his prowess on the water for nothing."

Pet refrained from tearing out her hair. "We can't go through a draugr-infested bog with Sidans on our tail." They'd be terribly outnumbered, battling on both sides.

Axel began walking back down the hill toward the ship. "Which is why we're going to get through the bog first."

ᚠᚾᚲᛟᚠᛁᛐ

PET SAT NEXT to Erik at the tiller, her back turned to the rest of the ship as she watched behind them for that screeching eagle or its gruesome prince. The scar on her abdomen gave a phantom twinge as she watched for the man that gave it to her. Axel stood at the stem as the crew's eyes and ears. Though Pet couldn't see him, she knew he was signaling to the rest of the crew where to move based on the way the rudder shifted under Erik's guidance. Her gaze stayed glued to the bog at their backs. The water rippled quietly as they drifted, gently stirring up the soft silt layered over the peat covering the bottom of the riverbed. A soft current carried them most of the way, but it was dissipating the farther into the bog they went. What started out as a glide had trickled to practically nothing. The trees blocked most of the wind, only the tops faintly rustling with whatever gusts snuck past them.

Erik nudged the tiller, the scrape of reeds brushing against the hull of the ship making the hairs on Pet's arms stand on end.

When the muck settled over the peat under the water, Pet's entire body seized.

At the bottom of the riverbed lay a man.

Based on the rough style of his ragged clothing, he was old. Older than should have been possible. Moss wove between the strands of his white hair. His bloodless eyelids remained closed, as if he was simply taking a rest under the water and would come up gasping for air at any second. But the gaping cavity that had once been his chest didn't hold any air.

This was the main reason Doran had taught them to communicate silently. While the hand signals and facial cues did help them when being discreet around the enemy, they couldn't risk a peep when faced with draugr infested waters.

The body disappeared as Erik navigated them around a patch of thick grass. Limbs swayed alongside the reeds under the water, some of the skin having tanned dark with age. Draugr skin did that as it mummified, until the monsters couldn't move anymore. After that, they just waited for their brothers and sisters to feed fresh blood to the water.

Pet and Axel had fought a horde of them once. They were clumsy creatures, easily decapitated then left to finish rotting. But a whole horde? It was dangerous to say the least. Axel had been able to fight them en masse, his skin impenetrable to their deathly bite. Pet had had to use a bow and pick them off one by one from a greater distance with the villagers they had been plaguing. Nasty creatures. Axel's clothing had smelled of rot and disease so badly they'd simply thrown every-thing—boots and all—into a fire.

Pet slowly drew out one of the axes from her waist. If her inner map was on track, they were likely in the center of the marsh. The water here was mostly fed by the runoff from the mountains now instead of the sea. Mountains which housed Ljust Löfte on their southern peak. Pet resisted the urge to turn and look at them.

What was the colony like? If she remembered right, she'd helped smuggle two dozen women and girls to the Great Mother over the last three years. Many of them had gone with entire families, which had been difficult to smuggle out in the more densely populated areas. How many of them were still there? Some of them had defected to Sida, willing to put their trust in a king who wouldn't murder them. At least, not yet. But who could say the future kings would be the same? The Great Mother's idea to simply separate from society as a whole seemed wise.

Erik shifted the tiller again and the hull of the ship scraped against reeds on the right. Pet refrained from hissing. The sound was too much. Her eyes snapped to one of the bodies under the water, but it didn't stir. She still didn't let out the breath she was holding.

They straightened out into the deeper parts of the marsh. Pet prayed the wind would stay with them, pushing them toward the peaks for just long enough to get past the largest parts of the water. The crew could fight off whatever dregs of the draugr they found as they got closer to the mountain, but it wouldn't do to alert the creatures right there in the middle of it.

Pet's attention snagged on movement.

Hel's bloody halls.

Sida's Shield crept into view.

Pet tapped Erik on the shoulder. He looked back and his face reflected all the creative curse words she knew surfaced in his mind at the sight of the Sidan ship. He turned back and tapped on Little Hal's shoulder who would deliver the news to Axel.

But Axel couldn't get rid of them. If they even so much as stirred too much of the water or made a splash, the draugr below them would waken, and every person on both ships would be fighting for their lives.

Little Hal tapped her arm, and she turned to see him pointing at Axel.

Axel's eyebrows furrowed. *What do we do?*

She held out her palms. *You think I know?*

A smirk. *You always do.*

While Pet might have appreciated his confidence in any other situation, this time it made her chest tingle—and not in a way she found comfortable. She turned back to look at the Sidans. A head of black hair popped up next to the stem. *Prince Enzo.* She would recognize that hawkish nose all the way across a battlefield. *Scourge* was too nice a term for the man. She hoped the draugr ate him. Another head popped up behind him. One of the crewmates it looked like. Both heads ducked back down. If only she had the ability to hear what they were saying.

How was she going to get the crew out of this mess?

On the other ship, heads started moving about. She watched as they slowly collected materials. A rope. A long bow. A bucket of pitch. A lantern.

Oh, bloody rocks. They were going to try to light *The Phoenix* on fire.

Pet spun from her perch. She found the largest, lightest thing she could see on deck.

One of Erik's peg legs.

She grabbed one from where it hung, strapped to the side of the ship under Erik's rail. She cut the thing free, not bothering with the knots, and lifted it over her head.

Erik tried to grab it from her, but she hurled the thing as far as she could toward the Sidan ship. It landed right between the two ships with a splash.

The Sidans stopped moving, their faces all turned toward the sound.

Chest heaving, Pet watched the peg leg float back up to the surface, the water rippling around it.

A white hand shot out and wrapped around the wood. It disappeared under the water, taking the peg leg with it.

She closed her eyes, listening, but the sound of the blood in her ears was almost too loud. Hands grabbed her shoulders and spun her around. Her eyes flew open, and Axel's enraged expression took up the full scope of her view.

Pet jerked when she heard the first scream.

She whirled back around, glancing at the Sidan ship.

A draugr pulled itself up over the side of *Sida's Shield*, launching its legless body into the mass of Sidan sailors.

The Phoenix rocked under Pet's feet.

Axel grabbed her arm, hauling her over to where Ella now stood near the mast. Little Hal joined them as the rest of the crew drew their blades and formed a tight circle around them.

Axel tilted his head left, then right. "Don't let them bite you."

The first draugr leaped out of the water.

It had once been a woman, the sag of her chest over her bared ribcage the only indication she'd once lived as a normal person before being relegated to this nightmare. The draugr's filmy eyes were wide with frenzy, and it charged Axel first.

Ella screamed and Pet slammed her hand over the girl's mouth.

Axel cut the head off the creature's body in one fell swoop. While the draugr were abnormally strong, their clumsiness made them slow. Much slower than Axel.

Another dragged itself over the side of the ship with one arm, the other limb hanging off its shoulder by a single tendon. Big Hal disposed of that one. But they kept coming. First in twos, then threes. Pet kept Ella pressed against the mast, her eyes taking in every single draugr that popped over the side of the ship.

Erik eventually left the tiller, scrambling for the Erik-sized hatch in the deck floor they'd had made for these situations. The man wasn't an idiot. He knew better than to try to fight these beasts. Best to let the ship drift than die then and there.

The circle of crewmen spread out over the ship. One of the draugr tackled Ludvig and another used the opportunity to sneak past toward Little Hal.

Little Hal raised his short sword, but Pet swung her ax and buried it in the draugr's skull. The creature fell and Little Hal separated the head from the body before it could get back up again. Decapitation was the only way to make sure they didn't. Pet flicked her ax, and the head rolled onto the deck right as another came at them.

The ship was beginning to slow, the weight of the draugr pulling the hull down into the water. Pet kept checking how far the Sidans were behind them, but there were enough draugr keeping them busy. *The Phoenix* just had to survive the bog.

A scream sounded from Pet's right, and she saw Hemming dragged over the side, his fist swinging at the creature with its jaws wrapped around his arm. Axel tried to get there, tried to save him from being ripped to shreds, but three draugr filled the space where Hemming had just been. It would have been too late anyway. Even if Axel had been able to save him from being devoured by the beasts, one bite from a draugr was deadly enough on its own. Pet prayed the man's death was swift.

She hacked off another draugr's head and moved around the mast. More broke through as the crewmates began to tire. One reached out for Little Hal, grasping a fistful of the lad's shirt, but before Pet could help him, Little Hal knocked the draugr back and lopped off its head.

Ella screamed again, and Pet saw the girl go down as a legless draugr grabbed at her skirts. Pet raced over and kicked the thing off. Ella scrambled away as Pet raised her ax to take its head.

Another body slammed into her.

She went down onto the deck, twisting this way and that, trying to guard any exposed skin as she fought the creature on top of her. She got her ax up right in time to stop the thing from biting off her nose. Bog water dripped into her eyes as she tried to push the murderous beast away. Its boney fingers dug gouges into her neck and arms as it tried to get its teeth in her flesh.

"*Pet!*" Axel's voice boomed over the clicking of the monster's teeth.

Pet screamed a battle cry as she pushed. This thing was not going to beat her, no matter how long she had to hold it here.

With a screech, the creature fell to the side.

Pet took in a full gulp of air as Little Hal fought the thing back with his sword. Ulf joined him, and the two of them finished it off. She pushed herself up—the scrapes on her neck and arms screaming— ready for the next creature. Her nose was bleeding, and she wiped the blood from her mouth.

Light bloomed around them.

Pet ducked down as fire spread over the water all around them.

Rocks. Rocks. Rocks.

Åldran Fire.

Pet looked toward the Sidan ship and watched as they dumped the liquid onto the water and fed the flames. How they'd come in posses- sion of the liquid fire, Pet could only guess. It was supposed to be one of Åldras's closely guarded secrets. *Bloody Sidans.* Her teeth ground together, but she couldn't help but send thanks to the gods above for the Sidans' thieving ways.

The draugr wailed, those hanging off the edges of the ship falling back into the water to try to douse the flames licking at their skin. The draugr still on the ship fought, but once they went down, none took their place.

Pet chopped the head off one, throwing the skull back into the water. She grabbed one of the thick furs at the front of the ship and wrapped herself in it, not allowing even the hint of a flame to touch her skin. She glanced back at *Sidan's Shield* only to watch that screeching eagle turn tail and run the other way through the flames. The crew on *The Phoenix* took turns disposing of the last few monsters left on the ship and took up the other furs and canvas bags to beat back any of the flames trying to eat at the deck. The outside hull of *The Phoenix* had a coating that made it flame resistant—thank the dwarves that made it—but the inside was still vulnerable to fire.

They weren't too far from the base of the mountains. Only another twenty minutes or so by the look of it. Hopefully, Erik would find a safe spot to beach and the draugr wouldn't be too much of a problem.

Pet found a spot in the middle of the deck, near the hold, and hunkered down. Her nose still bled profusely, and she tried to staunch it with her shirt.

Ella plopped down next to her, brows creased. The girl's shoulders were hunched over, her face whiter than the sail above their heads.

"You saved my life, Petyr."

Pet waved her off. She could live the rest of her life without the princess admiring her for simply doing her job. Or admiring her at all.

Ella looked at her. "Are you all right?"

"Pet?" Axel called.

She looked over at where he stood next to Erik, who was studiously watching the rudder for any chance of the flames catching. The rudder had been soaked in whatever magic it was that made the ship flame repellant, but that didn't mean the old man wouldn't be watching everything like a hawk.

Axel strode toward her and pulled her shirt from where she'd been pressing the collar against her nose. "Let me see."

Pet tried to push him off, but he grabbed her face in his hand. The tunic came free, exposing the rest of her face.

Axel's eyes widened as he ran a finger down her left cheek. It came away bloody. He let go of her face and started tugging at the fur wrapped around her. "Let me see, Pet. Take that off right now."

Pet did as he asked. Her arms were sticky against the fur. She shrugged out of it and found her skin caked in red.

Her stomach dropped to her toes.

Ella gasped and scrambled to her feet. "What on Midgard?"

Axel grabbed her arms and pulled them away from her body. "Where is it, Pet? Where—" He turned her left arm and found what he was looking for.

A perfect circle of teeth marks around the inside of her arm.

How had it gotten there? When?

"By the Allfather..." Axel looked up at her, his eyes filled with an emotion Pet had never seen there before.

Terror.

Pet looked down at her body. She saw the scratches slowly dripping blood from where the draugr had gouged her with its nails, but that wasn't all. Scars that she'd gained from fighting over the years began to open up along her knuckles, her hands, her arms. They turned from white, to pink, to red.

The draugr sickness.

She set a shaking hand to her torso. It came away wet.

She looked back up. "Axel."

He jumped to his feet. "I need our entire chest of medical supplies, now! Clean gauze, and every bloody poultice we have available!"

"Axel."

"Erik! Put your legs on your neck and get us to the base of the mountain. We need a healer. I don't care if the Sidans follow us all the way there and burn *The Phoenix* to bloody ashes. We need to get—"

"*Axel!*"

He spun back to look at her.

She touched the wet spot on her stomach again. The same spot where she'd gained the massive scar fighting Enzo all those years ago. Her vision went dark at the edges.

The last thing she saw was Axel rushing back toward her.

CHAPTER 26

SECRETS

There is nothing that will kill a man faster than the cursed bite of a draugr. Their magic is tied to Hel's, their spawn the victims of their curse of death. I've seen men bleed out of every cut they'd ever sustained, every wound they'd ever taken in battle. Their life drained from them faster than Hermod could ride down the Great Tree upon his father's steed. One bite, and they're gone. It's easiest to cut off their heads in the time between the last beat of their heart and the first twitch of their limbs.

— FROM THE WRITINGS OF DORAN FINNSSON, THE
LAST KING OF GROVÖ

Axel caught Pet before her head hit the deck. The crew began rushing about, grabbing supplies and dropping them at Axel's side. He ignored them as he laid her on her back and tugged her shirt out from under her belt.

Ella came up next to Pet's head. "How can I help?"

"Can you even use that gods-given magic to heal him?"

She shook her head. "I don't even know where to start!"

"Then hold his head up so the blood doesn't go down his throat and choke him." Hel's bloody halls, the girl was useless. Pet needed a healer. She needed one *now*.

Ella lifted Pet's head and situated herself so she could keep it elevated, Pet's blood smearing on her sleeves. Hel's halls, there was blood everywhere.

Axel yanked the fabric of Pet's shirt up. Underneath, the tight, linen wrap was soaked through with blood. Rocks, she'd need new bandaging to keep the wounds from growing infected.

Axel cursed. "Little Hal! I need fresh linens and a suture kit *now*!" The wounds wouldn't heal and where the needle went through would still bleed, but the sutures would keep more of the blood in her body rather than let it leak out. Praise the Allfather she'd never had any arteries nicked. He just had to get her to a healer. She wouldn't die. She would be fine.

Little Hal ran up with a small chest and handed it to him. Axel passed it to Ella and drew the small knife he carried in his boot. He clenched his jaw as he looked down at the wrappings and then at Pet's face. Wōden's eye, she was going to hate him for what he was about to do.

He grabbed the bloody wrapping and sliced through it. He sawed all the way through, working from her naval up to wear her tunic sat on top of her chest. He reached under her tunic and cut at the rest of it until everything fell away.

Ella gagged when she saw the scar—or rather what should have been a scar. The wound was opening little by little, slowly draining Pet of the blood that kept her alive.

Axel snatched the chest from Ella's hands. "If you throw up, I'll kill you right here."

Ella's already pale face went whiter, and she closed her eyes against the sight of Pet's wound.

Rocks, it was almost worse than when Enzo had given it to her. Axel grabbed the suture kit from the supplies and began threading the needle with catgut.

Doran approached from behind Ella, who had begun to sway. "Give him to me, Your Highness. I can hold him up while Axel does his part."

Doran began to take Pet from Ella's arms.

Axel froze. "No, wait—"

But Doran had frozen too, his eyes on the open collar of Pet's tunic as he held her from behind. He blinked. Then blinked again. He raised his head up to look at Axel, shock stark on his face.

Axel met his gaze, hoping his expression told Doran exactly what he could do with his shock.

"Axel—"

"Do not say *a word*," Axel hissed, returning his gaze to the wound on Pet's stomach. "We need to get him to Ljust Löfte and quickly. We don't have time to—"

"*Him?*" Doran demanded. "Thunder's beard, Axel. How did this happen?"

Axel could have punched the man right then in there if he hadn't been holding Pet's life in his hands. "Do you really think now is a good time?"

"Don't patronize me, Axel."

Axel quickly set to stitching up Pet's midsection. She moaned slightly but didn't wake. Axel searched his memory for the other wounds he'd helped stitch or fix. He knew there were slices on her legs he'd have to get to, but he'd get this done first and take her somewhere no one would see when he had to remove the rest of her clothing to stitch her up. He tied off the catgut and reached for the supplies.

Doran leaned forward to try to distract him. "Axel—"

Axel drew his knife again, angling it at Doran. "If you keep pushing this right now, I swear I'll slit your throat and throw you to the bloody draugr."

Doran glared at him. "Fine, but we will talk about this later."

Axel bared his teeth right back, the hairs of his neck rising. "Fine."

Doran backed off, but Axel didn't like the look he cast at Pet. One of sorrow, but also one of betrayal.

No, Axel didn't like it one bit.

ᚠᚾᚲᛟᚠᛁᛚ

AXEL LEAPED OVER A FALLEN LOG. He softened his feet as he landed, doing his best not to jostle Pet who hung from a sling of fur and rope Doran had tied to keep her strapped to Axel's back. His tunic stuck to his skin, but it wasn't with sweat. Her chest was pressed against him, and he prayed that the erratic beat against his ribs would somehow keep her heart from giving out.

"Just a little farther, Pet. You've made it this far. Just a little farther."

He traded the smell of burning flesh for the smell of earth and trees. He'd left the entire crew with the ship down at the base of the mountain, knowing they would simply slow him down. He came up against a small cliff face and hauled himself up and over it.

Faster.

Faster.

Faster.

He stopped at the top, looking about for any sign of the small colony. They were nearly halfway up the slope of the mountain already, but Pet's breathing had begun to slow.

Oh, Great Allfather, do not let her die.

Axel continued up. The map hadn't specified where on the mountain he would find the colony, only that it was on this peak that the Häxa had made their home.

He growled in frustration as he continued without any hint of his destination in sight.

But then he smelled it.

Smoke.

Not the smoke of the bog he'd left behind. Of dying things. This was woodsmoke. The smell of the living.

He followed his nose as he sprinted to the east side of the mountain. The smell grew stronger and soon enough, he heard the people.

His feet flew over the ground, the soles of his boots barely brushing over the pine needles before he was already away. He could feel Pet's heart start to pound with every yard he spanned. If it beat any harder, it would give out.

"*Stay with me, Pet!*" he yelled. If she could hear him, she didn't stir, but he prayed one of the gods in the branches of the Great Tree above him would. She had to live. She had to stay with him.

Pine trees flew past him until he broke through into a clearing. It was almost instantaneous, as if he'd entered another world and left the forest behind him. Where there had been trees and brush, now there were homes and humans.

People paused and stared as he raced past, not able to stop. He zipped past house after house until he found what looked like a village square. He dug his boots into the ground as he stopped just in front of a large plinth set in the very center.

"Please!" he hollered. "Please, I need the Great Mother!"

A few of the townspeople looked about, but others began making their way toward him, wariness in their eyes.

As if by magic, the Great Mother stepped out of a building not half a dozen yards away.

"Great Mother!" he shouted, pushing his way through the growing crowd.

Her face turned down in a frown as she took him in. "Axel? What—"

"Please, Great Mother. Pet needs a healer."

She stopped when she caught sight of Pet hanging from his back. Her eyes widened and she hurried toward him. "This way. Put your legs on your neck." She pointed at one of the buildings in the square. Darting that way, she waved off every person that attempted to waylay her. Praise the Allfather.

Axel followed the Great Mother, oh so tempted to grab the frail-looking woman around the middle and haul her to wherever she was leading him. He shifted Pet on his back and felt the cold wind chill his blood-soaked shirt. Gods, how much had she already lost?

The Great Mother stopped at a nondescript door and shoved it open. The scents of camphor and peppermint punched Axel right in the nose. It was definitely a healer's house. Axel spotted a clean cot across the room and strode in that direction as the Great Mother called for whoever was in the house. Axel crouched down by the bed and pulled apart all the knots he'd had Doran tie.

Bloody Doran.

Bloody draugr.

"Just here," he heard the Great Mother say. She led a middle-aged man into the room, followed closely by a woman of similar years. Axel's eyes stayed riveted to her. She was the Häxa that would help Pet after all.

The woman gaped when she looked at them and hurried over. "How long has she been bleeding?"

"She was bitten a little over an hour ago," Axel replied, breaking one of the ropes he had trouble untying, "and I've done my best to staunch it, but the disease…"

The woman supported the back of Pet's head as the sling loosened and gently laid her back. There was only the slightest rise and fall of Pet's chest now, and Axel was sure he wasn't the only one in the room that could hear the pounding beat of her heart. The woman dug into her pocket until she pulled out a small pouch of seeds. She dumped the tiny things into her palm and set the other hand on Pet's forehead.

Axel went to his knees by the bed, his blood-coated hand taking Pet's. Her fingers were deathly cold, and he tried to rub some of his warmth into them, avoiding her wounds as best he could. The cuts on her fingers were caked in dry blood, though the scratches weren't healing over.

"By the Allfather." The healer's eyes shot open. "Her right kidney is starting to fail, and the left isn't far behind." She turned to the man. "Quickly, Kristoffer. I'm going to need hot water, rags, and my ginger-peppermint poultice." Her gaze swiveled to the Great Mother. "Call for the rest of the healers. I can't do this alone."

The Great Mother raced back to the door with a speed that belied her age.

The healer set a hand on Axel's shoulder. "We need to get her closer to the fire. It will help keep her warm while we work."

Axel shook his head. "She hates fire. She'll only get distressed if you put her anywhere near the flames. They nearly make her sick if she gets too close. She hates it."

The healer's brows furrowed, but she quickly circled the cot and grabbed the end by Pet's feet. "If you grab that end of the cot, it'll be easier to move her."

Axel acquiesced and grabbed the top of the cot frame and helped the healer move Pet closer to the flames.

The Great Mother burst back in, followed by a trio of women. All of them caught sight of Pet and went wide-eyed.

Axel turned to the Great Mother. "What can I do?"

The Great Mother watched the women get to work, the folds of skin between her brows carved deep with worry. "You can come with me so these talented women can do their work."

Axel's head was already shaking. "I'm not going to leave her here alone."

The Great Mother raised her brows. "Are you disregarding my order?"

"Of course not. I just—"

The Great Mother took his elbow, which nearly hung at the same level as her head. "Then you'll leave these women to do what they do best and give Pet the privacy she needs. Do you think she would appreciate having you around while she's in such a vulnerable state?"

Axel paused at the threshold of the healer's house. "She's trusted me this far."

The Great Mother tutted. "Yes, as needed, but do you still think she would be happy to know you watched her be stripped bare and her body traumatized while you simply stood by and watched?" She shook her head. "Allow these sisters to do their work. I promise, straight from my liver, that they will take care of her. They know what's best, and you can return when she's been properly healed."

Axel looked back over his shoulder at Pet. Three of the women were already gathered around her. The other—the one whose house they were in—stirred the fire up to get the flames roaring. He took a deep breath and shut the door behind him.

The Great Mother patted his arm. "There's a good lad. Now, while I know you don't wish to go far, I need you to get some ice in your stomach so we can get you cleaned up and in a new set of clothing. We need to make sure none of the disease survives."

Axel stopped himself from running a bloody hand through his hair and followed the Great Mother away, doing his best to follow her advice to stay calm.

Gods, please save her.

Chapter 27

A Woman

Pet slowly realized she was awake. She was awake and she wasn't on *The Phoenix.*

It wasn't that her eyes were open and she could take a glimpse of her surroundings. Oh no. Her eyelids likely weighed more than Firmin and Anders combined. It was the way her body felt so still. So warm. Freyja's golden tears, she hadn't felt so warm in ages.

"Pet is a smart lass, Dagny, just like her..." Pet faintly recognized the wizened voice, even though the words faded in and out. "I'm sure... already knows."

Oh. It was the Great Mother. They must have made it to Ljust Löfte.

Wait. When did they get here?

"But does she understand what the magic..." That voice, Pet definitely didn't recognize, and it was growing harder to focus. "It took so much longer...Look at her...If I hadn't gotten the fire going so hot, we would have lost..."

Pet's pulse skipped at the mention of fire. She tried to push her eyelids open and succeeded with a slight flutter.

"Hush. There's no cow on the ice now," the Great Mother said. "You were able to purge the disease and that's all that matters. Go join the others...get some rest. I'm sure I can attend to her...Axel has gone to see to his needs."

A small portion of relief burrowed itself into Pet's chest. Axel was there. She wasn't alone.

"...think he knows?"

The scuffle of dragging feet faded, and Pet realized the other woman had left. She really needed to get her eyes open if she wanted to figure out what on Midgard was going on. A small groan slipped through her lips.

"Pet?" the Great Mother asked.

Pet tried to speak coherently, but she didn't know what to say so it slipped out as another moan.

A weight settled next to her. "There's a bit of valerian root in your system, which will make it feel like you drank a full barrel of mead last night and aren't quite orange free yet. You can go back to resting if you wish."

Pet didn't want to go back to resting. She wanted to know what was going on and where she was.

But she must have dozed off for a moment, because the next thing she knew there was a warm hand encircling hers and the fresh smell of pine and linseed oil brushed over her senses.

"She stirred?" His voice rumbled through their joined hands.

"Only about half an hour ago," the Great Mother answered.

Half an hour? Pet so wanted to open her eyes and see Axel's face. Show him she was fine.

"Dagny said it might be a few more hours until she's completely awake. Her body is still replenishing the lost blood. The magic will continue to run its course until every injury has been healed, but that takes a toll on her energy. It will be a slow process, and we'll need to watch her for a few days, but she's got a good nasal bone, and I think she'll recover quick."

Pet commanded her fingers to squeeze Axel's. Just one tiny squeeze. With what felt like a jötunn's effort, her fingers gave the gentlest curl.

Axel's other hand came to join the first. "Pet?"

But she was already sinking back into the dark.

ᛉᚻᚲᛩᚠᛦᛏ

FINALLY, her eyes opened of their own volition.

Pet blinked back the grit that gathered at the corners and tried to wipe it away with the back of her hand. Her mind remained in a fog, however, and it took her a moment to remember where she was.

Ljust Löfte.

She didn't sit up but turned her head to look around the room. The cot she lay in squatted near a fireplace to the left of her. No flames licked at the edges, but she could feel the warmth still emanating from the coals and saw a large burn mark in front of the hearth. Herbs hung in a long line above the mantle, little tags of cloth hanging from each bundle. It smelled and looked like a healer's hut, though she hadn't visited one since Axel learned how to take care of all their medicinal needs on his own. He'd helped the surgeons in the war camps on more than one occasion during their time under Doran's watch and picked up the skills quickly. They'd had to, in order to keep Pet's secret from getting out.

She looked over to the other side and found Axel slouched in a chair beside the bed. Thankfully, it was one with a back or he likely would have fallen over. His chin sat against his chest, his nose whistling just the tiniest bit with the soft, deep breaths of sleep. She watched him for a minute, not used to seeing him in such a quiet state. He was always moving, usually up with the dawn and running until the moon hung high in the sky. There was always something to do, someone to save.

A door opened, and Pet turned to see the Great Mother walk in, a basket on her arm and little Viveca, the girl they'd most recently saved, walking beside her. Viveca met Pet's gaze and beamed.

Axel stirred next to her, and Pet looked over to meet his bleary, green eyes. Wōden's eye, she'd never seen him so disheveled.

"Pet?" He cleared his throat, the sleep in his voice making it deep and gravelly. "Are you awake?"

"Oh good," the Great Mother said. "We were right on time with supper then."

At the words, Pet's stomach gave a rather outrageous gurgle. Viveca giggled and the Great Mother smiled.

Axel's hand settled on her shoulder. "I can help you sit up if you'd like."

Pet frowned. "I can sit myself up." She pressed her arms to the bed, but for some reason they buckled when she tried to put any weight on them.

"Don't be stubborn," Axel said, taking her arm.

Pet smacked at his hand. "Don't baby me, Axel."

He narrowed his eyes at her. "You've been unconscious for three straight days, and I've been out of my mind waiting for you to wake up. I've earned a bit of babying, don't you think?"

Pet stilled. "Three *days*?"

The Great Mother set her basket down on the table closest to them. "Yes, child. Your body had a lot of recovering to do, both inward and outward."

Axel took the opportunity Pet's shock obviously gave him to help her up. She didn't snap back at him, though she likely should have. "What happened?" she asked instead.

The Great Mother sighed. "If Axel had gotten you here even ten minutes after he had, you would have been dead. According to our healers, your organs had started to fail, and your heart was beating so fast it was nearly at its breaking point. You really shot the parrot with Axel bringing you just in the nick of time."

Pet was fully sitting up now, and Axel grabbed a pillow that had been laying on the ground. When he tried to place it behind her, it yanked on her head.

"Ow! What on—" Pet touched a hand to her head then slowly trailed down the length of her hair.

"My hair..."

Her *long* hair. Waves of brown fell all the way to her waist, curling around her hips. She hadn't had hair this long since before Holmberg. Since she'd been a child.

"Yes, well we had a couple hiccups during your healing," the Great Mother answered. "One of the sisters got overly enthusiastic and your hair growth sped up. Your nails were also affected, though we were able to trim those, along with your eyebrows, while you slept."

"Your nose is different too," Axel said.

Pet reached up and ran a finger down the bridge of her nose. She'd broken it too many times to count over the years and the resulting bump had disappeared. She looked down at her hands. All the scars and callouses she was so used to seeing there were gone, smoothed over as if they never existed.

Her chest tightened. "Does anyone have a glass I could use? Or anything?"

Axel grabbed a large metal bowl from one of the shelves above his head and handed it to her. She flipped it over and saw a *woman* staring back. Her nose was straight, the end of it pert rather than slightly sideways. The scar she'd had on her left cheek was completely gone, as was the tan color of her skin from living under the sun for so long. It wasn't a beautiful face, not in the godly way Axel's was or the exotic Lady Idalia's. It wasn't perfectly symmetrical or anything special. She still had her squarish jaw and large forehead, but the ruggedness had been smoothed away.

Thunder's beard, she looked just like Mama.

Tears burned at the backs of her eyes, and she shoved the bowl away from her. She refrained from lifting the smock she was wearing to check for the long scar on her abdomen. She could feel its absence. "How did this happen? It's like my entire history was just erased from my body."

"In a sense, it was," the Great Mother said, glancing at Axel before returning her attention to Pet. "The healing that saved you erased all the damage to your body, including that of previous injuries. We can't tell if the scars healed because they were no longer scars, or if they would have healed regardless, but yes, your body has been purged of every injury you've ever encountered."

Pet covered her face with her hands. She had never been proud of her looks. Thunder's beard, she'd had to overcome any kind of womanly pride when Doran had plucked them from Holmberg. However, she had embraced the mask her scars had afforded her. She'd earned every single one of them, whether from a brawl with a few of the other boys they'd trained with or from the battlefield. Every single one of those scars she'd fought for. Some she wouldn't even remember. Many came with memories she would never forget.

But this was too much. All of it was too much.

"Get out," she whispered.

"Pet—" Axel started.

"*Get out!*" she screamed. Something inside of her twisted. Shattered. A sob broke in her chest. She couldn't break down in front of all of them. She couldn't show them how weak she was when her appearance made it so obvious. "Please, just leave me alone. Just go."

They stood, but Pet didn't uncover her face as they shuffled to the door.

Axel's familiar stride stopped across the room. "I'll be just outside if you need anything." The door clicked shut.

Pet finally let the tears fall and curled up, her back turned to the cold fireplace.

CHAPTER 28

IDEAS

High up in the mountains, the breeze still held the chill of winter. Axel took a deep breath in, trying to soak up the peaceful air and tranquility, and let it out in a cloud of steam. After two weeks of outrunning Sidans, fighting magical creatures, and losing two crew members, they'd finished their mission. Stepping out of the Great Mother's house, he left Ella in her capable hands and went to check on Pet. She hadn't asked for him again after whatever happened that morning, and he knew better than to push her when she needed space. Instead, he'd gone down the mountain to check on the crew and fetch Ella.

He walked across the village square, nodding at the townsfolk all making their way to their respective houses for the night. Small fires sat in fire pits around the village. Axel spotted a large, dug-out space near the center of the square, likely for bonfires. He watched as a young Häxa woman guided a trail of water bubbles over one of the pits. The light caught on the water, casting ripples of color across the surrounding area, before she released it to douse the flames.

It almost made his stomach drop, the way some of these Häxa flaunted their magic. After living in Åldras his entire life, he was so unused to seeing magic in its rawest form and so casually exposed. He'd had plenty of interaction with the Häxa, but he'd never seen them so open with their gifts. So relaxed in their countenance.

Axel made his way to the healer's house. It was larger than the others around it, the front door a bright shade of green. A small herb garden took up what open space there was of the yard. The aroma of mint and chamomile swept around him as he quietly stepped to the door. He peeked his head inside and found Pet asleep in her cot once again. The healer, Dagny, had told him not to fret about her sleeping. It would still be another day or so before she would have the energy to get up and move more than just to the outhouse.

He shut the door behind him and crept into the room. A small pallet waited for him in the back of the house, but he hadn't been able to sleep on it. The chair next to Pet's bed was the only place where he'd felt even remotely comfortable closing his eyes. He settled onto the woven rawhide, quite the luxury considering most of the box chair seats he'd used in the past had been flax. He leaned his head back against the wall, but he couldn't help looking at Pet as she slept.

When he'd first seen her after the healers had finished with the worst of the wounds, it had been like he'd been shoved back in time. She looked so much like Mila it almost hurt. After so many years of war and ruin, Pet's face had taken on many of the scars of cruelty she'd been subject to. She even cut her hair in a jagged, sharp shape to keep other's attention away from the things she wished to hide.

But now that mask was gone, and it was Mila that had risen from beneath it.

Mila had been the only mother he'd ever known, the one woman in all of Holmberg who wouldn't let him charm her into giving him treats or let him sweet-talk his way out of trouble. His backside had met the end of her wooden spoon a good many times. She'd raised five strapping warriors, some of the best to come out of Holmberg if Father hadn't been exaggerating. Axel had fallen into their family as easily as if he belonged in it, raised side by side with the others. And Mila had never once told him he didn't belong with them. With Pet. She never once balked when he tore through a wall or accidentally broke one of the other boys' noses playing Knǫttr on the pond. He and Father had eaten many a supper at Mila and Mallory's table. Probably more than at their own in the great hall just up the hill. He remembered playing with Pet at Mila's feet, chasing Pet around the gardens outside the house as Mila and Pet's older brother Gram had tended to the small patch of vegetables.

The memories continued to swirl in his mind as he looked at her. They'd been so young when Holmberg fell. Children, really. Yes, even then she'd been the only girl Axel ever saw, but it wasn't until now that he realized how much she'd lost because of him. What would have happened if they'd told Doran she wasn't a boy? Would she be living a life of ease? Married with little lads and lasses running around her feet with green-blue hazel eyes? Would she have been happier if he'd let her go?

He watched the rise and fall of her blanket as his eyelids grew heavy, and he finally allowed himself to succumb to sleep.

ᚠᚾᚲᛟᛗᛏ

AXEL HELD himself under the water, waiting for even the slightest twinge in his chest to tell him he needed air. That if he didn't get out of the water right then, he'd disappear from off the face of Midgard and float all the way to Valhalla. But it didn't happen, and he finally grew bored enough to push himself to the surface. His head broke out of the water, and he wiped the water and hair from his eyes, then stilled when he caught sight of the audience standing a little way off from the riverbank.

"Shoo!" someone shouted, and a riot of squeals and giggles erupted as the Great Mother stalked into view. "Go on now, go to the forest! I know the lot of you have much better things to do than ogle a firm set of pecs." She shook her head as she approached the edge of the river and prodded Axel's clothing on the bank with the toe of her boot. "You've really crapped in the drawer, young man. You ought to know better."

Axel looked about to make sure there wasn't another young man she was chastising. "Me? I just came down here for a bath! I didn't realize I'd become such an attraction."

The Great Mother gave him a look that said she obviously didn't believe him. "No matter. We have much to discuss about what we're going to do with Ella now that she's here and what to do about Pet."

His stomach twisted slightly. "What do you mean 'what to do about Pet?'"

She turned around and began walking back in the direction of the village. "Get some clothes on and we'll talk at my house."

Axel quickly redressed and jogged back to the village, his wet hair soaking the shoulders of his tunic. He passed by more than one blushing young lady as he approached the Great Mother's house. He tried to give each of them a polite smile without simply ignoring them.

After a short knock, he ducked into the house before the Great Mother could even invite him in. The fire in the middle of the house was still roaring, chasing away the remnants of that morning's chill. Axel got as close as he could without catching his clothing on fire, hoping to dry the insane curls coming to life on his head. He always preferred to pull them back into a knot after they'd dried a bit more.

The Great Mother stepped out from a side door. "Ah, there you are." A lynx walked beside her, taking raw meat straight from the elderly woman's hand. The wild cat loped across the room and ducked through a small opening at the back of the house. A flap of thick leather covered the hole, and it smacked against the wooden planks of the house as it shut behind the ferocious looking beast.

"I've seen many a housecat in my day, but not one with such large teeth," Axel joked.

The Great Mother grabbed a towel hanging on a line along the wall. "I would not call Skuggi a housecat. More like a guard."

"Oh?" Axel looked from the flap back to the Great Mother. "Do you have many guards like him?"

The Great Mother wagged a finger at him, a mirthful smirk on her face. "You won't be learning all my secrets, my son. Some things you must trust your elders with."

He rolled his eyes. "Is this one of those 'I'll tell you when you're older' conversations?"

She laughed. "Of course not. What's hidden in the snow is revealed in the thaw. It's just that an old woman is allowed some secrets."

Ella stepped through the front door a moment later with a bucket of water in hand, her eyes bright. "Hello, Axel."

Axel folded into a slight bow. "Your Highness."

"Oh, no more of that, please. I'm simply Ella here."

That was probably for the best. Axel could easily imagine why she'd wish to let go of her title, especially in a place where people had run to escape Firmin's tyranny.

"I have a proposition for you, Axel," the Great Mother said, taking a seat at one of the benches scattered around the room. The Great Mother's house wasn't the main hall in the village—that sat in at the northern end of the village square—but she obviously had company often enough to warrant so many seats.

"I'm all ears," Axel replied, taking a stool across from her while Ella skipped over to a washbasin with her pail of water. She took up washing a set of clay bowls. It was good to see her feeling useful.

"The village council has decided we would like to put together a gathering of sorts. In honor of Ella's introduction to the community and the efforts of *The Phoenix* and her crew. Your men have helped so many of us over the last few years, and we feel we owe it to the lot of you to put together a celebration."

Axel narrowed his eyes. "You want to throw us a party?"

"Yes."

Axel deliberated over the best way to answer. "While I'm sure my men would be grateful for such an honor, we have much to do. This journey has taken twice if not three times as long as we were planning. There are matters to attend to at home, and we would like to leave as soon as Pet is recovered." He'd visited with Erik and the others—Doran had been off elsewhere, thank the Allfather—after getting his first full night of sleep since they'd arrived. They needed to get a plan set to move the ship. He'd done his best to scout out the path south of them. The marsh waters fed into a small river farther down. If what little information he'd gathered from the other villagers was correct, they should be able to travel south and swing past Sida instead of face the cursed storm they'd barely lived through.

"Pet is still recovering," the Great Mother said.

Axel nodded. "Yes, of course, but Dagny and the other healers expect all injuries to be properly healed within the next day or two."

The Great Mother tutted. "What is two or three more days after that, hm? Allow your men to come up the mountain, be fed a proper meal for once, and then you can take supplies with you."

"While I'm sure some of the crew might appreciate it, I can't speak for everyone. I would have to talk with all of them—Pet especially."

The Great Mother stood. "Then let's go talk to her."

A crash sounded across the room.

Axel shot to his feet, spinning to find Ella standing over a shattered bowl. The girl's eyes were wide when she looked up at Axel.

"*Her?*" she asked.

The Great Mother sighed. "Rocks, I forgot you wouldn't know."

Axel's stomach dropped. His gut reaction was to deny it, but the secret was out now. At least, here in the village it was.

Gods, what were they going to do if that knowledge left the village?

Ella looked between the both of them. "Pet is a *girl?*"

"Yes," Axel said. "It's a rather complicated situation."

"No need to walk like a cat around hot porridge about it," the Great Mother said. "It was for Pet's safety. She needed to stay with Axel, so they came up with the ruse. I'm sure if you asked her, Pet would be sorry for the deception."

Ella stared ahead, her eyes glazed over as if reviewing every moment since she met Pet. "She doesn't look like a girl."

The Great Mother snorted. "That was the point." She stood, tucking her hand into the crook of Axel's arm. "Come along, my son. We'll talk to Pet and get plans in motion."

Axel remained where he was standing. "Right now?"

The Great Mother tugged at his arm. "Yes, right now. If we're to put a party together, the sooner we can make plans, the better." She turned to Ella. "Will you go fetch Viveca for me? I believe she's about to be let out of lessons with the other children at the Great Hall."

Ella nodded and slipped out the door, her face still pale. Hopefully, the girl wouldn't think too harshly of Pet. It wasn't personal. Besides, the girl had a new life now. A new family. She would find some new boy here to give shark teeth to.

The Great Mother grabbed one of the half cloaks hanging from a hook next to the door. She nudged a bucket on the ground with her boot. "On with the butter. You can throw seed for the birds as we walk."

CHAPTER 29

AN INVITATION

P et stared at the unblemished skin of her hand as she brought the spoon to her lips. Dagny had announced her healed enough to have a proper meal, though Pet couldn't say that a bowl of porridge was what she would consider a *proper* meal. Freyja's golden tears, she could probably eat an entire elk right about now. But she didn't complain as she dug into her third bowl of the mush.

Thank the Allfather, she sat at a table rather than languishing in bed like an invalid. She felt almost normal in the trousers and shirt Axel had brought up the mountain for her. As if just with the change of clothing, she fit into her skin a bit better. She stuck the spoon back in her mouth with a growl. Gods, she really needed to get over herself. It wasn't like she suddenly became an entirely new person just because she looked a bit different. This face had always been hidden under the years of fighting beneath Åldras's banner. It was just so...*feminine.*

How had she never realized how much she looked like Mama? Da always said the two of them were a matched pair, but Pet had never seen it that way. Mama had been a mountain of stubbornness and wisdom. She could take every one of Kol's temper tantrums and the twins' ridiculous antics. Pet had seen Mama dress Dane down when he got too full of himself and even get Da to admit when he'd done something stupid. And every time, each of them had walked away knowing they could be better because Mama instilled that sense of goodness in them. She was the rock of their family—and in more ways than one.

But Pet had never been a rock for anyone. All she'd brought with her into this world was destruction. The mask of Petyr Mallorysson was the only thing that kept her from being the girl she'd once been. The girl she hoped to never be again.

Was that mask gone? What would happen when she returned to the ship? Would the rest of the crew notice? Hel's halls, of course they would notice. But would her ruse be up? She'd made it this far without any suspicion. She could lean on that, right? She could roll around in the mud for a bit, cover up her pale skin. Though, Erik might not let her onto the ship covered in muck.

A knock sounded on the door and the Great Mother stuck her head in. "Hello, dear. Mind if we come in?"

Pet swallowed the food in her mouth. "Yes, I mind."

The Great Mother came fully into the room. "At least the draugr didn't wipe away that prickly attitude."

Pet grimaced and pushed away the mostly empty bowl of porridge. If she never had to hear the word *draugr* ever again, she would die happy.

Axel stepped in behind the Great Mother and shut the door behind him. Pet really ought to apologize for the way she'd broken down the day before, but she wouldn't do it with other listening ears.

Axel took the rest of the bench next to her at the table, and the Great Mother took a stool across from them.

"How are you feeling today, child?"

She could answer that question a hundred different ways. *Unsettled. Awkward. Irritated. Scared.*

"Like I could eat an entire herd of reindeer, wash it down with a barrel of mead, and still not be full."

Axel laughed, which was what she'd wanted, but the Great Mother only studied her. "Yes, the magic used up many of your body's nutrients to heal you. I'm sure it will still be some days yet before you're feeling completely back to normal."

Any amount of normalcy seemed unlikely at the moment. Pet did her best to keep her expression neutral as she fiddled with the end of the braid she'd asked Dagny to help her with that morning. The weight on her head was still a shock, but for some reason she hadn't had the strength to ask for a pair of sheers just yet. It wasn't like she could keep the braid, but something about cutting it off felt premature. Besides, none of the crew were running around the village. She would certainly cut it before she saw them again.

"If you're feeling up for a journey is the better question," Axel said. "We've got quite a trek back to Åldras, and I'd hate to make you go too soon."

Pet swallowed. "Dagny said she'd need to monitor me only for one more day." She'd actually said, "at least a day more," but Pet didn't want to stick around longer than they had to. She could see the way Axel was itching to leave.

He stood up and began pacing. "The Great Mother wishes us to stay for another three or four days."

Pet turned back to the older woman. "For what?"

The Great Mother steepled her hands over the table. "I think it would be a great thing for the village to put on a feast in honor of *The Phoenix's* crew."

Pet bit her lip. While the crew would likely enjoy taking some time for themselves, a few of them might not be too keen on leaving the ship near draugr-infested waters—especially after being pursued by *Sidan's Shield* only a few days ago. "What do the others think?" she asked.

"I haven't discussed it with them yet." He bit the inside of his cheek. "Pet, there's something else. Doran knows."

Pet tilted her head. "Doran knows what?"

"He knows you're a woman."

Pet's stomach fell to the floor. "What? How?"

"It's my fault. I had to stitch you up when the draugr bite opened your wounds. He saw..." He shook his head. "It doesn't matter. He figured it out and he knows."

Pet's fingers clenched the edge of the bench beneath her. The mask she'd so carefully held onto was slipping from her grasp. "Does the rest of the crew know?"

He shook his head. "No, and I have no plans to tell them. I'm going to speak with Doran as soon as I can and make sure he keeps his mouth shut. I'll make sure he can't even write it down in his bloody journals."

Wōden's eye, how had everything fallen apart already? Perhaps it would have been better if the draugr had taken her out. She could have died as Petyr, and she wouldn't have to look in every reflection and see Mama. Wouldn't see the flash of sorrow every time Axel looked at her. Wouldn't have to deal with the ill fit of her skin over her bones.

"It's fine, Pet," Axel said. "It's all going to be fine."

She met his gaze. "Of course it is."

A lie had never tasted so sour on her tongue.

"Well, now that we've seen our Pet to the middle of the butter eye," the Great Mother said, "you ought to race down there and ask them."

"Right now?" Axel stopped pacing and looked Pet over as if looking for any excuse to stay.

She shrugged. He had to speak with Doran, didn't he? Had to make sure this bloody mess didn't catch fire and burn down their carefully crafted lie.

The Great Mother swatted at him. "Yes, right now. Go!"

"But—"

"*Go!*"

At the Great Mother's words, a group of mice crawled out from only the Gods knew where and charged at Axel. He gave the small creatures an unamused look and sauntered toward the door as they skittered over his boots. "All right, I'm going." He grumbled as he walked out the door.

Pet frowned down at the mice as they scurried out of view once again. Dagny would certainly be upset if they found their way into her pantry.

"Good, he's gone." The Great Mother leaned over the table. "The party was not the only thing I wished to discuss with you, child."

Pet met the Great Mother's honey-colored eyes. "What else do you need?"

"It isn't so much about what I need, my girl, but what *you* need." She reached out a wrinkled hand and set it on Pet's arm. "I'd like for you to stay."

Pet's brows pulled together. "I would like to stay as well, but it's not entirely up to me. The crew—"

The Great Mother shook her head. "Not for the party, dear. I mean for you to live here. Stay and become part of the community."

Pet had to take a moment to wrap her head around the words. Stay? Why? She repeated the words over and over again in her head, trying to poke holes in them. There was no way the Great Mother actually said that. "You're asking me to live here? With all of you?"

"Yes. I think you would be an excellent addition to our village."

A tightness took hold of Pet's chest as her stomach flipped. "But I'm not Häxa like these other women."

The Great Mother tilted her head slightly. "With or without magic, I'm offering it to *you*, Pet. As a woman who has done so much for this family, you deserve a place in it too."

"Why?" Pet asked. "Why now?" Why not when they'd first met? The Great Mother had known she was a woman since the first moment they met. She never outright said, but she'd known. She'd never called Pet "Petyr" or treated her like any of the other men. What changed? Just because a few more people knew her secret? Because she'd had to be healed?

"Because I didn't realize until your healing how much this life has taken from you." Her face fell into a sympathetic frown. "How much you've had to hide who you truly are because you had to fight for a place in a world you never belonged in."

Pet pulled her arms away. "I belong with Axel." He was her world. Her home. She'd fought every moment of the last eight years to stay with him. To stay at his side. She wouldn't just abandon that. Abandon him.

"Aye, but you can't go on living this lie forever, my child. Your mother would never have wanted any of this for you."

A single beat of her heart was all it took for the information to click in Pet's mind. "You knew her."

The Great Mother gave her a sad smile. "Mila was a great friend to many, even before she married your father. She and Axel's mother, Constance, grew up in the same village outside of Poppel. I believe it was Constance that helped arrange the marriage between your parents."

Pet had so many more questions, but the Great Mother raised a hand before she could put voice to any of them. "The time for questions will come, Pet. I promise you. But for now, I would like you to lay your head in the water and consider what I've asked."

The Great Mother stood, and Pet joined her as she made her way to the front door. "If I say no?"

"Then I'll make sure you have time for those questions before you leave, and I'll wish you safe travels." She opened the door, letting in an oddly warm gust of air and pursed her lips. "Those whisperers are going to loose the laundry if they keep up." She tightened her cloak around her shoulders and hustled after the whirling wind.

Pet leaned against the doorframe, watching her go and enjoying the mix of winds as they tousled the few loose strands of hair against her cheeks, bringing giggles with them. She grabbed the end of the braid still settled over her shoulder. What would it be like if she stayed? She didn't know who she was without Axel, without an ax in her hands and the song of death beating against her ribcage. The village wouldn't know what to do with someone like her. Someone who didn't belong anywhere.

But was going with Axel any better? Did she want to become a man again? Chest always wrapped and looking over her shoulder every time she had to use the outhouse? If Doran knew, how long would he be able to keep the secret? The Great Mother's offer was generous, and it came with a life Pet hadn't ever considered herself being able to have.

Axel would hate it anyway. He'd never want her to stay. It had always been the two of them. A team. She was his shadow, his second. There was no him or her, only *them*. Pet didn't know any better and neither did Axel. There was no other way for them.

The wind caressed her cheek again and she couldn't help but press her fingers to where it kissed her skin.

CHAPTER 30

APOLOGIES

The Häxa have always been a people of community. Before the reign of Anselm Häxasbane, the first king of Áldras to outlaw magic, the witches were often called to be the matriarchs of a town, always finding ways to encourage the growth of magic within the women under their care. Some Häxa would turn nomadic in their later years, going from town to town to spread their wisdom until the Valkyries took them to Valhalla, but most stayed in their communities, doing their best to teach the next generation.

— FROM THE WRITINGS OF DORAN FINNSSON, THE LAST KING OF GROVÖ

Little Hal jumped up and down near the fire, his scrawny arm waving back and forth over his head. "Axel!" The lad raced across the embankment where he'd been fishing. "How's Pet?"

"Pet's doing much better," he answered. "Hopefully, we can set sail sooner rather than later." He looked around at the small and empty campground a little way from the water. "Where are the others?"

Little Hal pointed toward *The Phoenix.* "Erik has been working on rearranging the cargo on the ship. Doran and Ludvig went hunting on the other peak for the day, and Big Hal and Ulf are watching for any sign of the Sidans or draugr."

Bloody Doran. He hadn't been there the last time either. How were they supposed to talk about Pet if he kept disappearing?

Axel ruffled Little Hal's hair. "And what are you doing out here?"

He held up his fishing pole. "Someone has to feed everyone when Doran comes back empty handed."

Axel chuckled and slapped Little Hal on the back. "Wise lad." They'd lost their best hunter when the draugr took Hemming. The man's death was another blow. He had been a good man, a good soldier. It was a sad day on Midgard when a man like him went to Valhalla. Axel would need to speak with Doran about that as well. The man was likely grieving his friend's death worse than the rest of them were.

Axel followed Little Hal over to where *The Phoenix* bobbed on the water. She looked worse for wear, her patches discolored from the Åldran fire and her usual glossy shine dull. As they drew closer, Axel could hear the rumble of voices coming from the boat.

"Not there, you rockhead," he heard Erik say. "If you put the barrels of pitch on the pickled herring, Little Hal will have a time getting us supper when we're in the middle of the bloody sea."

Axel swung himself up over the side and landed on the deck with a thump. The crewmembers turned at the sound.

"Ah, Axel," Erik greeted, "how is our Pet doing?"

Axel smiled. "Awake. He seems to be on his way to a quick recovery."

"Still 'he' is it?" Big Hal said, dropping a box on top of another. "From what Doran shared with us, I thought that might be changing."

Every fiber in Axel's body went still. "What?"

"Aye," Big Hal said, "he was going off about how you've been lying to all of us, and how Pet's been keeping a pretty big secret."

Axel whirled back to Erik. "Where is he?"

Ulf raised a large, placating hand and stepped between them. "Calm yourself, lad. What Big Hal failed to mention was the king accidentally let it slip. He called Pet a 'she' in front of the rest of us. He didn't betray whatever confidence you thought you had knowingly."

"But now all of you know?" Axel's knuckles popped as he clenched his hands. "Where did he go?"

Erik shook his head and hoisted himself up on a barrel. "I've seen that look, Axel. I'll not let you run off and beat that man to a bloody pulp."

Axel took a moment, holding his breath as if it would calm the raging torrent inside of him. He'd told Doran they would talk about it. When he came to get Ella, Doran had also been gone, but that wasn't Axel's fault. He had every intention of explaining, of bringing Doran in on their secret. But now, it wasn't a secret. Now the crew knew. Who would they tell? How long could he keep her safe if every man in Åldras knew? How long until Firmin realized what he could do with that knowledge?

But now it was too late. The control he'd had over the secret was gone.

"Axel?" Little Hal's voice broke through the tumult in Axel's head.

He let go of the breath with a groan. "Fine, I won't go running after Doran." But if he showed back up anytime soon, there was no telling what Axel would do.

"Glad you came to your senses," Erik said. "Now, sit down and tell us why you're down here instead of up on the mountain with Pet."

"The Great Mother has invited us to stay in Ljust Löfte for a few more days. Says she feels the village owes the crew a celebration." And it would give him time to knock Doran's head from his shoulders.

Little Hal jumped on his toes. "Can we go?"

"I thought I'd leave the decision up to all of you."

Little Hal turned on Erik. "Everyone will say yes, right?"

Erik's lips pursed. "Who will stay with the boat?"

"Everyone will have to draw for it," Axel replied. "They're wanting to put on an entire feasting night. We can take shifts to give everyone a chance to go."

Erik scratched at his chest. "Haven't had a good feasting night in a while," he mumbled.

"We don't have to take the Great Mother up on her offer either," Axel hurried to say. "With the Sidans only having been here a few days ago and the mission completed, we can leave as soon as Pet's ready to go."

Ulf and the Hals turned, waiting to hear what Erik would say. It wasn't that Axel didn't wish to go. He wanted Pet to reach a full recovery, for the men to have food in their bellies and smiles on their faces. The issue, he was starting to realize, was that he wanted to stay. He wanted to leave Åldras to its own problems. He wanted to abandon his kingdom and simply live out the rest of his days in this forest.

But that wasn't an option.

There were people dying every day in Åldras because the Sidans wouldn't keep their greedy hands to themselves. There were still Häxa being stolen away, still women and children being burned at the stake. So many people still needed him.

Father had died protecting their home, and Axel would stand in his place for as long as the Allfather deemed him able.

He needed to get away from this heavenly place and face the reality he wanted to leave behind.

Shaking himself from his musings, he looked to Little Hal. "If you think we should go, then we will."

Little Hal beamed, the first real smile Axel had seen from him in weeks. "Then we should definitely go."

"You heard the lad," Axel called to the rest of the crew. "We dine with the Häxa two nights from now."

Ulf and the Hals cheered, their faces bright at the sound of good food and proper beds.

Axel turned back to Erik. "When did Doran say he would be back?"

He shrugged. "Didn't say. Probably won't be gone past sunset."

Axel withheld the urge to grumble. If Doran had been there, he'd already have finished this business and gone back up to talk to Pet. Instead of simply plopping himself onto his trunk and taking a nap, he rolled up his sleeves. "What can I do to help?"

ᚠᚼᚲᛟᚠᛃᛚ

"I WAS WONDERING when you would show your face around here," Doran swung up over the side of the ship, a frown pulling his eyebrows low.

Axel dropped the three sacks of barley he'd been holding in order for Little Hal to get to the crate of clay jars he'd been looking for. His blood sang as he stormed across the deck. Ludvig stood at Doran's back, the bags slung over his shoulders a bit light. Just as Little Hal said they'd be. It only slightly appeased the buzzing in his limbs.

"Axel!"

Erik's bark came too late.

Axel swung a fist at Doran's jaw.

His knuckles only grazed Doran's cheek as the king dodged the swing.

"Hiding, coward?" Axel growled. He reached for Doran again, but Doran sidestepped the grab.

"I wasn't hiding," Doran snapped. "I have nothing to hide from."

Axel finally snagged the front of Doran's shirt. "You probably should have run."

"*Axel*," Erik warned.

Ulf and Ludvig drew their swords.

Doran brought up a hand to stop them. "No, it's all right." He let out a breath, meeting Axel's gaze. "I'm sorry Pet's secret came out the way it did, but I can't say I'm sorry I did it."

Axel yanked him close enough that Doran's weight was almost entirely lifted from the deck. "Excuse me?"

"You've kept this secret from all of us, Axel. For years." Doran narrowed his eyes, not even attempting to wriggle out of Axel's hold. "I still can't even figure out how all this happened."

"Well, when a bonnie lass and a strapping lad meet under a waxing moon—"

Doran finally moved, twisting out of Axel's grasp in a way that was so much like Pet. It was easy to forget he'd trained her just as much as he'd trained Axel. That he wasn't a king or a commander only because of his way with words.

He stuck a finger in Axel's face. "Don't even joke right now. You know what I mean. How were you able to keep this from everyone? Why didn't you tell us?"

"I didn't tell you because if you all knew, Pet would have never been allowed to stay with us."

"Bloody right she wouldn't have been allowed to stay," Big Hal grumbled under his breath.

Axel whipped around, but Doran grabbed his arm. "You can't beat every single man on this ship for feeling something at this news. Keep your fists to yourself for one bloody minute."

Big Hal's eyes narrowed as Axel stared him down. It only took a few seconds for the man to finally look away. Axel met the gaze of every other crewmember until he was sure they all understood what would happen if any of them spoke about Pet like that. Wōden's one good eye, he'd tear them apart with his bare hands.

Doran shook his arm, drawing Axel's attention back to him. His brow furrowed dangerously. "You didn't trust us."

"Did you expect us to?" Axel yanked his arm from Doran's grasp and ran a hand through his hair. "When we were on that island alone, I realized when someone eventually found us, they would separate us. She would find herself in a laundry house or as some kind of servant to a great family while I would fight. We would never see each other again." He took another step toward him. "We were thirteen when the Sidans destroyed our home and had never once gone longer than a day or two without seeing each other. She has always been my other half, my partner. I couldn't imagine my life without her and she without me. The both of us came up with the idea to disguise her and act as if she were my boy cousin. We practiced for months, going through every scenario, doing everything we could so we wouldn't have to rely on anyone else. When you arrived all those months later, we were terrified you'd see right through the lie. The fact that you didn't almost felt like a miracle."

Doran scrubbed at his face. "Freyja's golden tears, if I'd had eyes to see it, I would have. Perhaps it was part of the Allfather's wishes that I not see what was right before me. If I'd had my wits about me after..." He cleared his throat. "If I hadn't been in such a state when I found you, maybe I would have seen through the lie."

Axel shrugged, leaning against the wall of the ship. "Maybe, but once you took us under your wing, your word gave the ruse credibility. Not many questioned her gender since you said she was a boy. No one would argue with the King of Grovö."

"And then I turned her into a creature of war." Doran sighed. "I only thought it was that she was young. That the shadows in her gaze just needed some direction. She had such anger in her. I thought if I taught her to fight, to win against all the other lads, it would help her."

Axel's forehead bunched together. "It did help her. It kept her alive."

"But at what cost? While I'll never begrudge a woman for taking up a sword to protect herself or her loved ones, this life is hard. Brutal. It breaks men."

"You better not be saying she's not strong enough simply because she's a woman."

Doran rolled his eyes. "Of course not. She's stronger than half the brutes fighting under the she-bear's banner and can kill a man faster than any I've ever seen. What I'm saying is that if I'd known, I wouldn't have subjected her to the things I did. That anger in her has only been given more room to grow nourished by the lies. I should never have put her in this position."

"Because she's a woman?"

"Because women and men are different, yes. We all have a role to play here. Men bleed to send evil men from this world while women bleed to try to bring good ones into it. A kingdom will fall in moments without the women that hold it up. There is honor in fighting for the innocent, but there is also honor in being an innocent."

"So why should women not be able to fight for the innocent too? You say it's an honor to fight, but why can't that honor be given to the womenfolk?" Åldras didn't allow women to fight. It simply wasn't done, and Axel had never once understood that. Even before the Häxa had been outcast, women hadn't been permitted to join the men in battle. Some of the fiercest people he knew were women.

"I'm not saying they shouldn't be. The Sidans are right on that score. But they should still be treated with the respect their sex deserves. Mallory Alfriksson was a man of honor and dignity. He would have never wanted his daughter to live the life Pet has." Doran's eyes grew glassy. "I certainly would have never wanted my daughter to be put in the positions Pet has been subjected to. She could have found herself in grave danger, especially in the circles we often had to mingle with during your years in my company. Gods, I let her sleep in tents full of men that would have done unspeakable things to her if they'd known."

Axel folded his arms over his chest. "Pet would have protected herself."

"Our Pet today would have definitely taken care of any attackers, but the Pet of eight years ago?"

"She's the strongest person I know," Axel stated. "It's because of that strength that she lived through that year on the island. I have my magic, but her? It was all her. You weren't there. You have no idea what Pet is capable of."

"Axel, I'm not trying to diminish what Pet has accomplished. Only pointing out that this lie could have ruined everything for both of you."

Doran shook his head. "If even the lads the two of you trained with had found out, she would have been brutalized. A man's pride can be a dangerous thing, and there were more than a few of those boys that would have harmed her in unspeakable ways. I can count on both hands the number of commanders who would have slit her throat if they'd found out the lad that knocked them on their arses was a woman. She would have been charged with witchcraft. The Ekte would have taken her simply for the fact that she had fooled so many of us."

Axel stood, not able to keep still any longer. "But they didn't find out."

"And you should be singing praises to Wōden and Fulla that they didn't. It's a bloody miracle, but that miracle is running out."

Axel clenched his fists. "I know."

Doran stood and cut off Axel's pacing. "Do you?"

"Yes," Axel ground out. "Now that the crew knows, the secret won't last. People will learn of our deception."

"And what will the two of you do about that?"

Axel refrained from punching his hand through the gunwale of the ship. "She needs to stay here."

Doran's eyes widened. "I didn't realize the two of you had already discussed it."

"We haven't." Axel winced. "Not yet at least. But she'll see the wisdom of it, especially now that the crew knows."

Doran's mouth opened and closed a few times before he settled on any words. "I think you should try to have that conversation sooner rather than later."

Axel waved him off. "We will."

The unconvinced tilt of Doran's mouth gave away his disbelief, but he said nothing else. Instead, he grabbed one of the sacks Axel had dropped. Ulf and Ludvig followed suit.

Axel let out a breath and looked up at the stars peeking out from under the silky covers of the night sky.

How was he going to tell Pet?

CHAPTER 31

A DRESS

Pet tugged at the end of the long braid of hair pulled over her shoulder. She was getting used to the extra weight dangling from her head and it was convenient to be able to pull it all back into a plait. A shadow walked past the house, and she ducked back behind the curtain.

"You know you can leave, right?" a voice said from behind her.

Pet spun and found the Great Mother leaning against the doorway to her bedroom. The older woman had a smirk on her face. After Dagny had deemed her healed, Pet had moved into the Great Mother's house. Better to clear the beds of the healer's house to give room to others who needed it more than her.

Pet took a step away from the window. "I thought I heard something outside."

The Great Mother's smirk deepened. "I'm sure." She used the edge of a fingernail to dig something out between her teeth. "Then, I suppose you're waiting for all of the councilmen to arrive here for our weekly meeting."

"I didn't say that." In fact, that sounded like a terrible idea.

The Great Mother set her fists on her hips. "Then you ought to put your legs on your neck and get out. They'll be here any minute."

Pet grimaced. "You don't have to tell me twice." She opened the door once again and slipped out. The Great Mother's chuckles faded behind her.

Well, now what?

Axel wasn't in the village. The Great Mother had said he was still down the mountain talking to the crew. Not that she really wanted to talk to him anyway. Her skin still felt wrong against her bones, like her spirit didn't fit in her body anymore. She recognized the feeling. The same thing had happened after Holmberg.

Pet stepped out from under the Great Mother's short awning. Houses stood in clusters, their fires sleeping at this hour of the morning. Voices sounded from her right, likely the town council coming to meet with the Great Mother. *Best to avoid that scene.* Pet ducked around a corner and started through the buildings.

The familiar smell of lavender drew her forward. She'd always been able to find the laundry houses in towns because of the scent. It reminded her of days spent sitting at the edge of a bucket, her and Mama scrubbing away the sweat and mud the boys always had caked on their clothing from their practices.

Pet found the building and peeked through one of the windows allowing steam to escape the cramped space. Half a dozen women stood around vats of boiling water. One of the women flicked out an arm and a stream of hot water shot from one of the boiling basins to one of the wash tubs. A few others sat on stools next to wash basins, the suds of soapwort bubbling over the edges of the tubs as they scrubbed the muck from the fabric. There were looms set against a wall, none in use as the steam billowed about the room. A pair of women sat in one corner, re-shearing some of the woolen garments, as they'd grown quite dirty and had begun to fray. A group around one of the vats all took up an uproarious laugh, and Pet jumped back out of view.

She moved away from the window.

The Great Mother's offer sat at the forefront of her thoughts. She shouldn't still be thinking about it. She couldn't stay here. This place was full of good, innocent people with families and lives filled with a magic they adored. She didn't belong here. She still had to watch out for Axel and keep him out of trouble. The Sidans continued to be a problem, and she'd sworn to do her duty to fight at the frontlines of this war, even if she'd done it under false pretenses. There was still honor in it, still a purpose. Here, she would only get in the way, not having a place anywhere.

Axel was her place, and she would be lost without him.

Pet did her best to keep her head down, but her eyes flicked over the village as she walked. The sound of people swelled as the houses grew closer together. Pet kept to the shadows as she stepped out into a square—likely the center of the entire village. A large pit sat in the middle, a few men throwing logs into the bowl of it. Women scurried about, their voices calling over the crush of people and magic. One of the women stood to the east side of the square, her hands outstretched as she used the air around her to hang ribbons from a maypole. It was a little late in the month for a maypole dance, but the air buzzed with excitement as each colorful ribbon streamed down from the top. A rain cloud hovered after a small crowd of girls who were growing colorful things in planters hanging in windows and from poles.

Pet nearly smiled when she saw the head of bright-red hair in their midst.

Ella's gap-toothed grin sparkled as she listened to the girls around her. They tittered over the flowers in their baskets, their faces shining as they allowed the magic within them to work over the plants.

One of the girls handed Ella a basket and pointed toward one of the houses along the square. Ella turned that way but stopped when her eyes met Pet's.

Pet pulled back slightly but did her best to look nonchalant. The girl wouldn't recognize her, not with her hair and her face. She would look away at any moment.

Instead, the princess's eyes widened as what looked like recognition finally sparked and pink crept over her cheeks.

Pet's spine stiffened. There was no way. How did Ella know? Axel said Doran was the only one. Pet took a deep breath. Perhaps the Great Mother had told her in case they crossed paths while they were both here.

She ducked her head and shuffled in the direction of Pet's corner of the square. Pet didn't move an inch. The girl looked like she wanted to flee, but she planted herself beside Pet, tightening her hold on the basket of greenery in her hands.

"I'm glad to see you so well, Pet," Ella said, still hiding her face. "Though, I didn't expect you to look so..."

"Different?" Pet offered.

"Yes. I should have thought you would. Once I heard about..." Ella looked up at her then, her blue eyes fastened on the end of Pet's braid. "Your hair grew so fast."

Pet flicked the plait back over her shoulder. She really ought to chop the bloody thing off. "How did you find out? Who else knows?"

The mask she'd been trying to hold onto slipped from her grasp just a bit further.

"Axel and the Great Mother told me after I arrived in the village. I don't think anyone but them really knows."

Pet's chest loosened. Good. This was good.

Ella finally straightened, looking at her full in the face. "I feel I need to apologize, Pet. Well, if that is your name."

Pet shook her head, tapping her fingers on her chest but realized she still didn't have her vest of knives. She dropped her hand. "There's no nee—"

"I thought I liked you!" she blurted out. "You were so nice, and I felt so alone and—"

"Ella, please."

"And you saved me and for some reason I thought it might be just like in the ballads—"

Pet grabbed her shoulders. "It's fine."

Ella's words finally faltered. "But I thought you were a boy."

"Which was what I wanted everyone to think, so I can imagine it was easy to be confused."

"I thought I was falling in love with you."

Freyja's golden tears. "Ella, you're fifteen years old."

"What does that have to do with anything?" She crossed her arms over her chest. "Fifteen-year-olds can fall in love with people their own age."

"I'm nearly twenty-two," Pet answered.

Ella's jaw dropped. "What? I thought you were eighteen."

Pet shook her head. "I turn twenty-two the day after summer solstice." She was actually older than Big Hal too. He probably wouldn't be happy if he ever found that out.

"How long have you had to pretend?" Ella asked.

"Since Axel and I were picked up from Holmberg." Pet moved to take a step back, but Ella set a hand on her arm.

"How did you do it? How have you survived this long?" Pity softened Ella's face.

Something in Pet's gut burned. "What does that mean?"

Ella drew back at the sharp bite in her words. "You've had to pretend to be someone else for so long. Petyr isn't your name, and I bet Pet isn't either." She took another step closer. "Why did you pretend?"

The words felt like a blow to Pet's chest. The back of her neck grew hot. She yanked her arm away from Ella's and stepped around her.

"I have to go."

"Pet, wait!"

She ran.

Out of the shadows and straight through the center of town. Eyes turned her way, and she ducked onto a path away from the stares. She ran, dodging others as she wove through the buildings toward the trees. A scream built in her chest, but she couldn't let it out. She wouldn't let it out. She'd keep it tucked away behind the wall where she'd kept the truth secreted away for so long.

She couldn't let the past out. It would burn her alive if she did.

She came across a shallow river, cattails and reeds lining each side. Without even removing her boots, she splashed into the frigid water, submerging her body as fast as she could. The cold water only washed away some of the heat building in her center, the fire in her gut slowly fading until all she felt was a vice around her chest and a burn at the back of her throat.

She shouldn't have reacted so harshly to Ella's prodding. Even if it had felt like the princess's questions were peeling away every lie she'd told and finding the truth of it all underneath. The questions were harmless, but the truth was ugly when brought to light.

It was better to keep it in the darkness.

Pet pushed herself up to the surface and nearly screamed when she came face to face with the Great Mother standing on the banks.

"At least you're clothed."

Pet quickly tucked her arms around herself, feeling a bit indecent with how her tunic clung to her unwrapped chest. "Great Mother, I thought you were still in your meeting."

One white eyebrow rose on the matriarch's forehead. "You think I would have a weekly session with the town council that would last longer than an hour? Those meetings are the sausage of death, and I would rather garden in Hel's pepper fields."

Does Hel have pepper fields? Pet shook her head, ignoring the Great Mother's way with words. "Do you need something?"

"You can get out of that freezing river for starters." The woman touched the water with a finger and jerked it back. "Thunder's beard, it's chillier than a Hrimthursar's toes. We don't need you catching cold after the healers just fixed you up."

Pet grimaced and began walking back to the shore, the silty mud of the riverbed sucking at her boots.

"Come to my house. I'll make some tea, and we can send for a fresh set of clothes."

Pet nodded, following the elderly woman back into town. Apparently, the Great Mother was very practiced at sneaking about unnoticed, because they didn't come across a single person on their way to her home.

Good. Pet didn't need anyone else looking past her breaking mask.

Hel's halls, what would she do when she saw Doran? He would see straight through the lies, wouldn't he? Perhaps she should avoid him at the feast. Perhaps she would avoid the crew entirely. She could shut herself up in the Great Mother's house for the night. Or watch it all from afar.

The Great Mother opened the door. "Quickly now. You're already shivering."

Pet hadn't even noticed, but the moment the words crossed the Great Mother's lips, she felt her teeth clattering together.

The Great Mother pulled the door closed behind them and shuffled over to the fire. With a few good pokes of the coals and another log, she brought the dying embers back to life. Pet took up one of the benches farthest from it, though the heat would still reach her even from that far once the flames started rolling. The Great Mother grabbed a large fur and set it over her wet shoulders.

"Let me check my things. I think I may have something that will do while we wait for your clothes to dry." The Great Mother swept out of the room.

Pet's gaze fell to the fire. The flames shifted from white to yellow to orange, mesmerizing as they danced. Pet closed her eyes and set her head against the back of the chair with a groan. The cold still wrapped itself around her, shielding her from the heat of the flames. Would it always be like this? Would she always flinch at that crackle of burning wood? Duck her face at the kiss of heat on her cheeks?

It felt like ages before the Great Mother reappeared. "Apologies for the wait. You're so tall, I wasn't sure I'd find anything, but these should fit like a fist in the eye."

"Thank you," Pet said, taking the proffered clothing. She unfolded the clothing and nearly dropped it. A cream-colored smock and a plain, brown dress unfolded onto her lap. It hadn't really crossed her mind that the Great Mother would bring her a dress. She nearly handed it back. While she'd worn a dress when disguised as a laundress in Stern, this felt different. This felt like she was giving up the mask.

"The clothes won't bite you, child," the Great Mother said. "I can try to find something else if it really doesn't suit you."

Pet's hackles rose and she shed the fur. "I'm not afraid of a dress."

The Great Mother shrugged. "My mistake." She pointed toward one of the doors along the wall. "You can change in there if you like. We'll put your wet things next to the fire to dry."

Pet gathered the clothing in her arms and ducked into the room. She quickly shucked her wet tunic and trousers then pulled the smock over her head. The skirt fell to her calves. She was tall, but she'd nearly forgotten most women weren't the same height as the men they knew. She shook her head and pulled on the strapped overdress, grabbing the belt from her own things and cinching it around her waist as she'd seen other women do. With still-shaking hands, she pulled the leather string from her hair and unraveled the plait. She squeezed out the excess water then gathered her clothing to hang.

As she stepped out into the main room, a knock pounded at the door.

The Great Mother stood. "Put your things on the drying stand, child." She waved a hand toward a little rack sitting beside the fire as she swept toward the door. "I'll tell whoever it is to go."

Pet dropped her boots underneath the rack and set to work gingerly hanging her things up to dry, her eyes on the flames before her as the Great Mother opened the door.

"Ah, my son. You've returned."

Pet let out a small breath of relief as Axel walked in.

He passed through the threshold and froze, his eyes on her. "Pet?" He swallowed, looking her up and down. "Why are you wearing a dress?"

Pet rolled her eyes and straightened her trousers on the rack. "My clothing is wet and since you brought me only one set, I've had to resort to borrowing some of the Great Mother's things." She tried not to fidget in the smock. "Since it seems Ella already knows my secret and the crew is all still down the mountain, I'm not in too much danger."

Axel cleared his throat. "I suppose you're right."

The Great Mother clapped. "Excellent. Now that we've got that bit of ridiculousness out of the way, I'm famished, and we should all have supper."

Pet folded her arms over her chest, tilting her head to draw Axel's gaze up to her face. *Are you going to keep staring?*

Axel shook his head and looked away.

CHAPTER 32

WOMEN

Axel felt his gaze flicker over to Pet for the hundredth time since he entered the Great Mother's house. It wasn't that he'd never seen her in a dress. Wōden's eye, Stern hadn't been the first time they'd enacted the laundress ruse, but this felt different. They weren't hiding. Pet wasn't a woman pretending to be a man pretending to be a woman. She was...just Pet. The Pet he'd played with as a child. The Pet who had made him and all her brothers wear crowns of flowers she'd woven for her ninth birthday. Who had danced the maypole after she'd turned twelve and had bested him at hnefatafl a hundred times over. Wōden's eye, when had she disappeared, and why did it feel like she was coming back to him now?

Maybe Doran was right. Maybe the life he'd thrust on her hadn't been the right one.

The Great Mother handed Pet a knife and a cutting board. "Take these to the table. I've got some onions that need chopping, and we can fry them up with some of the herring I have." She shuffled back to another room while Pet set the supplies down.

Axel walked over to them. "I can cut onions."

Pet looked up at him. "No, you can't. You always cut them way too thick."

He grabbed a strand of hair hanging off her shoulder. "Why is your hair so wet?" He looked over at her clothing. "Did you fall in the river?"

Pet snatched the hair back. "No, it was completely intentional."

"So, you dove fully clothed into the river?"

"Yes."

Axel blinked. "Why?"

Pet shrugged, looking away from him. "Clothes needed washing."

"I just brought them three days ago and from what I'd heard you hadn't left the healer's house until today." Which was why he'd been so caught off guard to see her here. He'd come to talk to the Great Mother about helping him convince Pet to stay behind. Instead, he'd found her standing in the middle of the house in a dress.

A very flattering dress.

While it only hung down to her ankles, it hugged her curves in all the right places. Her belt cinched tight at her waist and the neckline exposed the barest hint of her collarbone. She looked like every wonderful childhood memory he had and a future he wanted so badly yet could never reach. If he wasn't careful, he'd keep staring at her.

Pet sighed. "I don't know why I plunged myself into the river, all right? I just needed to...just...not think. Needed to get out of my own head."

Axel touched her elbow, sending a jolt up his arm. He dropped his hand but moved closer to her. "Talk to me, Pet."

Pet shook her head. "I don't know what to even talk about."

"I found just what we need," the Great Mother said, returning to the room.

Pet took a step away, and Axel held back a sigh.

"Here," Pet said. "I'll take care of the onions."

The Great Mother passed the bulbs over then plopped a wet sack with half a dozen herring onto the table next to the cutting board. "Axel, why don't you set to scaling the fish. I'll get the pan hot and the bread from this morning warming by the fire."

Axel settled himself onto the bench across from Pet, grabbing the first fish and a knife. He stripped most of the scales into the sack the Great Mother had brought the fish in, but some still escaped, shimmering as they flew through the air.

The three of them worked in a semblance of silence, only speaking when they needed something passed to them or asking about how they liked their fish seasoned. It gave Axel way too much time to think, but he couldn't break the obviously wished-for silence. How was he going to convince Pet to stay with the Häxa? To leave everything she'd fought for behind? She didn't belong here. She belonged with him.

Her skirt moved over her calf, and he couldn't help glancing at the bare skin of her leg. He followed it up to her skirt. To her waist. To her shoulder. Her neck. Her cheek.

Or did he just belong with her? How would he leave her behind when he did go?

Once the food was done, the three of them gathered around the table, and the Great Mother offered thanks for the meal.

Axel tucked into the food quickly, keeping his eyes on his plate. He hadn't eaten since Little Hal had made him breakfast that morning. Doran had talked him into scouting the path out of the bog with him, and he'd skipped lunch, hoping to get back here quicker. Now that he'd fixed things up with Doran, he needed to talk to Pet. The conversation would be ugly. He'd have to get her by herself.

But when he allowed himself to meet her eyes across the table, he wasn't sure he could be alone with her without doing something very foolish.

"Have your men accepted our invitation to feast tomorrow night?" the Great Mother asked, drawing him away from Pet.

Axel swallowed the full bite of fish in his mouth. "Yes. Little Hal didn't give them much choice."

"Good," the Great Mother said. "Now the girls won't go pouring water out of their ears that I made them clean the guesthouse."

"How did you know for certain they would say yes?" Axel asked.

"Please," the Great Mother drawled. "I knew the moment I said there would be food that they would agree." She leaned over toward Pet. "You can always bribe a man with food."

"We won't be staying long after though, right?" Pet asked.

Axel thought over his words carefully before he said anything. "The crew has decided to leave the day after the celebrations. We don't want to stay longer than necessary."

Pet tilted her head. *What?*

Axel shrugged. *What what?*

Her eyes narrowed. *Why are you flinching?*

The Great Mother blessedly stood, cutting off their silent conversation. "I'll need to run to the bakery and get that cake ordered for the celebration. The crew will want to come up and bathe the day before. I'll make sure the guesthouse has fresh linens and things."

"Is there anything I can do to help?" Axel said, standing as well.

The Great Mother grabbed her bowl and handed it to him. "If you wash out the bowls quickly enough, you can both come with me."

Pet darted for the door before Axel could beat her to it.

As if she couldn't be alone with him either.

ᚠᚾᚲᛟᚠᛁᛚ

THE NEXT DAY passed in a blur of party preparations and Axel trying to convince himself to talk to Pet about staying in the village. At least three times, he'd tried to pull her away from one thing or another to talk to her, to go over his thoughts with her, but it didn't happen.

He rolled over on his pallet bed. Pet slept in the pallet next to his, her back to him and her shoulder rising and falling with her breaths. Hints of the coming sunrise lightened the room just the smallest bit, settling over her sleeping form next to him. He gently reached over and brushed a finger over a strand of hair laying on her pillow.

What was it about this place that made him feel like the world outside didn't exist? That he could be something else besides Mighty Axel and she could be someone besides Petyr Mallorysson. It was almost like looking into someone else's life, someone who didn't have the history they did. The lies they did. He rolled back over, hoping that not looking at her would help him stay focused. He needed to talk her out of coming back to Åldras with him. He needed her to understand that the Great Mother could offer her a new life. One where she didn't have to hide anymore. He didn't know if he was trying to figure out how to talk her into it, or if he was just trying to convince himself.

He swung his legs over the side of the bed and stood. Laying there would drive him insane. If he couldn't go back to sleep, perhaps he'd go back to *The Phoenix*. He could take down some supplies. Help the men so they could make the hike up the mountain with time to spare.

A rooster crowed outside, and Pet stirred.

"Hello?" she asked in a hoarse voice.

He bit the inside of his lip, but before he could decide whether or not to answer, she flipped over, her eyebrows bunched together, and she sucked in a sharp breath. "Mama?"

Oh no.

It had been a long time since Pet had spoken in her sleep. She only did it with the worst nightmares. The ones that she couldn't escape.

Axel jumped toward the bed, placing his hands on either of her shoulders. "Pet!" he hissed. "Wake up."

She whimpered. "Mama. It hurts, Mama."

He smacked each of her cheeks. "Pet, wake up. It's just a dream."

"Mama, please!" she cried out. "Don't leave me!"

Light bloomed from behind him and the Great Mother's gait sounded at the door. "What's going on, Axel?"

"Pet's having a nightmare." He pulled her up to sit. "Wake up!"

She didn't open her eyes. She started crying, small screams breaking up the sobs as she fought off the memories he knew haunted her sleep. He knew because it haunted his too.

Axel pulled Pet into his arms. "Come on, Pet. It's not going to hurt you. I'm going to protect you."

She still cried, but her screams had nearly stopped, turning into shaky breaths. He could tell she was still asleep, the way she sagged like a cloth doll against him was so different than her normal stiffness. He laid back down on her pallet, tucking her against his side as her breaths continued to slow. Hopefully, she would stay asleep. The Great Mother disappeared with her candle and the dawn's light slowly stretched toward them.

Axel stared as sunlight kissed the edges of the front window.

He watched as it haloed the top of Pet's head, banishing the shadows of the nightmare that had plagued her. Now, all he saw was her.

As the years after Holmberg had passed, he'd done his best not to give his heart any attention. Anytime Pet walked into a room, he'd have to think of something else, anything to occupy his mind until his heart could slow back to its steady rhythm. He avoided staring at her and allowing himself to take in her features.

But he couldn't stop now.

It took every ounce of strength he possessed not to reach out and run his finger down the bridge of her nose. Not to twist the loose hairs around her cheeks. Not to press his lips to the top of her head. He couldn't even move, afraid the slightest twitch would break every fragile wall of his resolve. He focused on the rise and fall of her shoulders as she breathed. A small snore whistled out of her nose, and he smiled. It wasn't anything like the snores she'd made with her crooked nose, but it was still so very much *her* snore.

By the gods, he could lay like this forever.

He would if Pet would let him. He would lay here with her until the world burned down around them.

How was he going to leave her?

After what had to have been less than an hour but felt like only a moment, Pet's natural stiffness settled in between them. She jolted upright. "What are you doing?"

With a sigh, Axel sat back up. "You had a nightmare."

Pet froze. "What did I say?"

"You just called out for Mila, same as always." The nightmare hadn't changed in the last eight years. Not even after the battles they'd seen. Not after her near deaths. She only ever cried over one name.

She shook her head. "I don't even remember it."

Axel shrugged. "That's a good thing, right?"

Pet pulled the length of her hair over her shoulder. "Sometimes I wish I could remember, just so I could push away the lump in my throat easier."

He studied her for a moment, watched as her mask slipped back into place and her shoulders straightened. He watched his best friend turn back into the warrior. He watched *her* disappear.

Tonight. He'd talk to her tonight. No matter what happened.

CHAPTER 33

A NAME

If Axel's prophecy ever does come to pass, I can see how his fall would bring about Áldras's destruction. While I have tasted the sweet fruit of true love, I can't find it in my selfish heart to wish it for him. I can still see the frustration the lad feels anytime it's brought up, but I can't help but be grateful for it. He's careful. I've never seen him do more than glance at a woman that bats her lashes his way. But he's the thread holding together the tapestry of our kingdom by mere will alone, the flag we follow as we charge into battle. I can't fathom how we will win this war without a man like Axel. Not when we must fight with only our steel and our blood as our enemies continue to gather more Häxa to their side.

*— FROM THE WRITINGS OF DORAN FINNSSON, THE
LAST KING OF GROVÖ*

Pet smoothed down the edge of her brown tunic. The dress the Great Mother had loaned her sat folded on the edge of the bed. She wouldn't need it after she left tomorrow. Pulling her hair over her shoulder, she braided it back into a simple plait. She'd need to borrow some shears. Perhaps someone could do it for her. She didn't want to miss any of the hair.

A knock sounded on the door and the Great Mother poked her head in. "Are you—oh, no that won't do at all." She came fully inside, a swath of blue fabric draped over one shoulder and a basket of flowers in her hand. "Today we are celebrating the wonder of life, and the glorious gifts Freyja has bestowed upon us." She set the basket down and shook out the blue fabric, revealing a long-sleeved dress.

Pet was already shaking her head. "I'm not a member of your coven."

"Now, don't go trying to make a hen out of a feather," the Great Mother said. "Everyone will be in their finest things. I won't see one of the guests of honor in simple garb. We've already put blues aside for the boys on the crew—though one of the girls is still sewing up Axel's tunic."

The men would appreciate such a gift. Blue dye was rare, so the fact that the villagers of Ljust Löfte were willing to allow the crew to borrow such fine clothing was an honor.

"I'm not a girl that can put on pretty dresses and weave flowers into my hair for a night of revelry. Besides, the men will be there. They don't know about me."

The Great Mother clicked her tongue. "Perhaps out there you are someone who must guard herself and put on a mask, but here you're safe. You're appreciated for *who* you are and not *what* you are. You're more than a girl pretending to be a man. Don't allow the mask you've worn for so long dictate who is underneath it. You're not only Mallory's son but Mila's daughter as well." She set the blue dress down on the bed and reached into the basket. "But, I did have an extra tunic made. I want you to have an enjoyable evening, no matter what you wear."

She set the tunic down beside the dress. "Now, I won't force you into anything, but I will say that perhaps we don't need to tell your crewmates who you are quite yet. Why not allow yourself to be you for one more night, hm?"

"I—"

"I'll fetch one of the other girls to put up your hair or cut it if that's what you decide. My old hands aren't as deft as they used to be, and if you insist on going back to being Petyr for this very ostentatious event, at least your hair will look presentable. Be back in two shakes of a lamb's tail." Before Pet could open her mouth to argue, the old woman slipped out of the room.

"Bloody woman," Pet grumbled. She glared at the dress laid out on the bed. She hadn't noticed it before, but gold thread decorated the hem and ends of each sleeve. The thread swirled over the blue cloth, vines and runes circling the cuffs while waves and clouds bobbed at the bottom of the skirt. The artistry was beautiful, but Pet could barely run her fingers over it. While she'd worn the borrowed dress the Great Mother had lent her, this felt different. More final. Like if she went out in this dress, she was allowing everyone to see she wasn't just Pet. That she was more than the fearsome warrior of Åldras, the shadow of Mighty Axel Ashersson.

She studied the runes on the sleeve. Pet had a vague memory of Mama dressing up for a Yule celebration, her dress twirling and small bits of some kind of greenery woven into her hair. Pet touched her nose again, her very uncrooked nose, then her cheek.

Maybe the Great Mother was right. Perhaps the disguise was warranted. She could avoid the crew for tonight. Have Axel tell them that she didn't want to participate in the revelries and that she would join them again tomorrow. Perhaps just tonight, just to live out the memory of Mama one last time, before the future finally faded those memories from her mind.

ᚠᚢᚲᛟᚠᚤᛚ

PET TUGGED at the sleeve of the dress, doing her best to tuck herself into the shadow on the outskirts of the village square. The Great Mother was only a few steps away, having been caught by one of the other villagers as she entered the circle of light the bonfire cast around the square.

Tables bowed with loads of food—breads, fruits, meats, nuts, every good thing the village had to offer piled on top of the creaking table-tops. Empty tables were sprinkled throughout the square, giving folks a place to sit and enjoy the food and the company. Children darted between couples, and somewhere a fiddle was being masterfully played, though she couldn't see by whom. Only the sweet notes of a lively dancing song gave the player away. A maypole stood above everything else, the ribbons tied to the top slowly weaving down as young ladies twirled underneath. Pet caught a flash of Ella's bright-red hair between the other girls circling the maypole.

I should go back. The words repeated themselves over and over in Pet's mind. She was exposed, her soul laid bare and her secrets out for everyone to see. If she got too close to that fire, everything would be undone. Everyone would see her for the vile thing she was. The liar. The murderer.

A large group entered the square from the west and Pet's gaze caught on the riot of curls reflecting the fire like molten gold. Axel looked about, his eyes scanning the faces around him. His blue tunic stretched over his shoulders, fitting perfectly. A long dagger sat against his thigh, but he'd left his lysande sword behind for the feast. He looked completely at ease. Like he belonged in this space. In this moment.

Pet nearly bolted then and there. He couldn't see her like this. He would know for sure. He would see through every wall she'd ever put up. She took a step back the way she'd come.

But his gaze found her before the shadows could swallow her completely. His eyes went wide, and a smile stretched across his face. Not the charming one he flashed at all the other ladies or the one he bared at his enemies. This was the one that radiated actual happiness. He saved it for when he watched a family reunited or when he heard a good joke from one of the crewmen. It was the one he couldn't help, the one that shone from his face with abandon. The smile stayed with him as he wove through the quickly growing crowd in her direction.

She folded her arms over her chest and lifted a brow as he reached her. "I didn't realize you were all already here," she said, nodding to the rest of the crew being led toward the feasting tables.

He looked back at the crew. "The Hals nearly ran the entire way."

Pet looked over each one and frowned. "Where's Erik?"

Axel leaned against the wall she'd been hiding next to. "Stayed with the ship along with Ludvig. He didn't want to make the trek up the mountain, and he would rather feed himself to the bloody draugr than let Big Hal or I carry him up like a babe. Little Hal and Ulf promised to take them some food later."

Pet nodded, unsurprised. Erik hated when he had to be harnessed to someone's back for the tough climbs. She watched Little Hal scamper over the tables, filling a large bowl someone had put in his hands. The lad grabbed an entire leg of lamb, trying to balance the humongous slab on top of his mountainous pile while shuffling in the direction of one of the eating tables. Big Hal followed behind Little Hal, his plate nearly twice as large, and Doran joined them a moment after. Ulf had found the mead and brought everyone at the table their own cup. The townsfolk encircled them, shaking hands and giving small tokens. Pet recognized one of the younger girls as she gifted Big Hal a crown of laurel leaves. He'd helped break her and a couple of other Häxa girls out of a dungeon last summer while Axel and Pet had distracted the guards. Big Hal's face stretched in a toothy grin as he bowed to her.

Axel straightened, brushing off the sleeve of his very well-fitted blue tunic. "So, are we just going to stand here and watch everyone else eat or are we going to partake in the mouthwatering feast everyone has made in our honor?"

Pet's chest tightened and she looked down at the skirt falling to the top of her boots. "You go ahead. I think I left something at the Great Mother's house."

"Pet."

She looked up at the softness in his voice. His green eyes seemed to take all of her in at once.

"You look..." He seemed to mull over his words and his eyes sparked with mischief. "Well, you look bloody terrible. A ridiculous mess. Why are there leaves in your hair? Did you roll around in the bracken by the river? And a fine blue dress? How dare you! You'll get gravy all over it, slob that you are." He grabbed her shoulders and spun her around. "Go back and put something else on before anyone sees you."

A grin cracked across Pet's face. While the words would have hurt any other girl, it was just the thing Pet needed to hear. "To Hel's halls with you, Axel. I can wear whatever I bloody well please." She ducked past him and took a step out into the light, the small spark of rebellion giving her just enough courage. Holding in a deep breath, she plunged into the crowd toward the crew.

The light from the fire grew hotter as she drew closer. The flames spat and crackled, ringing in her ears. Cold sweat broke out along her spine, and she did her best to keep to the edge of the square. She refused to look at it, even as the heat brushed against the side of her face, making her skin prickle.

She swept past the table and a few of the men looked up, but they looked away without recognition. Good. They didn't need to know it was her. Her plan was working wonderfully. When she came up beside Little Hal, he looked up at her. She didn't look at him, waiting for his attention to shift to the next face.

But his eyes narrowed.

"Pet?"

Her heart skipped a beat in her chest. Not allowing herself to look up, she kept walking, but she heard the patter of Little Hal's steps after her.

"Pet, is that you?"

Before she could get too far away, a hand grabbed her by the shoulder. She twisted, dislodging it, but found Axel's large frame between her and the men.

"Don't let them see you talk to me," she hissed.

"Pet." His voice was low. "They know."

The world around her froze.

The sound of laughter, of merriment, faded into a dull roar.

Her chest squeezed until she couldn't get enough air into her lungs.

"How?" It was the only word she could push between her lips.

Axel winced. "I've been meaning to tell you, but—"

She held up a hand to cut off his words. Taking a deep breath, she shifted so she could glance at the rest of the crew. A few of their eyes darted away from hers as she met them, but others at least attempted a smile. The corners of Doran's lips pulled up, but she could still see a glimmer of the hurt she knew he felt at being betrayed.

Without another word, she ran.

"Pet!" Axel called after her.

She ignored him. The rocking idiot had let her get all dressed up in this bloody disguise and for what? To look like a fool in front of the men? To prove all the things they'd probably been thinking since the moment they found out? Gods, he hadn't even had the decency to tell her that they knew. That the secret—*her* secret—was completely out.

Even though she couldn't see them any longer, she still felt their stares. Freyja's golden tears, this had been such a mistake. She shouldn't have allowed herself to be, well, *her*. She should have returned to being Pet. The warrior. The shadow. The man. She started back toward the Great Mother's house, but as she rounded the corner, Axel stepped out and blocked her path.

"Where are you going?"

She turned the other way. "Anywhere but here."

Axel caught up to her. "Pet, I'm sorry."

When she was finally out of the firelight, she filled her lungs with air. She tried not to think about it. She tried not to picture Doran's hurt. Big Hal's roaring anger. Erik's narrowed eyes and Little Hal's darting glances. Wōden's eye, how was she going to convince them to let her back on the ship?

Axel stopped her at a copse of trees, the light from the fire completely hidden by the large trunks. Only moonlight lit up the space, bathing Axel in its glow as if bestowing a blessing on him.

Pet stayed in the shadows. "What are we going to do? How are we going to keep the rest of Åldras from finding out?"

Axel gave a sigh. "I don't know."

"Why didn't you tell me that they knew?"

He took a step toward her. "I messed up, all right? I forgot to tell you."

Pet rolled her eyes. "Yes, because it's so hard to say 'Hey, Pet, the men know you aren't a man.'" She thrust her hand back in the direction of the village. "I looked like a bloody idiot back there. How am I supposed to return to the ship when they're looking at me like I kicked their favorite kitten? Or like I'm something to be pitied?"

Axel remained quiet, his face turned down and hidden in shadow.

"Well?" she demanded.

His head began to shake. "I don't think you should return to the ship."

A stone sank all the way down to the bottom of Pet's stomach. "What?"

"I said I don't think—"

"I heard what you said," she snapped. "I just can't believe the bloody words came out of your mouth."

Was he really planning in that thick skull of his to leave her here? To abandon her to these people she could never live with? Wōden's one good bloody eye, had the Great Mother told him to convince her? Had they been plotting this the entire time?

He took another step toward her. "The secret is out. We can't trust all our men to keep their mouths shut about it. There's too much at stake."

Pet stared at him. Her words tumbled around on her tongue, trying to find purchase, to find coherency so she could hurl them in his face. "So, now that I'm a woman, you can just throw me away?"

"No!" Axel crossed the remaining steps between them until they were toe-to-toe, and she had to crane her neck back to look at him. "Why on Midgard would you say that?"

"Because there's no other reason for you not to let me go back to *The Phoenix*. Nothing else has changed except for the fact that the crew knows I'm not a man. That I'm not as valuable as them."

"I don't believe that. They don't believe that. You're so much more than you realize."

"Then why are you going to leave me here?" She clenched her fists so tightly, her fingernails dug into her palms. "Why can't the crew just keep their mouth shut? If it's so hard to keep it a secret, just let it out! So what if I'm a woman? The Sidans allow women into their army. Perhaps it's time to follow suit."

He ran both of his hands through his curls. "We can't do that."

"Why not?" She stood on her tiptoes, bringing her face within inches of his. "Are you scared? Are you afraid just like all those other men—like Firmin and Anders and all their rocking friends?"

His eyes flashed. "Pet—"

She cut him off with a derisive snort. "You can't even use my name, Axel. Even in these woods, hundreds of miles from Åldras, you can't look at me and see *me*. To you, I am a pet, a plaything."

"You know that's not even close to the truth."

"Since Holmberg, I have been at your beck and call. Everyone on the Vit Sea knows I'm just your errand boy. But maybe I can't do it anymore. Maybe I can't be Petyr. I can't be Pet."

"Then what do you want to be?"

The question startled her. Did she even truly know? She'd never been able to choose, not really. Her brows pulled together as she continued to stare up at Axel. "There are a lot of things I want to be. I want to be more than just a girl who survived something terrible. I want to be Åldras's demon. Mighty Axel's shadow. I want to be the one who helps end this war."

He shook his head. He just kept shaking his bloody head. "You'll be killed for it. There's no room in this world for a woman who can do the things you do. You can't be...you can't be *her* and be the warrior you've become."

Pet laughed, the sound of broken shards of glass rather than the chime of bells. "You can't even say it."

"Say what?"

"You can't even say my bloody name! You don't even know who I actually am anymore!"

"Yes, I do."

"Then say it." She bared her teeth. "Say my name. Call me the thing you haven't called me since I was that girl you played with in Holmberg. When I was Mallory's daughter and not 'Petyr,' your fabricated cousin."

"You've always been Mallory's daughter."

Pet broached his space, so close her chest brushed against his as she glared up into his eyes. "Then say it, *coward*."

His brows drew low over his eyes, darkening his expression. His hands took hold of Pet's arms, keeping her cemented in place as he swallowed thickly, his Adam's apple bobbing slowly down his throat. He leaned in, his cheek brushing against hers as he settled his lips at her ear. She heard them part, and he took a deep breath. She closed her eyes, waiting, praying for him to finally release her from the shackles she'd worn for what felt like eons. For him to break down the secrets that had created this life they'd lived. For him to destroy everything in a single word.

"Petra."

Petra jerked, almost tearing herself away, but he held her to him.

That was not how she remembered her name. Her name was ice breaking apart and crashing into the water. It was a war cry with sharp edges and jagged teeth. The call of the wild, of freedom.

Not what Axel just gave her. Not a prayer over an altar. Not an oath to the gods or the sound of a crackling hearth in a warm home. Her name wasn't a caress. It wasn't a supplication, a dream on faraway stars. It wasn't whatever he just said it was.

She turned her face, her nose nearly brushing his as she met his eyes.

Then she saw it. A well of pure, raging desire crashed through the emerald green of Axel's gaze.

Lightning raced through every limb, charged wherever Axel's body brushed against hers. Petra's breath caught in her chest, her every sense tuned to him as he stared at her.

"Petra," he said again, though this time it held all the aching and wanting his eyes did.

Without another moment to breathe, he captured her lips with his.

All the emotions and sensations he'd shared in his gaze came crashing into her. He felt like a prayer, an oath, a dream. He was home and she'd finally walked in the front door.

His lips were demanding, silencing every retort before it could fully form on her tongue. His hands went from her face to her hips, pushing her until she backed against a tree, and he could demand more of her. And she demanded just as much, her hands wrapped in the soft fabric of his tunic as she pulled him closer. As she told him, all she wanted was to stay with him. That they were nothing without the other.

And she knew. Even as she deepened their kiss and poured every piece of longing that had burrowed so far into her heart, she hadn't even realized it was there. She knew why he'd never said her name. Why they'd played this charade for nearly a decade. Why she always had to be a man, a shadow, a warrior.

It was her.

She was the one who would fulfill his prophecy.

She was the one he would die for.

CHAPTER 34

RUINS

The only thought circling in Axel's head was *finally*.

Finally, he didn't have to pretend.

Finally, there weren't any more walls between them.

Finally, he could kiss her bloody senseless like he'd wanted to for years.

The kiss deepened and her fingers came up to curl into his hair. He answered in kind as he wrapped his arms firmly around her waist and pressed her back against the tree. Gods, it was like drinking in sunlight or tasting the golden apples of Idunn. He could live forever in this moment. This kiss. He'd dreamed about doing this for years, but those dreams had been paltry in comparison to this. To her.

A small moan slipped from Petra's lips, and he captured it with his mouth. Petra's hands slid from his hair down to his neck. His shoulders. His chest. Warmth spread from everywhere her fingers brushed against his body, igniting a fire he'd done his best to smother all these years.

Gods, she felt so right in his arms. Like he was holding the whole world in his hands. She was Valhalla. Perfection. His heart raced as his lips told her over and over that she was all he wanted. That he would do anything for her. That she was everything to him and without her he was nothing.

She shoved at his chest, wrenching herself from him. His arms dangled, empty, as she twisted and bolted away from him. His entire being revolted at the lack of her touch. The ache in his chest came roaring back. The need to touch her again beat against his ribs. He turned toward her, but her hands were up, warding him off.

"No. No, we can't do that."

His mind was still trying to catch up to what just happened. "What?"

Her fingers brushed against her lips. "We can't kiss. We can't touch each other."

His rapidly beating heart stilled in his chest. "What do you mean?"

Her eyes, dark in the faint light, finally lifted to his. Terror cut across her gaze. "We can't be together. I can't be with you, and you definitely can't be with me."

"And why not? I wasn't the only one taking part in that kiss, Petra." He stepped toward her. Her name felt so right on his lips. How had he forgotten how it tasted? Like sunlight and warmth. Like fire under his skin. He had to curl his fingers into his palms to keep from reaching for her again. "You met me every step of the way."

She shook her head, tears pooling above her lashes. "You shouldn't want to kiss me, Axel. Whatever this is that's starting needs to stop right now."

His chest tightened even further. "And what if I don't want to stop? What if this is exactly what I want?"

"It can't be." Her hand sliced the air between them as if cutting his words with her ax. "Forget what I said before. I'll stay in Ljust Löfte. I'll be Petra again. Just don't come back here. Go back to Åldras. Get back on *The Phoenix* and sail far, far away from here."

Axel took another cautious step forward; afraid he'd scare her off if he moved too suddenly. "You can't have changed your mind that quickly. What's wrong?" Had he hurt her? There was obviously something she wasn't telling him. Had she not wanted him to kiss her? It hadn't felt that way, but he hadn't kissed anyone like that. Ever.

A tear finally fell onto her cheek, but if he hadn't been looking, he'd have missed it. Pet wiped it away so fast she left a red mark on her face. "You can't fall in love with me, Axel. You can't. I'm nothing but a soulless killer. A murderer."

"Just as much as I am," he retorted. Heat built up in his throat.

"I've been on every battlefield with you. I've killed twice as many men as you."

Her eyes flashed. "This isn't a bloody competition, Axel. You don't know what I've done."

"Of course I do. I've been by your side this entire time."

"You don't!" she insisted.

"Then *tell me*!" he shouted. "Give me one bloody good reason why I shouldn't be allowed to fall in love with you. Why you've stopped fighting me on making you stay. Why you can't just let yourself have one good thing."

"Because I killed them!"

The words rang around the clearing, Petra's voice raw. Broken.

Axel watched as her eyes widened. Her hand came to her mouth as if she'd just said the most heinous of words. As if the gods would strike her dead, then and there.

"Who?" he asked. The Sidans? Yes, so had he. They'd both fought on battlefields of grass watered with blood rather than rain. They'd sent men to their deaths in the middle of the sea. It was war. People died. Good and bad, men and women, people died, and his hands were black with their blood.

Petra fell to the ground, her blue skirts falling into the dirt and grass. "It was me, Axel." She buried her head in her hands and sobbed. "All of this is my fault."

Axel crouched next to her. "I don't understa—"

A scream cut off his words.

Both their heads whipped in the direction of the village. A glow started up above the trees. The sound of screams rang out over the quiet forest.

Petra was already on her feet, running toward the light. Axel was a step behind her, keeping pace so he wouldn't lose her like he would if he ran at full speed. They scrambled through the brush, the bracken grabbing at Petra's skirt, leaving behind a trail of linen in her wake.

A goat passed them, running in the other direction. Then a cow. A horse.

Petra broke through the edge of the trees ahead of him and stopped. He reached her and nearly cried out. Fires burned all around. Homes went up in flames. Axel grabbed her hand and pulled her to the side. She was shaking, her eyes glazed as she stared at the fire.

He stepped in front of her and grabbed her face in his hands. "Petra, look at me."

She looked up, her eyes wide with panic.

"It's all right." He moved his hands to her shoulders. "Just stay with me. We need to find the others."

She nodded, but he could see the sweat breaking out across her brow. He could practically smell her fear. He took her hand again and pulled her along the outer edge, away from the flames. *Where are the villagers?*

A shout pierced through the crackle of the fire and Axel changed his trajectory. Petra's hand in his was slick with sweat, shaking as the flames grew hotter around them. He tightened his hold and pulled her behind him.

They found the edge of the fire. A team of water wielding seers stood guard at the east side of the village square. A wall of water stood between them and the fire. They had already made progress putting out the flames, but they still had far to go. The rest of the village pushed to the west, fighting a group of men. Magic flew through the air—water, earth, and air all barraging the group of men from above while animals and plants attacked from beneath—but it did little against the force pushing through them. Large shields formed a line, each brandishing the visage of a roaring bear. Shouted orders cut through the clamor of battle as they pushed through the Häxa. Their scarred faces were smeared in ashes.

Ekte. How had they found them? Where had they even come from?

Axel spotted Big Hal's tall form over the crowd, surrounded by the crew that had come up for the feast. Doran stood in front of him, his hand wrapped tightly around Little Hal's arm. The lad's face was pale as he and the rest of the crew stared across the still-roaring bonfire, where the maypole burned.

There, right under the maypole, stood King Firmin. A leering grin stretched across his face as he met Axel's gaze. Three guards stood around him, their shields up as they guarded the king.

"Da! Stop!" Ella raced toward them, her face smeared with tears. "They didn't do anything!"

The king's head snapped in her direction. "Do not call me that! You're nothing but a cursed wretch of a thing." He spat at the ground.

"Da!" She fell to her knees. "Please! Just stop them!"

Axel took a step toward her, but one of the High King's guards pointed his halberd at her, stilling him. Would the king kill his own child? Axel wouldn't put it past him.

Firmin turned away from her, glancing once again at Axel before facing the fight. "*Silence!*" he roared.

His booming voice had the entire square halting. The concentration of the Häxa faltered, and the Ekte turned toward the sound of their king.

"Our friends have joined us at last!" He gave Axel a haughty tilt of his chin then looked at Petra. His eyes glittered. "Old *and* new friends."

Axel stepped just in front of Petra, drawing the king's attention back to him. "What are you doing here, Firmin?"

"Well, I heard there was a celebration, and I've brought you a gift!"

Without breaking eye contact, he held out a hand to one of his men. A dark-colored sack plopped into his hand, and he drew out what was inside. The guards around him recoiled as he held it aloft.

Axel's entire body went cold even as the roaring fire at his back devoured Ljust Löfte.

A head.

It couldn't be.

From somewhere in the crowd, he heard Little Hal scream.

Firmin tutted. "You really ought to take better care of your crewmates." He tossed the head at Axel's feet.

Olav's head.

It had been weeks since they'd lost the man to Donar's Storm, but this kill had been recent. Hours, if not days.

"The Sidans found him in that storm," Firmin explained. "Brought him to me, believing they were doing our kingdom a service. After all, you'd kidnapped the princess, hoping to frame the Sidans to restart the war."

Axel's stomach dropped and he pulled his gaze away from Olav's face to look at the king. "What?"

Firmin shrugged. "Prince Roman was very concerned when he woke the morning after the feast to discover Ella had disappeared and *The Phoenix* was nowhere to be found. He asked me what had happened and, of course, I could do nothing but tell him you'd taken her from her home. The prince was very concerned, especially when he realized how you could use the brat as a way to break the armistice. When Prince Enzo arrived at the docks in Harligdam, the princes insisted they help us go after you. Prince Enzo's ship was already prepared to go. I couldn't reject such help. He took the lead while the rest of us followed behind. When Prince Enzo discovered you sailing toward Sida, he realized what it would look like for the princess to be captured and discovered in his kingdom. The armistice we had worked so hard for would be ruined."

There was no air in Axel's lungs. No blood in his veins. He was nothing but ice and fury.

"It was fortuitous the Sidans that chased after you discovered your man in the water. Nearly half drowned. They brought him back to my ship so I could find out where you would be taking the princess while Prince Enzo braved Donar's Storm to chase after you. Lucky me, your man gave us the directions we'd need to make this reunion possible."

Without breaking stride, Firmin pointed at the rest of the group. "Now, what am I to do with the lot of you?"

"You are going to leave us this instant." The crowd parted and the Great Mother stepped forward.

"Ah," Firmin said. "The Grandmother, is it?"

The Great Mother didn't even flinch at the slight. "You are not welcome on this mountain, Häxa killer."

Firmin's lip curled up in anger. "I can go wherever I bloody well please."

The Great Mother turned and spotted Axel. Her amber eyes were creased with worry but glittered with anger. She looked past him to Petra, and back to the king. "Pride will be the fall of Åldras, mark my words. It is souls like you that bring about the fall of great empires. You will be the last king of Åldras."

Firmin's face purpled with rage. "Do not threaten me, witch!" With a flick of his wrist, he flung a dagger at the matriarch.

The ice in Axel's veins shattered. He moved as quickly as he could, but he only made it halfway to her when the blade sank into her chest. She staggered back, her eyes wide as he imagined the pain hit her. He reached her as she fell, grabbing hold of her before she crumpled.

The Great Mother wrapped a hand around his wrist. "I'm sorry, my son." She gasped and set a hand to where the dagger protruded from between her ribs. "I couldn't stop what is to come, but your strength will...will..." Her eyes rolled into the back of her head.

"Mormor!" Viveca slid on her knees into place across from him, her hands shaking as she hovered them over the Great Mother. Her fingers shifted from human to wolf and back again. A low growl rumbled in the little girl's chest, far more animal than human.

A cheer went up from among the Ekte, their bloodlust only heightened. Axel gently laid the Great Mother down. The frost that had sunk into his gut burned away. Firmin had finally met his end. Axel reached for the long dagger strapped to his thigh.

"*How dare you!*" Petra screeched. Before anyone else could blink, she grabbed a knife from her boot and threw it in Firmin's direction, aimed right where he'd hit the Great Mother.

Firmin dodged the blade. It sank into the chest of the man behind him.

But Petra was already moving.

She snapped the neck of the closest Ekte and snatched his halberd as he fell limp to the ground. Two others charged her, followed by their comrades as they rallied to their king, but she quickly cut them down, using their own weapons against them.

A pair stepped forward to take the place of the fallen Ekte, but Axel grabbed the back of one's shirt, hauling him backward to stab him in the throat and kicking out to shatter the knee of the other. The man fell, howling.

Petra dodged past him and engaged King Firmin.

Doran flew past Axel, trying to get to Petra and the king, though to save which, Axel didn't know. He tried to follow behind, but Ekte swarmed them, blocking his path. With a roar, he charged into the fray, sending men flying as he pushed to get to her.

A howl sounded from somewhere in the crowd, and the Häxa

engaged the closest Ekte, their magic clashing against the shields and weapons. Even the men of Ljust Löfte brandished hammers and axes. The fire around them seemed to heighten, as if the surge of Häxa magic called to it.

Axel saw Big Hal next, throwing himself against one of the shielded soldiers and the rest of the crew joined in.

"Stop or I kill her!"

Axel froze and the men in front of him scrambled back.

Firmin held Petra against him, his fist in her hair and a knife pressed against the beating vein of her throat. Blood already dribbled into the blue cloth of her collar, showing how hard she was fighting against his hold but also how quickly Firmin could end her life. Doran stumbled to his feet next to them, shaking his head. Blood dripped from a cut on his temple down into his eye.

Axel threw up a hand. "Halt!"

The crowd around them stilled again, their faces turning to the king that held one of their own captive.

None of them likely realized she wasn't theirs to begin with. She had always been his.

Firmin's eyes flashed at Axel. "Drop the blade."

Axel did so immediately.

"And tell Petyr to stay in whatever hole he's tucked himself into."

Axel met Petra's eyes, nearly sagging. Firmin hadn't realized. Not yet at least. "Stay where you are, Pet," Axel called out, though he kept Petra's gaze. If she didn't stay put, she'd get her throat slit.

Petra gritted her teeth in rebellion and grabbed the arm holding the blade. With practiced movements, she pulled it to the side, doing her best to dislodge the High King. However, he anticipated the move and pulled her hair tighter, making her cry out.

"My, the woman is fiery!"

The men around him laughed, but their laughter died off quickly as Axel glowered at them. Only a dozen or so were left standing, the others either detained or on the bloody ground.

Axel returned his glare to Firmin. "It's time for you to leave this place."

Firmin's brows lowered, looking over the group of men left standing. "I think you may be right." He took a step back, taking Petra with him.

A growl rumbled in Axel's throat, halting the king. "Let her go."

Firmin smirked. "No, I think not." He lifted his head. "Let this be a lesson to all of you! I will no longer sit by while you witches join with the other Häxa in Sida. This war has nothing to do with you, but if you can't keep your bloody magic out of it, I will be back, and I'll take more than one girl with me."

Axel took a step forward, his eyes on the knife at Petra's throat. "I won't let you take her."

"Oh, silly boy, you have no other choice." He lifted the knife, drawing the flat of the blade along Petra's cheek. "I saw you come out of that forest with her hand in yours, Axel. I saw the way you tucked her behind you. I know what that is, and for a man whose true love is the key to my kingdom's destruction, it would be...foolish of me not to make sure she isn't put somewhere for safe keeping."

Petra grabbed his wrist and dragged his arm down, taking a small cut under her eye before she dug her teeth into his hand.

Firmin howled and dropped the blade, but he took a firmer grip of her hair and ripped her mouth away. She let go, but she bared her teeth at him, stained red with his blood.

"Don't think I won't kill you in front of your lover, woman!"

Axel charged forward, but two Ekte stepped into his path. Shields poised in front of them. He raised his sword.

"Stop, Axel!" Doran barked.

It was only because the man had drilled it into Axel's head to listen to his command that he stopped. He looked to where Doran had pushed himself to his feet, but Doran wasn't even looking at him.

He was looking back at the rest of the fight.

Out of the corner of his eye, he saw what Doran did. The Ekte outnumbered them three to one. Even with the Häxa's magic, the Ekte were trained to fight against magic. Not to mention the crew. Big Hal stood between three Ekte. Little Hal's face was stained with tears as he glared at the High King. The lad would get himself killed. And the gods only knew if Erik had been attacked down at the ship.

There was more at stake than just Petra. Axel's teeth ground together as he turned back to her.

Firmin brought the blade up again, this time, leaving it at Petra's throat. "I'm going to be leaving now." He took a step back. "If anyone decides to try to stop us, I'll immediately kill this little witch."

Axel hit the shield of the Ekte to his right. "Hel's bloody halls, she's not even a witch!"

Firmin let out a chuckle. "Is that how you caught him, little vixen? Pretended to be a normal girl in a sea of witches?"

Petra lifted her knee and stomped the heel of her boot into the top of Firmin's foot.

The king roared and practically shook her. "Try something like that again and I will gut you so quickly not even Mighty Axel will be able to keep your guts from spilling out."

Axel saw the spark of defiance in her face, but before she could do anything, he caught her eye. *Don't. Please, don't.*

Her lips bunched together in a furious line. *He won't beat me.*

Axel gave the smallest shake of his head. *Me neither.* His eyes flicked from side to side, taking in the bedraggled Häxa before returning to her. *But we can't risk them.*

She closed her eyes and gave the smallest bob of her head.

Axel shoved past the soldiers standing between him and Firmin, their halberds slicing at his clothes but only brushing against the first layer of his skin. He stopped a step away from Firmin, towering over him. "You will pay for every single drop of blood that you draw from her." He glared at the cut across her cheek and the blood staining the collar of her dress. "Starting with that."

Firmin's haughty expression fell for just a moment, a sliver of fear burying itself in his eyes before he puffed out his chest. "Behave, and no harm will come to her."

"I don't trust the word of a tyrant," Axel snapped.

"Then trust the word of a warrior. She loses value if I kill her, but her pain is priceless to me. I'm sure we'll have such a great time together, won't we lass?"

Petra gritted her teeth, murder shining in her blue-green eyes.

Not yet. Axel wouldn't allow Firmin to get away with this. With any of this. The man would pay in blood and pain, and it was only a matter of time before his guard was down just enough for Axel to slide a blade between his ribs.

Firmin took another step back, Petra falling in step with him. "As for the rest of you, if you would like to avoid a repeat of tonight's events, I suggest you cease your dealings with the Sidans. I don't care what hole you hide in, but if any one of you steps foot in my kingdom again, I will return, and it won't only be houses that burn."

CHAPTER 35

A SHADOW

Petra had to tell herself over and over again not to break every single one of King Firmin's fingers wrapped around her upper arm.

She had to remind herself it was important she not fight while the Häxa were still in danger.

That if any of the familiar faces around her recognized her, she would be dead.

Then *The Phoenix*'s crew would be dead.

She repeated it over and over as Firmin pulled her down the mountain.

"Put your legs on your neck!" Firmin barked. "If Axel or his crew get within an arrow's distance, they'll tear the lot of you to bits."

That got the Ekte running. Petra did her best to drag her heels, but Firmin's gait and the grip on her arm were merciless. She didn't speak, afraid Firmin or one of the others would recognize her voice. Not that she ever spoke much to any of them. Praise Loki the healing she'd gone through had practically reconstructed her face. Hopefully no one would look too closely at her.

She stumbled over a root in the dark but caught herself quickly. She couldn't risk any ire from King Firmin. Not when she could feel Axel's gaze on her. If he tried to take her, there wasn't anything stopping Firmin from slitting her throat. From going back and razing the rest of the village to the ground. From throwing her onto the flames. She shuddered at the thought.

If only she'd gone back to being Petyr again.

The men hurried down the mountain, descending ten times faster than Petra would have liked. Her hair finally fell from its wreath of braids. She captured one of the crocuses before it fell, the red stems bright in the moonlight one moment, then invisible once she was yanked back into the shadows of the trees. The petals crumpled as she smashed them in her fist.

How had this happened? How had she allowed herself to get captured? King Firmin was a warrior king. A master with the sword. He wasn't known as *Witchkiller* for nothing. Yet she'd still run into his open arms, believing she could fight him in a bloody skirt. But watching the Great Mother fall had shattered whatever good sense she'd had, and now she was being used against those she'd been trying to protect. Like a bloody damsel in distress.

She should have never put on the dress. Should have stayed in the Great Mother's house. Should have never kissed Axel.

The ground grew less rocky, the soft loam of the bog sucking at her boots. The Ekte's voices shifted from prayers to jubilation, their fears eased as they neared the water and what Petra assumed was their boat.

But she still felt those eyes on her, and she assumed the king felt them as well.

"Quit your yammering!" King Firmin barked. "Don't even think we're safe until we touch the waters of the Vit Sea."

The idiot at least had a sliver of self-preservation.

Máni's moon raced ahead of them, breaking past her highest point in the sky. They reached King Firmin's ship, *The Sceptre*, as the shadows receded in Máni's full light.

The king finally let go of her, thrusting her toward one of the other men. "Put her at the stem. I want eyes on her at all times, and I won't tolerate any mischief from the men, you hear?"

The Ekte agreed, hauling her in the direction of *The Sceptre*. It was a lighter vessel than *The Phoenix*, the snekkja used for cutting across the water quickly and beaching on even the shallowest shores. With the way the ship had beached, it had come from the south, the way Erik had first planned to go before they'd been cut off by the Sidans. It would have been faster with the currents of the Stiga Sea. How long had it taken *The Sceptre* to get here? A little over a week? How long had Olav been with them?

"Come on, woman," the Ekte said, pulling her to the rope ladder a few of the men were using to climb out instead of leaping over the side.

Petra used the ladder this time, the weight of her skirts and the exhaustion of the run down the mountain weighing her down. Once on deck, she was shoved toward the front of the boat, where a pair of rusted shackles were bolted to the planks of the deck. Seemed King Firmin kept prisoners often.

The skipper called for the crew to ready, snapping at the men who were pushing the ship out onto the water to move faster. A few remained on deck, making it harder for the men below to get the ship off the beach.

The Ekte stopped her at a set of ankle shackles attached to a small length of heavy chain bolted down near the stem of the ship.

"Your boots," he said. "Take them off."

"No." These were her best bloody boots, and she knew if she took them off another man would claim them for himself.

Firmin swung himself over the side of the ship. "Why isn't the witch in shackles, Leif?"

Leif glowered at her and reached for her boots.

She punched him.

He staggered back, his eyes watering as he cupped his scarred nose. The Ekte around him laughed, but Firmin wasn't having any of it. He stomped toward her, his knife already in his hand.

Before Firmin reached her, she crouched down, untying the knots with shaking fingers and slipping the boots off her feet.

Firmin glared at her, then looked up to the line of trees. "Get those shackles on her, now!"

The chains clanked as the still-bleeding Ekte grunted and locked the iron clamps around her ankles. A shudder went up her spine—and it wasn't only caused by the cold metal against her skin. Crudely carved runes marked the cuffs, the same ones carved on the face of the Ekte who tucked the key into his pocket.

The skipper called for men to take up the oars as the boat pushed out onto the water. The crewmates scampered up onto the deck, finding their trunks and locking the oars into their oar ports.

Petra tied the laces of her boots in a series of complicated knots and set them at the very corner of the stem. Perhaps the crazy knots would keep anyone from pilfering them. She finally glanced over the side of the ship. Smoke still plumed into the sky from Ljust Löfte on the peak above her. Her gaze moved down the mountain, stopping at the line of trees marking the edge of the water. A shadow stood under one of the large birches.

It wasn't long before the sail was dropped behind her and filled with wind. She tilted her chin up, doing her best to give her haughtiest expression.

It still didn't stop the small tremor in her fingers.

The ship rounded a bend, and they turned out of sight. Petra plopped herself down into the small nook the gunwale of the ship created at the stem. She hugged her boots to her chest and tilted her head back, finding the stars above her twinkling with laughter. Ah, yes. The stupid girl who pretended she was a man had finally been caught. She tucked the torn skirt of her dress around her legs, closed her eyes, and let herself fall into the waiting nightmares.

CHAPTER 36

RESOLUTIONS

Axel's fist punched all the way through the large tree trunk stuck into the hull of *The Phoenix*. The Ekte had rammed the bloody thing nearly all the way through to the other side, not only shattering the gunwale, but the deck as well.

The crew all stood a dozen or so ells away, watching him as he broke the bloody trunk piece by bloody piece.

Firmin had taken her.

Smash.

After all this time, all the deceit and the secrets and the disguises, right when he'd told her to let her guard down, it all went to the bloody, rocking fishes.

Smash.

"Axel."

Smash.

He could still see her face as the boat sailed away, that stubborn tilt to her chin.

Smash.

"Axel."

Smash.

Firmin would kill her the moment he found out. He wouldn't tolerate allowing her to live if he knew she was Pet. His pride wouldn't allow a woman to hold the reputation *Petyr* had.

"Axel!"

He paused, finally turning to where Doran was standing, an ax in his hand. "What?"

"Can the rest of us actually get the bloody tree out of the boat, or are you set on simply pulverizing it?"

Erik sat next to Doran, sporting a black eye and a bloody gash on his head that Little Hal had patched up. Ludvig's entire body was a tapestry of black and blue. Both of them had done everything possible to stop the bloody Ekte from attacking the ship.

But it hadn't been enough.

None of it had been enough.

Axel swung his arm one last time, cracking a large portion of the trunk off and shoving it aside. "By all means, sire."

Doran rolled his eyes and set to work on breaking off pieces of the ship sticking to the tree while the other men collected ropes to haul the trunk out. Axel tore off pieces of *The Phoenix* alongside Doran, his fingers ripping through the splintered wood. Firmin was a real piece of bloody work.

"So, what's our plan?"

Axel glanced up at Doran for a moment before returning to his task. "Our plan for what?"

Doran grunted and yanked his ax from a piece of the deck and swung it down again. "To get Pet. How are we going to get her back?"

Axel broke off a knot of the trunk, hurling it over the side of the ship. "We're going to chase after them."

"They'll beat us to Harligdam by days," Doran said. "This will take at least a week to repair."

"I'll build the bloody thing with my own two hands if I have to," Axel snapped. "Then, Erik will have us catch up to them and we'll take on *The Sceptre*. We'll get her back and bring her back to Ljust Löfte."

"You mean the place where he just took her from? What do you think would happen then? That he'd just let her stay?"

"Fine! I'll take her far away! I'll take her to the other side of the Stiga Sea if it keeps Firmin from touching her again."

They freed the space around the trunk, and Erik called for the men to begin to pull.

"Axel," Doran said in a low voice, "it doesn't matter if you planned to take her to the branches of Yggdrasil. The moment Firmin sees you, he'll kill her."

A stick snapped from where the trees stood away from the water, and Axel turned to find Ella stepping out of the shadows. "He's right, you know." She approached the ship. "My father won't hesitate to kill Pet if he thinks he'll lose his hold on you. If he knows he's in danger, he'll take her down with him."

With a roar, Axel slammed his foot down on the top of the trunk. With the other crewmen pulling, the tree practically popped out of the side of the ship.

Axel roared again his knees slamming to the deck. If he went after them, Firmin would kill her. If the king found out who she was, he'd kill her. If they got back to the city and put her on trial as a Häxa, he'd kill her. Every way Axel looked at it, Petra was going to die.

Ella came and knelt across from him. "There has to be something we can do; some way we can convince my father that Pet's not a threat. That it's in his best interest to let her go."

Axel lifted his head, meeting Ella's wide eyes. "Simple. If he doesn't let her go, I'll tear his bloody head from his bloody body."

ᚠᚾᚲᛟᛗᚤᛏ

IT TOOK them five days to get the ship rebuilt. Axel didn't sleep. He didn't eat. There was no point when his body could handle the lack of rest, and everything tasted like ash in his mouth. He poured every thought into getting the ship repaired and going after her.

His eyes never strayed from the side of the ship as he watched the seal tar dry on the wood. Erik had said it would need another hour or two, but Axel would watch for the exact moment it dried.

Ella had come again to speak with them the day before. The Great Mother wasn't responding well to the healer's care. Sometimes, not even magic could keep the Valkyries from claiming a soul. There had been a vigil at her bedside, but the woman had not woken, and they expected her to pass into Valhalla at any moment. The news only fed the already-increasing inferno inside of Axel.

The clack of canes proceeded Erik, who plopped himself down onto the pebbled beach next to Axel. The pegs on his legs no longer matched, Petra having used the one to draw out the draugr. Axel had carved the new one last night while everyone else had been asleep.

Erik pointed to the ship. "It's coming along. If those clouds stay out of the way, it should be ready in about half an hour."

Axel looked up at the threatening clouds, glaring as if he could will them away with his anger. If only his powers worked the same way as the other Häxa. If only the gods had gifted him something useful. He could have saved her. Could have stopped the fires destroying Ljust Löfte and the knife that sank into the Great Mother's chest. Could have kept Firmin from taking Petra.

"I don't think Firmin will kill her, lad."

Axel's head snapped in Erik's direction. "What?"

He shrugged. "Yes, His Majesty doesn't always make the wisest choices when it comes to people, but he is a warlord, a king, for a reason. If he thought killing her would help him, he would have done it up at the village. Instead, he kept her when he saw that he could use her against you." Erik threw a rock, sending it into the water next to the ship with a splash. "He's been looking for leverage over you for years. He'll not waste it now that he's found some."

Axel wiped a hand down his face. Would Firmin just keep her in Harligdam? Would she actually be alive when Axel got there? If Firmin wanted leverage, what could Axel bargain with to release her? The only things of value he had were his magic and his sword, neither of which would offer a good enough trade.

The thought continued to eat away at him even as the crew reassembled and they finally got the ship moving. If Erik's calculations were correct, it would be another two weeks until they reached Harligdam if the weather stayed mild and the ship didn't spring any leaks.

Axel prayed to whatever gods were listening that they would get there before it was too late.

CHAPTER 37

A PRISONER

A kick to Petra's foot sent her legs sprawling out in front of her and brought her dozing mind back to consciousness. The men on the boat snickered as she blinked herself awake. The sky had darkened since she'd last had her eyes open. *Rocks.* She'd been doing her best to stay awake, watching the men around her. It wouldn't do to let down her guard. Not on Firmin's ship.

The crewman who had likely been the one to kick her dropped a bucket beside her feet and leaned down to unlock the cuffs around her ankles. A long, white bone needle sat at the collar of his shirt, one used for stitching up sails.

Petra had been eyeing the little tool since she got on the boat. It would make for a good lockpick. She hissed as the man roughly jostled the aching skin under the manacles. She'd been careful with the shackles, but with the cold air chapping her skin and the loose metal always rubbing, the sores had continued to grow in the few days they'd been aboard *The Sceptre*. The sunburn around them only made it all worse. Most of her skin felt like it was going to peel off and leave her with nothing but the bones underneath.

The sailor dropped her freed foot and nudged the bucket next to him. "You'll be helping make the supper, lass."

Petra glared up at him. They couldn't really expect her to help with supper. Not after they'd forced her to cook the first night and she'd burned the whole pot. That had really riled the crew. The king had certainly not been pleased. He'd thrown his bowl at her, burnt slop and all, before raging at her. A bruise had blossomed along her jaw, she was sure of it.

The sailor rolled his eyes and pulled her to her feet. She allowed herself to stumble as he helped her, and she fell into him, her fingers deftly finding their way to his collar. With a mumbled apology she stepped back, pretending to regain her footing. The sailor's eyes wandered down the length of her before he grunted. He didn't even notice the bone needle making its way up her sleeve.

Perhaps, sometimes, it was a good thing to be a woman.

She snatched the bucket of oats and the threadbare blanket she'd been given two days into the journey after her skin had started burning from the harsh sun, the only mark of charity from any of these men. With the bucket of oats dangling from one hand, she used the ladder to climb out of the boat. Her ankles hit the shallow water, and she hissed as the salt found its way into her sores. The guard didn't wait for her to get her feet under her properly and hauled her toward the beach where the rest of the crew had begun preparing for supper. Stars already started to peek through the curtain of the sky. It wouldn't be long before everyone bedded down for the night.

She'd make her move then. It was time for her to get off the bloody ship.

The plan had been culminating in her mind for days, a tapestry woven together thread by thread. She still had her boots, which she kept hanging around her neck by their laces. It didn't matter that they were a nuisance. She needed them to get through the harsh wilds leading back to Ljust Löfte. She also needed supplies but only what she could carry. It was a good thing her brother, Gram, had taught her how to forage at a young age. Being farther south than most of Åldras, the climate was quite a bit warmer and there was much to scavenge from the land. If she got her hands on an ax and a length of rope, she could likely find everything else she needed on her way.

The guard deposited her next to the cook, who only grunted and grabbed the bucket from her. He knew better than to let her anywhere near their supper. Petra grunted back and found a spot to sit in the shadows outside the light of the cook fire as the flames began to catch on the logs gathered by the crew. Thank Wōden it was nearly Freyr's season. Petra would have lost her toes if the temperature on the sea was any colder. The appendages were numb much more than they should be anyway.

The smell of cooking food slowly drew the ship's crew closer to the fire. Petra did her best to tuck herself into the shadows, wrapping the thin blanket tighter around her shoulders. She needed to be invisible. The blue dress she still wore had picked up the grime of the sea and was now a splotchy gray. It would be difficult to get through the wilderness without proper clothing. She eyed the long, black cloak wrapped around the skipper's shoulders.

Tonight. It had to be tonight.

This was the last stop on the small continent where Ljust Löfte was located. If she didn't get away from the crew, she wouldn't be able to escape. Not when they'd be in Åldras.

The cook called for supper, and the men lined up with their wooden bowls. A few groaned at the sight of the oats being slopped into their dishes.

Firmin groaned the loudest. "Bloody oats again, Johannes? What on Midgard do I bring you along for if all you're going to feed the crew is this slop?"

The cook ducked his head, the skin of his neck turning a ruddy shade of red, but he didn't say anything.

"Like you could do any better," Petra mumbled under her breath.

Firmin's sharp glare whipped in her direction. "What was that?"

Petra bit the inside of her cheek and shook her head, keeping her eyes lowered. Wōden's eye, she needed to keep the attention away from herself. Just for tonight.

"That's what I thought," Firmin said.

The others lined up after the king, their grumbles about the food given fuel in height of Firmin's show of dissatisfaction. Little mimicking birds, the lot of them. Petra did her best to keep to herself, staying out of the way and not talking to anyone. When it was her turn to get her food, she scraped the crusty dregs out of the bottom.

As she settled back into her spot with her bowl, conversation took up among the crew.

"How long do you think it will take for Mighty Axel to catch up to us?" one of the men asked.

"Can't say," another answered. "We did a number on his boat. Would take weeks for a normal crew to repair, but we all know *The Phoenix's* crew aren't normal."

"Mighty Axel will likely supplicate Njord, and the boat will simply ride the wind instead of the sea."

"Honestly, Mighty Axel could probably lift the ship up on his shoulders and swim the sea if it took too long."

Petra tried to withhold a smile. How the men could talk about Axel as if he were some godly being made her want to laugh aloud.

"Who says he even needs his crew with him? The man's just as likely to walk over the waves on his own two feet and be here before we break our fasts in the morning." A few of the men laughed, but Petra peeked through the curtain of her hair to see more than a couple strain their necks to look back the way they'd come.

"Stop your bloody yammering!" King Firmin shot up from his seat on a rock and the laughs cut off immediately. "Axel Ahersson is just a man. He has to live by the laws of the gods, same as us."

"Don't know of any other man that can fight a bloody ice bear with only his hands and win," the skipper remarked.

Petra couldn't hide her grin anymore. Axel had done that when they were eighteen. The white fur of the beast lined the inside of his winter cloak.

"It doesn't matter if the boy can skin a bloody dragon with his teeth," Firmin spat. "He's not a god any more than you are. We proved that on that mountain. The boy has weaknesses." Firmin's gaze landed on Petra. "Just like the rest of us."

Petra glared back.

Firmin cocked a brow. "Not only did we take his lass, but the blow we delivered with that bloke's head..." Firmin began to laugh. "I'll never forget the shock on Axel's face."

Petra didn't know when she'd moved, but one moment she was at the water's edge, and the next, her fist slammed into Firmin's ruddy face.

The king stumbled back as the men around them caught onto what happened. Hands grabbed her arms and waist, dragging her away from the king. She landed a few more hits before they got her on her knees in the sand.

Firmin shoved the man trying to help him up and charged her, violence flashing across his face before he even slapped his hand across her cheek.

She took the hit, knowing if she showed any more rebellion that night, her plans would be foiled before they even started. The blow knocked her to the ground, her hair a riot of snarls around her. A couple of the men jeered as she lay in the dirt. She pushed herself up to her knees, ready to knock the bloody smiles off their faces.

King Firmin's fingers dug into her upper arm, and he lifted her to her feet. "Don't you *ever* try something like that again. I am a *king*, and you are nothing but a sniveling wretch only good for warming a man's—"

Petra's forehead smashed into the king's face.

King Firmin threw her away from him with a roar. Two of the crewmen grabbed her arms, and she let them drag her away as she grinned at the sputtering king.

Maybe she didn't need to escape tonight after all.

A few of the other crewmen jumped to attend King Firmin, who now had blood running from his nose. The king shoved them away from him. "Get that demon woman locked back up!"

Petra held back a groan as they hauled her back to the ship. She could feel the lump forming on her forehead. The king's face was a solid rock.

The Ekte shoved her over the gunwale into the ship. She glanced around. No one else remained on deck. Not even the skipper attended the tiller as Erik would have, no matter if everyone else was on land. It wasn't wise to leave a ship unattended.

The Ekte clamped the shackles around her ankles once more. Petra allowed her head to fall back against the side of the ship. Freyja's golden tears, why couldn't she have just left the king's face intact?

The Ekte turned and jumped back over the side of the ship, leaving her to the stars above. A draugr could jump over the side and gnaw on her arm before they even heard her scream. Not that she would let a draugr get their teeth on her a second time, but it was still rather short-sighted of them.

The faint bit of light she could still see from the fire on the beach slowly faded along with the sounds of the crew and Firmin's guards. Only the rumble of Petra's empty stomach kept the silence from fully descending. When the rumble of snores crescendoed and the hour grew late enough for the crickets to reach the peak of their symphonies, Petra grabbed the short end of her chain and rattled it. She waited a moment, then did it again two more times. No one hollered from the beach. No one came to check on her.

Petra licked her dry lips and tugged the bone needle from her sleeve. Quietly, she twisted the shackle on her ankle until the small keyhole was visible. The needle slid into the hole. It was only one piece, but the locks on the shackles were rudimentary. She had both ankles free within moments and shoved her feet into her boots.

Praise whatever good luck hamingja was looking over her, she had the whole bloody ship to herself. Moving through the chests and supplies strewn about across the deck—Erik would have thrown an absolute fit over the untidiness—she collected a small hand ax, a good length of rope, a pair of trousers, and a brown cloak. Wōden's one good eye, it was like they were just asking to get robbed.

With her newly acquired goods strapped to her, she quietly crept over the side of the boat where the stem of the ship hovered over the embankment. She kept her eyes on the sentry, who was focused on the water they'd already traversed rather than the ship itself. They probably had special instructions to watch out for Axel.

Petra crept through the shadows, finding any rock or short shrub she could use to disfigure her vague silhouette in the darkness. A line of trees awaited her a way off, and she trundled her way toward them. While the clouds blocking the moon helped, anything she could do to not look like a human sneaking through the tall grass would benefit her escape. The weirder she looked, the better. They might watch her, but if they mistook her for an animal or one of the creatures roaming these lands, all the better.

Something splashed onto Petra's cheek, and she quickly wiped at it. Another hit her hand, and her gaze shot up to the sky.

Bloody rocks.

She ran, giving up all possible pretense that she was anything other than a person. Firmin's men would find her missing the moment they went to the ship to collect their tents. Drops fell from the sky faster as she ran toward the safety of the trees in front of her. The men couldn't be farther than two or three spans of *The Phoenix*, but they felt a few steps away when the shout went up behind her.

She didn't look back.

The trees loomed above her, their shadows reaching out with their arms toward her.

She smiled as her boot landed in the first patch of darkness.

That smile filled with dirt as she was tackled to the ground.

Her heart shot into her throat, coming out in a growl as she twisted in her attacker's grip, the wet ground making it easy to wiggle out of the Ekte's grasp. She broke free and rolled, sliding the ax she'd stolen from the knot she'd tied in the rope. Her ax met flesh as she swiped at him and turned to jump back into the shadows.

Another Ekte met her there, hands reaching for her shoulders.

She swung the ax and slit his throat before she took off into the trees.

The crash of thunder and the torrent of rain made it hard to hear any pursuers, but it would make it difficult for them to keep track of her. She wove through the trees, hoping to confuse anyone behind her. At least there weren't hounds.

Her boots slipped on the wet ground, and she nearly fell into a small ravine a dozen or so ells deep. She turned sharply before the ground ate her whole. While the height wouldn't kill her if she fell, she'd still rather not break any bones as she fled. Not with Firmin's men right behind her. She followed the ravine, watching closely for any soft ground where it might break off and tumble into the hole.

The adrenaline of the fight ebbed, but she kept running, watching the ground at her feet.

A small bolt of Donar's light crackled in the sky, lighting the forest around her and the shape of a man launching himself in her direction.

She only had enough time to blink before Firmin tackled her into the ravine.

A growl tore at her throat as they fell. Firmin held onto her as if he could plunge her down the roots of Yggdrasil himself. She hit the bottom of the ravine, a *pop* near her left ear making her mouth widen in a scream, but there was no air left in her lungs to give the cry life.

Firmin's body pinned her to the ground. Her chest ached with the lack of air.

Firmin pulled away from her, but not far before he grabbed a fistful of her hair. A screech finally tore from her lips as he yanked her to her feet.

"*Bloody witch!*" he snarled.

Petra punched him in the jaw.

He howled and released her.

The wet ground made it hard for her to keep her balance, and she slipped a bit as she tried to scramble away, reaching for her ax with her right hand. Her left arm shot out to steady her, but she fell to a heap when blinding pain seared through her at the motion. She grabbed her shoulder, feeling the bones and joints out of place. The bloody High King had dislocated her left shoulder.

"To Hel's bloody halls with you!" Firmin growled as he grabbed her again, taking her by her injured arm.

Petra cried out as he hauled her to her feet. Black crowded the edges of her vision, but she shook it off and pulled the ax from her hip.

Firmin let go of her arm and sidestepped to avoid the blow Petra swung toward his middle. He drew his own sword, the lightning flashing above them glittering off the steel.

Black spots danced in Petra's vision, but she bit her cheek hard enough to keep her head and raised her ax.

"Halt!"

Petra barely registered the voice and looked up to find three long halberds pointed right at her from the top of the ravine. Her chest heaved as she stood, frozen. She wasn't Axel. She didn't have his strength nor his speed. She could dodge one of the spears on a good day, but not all three in the mud with pain clouding the edges of her mind. Her fingers tightened over the stolen ax in her hand, and with a roar, she buried it in the ground at her feet.

Firmin took a step toward her, and a vicious smirk spread across his ugly face. His eyes flashed with victory and barely suppressed fury.

"Smart witch."

CHAPTER 38

PLANS

Today, I realized there is nothing Axel Ashersson will not do for those he cares about. I watched the fifteen-year-old lad pommel six boys his own age and four full grown men in the time it took me to run the twenty ells down the hill I'd just crested. Petyr was on the ground, blood seeping from a broken nose and bruises blooming across his jaw. Not a mark marred an inch of Axel's shirtless torso, even though I could see the swords the others had unsheathed scattered around them. When Petyr came to, he gave Axel the verbal lashing of a lifetime. I've never heard so many words cross the boy's lips. I learned later that Petyr had been the subject of torment from some of the other lads at camp. I'll be glad to set sail within the fortnight, but I don't foresee any more problems while we are here.

— *FROM THE WRITINGS OF DORAN FINNSSON, THE LAST KING OF GROVÖ*

Axel pulled at the oar, his arms moving to the rhythm Erik's voice set. The other men around him grunted as each pair pushed their oars through the water.

Faster.

They needed to go faster.

It was like Axel could feel her getting farther away. Like if he didn't get to her fast enough, he'd never see her again.

After five days on shore and three more after that to get out of Isberg and across the small stretch of the Stiga Sea, Axel felt his patience fraying worse than bad wool.

Five bloody, rocking days that Firmin had ahead of him. They were likely only another five or so days out from Harligdam. His fingers tightened around the oar and the wood squeaked its disapproval.

Erik called to the men at the rigging and the sails unfurled above Axel's head.

He allowed himself to look back, just once, and think about Ljust Löfte—the one place in this whole world where he had felt happier than he had in nearly nine years. Where he'd finally been able to cast away every bloody mask he'd ever had to wear. Where he could be just Axel. Just *hers*.

Then he turned away.

The scene in the forest played over and over in his mind. The fight. The kiss. His hands at her waist. Her fingers digging into his hair. Her pushing him away. The hurt in his chest. The pain in her eyes.

It was me, Axel.

All of this is my fault.

He still didn't understand, but it was one of the many things they would discuss when he got her back.

The Phoenix pushed through the strait leading out to the Stiga Sea. From there, they would turn west, heading through the channel above Sida until they were back into the Vit Sea, back towards the waters of Åldras. It took them two weeks to fight their way to Ljust Löfte. Having to fight against the currents along Isberg until they hit open water, it would take them seven or so days to get to Harligdam.

That gave Axel a week to come up with a plan.

While the thought of razing Firmin's ridiculous fortress to the ground was a tempting one, he wouldn't harm the townsfolk living within its walls. Axel couldn't hurt innocent people for the crimes of one man, no matter how nice the image might be. That left sneaking in, but how? Firmin might have been an idiot, but he was a conniving idiot. He would be waiting for Axel the moment *The Phoenix* was spotted in Åldran waters.

The sails above his head filled with the breath of Njord and pulled them out of the channel and into the Vit Sea. If it had been any other time, Axel would have closed his eyes and taken a deep breath of the familiar, salty air. The first taste of home in months. Instead, he pulled the oar back into the hull, securing it into place as the others around him did the same, not once taking in the view of the waters.

Axel heard Doran's familiar step before the man sat on Petra's trunk next to Axel. A growl hummed in his chest, but he didn't give it voice as he turned to find Doran's plotting face on in full force, notebook in hand.

"I've been trying to come up with a plan."

Axel sat on his own trunk. "Not surprising." Petra and Doran had always been the schemers and Axel the blade they wielded.

"I don't know that there will be anything to barter for her release."

Axel had already come to that conclusion as well. What would Firmin want more than having something to dangle over Axel's head? The High King knew Axel's allegiances weren't to him but to Åldras and her people—including the Häxa. Having Petra in his grasp would allow Firmin to have some control over Axel. Even if he hadn't realized who she was, Axel's reactions to her alone had given Firmin enough of a reason to take her. The king would keep her in a tiny cage, like a rare bird to bring out only to flaunt in Axel's presence.

"We'll have to break her out," Axel said.

Doran untied the string of his notebook and flipped through the pages until he found what he was looking for. He spun it around so Axel could see the detailed map of Firmin's fortress, labeled with the names of every building. How Doran could map out every building he ever stepped foot in remained one of the most impressive things the man could do—though Petra had taken after him in that.

"If I know Pet as well as I thought I did, I imagine she would have gotten into mischief on *The Sceptre*." Axel's stomach tightened at the thought of Petra putting herself in danger, but he knew it was likely true. Doran's finger tapped at a portion of the wooden wall. "I think he would keep her here, in one of the watchtowers. There are small cells used for temporary holding of prisoners. I don't know what he plans to do indefinitely, but I imagine she'll be there at first."

"Were you able to see the cells?"

Doran shook his head. "Not finished. I only know about them because I saw their frames when construction on the wall began. The watchtowers are the only things made of stone, so there won't be a way to smash through the walls either."

Axels' fingers tapped on his knee. "What if we impersonate the guards?"

"You don't think King Firmin will have every available eye on this ship the moment we get into harbor? We will be tailed, and our tails will have tails."

"Perfect. They would give us the clothing we'd need for disguises."

"Firmin will have a dozen men on that watchtower on alert for anyone trying to get in. He's probably already got a tight rotation on it."

Axel's teeth squeaked in his head as he ground them together. "Are you here to discourage any plan I bring up, or do you have a proposal that brings with it a modicum of success?"

Doran scratched at his jaw. "I think you are going to have to grovel."

Axel's hackles sprang up. "Excuse me?"

"I don't know that it will even work, but if we want her to be treated well, we need to proceed with caution. Playing on King Firmin's pride will be a good start. If we can show him you're willing to—"

Axel shot to his feet. "There isn't *anything* I would be willing to do for that man after he's taken her."

Doran frowned. "But is there anything you'd be willing to do for *her*? Those cells in the watchtower are temporary for a reason."

The raging fire in Axel's chest went out. He slumped back onto the trunk, his face in his hands. Firmin, and the kings before him, weren't known for doling out light punishments. Most people lost limbs if not their life if their crimes ever made it to the king. Cold seeped into Axel's skin. The image of Petra, bloodied, on the ground of a dank, cold cell flashed through his mind. Bloody rocks, he'd pull his still-beating heart out of his chest and place it in Firmin's rotten hands if he knew it would keep Petra safe.

Axel dropped his hands from his face. "What would you suggest?"

"First, a gift. We need to at least appear to be apologetic."

A gift. What ridiculousness. "You think a trinket will appease him?"

"I think it will be a start. Most visitors bring some kind of tribute, you know. I heard Prince Roman arrived with a dozen head of cattle along with a large bouquet of rare blooms for the queen."

"Oh, perfect! I'll just go round up some cows and pick some heather then. Hopefully, that will appease the brute who invaded an innocent village of witches and likely killed their matriarch."

Doran cuffed the back of Axel's head. "Don't be an idiot, Axel. We need something to bring his guard down the smallest bit. Something he wouldn't expect you to be willing to give up."

Axel's gut clenched. His eyes flicked to the hold of the ship. "I have my father's shield."

Doran followed his gaze. "You still haven't given it to him?"

Besides the lysande sword, it was the last thing he had of Father's. He'd found it on the beach a few days after the battle. Father must have dropped it in the water sometime during the fight, because it had only slightly been damaged by the flames instead of ruined like all the others.

"I wasn't going to let that monster hang my father's shield in his house like a trophy."

Doran slowly wrapped the leather tie back around his notebook. "It would certainly accomplish what we're trying to do."

A lump formed in Axel's throat and sank down into his stomach. "But will it be enough to get her out?"

Axel could read the calculations running through Doran's head in the twitch of his eyebrows. "No, but it will definitely catch him off his guard. It may even give you long enough to try to talk him into letting you see her."

"You don't even think he'll let me see her? Even if I say I need proof of her life?"

"I honestly don't know, Axel." Doran sighed. "I thought I was good at anticipating high King Firmin's movements, but his arrival in Ljust Löfte surprised me. I don't know that I can predict what he will or will not do."

Axel tried to swallow back the burn in the back of his throat but found it difficult. If Doran couldn't figure out how to save Petra, what chance did Axel really have?

"What are we going to do, Doran?"

"The only thing we can do," Doran said. "Pray."

And he did. Axel sang prayer upon prayer to Njord, but either the song was stolen by another god before the wind could deliver it, or it fell on deaf ears.

Axel could feel the eyes of the gods upon him, seeing what he would do next. As they drew closer to Harligdam, all he could think about was carnage. Father had always warned that there were times when violence would feel like the right answer. It was easy access to power, to garner respect—though grudging it might be. He had cautioned that Axel would likely suffer with it, his abilities far surpassing those of even great leaders. He'd taught that while fear and brutality could lead to power and glory, it led to destruction as well. Axel had learned simple communication, one man to another, often resolved more conflicts than fists or swords ever did.

But now, he was done talking.

He would take Father's shield, but if Firmin gave him even one inkling that he would harm Petra, Axel would shred Åldras into pieces with his bare hands.

CHAPTER 39

A LEASH

P etra allowed herself a small sigh when the guard unshackled her ankles. After the longest ten days of her life, they'd finally made it to Harligdam. The journey had been filled with calm skies and good wind. Petra didn't know what King Firmin had offered the gods for such an uneventful trip, but whatever it was, it must have been good. They hadn't even gotten close to any Sidan ships. As if Loki had draped himself over *The Sceptre* and pushed them through the Vit Sea.

The second shackle fell from her ankle, and it was like Petra could take a full breath again. While her ankles were still sore, she'd been permitted to keep the trousers she'd stolen, Firmin saying it served the crew right for allowing them to be taken. But she knew that wasn't the real reason. He didn't want the men to forget that she'd stolen from them, and he wanted them to watch her. What better way to do that then keep her dressed in the things she'd taken?

Firmin stomped toward them. "Put your legs on your neck and get the girl off the ship. Up! Up!"

The guard grabbed Petra's arm and hauled her to her feet. She swayed slightly, legs wobbly under her and gaze blinded by tiny lights as pain shot from her shoulder. The surgeon on the ship had reset the joint, but it still hurt like bloody rocks. She shook her head, attempting to cast the spots away when Firmin yanked at her free arm.

"I said—"

Petra yanked her arm away from the guard and slammed the heel of her hand into the king's throat.

It was almost instinctual. She'd done her best to keep to herself throughout the rest of the journey. She'd hardly spoken. But the High King...well, the bloody High King had spoken plenty, and Petra was through with it.

Firmin's meaty hands grasped at his neck, his face purpling with lack of air. He stumbled back, knocking into a man and sending them both tumbling into a pile of sacks. A guard rushed to help the High King, but Firmin shoved him away and got to his feet, hands on his knees. The rest of the crew gaped as their king finally wheezed in a breath.

He stood straight and marched back toward Petra. She bared her teeth at him, but it did nothing to deter him. He raised a hand, which she dodged. With the shackles gone, she bolted for the side of the ship. Grabbing the top of the gunwale, she pulled her legs up.

Hands grabbed her before she could jump.

Two Ekte yanked her back onto the deck. She grappled with them, kicking out one pair of legs.

A hard slap sent her sprawling to the ground, the lights returning to her vision.

"*Enough!*" Firmin bellowed from where he stood over her. "Get this wretched creature out of my sight."

The Ekte retook her arms and yanked her to her feet. "Where are we to take her, Your Majesty?"

"The fortress, the cells, even a bloody hole in the ground! As long as she stays out of my sight, I don't bloody care. Just make sure, wherever it is, it's guarded, and no one can get in or out of it. Do I make myself clear?"

The men bowed to the king and hauled her to her feet, even as her head spun. The docks were filled with people, their eyes trailing her as she was dragged across the city, three swords at her back.

Wait.

The smell of the sea was replaced by the stench of too many people.

Wait.

Harligdam passed by her in a kaleidoscope of whispers and glares.

Wait.

When the walls to the fortress came into view, Pet yanked her arms down. The Ekte holding each of her arms had grown relaxed as they walked, and they stumbled into one another.

She reached around the waist of the one to her left and wrapped her hand around the hilt of his sword.

A blade settled at her neck. "Not a move, witch."

Pet pulled the sword free and met the blade.

The Ekte on her right slammed the hilt of his sword into her shoulder.

She screamed, her hand spasming and releasing the sword.

The Ekte descended on her, each grabbing her limbs as she fought to free herself.

She got her teeth around one of their arms.

"Hel's bloody halls!" he hissed.

An arm wrapped around her neck as they dragged her into the walls of the fortress.

Her vision darkened at the edges as they wrangled her through one of the doors set into a stone tower.

A room of cells greeted her, the stench of human waste and mold stuffing her nose.

She writhed. She couldn't go into one of those cells. If she did, the gods only knew what they would try to do to her. What she would do to them the moment they laid their hands on her. She needed to get out of here. Needed to get far away from here.

The Ekte threw her into one of the cells. She hit the stone floor and any air she still had in her lungs left in a *whoosh*. The lock on the door slid into place as Petra got to her feet. She raced for the door, sticking her arm through the small window to try to grab the guard.

He jumped back before she could do more than brush a finger over his tunic. "Nice try, little witch, but you can't catch a quick one like me." He tapped his finger to his nose, but Petra only snarled at him. The man blanched and scurried out of the room.

Bloody idiot.

Petra's legs finally gave out, and she slid down the hard, wooden door. Any energy she might have had evaporated.

A tear leaked from her eye, and she swiped at it before it could so much as touch her cheek. She was not weak. She would not break. She would get out of this bloody prison and back to Ljust Löfte or wherever else she needed to go to get away from all these bloody men.

Her vision faded in and out, the hard lines of the stone under her knees fading as she stared. She didn't know how long she sat there before a door shut outside her cell. Petra pulled herself to her feet. She blinked at the sight of Queen Eva standing on the other side of her door.

"Hello there," the queen greeted.

Petra's eyebrows pulled together, but she didn't speak.

"All right. Well, I'm supposed to conduct some tests on you." The queen chuckled, her blue eyes glittering. "It's actually quite funny. See, the king usually has his regular testers do it, but when I heard about how you quite decently thrashed the king, I volunteered."

"Why?" Petra asked, her voice cracking with disuse.

Queen Eva shrugged. "I wanted to see the woman who had driven the king to such outrage. Not very many of us get to do that."

A breath of a laugh escaped Petra's chest. "Well, here I am."

"Here you are." Queen Eva studied her through the small window. "You look very familiar. Have we met before?"

Petra's chest seized a bit, and she shook her head. "I think I would have remembered you."

The queen sighed. "I suppose you're right." She leaned down and set something on the floor, though Petra couldn't see what. "Now, I'm supposed to conduct some experiments to ensure you're a witch."

Sweat beaded on her palms. "What kind of tests?"

Queen Eva held up a small vial of what looked like ink. "I'm to see if the elements react to you. Water, stone, plant, bone. You know. The regular things." She held out her hand. "If you wouldn't mind simply sliding your arm through the window, we can begin."

"What if I don't?"

"Then the guards outside are ordered to come in and make you. I did talk them out of coming in with me, much to their disappointment. A few of them looked eager to get involved."

Petra grimaced and stuck her hand through the window. Her fingers trembled the slightest bit, but she kept her face impassive.

The queen took her hand and shook it. "I'm Queen Eva."

"Kelsye." The name slipped off her tongue. It took her half a second to place it, but she remembered where she'd heard it before. It had been the name of a girl in Holmberg. Dane had been planning to court her before the chance had been stolen from him.

"A pleasure to make your acquaintance, Kelsye." She let go of Petra's hand and undid the cork on the small vial. "I have to draw a rune on the back of your hand. It will make the magic more receptive to the elements for testing."

She proceeded to dribble the contents of that vial over her fingers and traced a dark mark on the inside of Petra's wrist. It was warm. The moment the queen finished, it grew hotter.

"Now," the queen said, "if you'll continue to hold your hand there, we can begin."

She started by rubbing runed rocks across Petra's arm that turned her skin red, jabbing the end of a finger with a small thorny vine until it bled, placing a feather in her palm, pulling out a caged mouse and letting it bite her. By the gods, if Petra died by some kind of infection in this hole, she was going to come back as a draugr and bite Firmin's giant nose off. Every failed test smoothed out the hard furrows between the queen's brows until they had all but disappeared.

When the queen had exhausted the somewhat extensive list of trials, she smiled. "Well, there's no sign of any magic. I'll let the king and his men know."

She stood to go, but Petra grabbed her shoulder. "If you can't prove I'm a witch, will the High King let me out of here?"

Queen Eva's face fell. "The High King and his brother aren't known for letting women go easily."

Petra's fingers tightened slightly. "Listen, whatever your husband thinks he's going to gain by keeping me here, he's wrong. All he's going to do is force Axel's hand, and I don't think this kingdom is ready for that battle, do you?"

"You're obviously not from around here if you think I have any real power over the High King."

"You may not believe you have power, but I bet you have more control over your husband than you believe. No woman would have made it this far with that rat for a spouse if she didn't."

The queen studied her, eyes much like Ella's flicking over Petra's face. The steel Petra had seen all those weeks ago hardened.

"If I had any sort of power to free anyone, don't you think I would have left long ago?"

With those final words, she turned and fled the watchtower.

ᚹᚾ᛬ᚲᚩᚠᛁᚠ

PETRA STARED at the corner of her cell where water dripped down onto the stone floor. Must have been a hole in the roof and no one cared that it was leaking through the floor above her. Water snuck through the floorboards and into the small wooden cup she'd kept from her last meal.

Drip.

Drip.

Drip.

She'd been in Harligdam at least five days if she counted right. They'd thrown her into the small cell in the watchtower quite some time ago, but without any sign of the outside world, she couldn't tell. Even the rotation of meals had been irregular and all they offered her was a hunk of barley bread and goat cheese every time, so it wasn't like she could tell the difference between breakfast and supper.

All she knew was the scratch of her broken fingernails on wet mortar. The water only slightly helped break up the paste keeping the stones together. It was slow work, but she had a stone halfway free from the floor. With it, she might be able to break the door where the bolt sat and get out.

A light scattering of straw dusted the ground, keeping the floor from getting too wet where she slept. Petra swept some back toward her when she heard guards rustling outside the cell door. The wooden barricade had a small, barred window. A silhouette came into view, filling the small square and blocking what little bit of light came through it.

Petra pulled her long hair forward to hang around her face. She didn't need any of these morons recognizing her. Not that they likely would. Not many men could tear their eyes away from Axel and those that did never held her gaze for long.

"Told you it was a witch," a voice hissed.

"Don't look much like anything if you ask me."

Petra turned away from the door, her fingers trailing across the cracks in the cell floor, searching for anything she'd missed on her first perusal. There wasn't a mattress, or she would have started taking that apart earlier to look for something she could make into a tool.

The guard pounded his fist on the door. "Hey, are you a witch?"

Petra ignored them.

"Of course she's a witch," a different voice said. "Wouldn't be here for anything else."

The guard blocking the doorway moved and another took his place. "It's certainly an ugly thing."

How many men were standing out there? Three? Four? She'd only ever seen two at one time, but it was good to know there were more within speaking distance. She fiddled with a piece of straw, pulling the fibers apart with her bloodied fingers.

"What kind of magic can she do?"

"Don't know. The High King brought her back from his trip while you were gone. Just said to find a cell to keep her in and left it at that."

"Haven't had a good witch burning in six months. The city will be thrilled."

The man at the window tapped at the small iron bars at his face. "Did you hear that, little witch? It's going to be right fun to watch you writhe up on that pyre."

The men laughed as if their comrade had just told the funniest joke they'd ever heard. *Idiots*.

"I'm sure their working on it now, piling up the logs just right to make sure the flames are hot as Muspelheim. What do you think? Will the smoke or the flames kill you first?"

Petra didn't even look up. Let these men try to scare her. Nothing they said meant anything. Nothing they said would harm her like they thought it would.

"I suspect it'll happen any time now, what with *The Phoenix* coming into harbor."

Petra was on her feet in a flash. She reached through the small window and grabbed the guard by the collar, tugging him against the door. His nose hit the wood with a crunch.

She shook him. "What did you just say?"

Another guard yanked his friend out of her grasp. Blood ran down the guard's face, and he glared at her.

The last guard laughed. "You heard him. Mighty Axel is coming into harbor, and everyone is waiting to see what he's going to do."

Petra's pulse rushed in her ears. Axel was already here. Rocks, she had to get out of here. Had to stop him from doing something foolish.

The door to the watchtower crashed open behind them, and Firmin stormed in. His dark eyes narrowed at the sight of the guards.

"What are you three idiots doing in here?" he snapped. "Get back to your stations! I'll make sure your commander has you out in the rain for the rest of the night!"

The guards scrambled for the door, not even daring to look back at the furious king.

Firmin watched them leave, then slammed the door behind them before he turned to face her. "Good evening," he sneered. "I'm sure those rockheads just spoiled my good news."

Petra allowed a small smirk to surface on her lips but didn't say anything.

Firmin's sneer sharpened. "I know you think he's going to walk in here and save you. That he'll simply saunter into my fortress, blade swinging, and deliver you from this sad, dank cell. Well, I'm here to squash any of those thoughts right now."

He strode toward the door until his face was level with hers in the small window. The sour stench of his breath made her want to gag, but Petra remained where she was.

"When Axel and his men arrive in port, I'll have every single member of his crew arrested and put under guard at the dock house. If any of them attempt to put up a fight, my men are to remind them you're sitting in a cell only a few doors away from an oiled pyre. Axel will be brought to the great hall, and he will kneel at my feet. The man will have to lick the hound dung from the bottom of my boots before I even grant him permission to speak. Then, and only then, will I let him to plead his case, beg me to allow him to take you back. Which I will firmly deny. I'll then send him out to find and kill a Häxa every week for the next five months. If he fails in this, I'll slit the throat of every single one of his crewmates and burn you at the bloody stake. Do I make myself clear?"

Petra felt the small bit of warmth in her body disappear, but she kept the smirk on her face. "Do you really think this will work?" She lowered her chin and took a step back, out of the light, making Firmin's eyes narrow. "You think you've gained something by taking me, but all you've done is made him furious."

Firmin shook his head. "Perhaps, but if I'm to fall, that boy will fall with me." He took a step back. "Oh, and I hope you weren't getting too attached to your new home." He opened the door, and four guards swept into the watchtower.

Petra scrambled for her half-dugout rock, but it wouldn't budge as the men filed into her cell and pulled her from it. She straightened and punched the first guard, knocking him into the wall, but another took his place, grabbing one of her legs and dragging her out of the cell. She flipped over, twisting her foot from his grasp and rolling to her feet. The other two guards reached for her, but she slipped between them, heading for the door.

She opened it, but before she could take a step into the cool night air, Firmin grabbed her. With a snarl, she whirled to gouge his bloody eyes out.

Firmin dodged her first swipe and slammed the butt of his dagger into her temple.

The world went dark.

CHAPTER 40

GIFTS

Axel readjusted his grip on Father's shield, glancing down at the blue-dyed leather decorating the two quarters of the shield opposite one another. The leather had a couple of rough spots on it, but Axel had oiled it and polished the steel umbo until it shone brighter than the stars overhead.

The docks of Harligdam glittered with torchlight. The dock workers bustled about, preparing the ropes and hooks to help pull *The Phoenix* up against the wooden docks, but something about them made him stare. They went about their business, but their heads were bowed low, and no one sang. While the hour was somewhat late, it didn't explain why the very wind itself felt like it was holding its breath.

"Something smells," Erik muttered, and Axel knew he wasn't referring to the stink of fish from the harbor.

Axel's hand reached for the pommel of his sword, but he'd tucked the lysande sword into a hidden compartment in the hold. Doran had thought it best he arrived unarmed to the fortress. Not that leaving behind his sword meant he couldn't wreak havoc on Firmin's great hall if he wished to.

The ship pushed the final length into the harbor.

The moment *The Phoenix* settled into place the docks erupted.

Guards swarmed from the harbor master's building. Several jumped out from behind crates and raced for *The Phoenix*.

The crew all shot to their feet; the scrape of swords being drawn ringing out across the deck.

"Hold!" Axel shouted as the first of Firmin's men climbed into the ship. A dozen followed after him and two dozen waited on the dock behind them.

"Axel Ashersson," the man Axel recognized as Captain of the Guard said, "His Majesty has ordered the men of *The Phoenix* arrested for crimes against Åldras and has commanded you and King Doran be brought to the great hall immediately."

Axel took a step toward him. "On what grounds?"

"On the account of conspiring with witches, kidnapping Princess Ella, and plotting against the High King, my lord." The captain's face didn't reveal whether or not he believed the charges, but he kept a hand on his sword.

Axel growled, but before he could say anything, Doran grabbed him by the shoulder. "We'll go, Captain. Where can we expect to find the crew when we are finished with His Majesty?"

The guard's stance eased only a fraction, but Axel saw it nonetheless. "They will be held in the harbor master's house until we receive further orders."

"Thank you." Doran turned back to the crew. "You may do as this man says. Everything will be fine."

Axel grabbed the front of Doran's shirt. "You think this is *fine*?"

Doran ignored him and looked back to the captain. "May we leave our skipper to watch over the ship?" He pointed to where Erik sat, still perched on his seat next to the tiller.

The captain eyed Erik for a moment, his gaze settling over the stumps of his legs. Axel nearly pummeled the man for his obvious prejudice, but Erik shook his head at him, keeping him from causing bodily harm to the man.

The captain sighed. "I suppose he can stay, but the rest of you need to come with us. Now."

The crew filed off the ship one at a time. The guards made Ulf strip every weapon from his person, which was not few. Ludvig grinned like he was about to go for a pleasant stroll. Big Hal put an arm around Little Hal's shoulders and made sure to keep him close as they were marched to the harbor master's.

"Where is Lord Petyr?" the captain asked.

A puzzled look crossed Doran's face. "What do you mean? Is he not on the ship?"

Wōden bless Doran's sharp mind. There was no way Firmin would believe Petra hadn't come with them. That she wasn't on the ship. Not when they had no idea they had her in chains. They'd prepared to face the question, but it still made Axel want to pummel something. Petra should be by his side. Should be safe.

"No, he isn't on the ship," the captain replied. "Do you know where he is?"

"Do you think I can keep tabs on Åldras's Demon? If he doesn't wish to be found, he won't be."

The captain narrowed his eyes. "Lord Petyr is expected to remain behind with the other crewmembers."

Doran shrugged. "If you see him before we do, be sure to tell him."

The captain's face paled slightly. Petra's reputation as a warrior proceeded her. Hopefully, the man would be wise enough to keep the fact that Petra wasn't with them to himself—if not to avoid her wrath, then to avoid Firmin's.

He called for one of his men, telling the man to double the guard on the prisoner. *Petra*. Axel took a step forward, but Doran grabbed his shoulder.

"Don't," he hissed.

The captain turned back and pointed toward the fortress. "This way, my lords."

Axel's grip on the shield tightened. Only the knowledge that this all might help Petra kept him from tearing the captain's head from his shoulders right there.

Doran took up conversation with the guard captain, drawing attention away from Axel as they wove through the city. Rats skittered through the mud left by rains that must have just passed over the city. A few people milled about at the late hour, but when they saw the retinue of guards, they quickly found somewhere else to be.

No one greeted Axel as he passed. No children waved and laughed as they skipped alongside him down the street. No banners hung in the windows and no songs wove through the air.

It was as if the Harligdam he loved had vanished, replaced by this empty husk of a city.

They arrived at the fortress much sooner than he had wanted to. The large, wooden wall stood tall, its sharp points threatening the stars above them.

As the captain went to address the men at the gate, Doran slipped back to stand beside Axel. "I'm as furious as you are, but you can't let it get to you. Your patience is the only thing keeping any of us alive."

"Don't you think I know that?" Axel snapped.

"Some things need spoken aloud sometimes." He watched as the gate opened. "I trust you with my life. We all do."

The words did steady something in Axel. This was about more than just him or Petra. This was about all of them. If he wasn't able to keep his head on straight, all of them were in danger. He'd implicated Doran, Ulf, and Ludvig in the crimes Firmin was accusing him of. The Hals and Erik would be disgraced. They could all lose their heads. All except Axel.

They marched into the fortress and Axel could swear the gate nearly snatched the back of his tunic with how fast it closed behind him. Torches lit the walkway to the great hall, but the crackle of the flames did nothing to calm Axel's racing pulse.

The great hall loomed before them, and it took every ounce of patience Axel had in his body not to storm in there and throw Firmin through a wall. Instead, he followed behind the captain as the door opened to allow them inside.

Axel nearly hissed when he crossed over the threshold.

All the kings and lords of Åldras had been gathered.

Axel slowly stepped into the room, head held high, eyes flicking over their faces. Firmin really had thought all this through. He'd made sure there would be witnesses—*powerful* witnesses—to whatever exchange would occur that night. Axel's blood boiled under his skin.

"Ah, Axel! Wonderful of you to finally join us." Firmin sat at the head of the room, his not-a-throne draped with the fur of a white wolf and rings glittering on his fingers. "Doran, if you would take a seat, I'm sure we would all appreciate your wisdom as we address the situation we've found ourselves in."

Axel watched Doran out of the corner of his eye. Doran's face had turned hard. He knew exactly what Firmin was doing. Making him pick sides. He'd always been one to stay out of conflict, doing his best to keep peace between everyone. This was Firmin doing everything he could to isolate Axel, and Doran would likely not stand for it.

"Sit down, Doran," Axel said under his breath. "I need you to start spreading good word through the other kings."

Doran's gaze shot to him for a moment, but Axel kept his face turned toward Firmin. With a nearly imperceptible nod, Doran slid past the other lords and kings until he found an open spot. Perhaps getting a few of the others back on their side would be enough to distract him while Axel dealt with the real threat.

Firmin's eyes narrowed as they caught on Father's shield. "Have you come looking for a fight, Axel?"

Axel spread out his arms, holding the shield in one hand and revealing there were no weapons on his person. "Of course not. I've never been received into Harligdam's halls with anything but welcome. Should I expect otherwise?" Axel sauntered the rest of the way through the hall and stopped a few paces away from Firmin. "I've brought you a gift, Your Majesty."

Firmin's brows rose. "This is a surprise."

With shaking hands, Axel held out the shield. "My father, Lord Asher Redbeard's shield. I thought it was time it graced the walls of this great hall, in honor of his memory and in gratitude for" —he cleared his throat— "for Your Majesty's great service to the people of Åldras."

A smile split across Firmin's lips. "A mighty tribute indeed." He called for someone to take the shield, and a servant arrived a few moments later. The lad held out his hands, his face impassive. Axel lifted the shield, staring at the shining face as he placed it in the servant's hands. With a deep breath, he let it go. At least he hadn't had to put it directly into Firmin's sausage fingers. He might have retched all over it.

"While I appreciate such a gift," Firmin drawled, eyes sparkling with victory, "I'm curious as to whether you believe this will absolve you of the crimes you've been charged with."

"After the way we left things last I saw you, I believed it would be best to come with a token of peace. To show I mean no ill will toward you." *Not yet at least.*

"That's interesting. I thought you would have used it as a ransom to attempt to pay for the prisoner I have locked in a cell."

A few whispers took flight behind Axel, but he didn't look at the crowd. "You mean the woman you kidnapped?"

"I mean the witch I apprehended."

The whispers grew.

Axel did his best to look confused. "I can most assuredly say that she is not a witch."

"Do you know how many fathers, husbands, *lovers*," he said, emphasizing the last word, "have come to me and said those same words? Yet they have all lied, bewitched by the women they believed were clean of magic."

Axel squared his shoulders. "Do you think me, the only son of the Häxa, would not recognize one of my own?"

"She was with others of her kind, Axel. It's obvious she is a witch."

"There are many who cannot choose where they live. Lord Gill lives on an island overrun by seagulls, yet he is not one himself."

Laughs erupted as Lord Gill half-heartedly objected.

"That isn't enough to convince me of the woman's innocence."

A few heads bobbed at Firmin's statement, but Axel quirked a brow. "Have you seen her use any gifts? I've known the lady quite a bit longer than you have and have never seen her use a drop of magic—well, perhaps besides her charming smile." More chuckles erupted, the tension in the room decreasing by a few degrees. "Have you any kind of testimony?"

Firmin's gaze snapped to Doran. "You were there when I apprehended her, so you know of the witch we speak of. In front of this court and the eyes of the gods above, do you swear you have never seen that woman perform magic?"

Doran's shoulders eased. "I swear to everyone in this room and to the gods in the tree above, I have never once witnessed that woman perform a lick of magic."

A few of the men turned contemplative, but Firmin thrust a finger in the air. "That does not excuse her from harboring other witches or from conspiring to kidnap the princess."

One of the other men, King Agnar, stood. "But the woman will not be subject to the pyre until it is proven she is a witch."

King Agnar's companion spoke up from beside him. "Have the tests been performed?"

Axel turned back to Firmin, whose face had turned a mottled shade of red. "Of course. They were indecisive."

Murmurs started up around the room. Axel couldn't withhold the small grin that played at his lips. "So, she's not a Häxa?"

"That's not what I said!" Firmin barked. "I said we don't yet know."

Doran stood. "If you cannot prove she has magic, why are you keeping her here? Why not allow her to return to her home?"

"Shut your trap, Doran!" Firmin snapped. "You need to keep your nose out of it."

Doran's lips drew into a thin line before he slowly sat back in his chair.

Axel's fists clenched at his sides. The bloody High King had brought Doran into this mess. It took everything he had not to pummel the man. He had to loosen his jaw before he could speak again.

"If she is not a witch, then why is she being treated as one?"

Firmin bared his teeth in what he probably thought was a smile but was more a snarl. "Because she was an accomplice in my daughter's abduction. You took her to a colony of Häxa, who have infected her with their awful curse. You planned on handing her over to the Sidans to use against us once the armistice ended."

A few gasps cut through the murmurs of the room.

"That is a lie!" Axel snapped. "That's not how magic works, and all of you bloody know it."

Firmin held out his hands. "How can we know the ways of magic? We long believed only women could be cursed with such things, yet here you stand. What if we've been blind to what the Häxa are truly doing? What if it was actually you who cursed her?"

The murmurs about the room rose, turning to accusations.

"Did he curse the princess?"

"Is she even now working with the Sidans?"

"If the curse is contagious, are our families safe?"

"Is the princess still alive?"

Axel held his ground, keeping his gaze firmly planted on Firmin. The High King leaned back in his not-a-throne, a smug tilt to his mouth. How much time would Axel have to escape if he simply walked over and snapped the man's neck? How long would it take the Sidans to learn of the High King's death? How long would the kingdom last under Anders's rule? Would Axel be able to escape with Petra and the crew if he killed both Firmin and Anders? How many men would it take to stop him?

A slight creak split the air between the lobbed questions and accusations.

Firmin's eyes shifted from Axel to the door behind him.

The soft patter of steps clipped across the stone floor, barely audible to Axel's ears over the voices of the kings.

But with every step, a voice fell silent.

Then another.

And another.

Every man's voice faded away until none of them spoke.

A dark skirt of pale-green fabric stopped just at the corner of Axel's view.

Firmin's eyes narrowed. "What are you doing here, wife?"

Axel finally turned to look at the queen standing next to him. The woman's blue eyes didn't stray from her husband, but the corner of her mouth ticked up slightly when Axel looked at her.

She folded her hands over each other at her waist. "I have come to make a confession, Your Majesty. I was the one who ordered Mighty Axel to take our daughter."

Even the few torches in the room went silent at the queen's words.

Axel blinked at her. What was she doing?

Firmin shot to his feet. "You don't know what you're talking about. Leave. Now!"

Queen Eva's face remained serene as she turned away from Firmin. "My lords, Mighty Axel is not the one to blame for the disappearance of Princess Ella. I am. I was the one who discovered she was a Häxa nearly six months ago, and I was the one who commanded Mighty

Axel to take her to the other Häxa. While he attempted to dissuade me at first, his sense of duty overcame any qualms he may have had. I was the one who put him in this position, and it was I who conspired with our enemies by forcing him to take her away. I went behind His Majesty's back to save my daughter from the punishment of the Ekte."

She fell to her knees before them, a tear falling from the corner of her eye. "In that moment, I did not act as a queen with concerns for her kingdom but as a mother with fear for her child. I was the one who gave the command. If anyone is to blame, it is me."

Thunder's beard, the woman was a master. Even Axel felt his heart soften toward the queen. It was only the fact that he knew what had actually happened that he could see past the act.

"Get *up*, woman," Firmin snapped, striding toward her.

"Is it true, Axel?" asked King Agnar. "Was the queen the one who ordered you to do it?"

The queen looked past her husband and up at Axel. "You can tell them the truth."

Axel looked to Firmin, who had stopped only a step away from the queen. The High King glared at him as if daring him to expose the lies that bound them together.

Axel smiled. "I swear on the name of my father that it was the queen who gave the command to take her daughter to the Häxa."

And it was absolutely true. Petra had stated they would only take Ella if the queen commanded it. Which she had.

It was bloody brilliant.

Firmin reached for the queen, yanking her to her feet. "You—"

"I'm so sorry, husband!" the queen wailed, grabbing the front of his vest and burying her face in his chest. "I couldn't tell you. I knew your sense of justice would be too great. That if you knew, you would have had to do the right thing and turn Ella in. I'm sorry I went behind your back. I will turn myself over for whatever punishment you and the kings deem necessary. But I did it for my love of our daughter and my love of our kingdom. Please don't let anyone else take the blame but me."

The air in Axel's lungs left with every word. The queen was practically throwing herself on Firmin's mercy. Sacrificing herself to free Axel. But why?

Firmin stared down at his weeping queen, his jaw working.

Axel had to bite his lips together between his teeth to keep from grinning.

Queen Eva had just presented her husband with a conundrum.

If Firmin told everyone Queen Eva was lying and that she was a traitor, he would lose his queen. That wouldn't be much of an issue except everyone in the bloody kingdom loved her. There would be riots if he executed her for being a traitor. It would also put a black mark on his reputation, considering the queen was also protecting one of the royal children, even if the girl was a witch. It wouldn't look good, and it certainly wouldn't help to stir up trouble during the armistice.

But, if he did let Queen Eva get away with her scheme, he would lose his game against Axel. He would have no argument to stand on. While he would save face, he would have no reason to continue to humiliate Axel or keep his crew locked up.

Firmin slowly looked up at Axel, his blue eyes bright with anger as he settled a hand on the small of the queen's back.

"As a High King, I must demand justice, but as a husband I don't know that I can cast judgment in this situation." He turned toward the rest of the kings. "So, I will present the choice to the council gathered here. What say you?"

Doran stood first. "I believe the queen should be pardoned. We cannot blame a mother for protecting her child nor a queen for protecting an heir, as is her purview. While the Häxa are forbidden in this kingdom on punishment of death, there is no law that states we must punish those who protect them."

One of the other kings stood. "Perhaps there should be an amendment to that law. If we have witch sympathizers, there could be cause for concern. We would not wish for the Häxa to believe they have a foothold in this kingdom. Perhaps we ought to make an example of the queen for those who would wish to help the evil in our kingdom."

A few murmurs broke out, but it was King Agnar that stood.

"Sit down, Tyrus," King Agnar said. "Just because you don't have a heart beating in that scrawny chest of yours doesn't mean you need to go about trying to break other folks'."

King Tyrus plopped down in his chair with a huff.

King Gudrun stood up beside Agnar. "All those in favor of

punishing our lovely queen by strapping her to a pyre like the lot of you would have done to her daughter if you'd caught her, say 'aye.'"

A few "ayes" smattered the room.

"All in favor of those who wish to show our love for our queen by letting her walk away with nothing but a smack on the hand?"

The room filled with a chorus of assent.

"Well, there you have it," said King Gudrun. "The queen now knows not to go about ordering our greatest warriors to perform possibly treasonous acts and we can all go home not feeling like bloody murderers."

A few chuckles rumbled through the room.

But not enough to cover up the threat Firmin uttered under his breath.

"If you think you've accomplished something here, *wife*, you will soon realize how much it costs."

Axel's blood turned to ice. He took one knee at the queen's side. "My queen, I am your humble servant. Anything you ask of me; I will make it happen." He did little to hide the open glare he gave Firmin.

She is under my protection.

The High King sneered, but Queen Eva only settled a hand on Axel's shoulder. "Thank you, Mighty Axel."

He could read the unspoken words in her thanks. *Thank you for trying to protect me. Thank you for saving my child. Thank you for caring even when we both know there's little you can do.*

Axel got to his feet, once again facing off with Firmin. "While I'm happy to be once again redeemed, we still have matters to discuss." He wouldn't leave here without Petra. Wouldn't let Firmin hold her for one minute longer.

Firmin's face darkened. "I think this meeting is adjourned."

Axel gritted his teeth. "Will you release the prisoner or not?"

"Of course not! She is my prisoner, and I'll do what is necessary in order to keep this kingdom safe."

In other words, Firmin would keep Petra there until he got whatever it was that he wanted. He would lock her in a bloody cage somewhere, let her rot, until she either died or Firmin did. All in the name of keeping the kingdom safe.

Axel would not leave her here.

All of Doran's cautions flew out of his head.

Petra would be leaving.

Now.

Axel's hand grabbed the front of Firmin's velvety tunic, and he shoved the man back into his not-a-throne. A few of the men shot to their feet, but they all knew better than to try to approach.

"Listen here, you maggot..."

CHAPTER 41

AN ESCAPE

My worries over Petyr continue, but I pray it is only the imaginings of a tired man. He's excelled at a rate I wouldn't have expected from a fifteen-year-old. He knows how to wield every weapon imaginable, but his sticky fingers may cause me more problems than I'd like with the other lords. He's kept himself out of scrapes with the other soldiers, but I learned it's because he's become somewhat of a legend, in spite of Axel's notoriety. There are rumors he's been running a gambling ring in the camp, but I haven't been able to get any more information out of anyone than that. He's become a fox among wolves. While Axel would tear your arm from your body and slap you with it, Petyr could cut the nose from your face, and you wouldn't even notice until you tried to blow the snot out of it.

— FROM THE WRITINGS OF DORAN FINNSSON, THE
LAST KING OF GROVÖ

Petra groaned as she ripped the canvas bag from her head, not that it did anything to help her see. Wherever she was, it was pitch black. Rope lashed her hands in front of her and chafed her already-sore ankles. Something earthy stung her nose, and as she sat up, she hit her head on a low counter. Something smashed to pieces next to her. Petra gently felt around until she could find what had dropped. Jagged pieces of what felt like pottery sat in a pile of dirt.

She was in some kind of garden shed.

Carefully, she grabbed the largest, sharpest piece of the pottery she could find and began sawing through the ropes tied around her wrists. It was tedious and the broken shard cut her hands as much as it cut the rope, but she was able to get one hand free and untie her ankles. She kept the shard in hand as she felt around the small shed. She had bumped the counter at the back, but the walls were lined with shelves of tools. Hatchets, spades, a dull knife, and a mallet. Plenty to get her out of this mess.

She tied a length of rope around her waist, cinching it tight against her hips. The dull knife and one of the spades slipped into her makeshift belt but she kept a hatchet in her right hand and the mallet in her left, weaker hand. Her shoulder still ached, and it probably still would for a good few weeks. Now that her eyes had somewhat adjusted to the complete dark, she saw the thin outline of the door, a sliver of moonlight barely sneaking through the cracks of the doorframe. It must be under a covering or inside another building.

As quietly as she could, she tried to push open the door, but it didn't budge. She found the small knot of rope that acted as a door handle and yanked, trying to see if there was some kind of locking mechanism attached. She felt something move on the outside of the door, but voices interrupted the sound. She released the rope and watched as someone on the other side checked it.

Perhaps subtlety was off the table that evening.

Petra lifted her foot and kicked the thin wooden door. Her boot went right through and smashed into whoever was on the other side.

A holler went up, and she pulled her leg back out of the hole and reached her arm through to find where they'd locked it. A small piece of wood sat in a slot not halfway up the door. She yanked the wood out of place and opened the door.

The guard that she'd kicked regained his footing as another raced toward them from the other side of the covered space. It was just a frame of a building, the roof having already been built but the walls open to the weather. She spotted three more guards as the two approached her.

"Listen here, little witch," the kicked one said. "If you go back in that shed nice and quiet, I'll pretend you didn't kick me."

Petra glared at him and raised her makeshift weapons.

The other guard drew his sword.

She charged before either of them could make another move.

Her mallet arced through the air, slamming into the face of the first guard, while she raised her hatchet to deflect the sword of the second. The first guard fell, and Petra caught another swing from the second guard with both her mallet and her hatchet.

The guard was only a hairsbreadth from her face as they locked weapons.

"You can fight?"

Petra headbutted him in the nose.

He staggered back, but a new guard took his place. His sword stabbed toward her belly, and she had to twist out of the way to avoid getting skewered.

Another guard joined the fray, his sword raised, but he stayed behind his companions. *Freyja's golden tears, how many are there?* Petra fought back the newest opponent. When she spotted the still-sheathed sword of the first guard, she smiled. Sidestepping another swing, she dropped her hatchet and grabbed the man's sword.

But he'd been ready for her. He grabbed her arm and punched her square in the face.

Petra felt the crunch as her nose broke. Her vision swam for a second, and it was instinct alone that had her rolling away, taking the brunt of her weight onto her injured shoulder. A sword nicked her upper arm, and she roared, drawing her knife and blindly throwing it. It must have stuck someone because she heard a scream.

She regained her feet and wiped the blood seeping from her nose. She could feel it already starting to swell.

The guards circled her, five to one.

"You shouldn't have done that, little witch."

One of them spat at her boots. "You're dead!"

Two of them charged her at the same time.

But Petra was done playing nice.

She raised her weapons.

It was over in seconds.

One severed tendon here.

One opened artery there.

Once she got ahold of one of their swords, she cut them down.

One by one, they fell.

She drew the sword out from the chest of the last man that had stood before her. Eleven bodies lay at her feet, each bleeding out. Each twitching as the last dregs of their live seeped into the ground.

Her eyes flicked up to the last still breathing. The one who had spit at her.

He crawled away, his hand holding a gaping wound in his side as he tried to escape.

Petra stalked behind him, and he looked back at her, fear making the whites of his eyes take up most of his face.

She grabbed a handful of his hair and yanked him up to his knees.

"Please!" he begged. "Please, don't kill me."

She plunged the blade through his spine.

ᚠᚾᚲᛟᚠᚤᛚ

PETRA RACED THROUGH THE CITY, dodging patrols and skirting around torchlight until she reached the dock and found the place swarming with guards. *The Phoenix* bobbed in the water, not a soul walking her deck. Where was the crew?

A guard stepped around the corner, and Petra tucked herself back into the doorway. This particular man looked older than the others, his eyes scanning the other men rather than the shadowy edges of the docks and the water lapping at the wood.

One of the other guards approached them. "Nothing to report, Captain."

The captain nodded. "Good. We can probably tighten our formations around the harbor master's house rather than leave everyone spread out. The prisoners are secure, and we can send the evening shift back for supper."

"Yes, sir." The other guard left, and the captain continued his walk.

Petra loved it when stupid people laid information at her feet.

She crept along the harbor, watching as some of the men were relieved of duty and sent home. By the time she reached it, the far end of the dock was completely deserted. She untied her boots and hung them from her neck. Carefully, she broke away from the shadows and darted to the first stack of crates standing at the edge of the small dock. She waited for the sound of alarm or the clip of steps on wood but heard nothing. She darted a glance around one of the crates and found the guards had pulled back all the way to the harbor master's building and the three main docks. Petra crept out onto the dock until the water beneath was deep enough for her to swim and the shadows hid anything that might be lurking beneath. Praise the Allfather it was hightide. With a deep breath, she slid into the water.

Each dock was three boat-widths apart, and she swam from one to the next, only stopping to catch her breath under the safety of the wooden planks. As she drew closer to *The Phoenix*, she used the other boats as cover as well.

"Did you see that?"

Petra darted back behind the ship she'd just kicked away from. Peeking around the side, she spotted two guards walking down the dock.

"What did you see?"

"I swear there was something in the water, just there." He pointed in Petra's direction.

She cursed under her breath as they walked along the other side of the boat and disappeared from view. She looked back to *The Phoenix*. *Only fifty ells away.*

Her lungs already ached from the swim, but she took another deep breath and sank back down. She cut through the water, her legs propelling her the final stretch toward the large shadow of *The Phoenix* ahead of her. Her lungs started spasming three-quarters of the way there and she kicked her way to open air. Her head broke through the surface near the rudder. She sucked in a lungful of air, then another, before she wiped her face and looked for a way up. The rudder itself could be an option, but with the way her limbs were quaking, she didn't know if she had the strength to pull herself all the way up. She might be able to sneak around to the side opposite the dock and use the lower part of the gunwale. There might even be a rope.

Her thoughts were cut off as something wacked her in the head. She looked up and found a rope ladder hanging over the back of the ship and the silhouette of Erik's head peeking over the edge.

"Put your legs on your neck and get up here," he whispered.

Petra grabbed the first rung and clambered up the ladder. When she reached the top, she carefully climbed over the side, not wishing to be seen by the guards.

"About time you showed up," Erik grumbled. "I've been waiting all night for you."

Petra pressed herself to the wall of the ship and looked up at him. "Me? Where's Axel?"

"Gone to try to convince the bloody king to let you go, but you and I both know that was never going to happen. I knew you'd break out and make it here once you knew this old bird was in the harbor. What I didn't count on was Firmin arresting the rest of the crew and stuffing them in the harbor master's cells until Firmin was done messing with Axel's head."

"He really arrested them?" Firmin had done many things to try to keep Axel from leaving port, but never had he laid a hand on the crew. The king was losing patience. "Well, I'm here now. How do we get word to Axel?"

"*We* don't do anything. I'm as stuck here as the rest of the men, and I don't think Firmin has any plans to let us go anytime soon."

Firmin's threats from a few hours ago echoed in her ears. He was going to do everything he could to humiliate Axel. But there was only so much Axel would put up with before he ripped the High King's head from his shoulders and if the rest of the crew was to make it out...

"Where's my trunk?" she hissed, already moving toward the rows of them on the deck.

"Same place. I'll try to cover up any sounds."

Petra reached her trunk, right where it had been before the draugr attack, as Erik took up a song. His low baritone rumbled across the deck, but the man never was perfect at finding the right pitch. Petra opened her trunk and pulled out a set of clothes, her cloak, and all her blades. Her eyes prickled when she slid her axes back into their loops at her waist.

A few of the guards started grumbling, shouting at Erik to quiet his racket. Petra hurried back to Erik before they came their way.

Erik's song died off. "Did you get what you needed?"

"Almost." She met Erik's eye. "I'm sorry."

Erik frowned. "For what?"

"I lied about who I was." And something about lying to Erik felt wrong. While she trusted the rest of the crew deeply, the skipper had always been different.

He chuckled. "Did you really think I didn't know?"

Petra blinked. "What?"

"I figured out you were a lass in my first three weeks aboard this ship."

Her mouth fell open. How on Midgard had he known? How had he kept it a secret all this time?

He winked. "Off with you now. Probably best to go back the way you came. There are too many eyes on the docks."

With his little revelation still sinking in, Petra climbed back over the side of the ship and slipped into the water. It was more difficult to stay afloat with all her gear, so she sent a prayer up to Loki and waded back to shore only halfway down the harbor. She pulled herself out of the water and tugged her cloak to cover her hair.

Oh, bloody rocks. Her hair!

Tucking herself behind a barrel, she bunched the strands of her long hair together at her neck. She slid one of the small throwing knives from her vest and set the edge just above where her fingers wrapped around the tail. It took a bit of sawing to get through all of it, but the blade cut through the hairs, the ends brushing her jaw in uneven waves. Chewing at the skin of her lip, she dropped the cut hairs into the sea beneath her. With a single crash of a wave, any semblance of Petra was gone, and Petyr was once again left in her place.

She pushed herself to her feet, her clothes heavy with water as she raced back through the shadows of the city. Her chest heaved when she reached the outer wall of the fortress, and rain started up again as she jogged down the wall toward the gate. Her steps slowed when she spotted two guards standing watch outside. *Rocks.* Each man had a torch in one hand and a spear in the other. The rain began to fall harder, and Petra saw them both tuck themselves closer to the wall to try to avoid the deluge.

Petra blew out a breath and tugged her hood farther down her face. She darted out of the shadows and raced toward the gate.

Both men turned in her direction and she raised her hands. "I've come with a message for Mighty Axel."

One of them stepped forward. "His Majesty said not to allow anyone through the gate until he said so."

Petra tried to hide her grimace. "Did he mean in or out?"

The guard opened his mouth but paused.

"I think he did say out," responded the other.

"No, he said once it closed, we weren't to allow any—"

Petra smashed both of their heads together.

They fell into a crumpled heap. One was unconscious but the other shook his head. Petra didn't let him get up before she punched him in the jaw and knocked him out. Axel wouldn't approve if he found out she killed them when they hadn't attacked her. She slipped the largest key from a leather cord wrapped around the older one's neck and slid it into the small door carved into the large gate, used for the guards to pass in and out of. The lock on the other side slid back and she pushed through the door, ax in hand.

No one awaited her on the other side.

Firelight flickered along the path to the great hall, but Petra skirted it, instead heading for the residences attached to the outside. She found a small servants' door and pushed at it. Unlocked. She slipped through and found herself face to face with a serving girl, a tray of mead hovering above her head. The lass blanched as Petra pulled back her hood. She obviously recognized Petra, or rather *Petyr*.

"Evening," Petra said, lowering her voice for good measure. "Can I take that?"

Before the girl could respond, Petra whisked the tray from her hands and marched toward the door leading to the great hall. As she got closer, she could hear Firmin's voice on the other side.

"I think this meeting is adjourned."

Petra's gaze shifted from the king to Axel standing only a pace or two away from him. Anger radiated off him in waves. She couldn't believe the room was still standing.

"Will you release the prisoner or not?" Axel asked.

"Of course not!" Firmin snapped. "She is my prisoner, and I'll do what is necessary in order to keep this kingdom safe."

In a flash, Axel had him thrust up against his not-a-throne.

Petra dropped the tray she was holding and hurdled over a table until she was at Axel's side. She put a hand on his arm. "Let him go."

Axel whirled, his green eyes wide as he met her gaze. She saw the fury replaced by shock then elation.

"You weren't invited to this meeting, Petyr."

Petra turned away from Axel and back toward the king. "I go were my lord goes, Your Majesty."

His face turned back to its mottled red but before he could begin his tirade, the doors leading to the royal rooms burst open, and King Anders stumbled in.

"She's gone!"

Petra felt her stomach sink down into her toes. She hoped they wouldn't discover she was missing until after she and Axel had escaped the fortress.

"How did the witch escape?" Firmin yelled.

"Not the bloody witch, Firmin," Anders snapped. He held up a crumpled piece of paper. "My wife! That bloody Sidan prince has stolen her away from me!"

CHAPTER 42

TRUTHS

A xel couldn't keep his eyes off Petra for more than a few seconds as King Anders went off about how Prince Roman had stolen his wife. Anders had returned from Oxe to see to all of this, but he hadn't brought his wife back with him, giving Prince Roman the chance to take her. *Serves the bloody rockhead right.*

Petra remained focused on the two brothers, her blue-green eyes flicking between them as she gathered information. Axel studied every inch of her. Her hair was short once again, the ends jagged as they rested against her neck. Her nose was crooked and swollen, two spots of purple blooming under her eyes. He'd kill whoever broke her nose if she hadn't already. There was a lump on her forehead as well and a number of cuts on her skin. Her fingernails were worn to the nub, cracked and scabbed over.

What had she endured at the hands of their so-called High King?

He tapped the back of her hand, and she finally looked up at him. He tilted his head. *You good?*

A twitch of a smile. *I'm good.*

Axel allowed a small fraction of ease to loosen his chest. He would still kill whoever touched her, but he could wait a bit longer.

"They're likely already halfway to Bellator by now!" Firmin roared.

"I don't care what it takes!" Anders screeched back. "This is your fault for bringing bloody Sidans into our halls. You'll send whatever men necessary to sink his bloody ship and bring me back my wife!"

Firmin grabbed Anders by the front of his shirt. "You think I can just send ships to attack a Sidan prince? By the time they catch up, they'll be in Sidan waters. It will be construed as an act of war, and Enzo the Scourge will come knocking at our door."

Anders shoved him off. "I don't care. He stole what's mine, and I want it back!"

Firmin growled, but before he could cause his brother any more bodily harm, Queen Eva's voice broke over the cacophony. "Might I make a suggestion?"

Both brothers whirled on her. "What?" they snapped in unison.

The queen gestured to Axel and Petra. "Perhaps you can send *The Phoenix* and her crew after them."

Axel spun toward her. "What?"

"You can't be serious," Firmin growled.

Doran stepped up next to the queen. "Her Majesty makes a wonderful suggestion. *The Phoenix* is one of the quickest ships on the Vit Sea. Her crew could easily retrieve Lady Idalia."

Was the man rocked? Axel would never step foot in that godsforsaken wasteland. The moment he did, they'd probably try to kill him, which would be tedious, and he'd have to kill everyone right back.

Doran continued laying out a plan he was likely coming up with as the words left his mouth. Timelines, possible routes the Sidans could have taken, where they would keep the lady.

A slim hand wrapped around Axel's arm. "Listen to me, Axel," whispered the queen. "That foolish girl just marked us for death. If Anders doesn't get her back, he'll rally his men and march on Bellator. Firmin will be only minutes behind him. While the two of them are at odds more often than not, they're loyal to one another above all others. The moment either of them sets foot on Sidan shores, they'll announce the break of the armistice. That can't happen. Áldras needs every second we can get before we go back to battle. Get Idalia. Get her back here as quickly as you can. I'll hold off my husband and his brother as long as I can. Don't let our kingdom fall because of Idalia's foolish pride."

Hel's halls, Lady Idalia had practically thrown their kingdom into the fire. Anders would restart this war over this. There was no doubt. Axel couldn't let that happen. He'd drag the lady back kicking and screaming if it would give them more time. It made something in his chest tightened, remembering how Anders had treated Lady Idalia at the feast weeks ago, but he could find a way to save her from her husband *after* he freed her from the Sidans.

Rocks, this was getting bloody complicated quickly.

"Bring her back here," the queen repeated. "Don't let all our hard work be for naught. Don't let my sacrifice be for nothing."

Axel looked down once again at the queen. How had he never realized how much she truly cared? How much she knew? He could see the resolve in her. The steel of a blade and the heart of a she-bear.

He bowed his head. "I give you my word."

She gave him a nod of thanks.

Firmin stepped away from his brother and pointed at Axel. "After what this idiot has done, do you really think I'm going to let him take charge of something like this?"

Axel bristled, but Doran raised a hand to keep him from speaking. "I think the gods have given us a boon. What better way for Axel to show his allegiance than for him to cross into enemy territory to retrieve our beloved lady? After all, he's sworn his allegiance to our kingdom. Our queen. If you order it, he'll see it done."

A few of the other kings murmured their agreement.

Firmin glared at each one before turning back to Doran. "How do I know he won't betray us and join the Sidans?"

Indignation rose up in the crowd behind Axel.

"You would question him on that?" one said.

"Axel would never—" another started

"Mighty Axel Ashersson," King Gudrun said, "the Sidans' Bane, and hero to all of Åldras would never turn his allegiances to the Sidans."

Axel bowed his head to the king in appreciation.

Firmin raised both hands to quiet the protests. "All right!" he barked. He turned back to Axel. "You want to prove your loyalty to me and the rest of Åldras? You want to convince me of the witch's innocence? Go to Sida. Bring back Lady Idalia. If you succeed, you'll be restored into my good graces, all offenses against me forgiven."

A few of the men gave a hearty agreement.

Firmin stepped closer and lowered his voice so only Axel could hear. "But if you fail me in this, I will carve my name into every inch of that woman's flesh before I strap her to a witch's pyre. Do I make myself clear?"

Axel met the king's eyes and bared his teeth. "Crystal."

ᚠᚾᚲᛟᚠᚤᚠ

AXEL AND PETRA flew through the streets of Harligdam, Doran only steps behind them.

"How long until you think they'll notice you've escaped?" Axel asked.

Petra shrugged as much as she could as she ran. "An hour, maybe more. They had me in an unfinished building on the west side of town."

"Then we only have so long before they come looking for us." Firmin would be absolutely livid when he found the one thing he could hold over Axel was no longer in his grasp. If they didn't bring Idalia back, there would be more than just Hel to pay.

Petra smirked. "Good thing we'll be out of this city before then."

He laughed, the sound freeing as the stress and anger fled from his chest. Wōden's eye, it was so good to have her beside him again.

They made it to the docks and Axel thrust the release orders from Firmin in the face of the first guard they saw. "My crew is to be released immediately." He didn't even wait for the man to speak before Axel turned and sprinted for *The Phoenix*. Dawn was beginning to color the horizon.

Doran caught up to them. "Take Ludvig and Ulf with you. The journey to Sida will be rough and you need all the men you can get."

"You're not coming with us?" Axel asked. He had assumed Doran would, especially after what just happened in the great hall.

Doran shook his head. "You need eyes and ears here, especially in the aftermath of Pet's escape. I'll keep an eye on the queen and figure out how to cover up Pet's disappearance. I can watch the kings and continue to garner their favor back in your direction. Bring Lady Idalia back so we can all get on with our lives."

Axel offered his hand and Doran grasped it firmly. "I'll send word once we reach Bellator."

Doran released his hand and looked to Petra. "Keep yourself out of trouble."

Petra nodded.

After Doran departed, Axel pulled himself over the side of the ship and grabbed Petra's arm.

She hissed and tried to shake him off. "I dislocated my shoulder, you bloody idiot! I can get on the bloody ship myself."

She'd dislocated her shoulder? He ignored her demands that he leave her be and hauled her up onto the deck, doing his best not to jostle her too hard. Dropping to his knees, he dragged her down out of sight with him. His arms wrapped around her gently, and he tucked her head under his chin. "Gods, I'm so glad you're all right."

Petra's stiff form sagged into his chest, and she wrapped her arms around him.

"If you two are done snuggling over there, we need to get this ship ready before a certain king figures out what's actually going on and all our plans go to the fishes."

Axel laughed and turned to where Erik sat at the tiller, buckling his harness into place.

"Right you are, skipper."

Axel let go of Petra and they followed Erik's barking commands until the rest of the crew joined them only minutes later. Apparently, Firmin's orders had emphasized their haste to depart.

Big Hal tossed Little Hal into the ship and clambered up behind him.

"Pet!" Little Hal shouted and raced over but stopped before he ran right into her. "I'm glad to see you."

Petra ruffled his hair. "As I am to see you."

"Now's not the time for reunions!" Erik snapped. "Get the oars through those ports! Pull the anchor!"

The crew scrambled to follow every order, and soon they were out of the harbor and headed for the open sea.

As the wind filled the sail, Axel tied down the oar and turned to look at Petra, who stared out over the side of the ship. Axel finished and slid closer to her. She jumped as his shoulder brushed against hers.

"I have some questions," he said.

She slowly turned back toward him. "What questions?"

So many flashed through his head. What happened while they'd been separated? What had Firmin done to her while she'd been trapped? How had she escaped? Did she remember their kiss?

But the one that fell from his lips was "Why did you say all of this is your fault?"

A line formed between her brows. "What?"

"In Ljust Löfte, after we—"

"Don't say it," she hissed, her gaze flicking around at the crew. Her shoulders bunched up at her ears, and Axel watched the blood drain from her face.

"You said all of this is your fault. That you killed them. What did you mean?"

"Nothing."

Axel wrapped a hand around her forearm. "Don't lie to me. It didn't mean nothing. What were you saying?"

He saw the moment the shadows of the past came over her. Most of the time, they were only a flicker, there for a moment and gone just as quickly. But now, they sat dark and heavy in her gaze.

"It's my fault they're gone, Axel. Your Father. Da. Dane. Kol. Brand and Corey. Gram." Silver lined her eyes, and she swallowed hard. "Mama."

"Petra, you didn't kill them."

Two tears fell on either side of her face. She blinked and two more followed, the color of her irises more blue than green with the shadows swirling in them.

His chest seized. "You didn't kill them, right? It was the Sidans. They invaded Holmberg. They killed our family."

Slowly, almost like it pained her to do so, she closed her eyes and hung her head. "No, Axel. The Sidans didn't kill them."

His chest heaved with the effort of trying to draw air. "But you couldn't have killed them. Petra, there's no way a thirteen-year-old could have done what was done to Holmberg."

Her head lifted slightly, her eyes flashing to his.

"No, but a thirteen-year-old Häxa could."

A Fire

"Not there, Little Dove." Da moved the dark piece back across the hnefatafl board. The stout wooden boat looked fragile in his large hands. "If you move him, the king can easily be swallowed up by my left side. You must find another way."

Petra grumbled incoherently at the game in front of her. She would much rather be outside, playing with Axel, than sitting in place for so long—especially as Da tried to teach her to play this stupid game.

"Don't whine, Petra," Mama called from where she stirred their dinner over the fire. "If you want to beat Gram next time, you'd best listen to your da. He's smarter than he looks."

Da let out a booming laugh as Petra attempted to shrink her head into her shoulders. "Why do I have to learn to play this silly game? Axel says these games are for children and the elderly."

Da's blue-green eyes sparkled at her. "And since when has Axel become the lord of fun? Yesterday, you begged me to stay up and play far past sundown."

Petra's lips quirked. "Only because yesterday I was winning and didn't want you to snatch my victory out from under me."

Mama's spoon clanged on the edge of the pot. "She gets that competitive streak from you, Mal."

Da's large frame nearly toppled from his chair as he laughed. "If she

341

gets her competitive spirit from me, she certainly gets her stubbornness from you, my love."

The clang of the spoon ended only to be replaced by the sound of the door bursting open.

"What's that smell?" Petra knew Brand's voice anywhere. It had always sounded like he was halfway to laughing, just like Da's.

"I'm starving," Corey moaned.

"Move out of the way!" Kol hollered.

Eventually, all five of Petra's older brothers tumbled into the main room of the house. Kol raced off toward the door leading to the boys' rooms, a pile of gear in his hands. He squired for Dane, their oldest brother, and often came home with all their gear. If he didn't put it away properly, Dane would have his head.

Brand and Corey, the twins, were the first to circle the large table at the head of the room, their impatient hands reaching for the food.

Dane knocked their heads together. "Wait for the rest of us!"

Gram entered last, heading straight for Mama, and kissing the top of her hair. Even at fifteen, he was nearly two heads taller than her. "Evening, Mama."

She gave him a smile before turning to the rest of the room, spoon waving as efficiently as Da's sword. "Food will be ready in two minutes, and I expect to see clean hands and clean faces."

The boys ran back out to the water pump. Even Kol had heard Mama's demands from the other side of the house and was quick on their heels.

"I think it's time to admit defeat," Da said, drawing Petra's attention back to the game.

Petra groaned, knocking over the king with her own finger. "I didn't even make it out of the middle that time."

"Can I show you where it went wrong?"

Petra nodded and Da shifted the pieces on the board, returning them to where they were four moves ago.

"If you would have moved this defender here instead of taking my attacker there, I wouldn't have been able to block your path to the corner in two more moves."

Petra stared at the board. He was right, of course. She could have gotten her king to the safe corner in no time. "How did I not see that?"

Da collected the pieces, setting them in their small wooden chest. "We often forget that being the most aggressive is not the only way to win a war. Sometimes, it can be as simple as putting men in the right places at the right times."

"Or just being the side with the most soldiers," Brand said, strolling toward the dining table, hair dripping onto his tunic. "Why do you think Da asks to play white all the time?"

Petra narrowed her eyes at Da who chuckled. "I confess to nothing."

Mama gathered up an armful of wooden bowls. "Petra, come help me dish up."

Petra jumped up and hurried to Mama's side to help get the food into their bowls. The boys all gathered around the table. Petra sat in her chair across from Gram, Kol at her left, and Mama at the foot of the table on her right. Da sank into the chair at the head of the table and sent up prayers to the gods that watched over them. The moment he finished and picked up his spoon, the boys descended on their own bowls.

Petra tried to focus on every conversation happening around her, but the voices came and went like the waves of the sea.

Dane's voice crashed first. "King Asher asked if I was willing to go on a scouting mission at the end of the harvest. If I go, it should give me the opportunity to—"

"Do you think Brenna will like a guy with a scar?" Corey asked.

Brand smirked. "Not if she knows a thirteen-year-old was the one who gave it—"

"I know I'm your squire, Dane," Kol snapped, "but you can't boss me around all the time."

Gram leaned over toward Mama. "The leeks in the garden should be ready by week's end. Do you think we should pull the radishes too?"

Mama turned to answer but froze. "Hush!" she said over the cacophony of conversation.

A distant bellow of horns cut off every voice. The horns droned their song into Petra's breastbone. Da's eyes snapped from Mama's face to the door of the large house. He was on his feet as quick as a wisp and swung open the ornately carved wooden door. The sound of shouts and the smell of smoke wafted in on a breeze that chilled Petra to her very core.

The boys were on their feet, their half-eaten bowls forgotten entirely. They scattered through the house, strapping anything with a sharp blade to their belts and hoisting shields from their hooks on the walls. Petra followed Gram toward the door, holding his quiver of arrows as he strung his bow. All five boys marched out the door, Mama touching each of their arms in a silent farewell.

Pet bit back the goodbyes filling her cheeks. They would be fine. They'd been training to fight since each of them had turned twelve. There wasn't a foe on the planet that could face the wrath of a Mallorysson. Goodbyes were for grandmothers and old dogs.

Without looking back inside, Da reached out his hand. "Mila..."

Mama answered without a word. Da's large sword was thrust into his hand and with the other he swooped her into a fierce kiss, the only parting either of them needed.

"Don't open the door for anyone else but me or the boys." He lowered his voice. "Use the stones if you have to."

Mama's eyes widened. "And have Petra and I burned alive for it after?"

"Better to be alive and forced to hide than dead because you won't let your stones protect you."

She shook her head. "We'll be fine."

He looked back over his shoulder at Petra and gave her a wink. "Don't you dare think we won't be having a rematch the moment I get home, Little Dove."

Then, he was gone.

ᛈᚾᚲᛟᚠᚤᛚ

HOURS TICKED by as Petra waited with Mama. Their house stood tall in the middle of the city, near the main hall with the others that held positions in the city's leadership. As second in command to King Asher Redbeard, Holmberg's reigning warlord, Da had to stay close to his liege. If the attackers made it to this part of the city, the fight was already lost.

Mama peeked through the curtains of the window, watching for the signal to fight or flee. Two packs now leaned against the table where the hnefatafl board sat. Petra just hoped the boys could make it to them in time to leave with them if they had to go. If not, there were certainly other places to meet up after.

The ring of fighting and the screams of the dying echoed through the open door. Petra saw the faces of everyone she knew flash before her eyes. Something in her chest caught. Axel was likely in the thick of the fighting. As a thirteen-year-old, he'd only been officially training for a year, but could easily match the skill of men twice his age. Petra had heard all about it—both from her brothers and Axel himself. His mother, a Häxa, had prophesied many things concerning her son before she abandoned him, one of them being his prowess on the fields of battle.

Another horn bellowed, this one much closer than any of the previous had been. Mama shut the door. "Petra, gather up the packs." Mama knelt next to the door, pulling up one of the stones making up the floor of the entryway. She withdrew a small bag from the hole and replaced the stone.

Petra set the bags down by the fire in the middle of the room. "Mama, what are you—"

The front door caved in, and a large silhouette of a man backed by the torches of his comrades walked into the house. As more men filled the doorway, Petra took in their hawkish noses and their black eyes—demon eyes, she'd heard her father say. These men were Sidans, citizens of the southern kingdom with their eyes set on Åldras. She'd heard enough from Da and Dane. Since High King Firmin had taken the throne, the Sidans had been causing problems.

Mama rushed to Petra's side with a handful of stones. With a flick of her wrist, the stones skittered across the thrushes on the floor, each one etched with a rune. "Don't come any closer."

The man stilled in the torchlight, holding up a hand to stop his comrades. "Häxa stones." He met Mama's eyes. "I think there has been a mistake."

Mama straightened and pushed Petra behind her skirts. "Do not tempt the gods I serve with your small mindedness, Sidan. It will be your death they send their Valkyries for, not mine."

The Sidan shook his head. "I'm not here to kill you, my lady. I have been tasked with retrieving all Häxa—"

Mama hissed, drawing a long dagger from the folds of her skirt. "You won't be taking me from my home."

Petra reached for her own dagger at her waist but found only her skirt. She looked back over at the table, seeing the blade snug in its sheath. Her gaze returned to the invader and his comrades who were slowly making their way to the edge of the line of stones Mama had thrown.

"I swear to you," the man said, "we are only here to—"

Petra dashed for the blade, twisting away from Mama's skirts.

She'd forgotten about the bags at her feet.

Her boot caught on the largest pack, sending her sprawling.

Right into the fire.

She screamed as the flames flew toward her face. She shut her eyes, waiting for the sharp bite of pain. Her hands hit the burning logs, then the red-hot coals at the bottom. As soon as she was able, she pushed herself up from the flames.

Mama's arms wrapped around her waist, hauling her up.

"Petra!" she yelped.

Searing heat licked at Petra's arm. She screamed as the flame caught on the sleeve of her blouse only to spread up her shoulder. A pressure began building in her chest, causing her breathing to choke around her sobs of horror. Her screams grew more frantic as she tried to put the fire out only to watch it stretch across her skin. She looked to Mama, the pressure in her chest mounting, but found her staring back in a mixture of terror and sadness. Their eyes met.

Mama spoke quietly as she gazed at her with fear and love shining in her eyes. "Your förändra."

A flame jumped from Petra's arm to the ground, catching on the dry threshing coating the floor. A shout rang from the door, but Petra couldn't look away from the flames. They bounced off her and ate away at the packs at her feet. The floor. The walls. Screaming stung Petra's ears until she realized it came from her own lips. The flames grew as they continued to feast on Petra's childhood, on the dreams of her parents.

"Petra, look at me!" Petra's eyes fastened on the ferocious and serene blue of Mama's gaze, staring back at her from a few ells away. "Petra, my love, I'm so sor—"

The pressure in Petra's chest flung out of her with a resounding *boom*. Power pulsed out from under her skin and a wall of flame flew from her.

Straight into Mama.

"*Mama!*" The scream tore from her throat as another wave broke out from her chest, eating everything left in its predecessor's wake. Petra watched the left-over pieces of the walls of her house sway before crumbling down around her. The last thing she saw was the glitter of embers and stars as the building fell on top of her.

ᚠᚾᚲᛟᚾᛁᛚ

THE DARKNESS WAS ABSOLUTE. Petra was sure she was on her way to the Allfather's domain, following Mama to the waters of Valhalla. She did not expect the afterlife to hurt so horribly or smell so much like smoke. Perhaps she'd ended up in Hel's halls after all. She couldn't move any part of her body. Ringing clanged through her ears. A cough wracked her small frame, causing pain like she'd never felt to steal the little breath she had from her lungs.

After a moment, she realized what had caused her to float out of the darkness she had been swimming in. Shifting rocks scraped over the ringing in her ears and a ray of sunlight landed on her face. Her eyes watered at the brightness, blurring her vision. She coughed at the salty sea air she recognized as her home—tainted with the putrid smell of smoke.

"Pet!" The voice broke over her name. "Oh, Pet. Oh gods. Hold on." Axel left her sight, but she could still hear his cries as he walked away only to come back with a burnt cloak. "Here, I'm going to shift these last couple of beams and then you'll be out, all right?"

With a grunt, Axel lifted the beams that should have been impossible for his thirteen-year-old body to even budge. "Can you move?"

Petra slowly lifted her arm. Pain raced through her muscles and joints, but not enough to inhibit any movement. She finally nodded and began to sit up.

"Here," said Axel as he thrust the cloak in Petra's direction. Petra looked down to see her entire body covered in only a thick coating of soot. She gratefully took the cloak and wrapped it around herself as a breeze blew across her exposed skin.

Her heart raced as she looked down at her arm. There wasn't a burnt flake of skin or single blister marring any part of her body.

"Do you think you can stand?" Axel asked.

Petra tried to respond, but the words caught in her throat as she finally looked at their surroundings. Every house within a hundred yards had turned into piles of rubble and ash. Beyond that, Petra saw the streets charred and buildings still smoking with small fires.

"I don't know what happened," Axel said. "I was in the middle of fighting off the invading Sidan's on the beach when a huge wall of flame came roaring through the city. I never would have known it was coming if the men in front of me hadn't turned tail and fled into the water. I was the only one left on the beach and I only just made it below the water before the first of the flames washed over. The second wave took out half of the Sidan ships in the harbor and all the men on the smaller vessels. There is no one else left." Axel took a deep breath and pointed toward where Petra knew the harbor to be. "There's not a single boat left on the water."

Axel turned to her. "What kind of weapon did they use? Why would they risk killing that many of their own men? If they wanted to invade, why use something that would destroy everything they were trying to take? It makes no sense. Who would burn down an entire city and leave it in smoldering ash?"

Petra could feel the tears making tracks down the ash crusted on her face. It was then that she was able to push a semblance of noise past her throat. Her voice came out in the same creaking and broken sound as the city around her.

"I don't know."

Author's Note

Many of you already know I have a very deep and unhealthy obsession with Greek mythology. When the idea for *Children of Ash* came to me, I was watching *Troy (2004)*. I knew I wanted to do some sort of Nordic-inspired world, but what I hadn't had was the main characters or the plotline.

Then, Brad Pitt showed up, and I knew.

I found my story in the way Achilles hated the fate he had been dealt. In the way Odysseus kept the peace between the prideful warriors. How Patroclus jumped into action, even when it cost him. How Agamemnon lived for glory and glory alone.

I knew there was something there. My story brain started whirring, taking the pieces I knew from the story of the battles at Troy and started sticking them all together. I knew where I wanted this story to go and I knew I wanted to play in Homer's sandbox, take the things he'd created and decorate them a little differently.

When I was outlining the series, I thought I knew where the story started. However, it wasn't until I took a deep dive into the myths surrounding Achilles, that I found my story's beginning. Something about Achilles dressed up like a girl and hiding out in Skyros with the daughters of King Lycomedes made me laugh. The rest of that part of the story wasn't half as humorous, but I felt like I could see a character take form there. When I learned about Agamemnon getting Greece

Author's Note

cursed for killing Artemis's sacred deer, I found another piece of the plot.

After that, I continued to research the tensions between Agamemnon and Achilles, and it was there that I realized there was so much more to this story than just Paris stealing away Helen, or Hector and Achilles battling it out. So, this book was born. The beginning. Where the war really begins. Where fate grabs hold of our characters and takes them for the ride of a lifetime.

Acknowledgments

No book is written by one person. Ok, that might not be completely true, but it is for me. While I was the one with the crazy idea and the one who did most of the footwork, I had an entire team of amazing souls backing me up.

Thank you, Tyleah Merino. You are my north star and my guiding light. Thank you for always encouraging me, for telling me when my books are stupid, and for always listening to me when I have insane story ideas.

I need to thank my family, who puts up with the obnoxious writing goblin they all have to live with. Thank you, Eric, for everything. There will never be enough words to express how grateful I am for your love, support, and pizza-buying skills. I love you. My girls, you are my best cheerleaders. Thank you for helping me find time to write and for always being excited to go on book adventures with me. Thank you, Dad, for pushing me to do this. Thank you for telling me I could and for running this writing path with me. I'm so excited for all the good things coming your way. Thank you, Mom, for always taking my phone calls and listening to me talk about all things book.

Thank you to my amazing publisher and editors. Thank you, Oliver-Heber Books and Tanya Anne Crosby for taking a chance with me and for letting me try out something new. Thank you, Kate Ward, for making me do all of those edits. The book is so much better. Thank you, Sally O'Keef for finding all of my missing commas and for sitting on the phone with me while I banged my head against my keyboard. I trust you.

I also have so many author friends I need to give my deepest gratitude to. Thank you, Jeff Wheeler, for reading this crazy book and being so excited about it. I'm so glad you gave me permission to let Pet kill more people. Thank you, KayLynn Flanders, for sitting across the table from me in that ice cream shop at ten o'clock at night, telling me it was all right for me to write this as an adult fantasy. You were absolutely right. Thank you to my OSAWG group: Dad, Marci Johnson, Ben Bailey, Tracy Tyler, Aimee Hall, Robbie of the Beams of Stuffle, Jared Jensen, and David Haynie. You guys are the absolute best, and I can't wait to read all your books (looking straight at you, Marci)! Thank you to my Write Club: Bonnie Jo Pierson, Amber Marcusen, HR Boyd, Kayla Tillotson, Marci Johnson, Tarry Perry, Sally O'Keef, Lindsay Hiller, and—most especially—Kelsey Larson. You girls are my alchemy. Thank you for inspiring me every single day.

And last, but never least, thank you to my Heavenly Father for continuing to inspire me and for always answering my prayers. Thank You for trusting me and for continuing to guide me.

Also By Allison Anderson

Children of Ash

Children of Ash

Son of Steel

Daughter of Flame

The Cartographer's War

The Spring Maiden

The Shadow Lord

The Unseen King

The Unwanted Queen

The Cartographer's War: A Necessary Tragedy

The Seer's Assassin

The Fated Mage

About the Author

Allison Anderson lives her best life as a wife, a mom, a dedicated member of The Church of Jesus Christ of Latter-Day Saints, and a fantasy writer. As a lifelong fantasy nerd, she finds it natural to create stories of her own and you can often find her jotting down new story ideas or talking about dragons. She's spent most of her life across the southwestern United States.

https://www.allisonandersonauthor.com/

www.ingramcontent.com/pod-product-compliance
Lightning Source LLC
Chambersburg PA
CBHW050508110726
47899CB00005B/1375